Bhalchandra Nemade

COCOON

Translated from the Marathi original by

SUDHAKAR MARATHE

www.popularprakashan.com

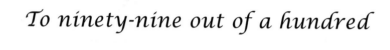

To ninety-nine out of a hundred

Woman, how can one explain to the living the attributes of the dead.
— *An aphorism said by Shri Chakradhara*

Where does the Wandering Spirit roam?
To the East? Or perhaps to the North.
To the West? Or perhaps to the South.
God's viands are scattered in every corner of the Earth, but you
cannot consume them, for you are dead.
Come, you Wandering Spirit, come, so you will find release at last
and you will make the path.
— A Tibetan Prayer

Published by
Harsha Bhatkal
for Popular Prakashan Pvt. Ltd.
301, Mahalaxmi Chambers
22, Bhulabhai Desai Road
Mumbai 400026
www.popularprakashan.com

First Published in Marathi, 1963
First published at Macmillan, 1997

Republished 2014

(4379)
ISBN 978-81-7991-819-7

Cover design: Nitin Dadrawala

Printed by
Avantika Printers
New Delhi

Introduction

Bhalchandra Nemade, with his *Kosla,* (meaning cocoon), made an unparalleled impact on the Marathi literary scene in 1963. The reasons are not far to seek. In the two decades immediately preceding the publication of *Kosla,* the Marathi novel was lost in a world of romantic day-dreams. Or it indulged in middle-class pseudo-idealism doling out quotable quotes as profound philosophical truths or as in the early novels of S.N. Pendse, it presented a linear, crude but reader-oriented notion of heroism. A denominator common to all these novelists was an engagement with the reader's interest in literature *qua* literature and not so much with the nature and quality of life. Artifice was thus more important than experience.

This led in the fifties to the emergence of a formalism which, through the growing influence of critical theories, became a strange conglomeration of Kant and Clive Bell, the aesthetics of Eliot and Pound and the New Criticism of Brooks, Richards and Tate. It also became a hallmark of modernism and appealed to a host of writers who in any case were no longer in touch with the changing realities of post-Independence Maharashtrian culture and society. The formalism and modernism of these writers meant that they derived their notions of literature from literature itself. With a vengeance, inter-textuality became more important than the interface between literature and life. Style —

not as a mode of revealing challenging perceptions of reality but as a device for sustaining the reader's interest, a blind borrowing of sophisticated techniques such as the stream-of-consciousness, artificial transplant of existentialism and absurdity — all these were aspects of that grand formalism-cum-modernism which held powerful sway in the fifties and the early sixties. True, there were some authentic native voices such as Vibhavari Shiroorkar and Vyankatesh Madgulkar and Pendse with his *Rathchakra*. But on the whole they were isolated instances in the wilderness of this modernism and formalism. It was only *Kosla* which responding as it did to a crisis in the cultural consciousness of Maharashtra, that opened up new, native possibilities of form and meaning and thus sought to change the direction of both literary taste and fictional tradition.

II

Kosla has no story or plot in the traditional sense of the term. Dedicated to the "ninety-nine out of hundred," the novel unfolds, by using the first person narrative mode, the life of twenty-five year old Pandurang Sangvikar. This narration of the hero's life is divided into six parts. The first part depicts Pandurang's childhood and his school education in Sangvi, a village in the Khandesh region of Maharashtra. The second describes the first two years of Pandurang's college life in Pune while the third part deals with the next two years of his undergraduate life. The fourth part shows Pandurang's educational life as a failed student (who has to repeat the examination) in the same city. The last two parts of the novel describe in minute detail Pandurang's life in his village after he returns to it from Pune. Thus though the novel does not have a regular plot, it does have a structure which builds up a consistent contrast between Pandurang's village life and his experiences of the city. Historically speaking, this structuring of the contrast between the rural and the urban can be traced back to the process of transition from tradition to modernity that Maharashtra went through during the post-Independence period.

As we have noted already, the novel has no story in the regular sense of the term. What emerges however, from a loose, episodic narrative, is the retrospective life story of the unheroic hero, Pandurang Sangvikar. The only son of a well-to-do farmer, Pandurang spends his childhood and his school years upto high school in his village Sangvi. His experience and memories of life in his village are far from happy. Subjected to the patriarchal authority of his father, and greatly attached to his mother and his younger sister, Mani, his emotional anchors were a poor compensation for the oppressions of patriarchal power, the hypocrisy, the false notions of respectability and in general the various forms of phonyness he sees around him everywhere. Except the sky above, he finds nothing that is pure and spotless in his village.

Things do not change very much when Pandurang, after high school comes to Pune to attend college. In fact, they get worse and sometimes even traumatic. Initially, in keeping with the middle-class ideals so characteristic of college life, Pandurang tries to acquire a public image by participating in a number of students' activities, but very soon realises the fallacy of this and gives it up. He finds his teachers equally hollow. He spends a lot of time with some of his friends on wild wanderings and hill climbing. He works as the secretary of the hostel mess only to be cheated and plunged into an embarrassing financial crisis. Disillusioned all round, Pandurang is traumatised when his younger sister, Mani, dies. His visit to the Ajanta caves sharpens his sense of death and meaninglessness.

After appearing for his B.A. examination as a failed student, Pandurang decides to leave Pune for good, and returns to his village. The village does not hold out — as in fact it never did in the past — any meaningful promise for him. His only friend during this period is Giridhar in whom he discovers an ideal and authentic being. But he knows that he has inherent limitations, and cannot therefore measure up to the ideal Giridhar embodies. Outside, the world continues to be full of hypocrisy, sham, incomprehensible suffering and meaninglessness. In such a mood of existential helplessness, Pandurang decides to say yes to everything that is essentially negative. It is precisely at this point that the novel ends.

III

The foregoing description of the structure of *Kosla* and its bare storyline makes it clear that what holds together a vast array of discrete events, memories and a large number of characters in the novel is not the Aristotelian principle of organic form but simply how Pandurang perceives them from time to time and shares them with the reader. This complex perception takes us to the basic theme of the novel — Pandurang's alienation and disillusionment.

What is more important however is to note the socio-moral nature of this alienation and the value-system implicit in it. It is not the product of attitudes borrowed from Western movements such as Existentialism and Absurdity. That is why early critics who tried to read *Kosla* in terms of the categories of the anti-hero, the anti-novel etc. could not come to terms with its real meaning.

Alienation in *Kosla* is the product of a grassroots crisis; and this crisis can be examined in both sociological and historical terms. In Maharashtra, in the latter half of the nineteenth century, the impact of British liberalism created a middle-class generation which seriously believed that it had a responsible role to play in society. Gradually however the Maharashtrian middle-class lost this social conscience and instead cultivated values of material success, careerism, social status and prestige. *Kosla* captures this historical impasse and the contradictions of the colonial legacy in the post-Independence period.

A tragic sense of this dead end and its contradictions are seen in the way in which Pandurang reacts against his orthodox, patriarchial Hindu family which has resisted the waves of liberal thought and action. The patriarchal family is a micro-copy of the received, official culture which perpetuates social authority by fostering the values of obedience and filial duty and by holding out the rewards of success, status, prestige and security. When Pandurang says in the opening part of the novel that he found his father "wicked and cruel, etc." he is reacting against a whole patriarchial order of power which crushes individuality and freedom.

Alienation in *Kosla* is thus not a product of metaphysical absurdity as in Camus's *The Outsider,* nor is it related to phenomenological angst as in Sartre's *Nausea*. It does share limited stylistic peculiarities such as the anti-climactic use of "etc." and "for example" with J.D. Salinger's *The Catcher in the Rye*. But Nemade does not propose, as Salinger does, an alternative world of innocents and saints. By concentrating on the primary social institution of the family, then moving on to the secondary ones and finally to the problems of history and time, *Kosla* offers a fairly wide context for its theme.

Given this essentially socio-moral background of the hero's alienation, it is not surprising that Pandurang Sangvikar has values that give his character a dimension of moral integrity and idealism. What hurts is to find that in the adult world that surrounds him, values are systematically distorted behind facades of social decency and institutional security. This hypocrisy blankets both the rural and the urban so that in *Kosla* there is no nostalgia for some kind of rural stability destroyed in the process of social change. This hypocrisy pervades every area of life — from agriculture in the villages to literary circles in the cities. It is this miasma of distorted values in a phoney world which makes Pandurang Sangvikar a progressively alienated being. He unmasks these perversions by using humour as a serious moral gesture. Thus he describes his participation in the college elocution competition in the following manner:

For instance, I began — Today the world is caught in a terrible predicament.

At the thought that I had uttered the crummiest of platitudes I started to laugh at myself. Fine, but how would every speaker laugh at himself?

Later I said, In the Upanishads is gathered the essence of all knowledge.

Laughter.

In them it is said — Sarvetra sukhinah santu.

Laughter.

Unless all men foster emotional ties among nations, there is no way out for mankind.

Guffaws.

Nationalism is a sin.

Hoots.

This kind of oblique, irreverent and eccentric humour effectively brings out the sensitive younger generation's disillusionment with the idea of the welfare state in post-Independence India.

This strategy of using humour for intensely moral purposes is further seen in Pandurang's parody of history. Pandurang and his friend Suresh imagine themselves as future historians writing about the twentieth century:

...And, at that time there used to be Centres of Higher Learning called Universities. Now you will say, What the dickens is this thing? So then, in Universities would go on study of some subjects. Now what does study mean? So, then, even a language called Marathi would be studied.

The people of those times used to take Exercise. We shall tell you in brief what Exercise means. Now for instance, Exercise means that thing by which people's bodies became tough. Indeed, some of them would do, for instance, squats, others would run, for days on end for no reason whatsoever.

Furthermore, these people would consider themselves either Hindu or Musalman. Every person used to know who his own father was. These people used to relieve themselves in closed toilets. That is to say, they used to do many things in such a way that others might not see them.

In the Twentieth Century, people used to even "marry." Now you will ask, what does this Marriage mean? So then, Marriage was such a thing that a man could only marry a woman. During these Marriages would be played loud band music. Moreover, large crowds would gather. This actually means that the same woman would cook the food for her married man and wait for the time when he would return home.

. . . .

These people were ill equipped to exist, to such an extent that they had annihilated, with their Guns and merely for

entertainment, great big Godlike creatures, White Tigers, Lions,
Elephants and Whales.
Now you will ask, what does Gun mean? And what is Elephant?
These you must see in museums. But what this God-Fish or
Whale was no one is yet able to say.

IV

Alienation in *Kosla* has dimensions other than the socio-moral.
It is not therefore surprising that having considered history, it
should go deeper — that is, to time itself Consequently, *Kosla* has
an existential (not existentialist) level where it examines, through
the eyes of the alienated hero, the problem of man's freedom in
relation to time and death. When Pandurang's younger sister
Mani's death traumatizes him, his response is not sentimental
but there is a good deal of emotional violence in it. Sangvikar's
realization of the futility of society, history and civilization now
escalates into an awareness of the futility of life itself. He thinks
he has become a ghost. This mood pervades the last section of the
novel. After failing his graduate examination thrice, Pandurang
comes back to his village to find not only hypocrisy and duplicity
but various forms of human suffering. He realizes that man's
original relationship with the universe, nature and with "the
other" is tragically lost in the modern world.

Pandurang's friend Giridhar is also an uprooted person. But
there is an important difference between him and Pandurang.
Like Dostoevsky's Kirilov, Giridhar believes that a man who
commits suicide undermines in that moment of decision
the power of death. Given this ability to decide and act,
Giridhar authenticates his freedom by leaping into the world
of non-institutional faith, and thus undertakes a personal
spiritual adventure. Pandurang suffers from socio-moral
and spiritual restlessness. But he lacks Giridhar's courage. He
realizes now that in the absence of such courage, he will be forced
to become part of the system he has been trying to reject. All this
however has not prevented him from believing in the possible

acts of "greatness", though the surrounding world is full of moral corruption and decadence. As he puts it:

Just as when a lamp is lit in a house we perceive the light from the windows, doors and and even the vents, even so from the behaviour of every great person, must appear some such illumination.

In other words, for others, there's no light within. Such a man is hollow.

Kosla is thus a comprehensive statement on Indian alienation for which there is hardly any parallel in Indian fiction. This is because Nemade's metaphor of the cocoon stands for the agony and crisis of a whole generation caught in the process of transformation from the rural to the urban, from the traditional to the modern in post-colonial India. Given the hero's moral idealism implicit in his rejection of society, history and civilization, it is clear that we cannot speak of any kind of European nihilism here. In this larger sense, *Kosla* is a major and influential example of modernism.

A few words need to be said about the language and style of *Kosla* for the simple reason that it is the only novel in Marathi in which linguistic experiments are simultaneously original and utterly unselfconscious. Rejecting all the established conventions of fictional language, Nemade uses in *Kosla* a language which absorbs the rhythms of colloquial speech, the slang of college students, while manipulating a whole range of stylistic levels from the purely discursive to the intensely lyrical (without any purple prose), and displaying a highly idiosyncratic but creative use of words like "for example," "etc.," "great," "terrific" and a host of other lexical items. This kind of language enables Nemade to use the strategies of incisive humour, and subtle satire to portray his hero's tragic crisis. Since this crisis is not just a personal one, but in a deeper sense, the crisis of a whole generation, Nemade's language in *Kosla* is a measure of his highly original perception of the Marathi culture.

After *Kosla,* Nemade did not publish any novel for a period of twelve years. But since 1975, three novels, *Bidhar* (1975), *Jarila* (1977) and *Zool* (1979), which are parts of a proposed quartet, have appeared. These novels examine the possibility of playing one's role, however alienated one's inner life may be, in relation to society and history. Nemade is today the only Marathi novelist whose sensibility has come full circle in the context of Maharashtrian culture and literature.

Chandrashekhar Jahagirdar
1996

Translator's note

Translating *Kosla* into English was an event in Marathi history, as also in my own personal linguistic-cultural history. No work is so good that it leaves nothing to be desired. But *Kosla* has satisfied far more questions in the process of modernizing Marathi literature than it has left unanswered. It is an event because it is the most discussed novel of the past thirty odd years; because it presents youthful consciousness in the process of cultural reassessment. And, perhaps surprisingly, it is even more genuinely Marathi than one might expect a novel to be which is set in a college campus. It is patriotic in the pain which not just youth but a whole culture has experienced in attempting to grow up to its time in history. And further it was an event because it makes the 'argument' that everything we take for granted must be questioned, from financial security to spiritual baggage, mother tongue to motherhood. *Kosla* was an event also because it made people sit up and take notice of its language, its irreverence, its plot without plotline and character without precedent.

For all these and other reasons, it became also a serious challenge to translators. The following translation must be read for what it is. And yet it cannot be read without either some knowledge or some sense of the original. In the effort to produce a version that might approximate to such expectations, I cannot sufficiently acknowledge the meticulous hard work the author himself has put in over a long year and a half, or the encouragement he has given me throughout. Without the trust he placed in me, as did Meera, Chandrashekar, Ravindra and many others, I could not have attempted this translation.

I take great pleasure in acknowledging Mini Krishnan, the Series Editor who has done the most scrupulous work I have seen any Indian publisher do and Macmillan India for encouraging the translation of *Kosla* into English. For any shortcomings in the translation, I must take responsibility

SUDHAKAR MARATHE
1996

ONE

Me, Pandurang Sangvikar. Today, for instance, I am twenty-five years old.

Honestly, there's only this thing worth telling you. Now, in this world, twenty-five years isn't such a great space. Still, even after spending ten-twelve thousand rupees of my Father's money, I've never really given examinations and such with seriousness. That's my own fault. I admit that. Though we are well off at home, in my family every one is always scrabbling for paise[1] and so on. I mean to say, of course, our farmhands and others are also included. A farmer must earn his hard cash by making sure of every nut, each ear of corn, every pod. This too I do admit. Besides, having spent so many years in the city, one should at least speak, dress, sport some flourishes, in style. But even these things I don't do. That's what they say.

I thought, I should tell all this. I mean of course I'll tell. Except two or three things. First, whatever I used to do in my room. Second, I mean, why I made bold to exercise, train regularly for a whole year or so. But, 'course, I shan't tell all. Because that, even my shirts know.

In this small village, to all appearances, my Father is an

established sort of bod. All the same, even he makes a visit to the temple each day. He's well thought of in our village, because, we are pretty well-spread, solid farmers. That's there, of course. But mainly, I mean for instance right from the beginning, that is my Grandpa's time, it's been our custom to keep things of general utility in the house. We have a huge big decorated floormat — at every wedding and such, of course, it comes in handy for everyone. Then, prior to that, we used to keep a monstrous large Nimari stud-bull. Perhaps you don't know but in the stud-show of 1950, our bull Budhya bagged the first prize. For instance, with suchlike property, we happen to be pretty useful to everyone in our village.

Father never sleeps during daytime. He has a hand in every caucus and plot in our village. But since childhood I have not seen eye to eye with Father. For one thing, his build is like a true Father's, terrifically sturdy and solid. At Pola, the bull-festival, grown-up men's games are held, *kabaddi*, etc. For fun, you see. Then his bare body seems obscene to me. If I happen to have a scrap or something with someone, guilty or not, he used to wallop only me! Yet from Granny I learned a thing about his childhood and since then I began to feel insulted to be slapped by him. I mean to say, he's a crook. So then, Father had hurt someone, hurling a terrific rock, and broken open a boy's eye. Then the boy with the split eye brought his own father. His Pa said, whoever ripped my boy's eye, I'll rip *his* eye open. Then Granny hid my Father upstairs in a great mud-jar. And said to that worthy, He's not at home. Then all day long, even at night, that chap remained at our door, and Father — in the mud water jar. That man only left when he was given ten seers of ghee in compensation.

My whole childhood passed in awe of my Father. He used to be wicked and cruel, etc. On the farm, once, having cleared a bit of ground, we children planted some flowers and such. So then, the moment he heard, he ripped them out and chucking them away, he said as he twisted my ear, If you plant ten banana stumps in this patch, that would at least fetch twenty-five rupees.

Now when I was learning to play the flute, perhaps everyone

in my family may have been disturbed, and so on. But handing me a tight whack my Father said, This isn't Krishna's Age,[2] is it? Take up your book. Throw away that bamboo. Having spoken thus, besides, he snatched the flute from me, broke it against the wall and flung it away.

For instance, once I played a part in a school play. That same night, I returned home excited. But then, telling me that I had spoken mincingly like a pansy, he gave me a scare for life.

Once, bright and early in the morning, Eknath and I went to see the hills and such. It was great fun on the hills — grass, terrific tall bamboos, small little khair trees, anjan trees,[3] etc. We didn't carry any bhakri[4] and such things. Still, we didn't feel a bit hungry all day long. But in the afternoon we both felt thirsty. Just where there might be some water, for example, we didn't know. Then leaving off appreciating the Beauty of Nature, etc., we scurried about in search of water. I said, Let's go down straight at an angle like this. So we'll descend without much effort. Might even meet someone. And, of course, we shall find water. But even after we had descended a good deal, we gained nothing at all. Then, of course, we became terribly scared. And then we saw some monkeys. Naturally, it was evening. After a while we saw a cowherd who showed us a deep pit in the dry river bed. We drank plenty of muddy water. On the way back home, we lost our way, and it got quite late in the night by the time we reached. My legs were throbbing. On top of that, of course, Father plied the switch. I may not mind anything else, but, I cannot take being struck with a switch. I shouted at him that this was hardly in keeping with our Hindu religion. Damn your daily prayers in the temple.

Besides, at that time, he was making me apply, under duress, for freeship at the high school — by showing a low income. Then my teacher was sure to call me names during class, as he taught the moral tales of Saney Guruji.[5] Father was most terrifically after money.

For my mother, though, I felt great love. Once, in the holidays, I went to Indore to my Atya's place. Father had just this one sister, you see. At that time Mother gave me thirty rupees and eight annas[6] — all the cash she had. Whenever I went to Atya's place, she'd teach me manners. One must not wash one's mouth noisily, one must speak pure language. She'd din this into me a thousand times, repeatedly. But I visited her infrequently. Because she and Mother had fallen out from the start. Because, you see, she came to us, as was the custom, to have her first baby. At that time — I was already born. But then Granny would not take good care of me, yet for Atya's daughter she cared very much. Besides, she'd had a girl, and my Mother, for example, — had me, a son. But Atya herself told me a story about Mother. That's good, really. In those days folk married in childhood. So then Father, Granny and Atya all went together without prior notice to my Mother's mother's place. Mother was playing outside. She cast just one glance at them. When they had gone into the house, Mother's folk called out to her to come in. But she wouldn't leave her play.

Our Granny and Mother squabble every day. Our lands are considerable. So Granny must accompany the farmhands. At home, for instance, a lot of visitors come and go. So Mother too has a great deal to do at home. Granny's point is that while she slaves in the fields Mother just sits at home, comfortably. Actually Granny only supervises the hands. Sits in some place in the shade so she can watch the road in the distance. And if she sees Mother or someone approaching then she hustles and hurries and slinks to some place where she can pretend she's really working.

Mother had noticed all this. And once on her way in she deliberately entered the field by another path. Having put down the *bhakris* in their place, suddenly from behind Granny she said, Yes, you really are breaking your bones working! Granny said, You came into the field by stealth. Sneakily. Tell me why.

Some stranger might think that this goes on really by way of entertainment. But Granny in fact hates Mother. Once in a way of course she does send Mother to the fields. But she doesn't know housework properly. Once for example an important guest arrived. At that time, after a quarrel, she had sent Mother off to the field. While serving the guest his lunch Granny said, Since morning I

Cocoon

have been breaking my back working. How much can I do! I will serve you just what we have ready. So when Mother arrived in the evening we told her about this. Then Mother said, You'd better stick to over-seeing the hands. We don't want to disgrace our house. Granny said, Who are you to say that? Isn't this my house, what? Then in a huff she went off to Indore to my Atya's. Came back after two months. That time she brought back an expensive piece of cloth for Mother. For my sister some red-and-yellow dolls, etc., and for me a talking parrot complete with its cage.

Beyond this I will not speak of any private matter about my home. For one, a person who tells such things usually happens to be a fool, and the listener is usually, for instance — a crook. Besides, I got into trouble once, having revealed private and secret stuff about my home. Some things I narrated to Eknath, innocently, and later when we had had a terrific quarrel he quite buried me for ever with frightening threats. This Eknath would seem a friend while he was one, and an enemy when he was an enemy. Having failed many a year in examinations he at last found himself in my class. From then till we went to high school he and I were a constant knot. Today, this Eknath seems to me like a nobody at all. Even then, I do not despise him. I do not myself have a degree or even a job. He and I used to go directly from school to take dips in the stream. Our Marathi school was just outside our village. The high school — that was in a neighbouring village. From villages round and about would come the pupils. When school gave over, Eknath and I always came back home after dark — gobbling this and that, tasting fresh goodies from the fields on the way, bringing down off trees tamarinds and berries. We were late every day. The other children would scamper home immediately after school. I never made friends with them. Once in the dark an enormous cobra crossed our path. At home I was never able to be by my-self. So I obtained that in this way, after school gave over. This fellow, by age and build and bone was the largest creature in our class. And me! My lankiness was a cause of derision for the whole class. If some day either he or I were on leave the boys would ask, Where's the wife today, eh?

From Eknath's time till today, I have found only one such friend at a time, a special one. I have never had two, three bosom buddies at one time. Now this is the sort of chum who in the end betrayed me most comprehensively. One evening he said to me, First go fetch that girl and then you stand guard here until we have finished everything. And if someone approaches, whistle. I asked, Where? I said, No. He said, Well, think carefully. I was nearly in tears with fright. He said, See, better think carefully. Don't want to? Then get out of here. I didn't quit, though. Just stood there, still, shivering. Because, what might not Eknath do to me tomorrow? He would reveal all my secrets. He started to leave. Then feeling pity for me or whatever, he came back and said, Don't weep, son. I only pulled your leg. Go, I'll manage all this without your help. Even so my arms and legs didn't stop trembling. I thought, He will reveal all. Yet how does he go with the girl and do these... things? So, for instance, what sort of a chap *is* he?

Yet Eknath himself revealed nothing. But then for a couple of years I thought he was a very old friend. Later, when we were in the seventh or eighth grade, from the Satpura Hills came a big troupe of tribal Korku[7] folk. Taking one of their girls, Eknath ran away.

At this time I had just begun to comprehend these affairs. So then I understood that this Eknath was in fact a very daring sort of young blade. Having kept even the police at bay, some two or three months later he returned alone. And having arranged a young bride for him his parents even rushed his wedding through. His father-in-law himself stuck him into a job in the railways. Still, as he had not given away my secrets, now Eknath began to seem great to me, and so on. And these secrets of mine... they were that in Grandpa's time, buried treasure had been found in my house. And that I used to eat, sneaking away to a halwai's[8] shop to do so, bhajis,[9] etc.— that was all.

Now, for instance, an introduction to myself. Ever since my childhood on and off I would have terrific dreams of a set pattern. Mother says that having risen in my sleep I used to chatter a great deal about matters-not-to-be-spoken-about-again. Then even Father's arms would ache from slapping me on my cheeks. Mother would weep. When I came to, though, I would fall asleep quite drained out. These dreams seem the same, the same. Some are vivid enough to be narrated, but Mother reports that I habitually shouted and howled in different ways. Sometimes, grabbing window bars and the like, I would sing without fail always this same hit song — "*O my darling is a rose, a rose.*" Sometimes I would keep repeating over and over things like aha aha wah wah wah. Or at other times, hooo…hooo...hooo....Like that. These dreams and such, I never did really manage to make sense of them.

In one dream I would feel that I was a creature like a horse,or something. And I would have to run a great deal. At a dreadful pace. Until my chest cracked. There is just open country about me, see. And even in this dream the terrified yelling, yowling — and waking.

Or may be not even like that.

— All the houses about me have, all of them on their own, started moving forward. A house or so among them is me. Some are strong houses. Some are high houses, rushing on and on, having flattened smaller houses to the ground. All the houses are shoving-butting each other like buffalo bulls. But how is it that nothing at all makes noise? So I would wake up, terrified, screaming.

Or perhaps not even like this.

— From waist up I am a cactus. Like a cobra's hood, growing, sprouting profusion. The roots have reached deep, deep down. And up above there's the prickly hood. My head, limbs wish to flatten this cactus, crush it, from within. Yet I also feel that I would grow, big, massive, and then explode. In the end I would be stretched out like a long rope or sideways like stretched rubber. Then I would wish in vain to wiggle my arms and legs. Just then I would wake up to sense my Father's hold on both my arms in one of his hands, while he let me have it with the other.

Or not like this either.

— In a glittering jewel set in a wall would be seen a building like the Taj Mahal. But someone says, Look behind. Then I do not see any building behind me at all. Only the reflection in the gem.

Or not even like this.

— A boulder, enormous like an elephant, tumbling over and over, down, down, smashing to bits as it comes. Those large and small bits — they are my body. But these fragments, scattered all over the countryside, have got to come together, they MUST. Yet the rock-shards don't have the strength to approach each other.

Or not even like that. While I was still at school there was a terrible threat hanging over me. One *halwai's* son would pester me, for no reason whatever. He was a chap who never had a bath, who would run after me, flicking licks of his hair up with one hand. Awfully cruel. I would become really restless when it was time for school to give over. Coming out, I'd pretend not to take notice of anything, having butted my way into a pack of boys. But this boy would come, without fail, running down running down off the patio of his shop, and he too would butt his way in straight and grab me. Then I would try walking on the edge of the crowd. Sometimes he would land a blow on my left arm, or whack me on the right shoulder, or at another time trip me over by thrusting his leg between mine. I'd say, nothing at all. Yet he would not spare me. Sometimes I'd say, What did I ever do to you? So then, tearing up my shirt he would say, You say 'What did I do?' Shall I give you one more? One more, shall I? Then I would start walking wordlessly on. Like this he would chase me quite far. Once, right in the school building, being terrified, I said to Lakhu, who sat next to me — Lakhu, let's not go home today.

Lakhu said, Today at my house we are having brinjal mess, so my mother has told me. I must rush.

I'd tell Ramesh, another friend, I don't feel like coming to school.

He'd ask, Why?

I would say, That halwai's brat hits me.

Then Ramesh would say, Why don't you yell? When someone hits me, I yell, loudly. Then he runs away. You should then pretend to wipe your eyes.

That day I tried weeping. The halwai's brat then filled my mouth with a fistful of dust. I came home spit-spat. Wiping my mouth so that no one would notice, I went in.

This last, of course, in my early childhood. Whether it was real or part of a dream, I don't remember exactly.

Meantime all this stopped. Because I began staying up all night. Truth to tell, that too is an introduction to me. Because there is no one else with such control over their sleep like me. I mean, when I stay up, including during daytime, I am up a couple of nights at a time. And when I do sleep, I am able to sleep — including night-time — for a couple of days at a stretch. Of course, now, I cannot manage all this at home. But let that pass. But this is a general introduction to myself when I am myself. Now, at home, once in a way having risen early and having performed my ablutions, I then feel, whatever shall I do now! Yet when I see some chap already up at six or seven o'clock, whatever might he not accomplish later on! At least for an hour, hour-and-a-half, though, he keeps doing any old thing, for instance.

So then until I matriculated, for instance, I did mostly pretty odd sorts of things. Later Father made sure that I would just study, and so on. But I must tell you something that I liked from before all that. But still, first I *will* tell you a tale that pleased me. Not that I have myself read it somewhere or something. Because, during that time I did very little unrequired reading. That is to say, I did read the *Geeta* which Jaganbuwa gave me. But as I looked for the meaning of the verses at the foot of the pages, there would be constant confusion. So then this story I heard from Girdhar, my friend at the time. He heard it in a monastery where a certain head monk was delivering a discourse on the Mahanubhava scriptures. Among all my friends I was most fond of this Girdhar. In general, in fact, he was quite obsessed with scriptures and such reading.

This tale is an example of the precept, *A Soul must in Godhead surrender*. In a cholera year a rich man's mother, father, children, wife, all, all died. Then bereft of hope, disgusted with life, he flung himself into a well by way of surrender. But once there, somehow regretting it, and so that someone might hear him and fetch him up again, he began to call out loudly. It was night. Those who did hear him thought it must be a ghost or something. So they ran away instead. Though it was bitter cold, this rich man did not stop his shouting all night long. Then next day, having heard this loud continuous noise, people gathered together and fished him out, the chilled rich man. He said, All this land and property of mine — crooks and thieves will grab it all! My ancestors acquired it by dint of labour, so I didn't feel like dying and surrendering it. Instead, suddenly he had felt like living. All the people said, Of course, that is right. Later after a couple of days, he died of fever.

This is certainly a queer old tale.

At our front door was a peepal tree. Its bole was extremely inadequate for its spread above, which was enormous. Once, because of a frightful wind-storm it fell — crash. Its farflung roots turned up cracking even one of our house walls.

This too is strange. But hitherto all is just an oral reckoning.

For instance, once again (and so on) I had been terrified. Let me tell you that one thing. When I was in my matriculation year, my third sister was born. That day Mother raised the roof. I was upstairs. Having collected from here and there some paper that was blank on one side, I was sewing it up into a huge big notebook. Just then, predictably, Father came there. Said to me, What, have you eaten? But Mother, who has always loved me, has now forgotten me. Isn't she anxious about something else now? Besides, into my mind were then beginning to enter some, like sensitive ideas, about birth-and-death also. I was, too, sewing that notebook in a determined mood. Even then Father said once again, What, have you eaten? At that, however, I just left in red hot temper. And wandered about here and there in the village until quite, quite late. Having come back, I learned that I now had a new sister. Later that night, having stayed up until very late, I prepared for the entire year a grrrrrreat timetable. Every morning, Algebra. Then school. In the evening, homework, etc. At night, English. Sunday, all other subjects. And no loafing about here and there, in the fields or in the village, for all the months until the exam was over.

This is, indeed, really bizarre.

And another thing.

About rats my opinion has not been good for — Oh, generations! Our Grandpa and two aunties and one uncle and his entire household had all perished in the plague. This is common knowledge. A rat makes its hole anywhere, it pisses anywhere, piles up its droppings anywhere, at all. Even all this one might on occasion tolerate. But to ruin good, quite good things without rhyme or reason is a terrible thing about rats. They will cut through *chappals*; by nibbling at the strings, they will drop a picture from the wall and break it; eat the lead in a red pencil; make holes in a new cupboard; bite your big toe; hop on to your body — so what if the rat is sacred, Lord Ganapati's mount![10]

Very early in my childhood something happened. From that time I made a resolve — A Rat is My Enemy.

The watchman on our farm once brought two baby hares that he had snared. One of them he must have eaten that evening. The other I brought home. I just *had* to. For the moment I placed it in a rat-trap. Its flashing red eyes, red-burst tongue! If I tickled it with my hand it would run so far away. And it would munch peanuts — *tuk tuk tuk*.

That night I slept with the rat-trap under my bed. Many a time before falling asleep I picked up the trap to look at him. Then he would suddenly start.

Very early in the morning I woke up to look again, but in the trap were two big, big fat hideous rats. And the poor bunny was lying dead, its wee feet turned up. Then I became most violently angry. The rats had bitten him in many places.

While it was alive I had not even looked at the bunny properly. The rats — they were rampaging about without a care in the world, in the trap. Ogre-like whiskers, ring after ring of their long black tails, and their sharp fangs biting at the wires of the trap, sleeky black hairy bodies. I will torture them to death. Mean to say, I *will* kill them. But the little dear's body must remain unmolested at least now. So then I took the trap to the water trough in the cattle shed. Even though I opened the trap door there, the rats refused to fall out into the trough. Many other children of my age were…gathered there, ready to kill…those rats. The rats would just scamper back and forth right over the bunny's body. But they would not come out. At last one boy shook the trap vigorously. We were all distracted. And so both rats, instead of tumbling into the trough, hopped along the edge and scuttled off unerringly towards the house, free.

Then, giving vent to my regret and all that, I really became mad at rats for ever. The whole lot is wicked. So thereafter I never wasted any opportunity to kill rats. Keeping a cat was not acceptable to Mother. Poisoning rats was disallowed by Father. A rat that had gone into its hole — Sumi and I would kill it together. She was the one to fetch and pour water. While I would lurk near the hole with a broom. Truth to tell, Sumi's task was awful. But in fear of me, she would fetch bucket after bucket of water. Once in a way, during the interval when she had gone to refill the bucket, that rat would emerge. And she would be so disappointed. I have killed rats from the trap by drowning them in water. I have waited with a stick, having determined the exact route by which rats came and went. And then — hammer, bump — at the rat just as it came out! That too I have done.

Once I poured kerosene on a rat and set it on fire. But he went directly into the house. And I received a great beating from Father. This continued right till the end.

But even then in my matriculation year I killed an overwhelming number of rats. Once one rat nibbled the bindings of all my books which I had stood all in a row, from the back. And separated leaf from leaf. Who will tolerate such liberty without protest? And there's another thing that's bad about rats. Mean to say, there's no telling exactly which rat has perpetrated such a thing. Because they are all alike, every one of them. Even then, keeping watch on the second and third night after that I saw one rat, for instance, stealthily scaling the books. And I thought, This has to be the selfsame rat, the Nibbler of my Books.

I used to study etc. on the upper floor of the house. Here, there was an awful clutter of things, stuff. Great cornbins and huge water jars, mud pots. And so on. But once the door had been shut then the rat had only one way to go — up along the wall. This rat stayed for a while on those books.

I had made all my preparations in advance. Stretching out an arm, I turned up the lantern. At this the rat promptly scurried behind a trunk. Then closing the door I flashed the torch on the trunk. Saying, Now you're well caught, Old Boy, I pushed the trunk, which had been pulled forward just for this purpose, right back up against the wall. With great gusto, I pushed and then waited for a short while. Then I again pushed the trunk to one side and took a peek. Well, there was nothing there at all.

Even if he had scuttled away where could the rogue have gone? I stood by, still. Then as expected there was some rustling at the back. In that corner was a row of mud pots and such. But to kill a rat there would be an awfully difficult task. Still, now I won't let even that rat's daddy get away!

Normally the rats would run over the pots and then along a bamboo stick hung to dry the washing, and so into the rafters. I now took the bamboo out of its place. Everyone else in the house was asleep. That was a good thing. Behind the large mud jar was a heap of sickles, useless axeheads, discarded pickaxes, iron scrap of a thousand kinds. Even after I flashed the light from above nothing could be seen.

Then with a long stick I banged about there a good deal, like. So then the rat emerged from one heap — srrrrr — and ran under another. So I sent the light down past another couple of jars. Just the tail of the rattie was visible outside the clutter.

If you look at it that way I am a pretty accurate marksman, actually. Holding the torch steady in one hand I advanced the stick very slowly, terribly slowly, in the direction of the rat's tail, and then suddenly smashed it down on the tail, BANG. Merely uttering a squeak and with a rustle and a jingle the rat disappeared in there somewhere, only a hollow tip of its tail came off.

Again I went inspecting, meticulously, behind each water jar and such. At last in a corner there was a vast storage jar. When I looked from one side for instance I saw nothing. Because behind this jar once again there was much junk and balls of paper, gathered by the rats.

When I sent the beam of light from the other side, then of course I saw the rat's back. So I closed that particular side by shoving a wooden board across by the side of the jar. At the same time I checked whether anyone had woken up downstairs because of this racket. Even from the other side — where I would not have found it easy to kill the rat — I jammed up the route by dragging a chest across.

Again I looked by torchlight. Because, otherwise, the beggar might have run away. But now his very face was indeed turned towards me. In the light his eyes were shining like beads, bright, very bright. I said, Just a wee bit longer now.

Then I actually climbed up on the huge bin, like. It was so high that if one raised one's head just a little bit one would touch the rafters. There somehow crouching hunched in the dark I let down the stick terribly terribly slowly. Whether the stick reached where I had intended or whether it just ended up short who knows, but I paused. Then I suddenly turned on the torch. This foolish creature had not the foggiest idea that the light might shine on him from above.

But, for instance, now two rats could be seen there — this was something novel. So when exactly did the second one arrive?

I mean to say, this really is charming. Then I poked the stick abruptly into the body of one and that one, of course, I killed quite dead.

The second one sought a way to escape. But all ways, everything was closed up tight. So then he climbed right up the very stick I was holding. Then, having cried out loudly, I flung the stick from my hand. The long stick went down with the rat. It must be retrieved once again. By good fortune he was now holed up behind some of the junk. This too was novel.

Then I myself jumped down — Thwack! — picked up the lantern quickly and placed it on the great jar. The rat had better not climb up just then. With another, smaller, stick I lifted up the long one, raising it upright. Again I picked it up in my hand. With this stick I churned the junk most terrifically. Still the rat would not come out. I was having to bend really really low. In that flutter and fuss the lantern even burned my shoulder. I really got mad. There wasn't time to put the lantern on the floor and then climb up once again. So after that I had to take constant care also to hold my shoulder away from the lantern. Then for instance by pushing with the stick I began to shove aside bits of the junk one by one.

The clutter in our house is infinite. And Mother says, The upper floor is not hers. Downstairs, though, she keeps everything really shipshape. Yet a thousand things end up here, just dumped, because they must not be seen below. This is something unique too.

I really lost my shirt.

I had now become really crazy. In the end while flinging each of the objects aside with the stick, I did see at least the tail of the rat. Just move one or two more things aside, that would do the trick. Then I wiped my sweat off. This was too much.

I pushed the lantern a little to one side. Holding the torch just so, I threw off an iron strip. Then for instance I saw the rat's back. This was another revelation.

It seemed to me that this had gone quite far enough.

His head was buried under the huge bin. But behind the bin I could see his bulk clearly, what about that, then? And the head remained hidden inside right where the stick stuck into his back. Then with a struggle the rat poked his head out. I pressed down the stick harder and harder. And after a while he was jammed there.

This is most terrific.

It does not end there, though. I had to climb down and push away the chest abutting the bin. Then I still had to drag out the two dead rats. For that I would have to climb up once again — incredible.

Then sometimes from behind the junk, at times shoving between things, I dragged out both dead rats. But these were altogether different rats. Incredible. Mean to say, the rat with the nipped tail was not one of them. That means — it had got away.

It was impossible to look for that one now. Because it was approaching daybreak. As usual having put these two rats on a piece of paper I went to the roof to throw them away. This was really getting out of hand.

Having flung the rats away, stretching lazily, I kept staring towards the east. There were tremendous stars there. Yet light was also spreading. My clothes were soaking wet. The cool, cool breeze on my face felt good. Being cool in the body now tired me, however. Then I lay down right there for a while, with my eyes open.

I thought, There's no sense in anything. So then I stretched my arms and legs out even wider and closed my eyes.

I thought, sleep is sure to come to me quickly. I was to have got up early in the night and finished my study of history. But this night is gone. This morning is gone too. The day will also pass in a daze. And again at night I shall be horribly sleepy. Forget rising early the day after — of course I would wake up late. And that will also be wasted. In sum, this was all too much. And then these cruel rats, their tails, this musty vast old house; these feckless stupid folk who gathered outside the village; and our ignorant farmhands. Not one worthwhile soul in this entire place. Rats, flies — no one kills them. All these heavy farm implements. This

Cocoon

village. The hideous barking and yowling of dogs that goes on all night long. This studying — all this is a useless burden. Let the examination take care of itself. I have been through a couple of revisions already. But I cannot now concentrate.

Then I turned on my side. A great thick stream of ants was passing in a hurry. It's still not quite morning. And these ants are already busily at work. They must have undermined this house. There are not just a hundred or two hundred ants. There must be millions. They must go on with this and that all night long. But this is good. At least this house will be razed to the ground, flat, undermined, that will be good.

Then I lay on my back again. Still some prominent stars. The morning comes first to the sky. Then whatever is left over comes to the Earth. How many such mornings have I suffered in this worthless place — who knows. Above these houses, above the village and rats and flies, in the sky all is spotless. Down below, though, snot, faeces, goo, mud, smoke, hundreds of niggling little noises, barking, yelling, yowling. All said and done, the waterwheels do sound good, though, as they draw water. But all in all this isn't really nice.

Must do something great. There has to be something that is great. Or it may be great to accomplish it. So I must do something like that. At least I must clear the matriculation well and escape from here. Otherwise Father is bound to say, There's such and such a six-month course in the agricultural college, you take that, that would do for you. What can be great in a six-month thing? Somehow, outside this village somewhere I must do something for years and years. There might be meaning in that — otherwise why bother to exist here uselessly?

Just then Mother herself came up. The lantern was still burning. She said, And why did you take off the drying stick? You mustn't study so far into the night. She said, Come down. So then I went down. In the morning as my eyes were about to shut, like, Father woke me up. I spent the day with my eyes strained open. And I also made numerous piddly little resolutions.

Then came the exams. Our exam centre was in Nasik. I had to have my eyesight tested by an eye doctor, too. So I went to Nasik. Sat the exam.

Fitted the glasses also.

But now this is all become too much.

TWO

Poona is the alma mater of learning. There I spent six years.

With me for the college admission and such rigmarole was sent a gentleman from our village. He'd spent a couple of years at college in Poona and after that he'd just sat at home. So it was appropriate that Father should send such a bod with me. But I was off to Poona for the first time so he ought to have described Poona to me or something beforehand, you'd think. But nothing doing. His notion was that I should ask him about his own history. And then he would tell me tales of his own college era throughout our journey. But I didn't ask any such questions. So he was annoyed with me. Mean to say, at Kalyan station when I broached the topic of tea he said, I've had tea at the last station. Or I said, You haven't ever been seen smoking cigarettes in our village but tonight you are smoking away. Then he said, The college office opens at eleven. First we'll go to your Maushi's[1] place.

The train arrived already full out of Mumbai. Even then we made pretty good room for ourselves. Then according to my youthful nature I felt hungry. Besides, I'd been feeling that in the midst of this vast crowd I was nobody at all. I'm not going to manage in this city world, really. Still, let's go on to Poona.

Then I slept with my head on my knees. When I woke up our gentleman had struck a pretty good friendship with a military man sitting beside us. Our gentleman was saying flippantly that there's not going to be a war, so you chaps have jolly good fun anyway, and so on. And the soldier was saying, in Hindi, Aw, forget that. He asked, Why are you going to Poona? So then our gentleman only said — Oh, for a little business. In Hindi, I'm going, you know, just like that.

Mean to say, these two thought nothing of me at all.

Through the window once in a way could be seen natural scenery and all that, but in the entire carriage I could only see one great man. Even though he was squeezed in among four or five others, he still looked great. Actually all those on his bench were dozing. But this chap had run his muffler under his chin and then tied it up to the handle of a trunk on the luggage rack. So no matter how much shoving and pushing occurred on his bench or how much the train rolled, his chin would happily float on the muffler and he himself was fast asleep. Besides, that large trunk above must be his too. Why would someone else let him tie his muffler to it this way?

Later, waking up, our gentleman said, Poona, Poona.

I'd planned that before we came to Poona, I'd wash my face and so on and freshen up a little before getting off. Instead we stumbled down, rubbing our eyes. Since our gentleman quarrelled with the porter or something, we came out of the station with my heavy trunk on my own head. A trunk on one's head... that's not quite right. Besides, it was so heavy my neck ached for the next two or three days. I entered Poona in this awkward way. Further, all the scurrying here and there looking for an autorickshaw. On top of all this we still had to go to Maushi's house — and Maushi just had to live up on the second floor.

Having got ready (and with better clothes and jacket than mine) our man started from Maushi's place for the college, with me in tow.

Our gentleman was walking in a lordly sort of way. When we met an old friend of his on the way our gentleman said to him, Come, let's have some tea. And the handsome looking friend said, Fine, having first scrutinized his watch.

Cocoon

I was eager to get to the college. But the chatter of these two was interminable. Then I felt, Perhaps we are still in the train. Now after reaching Maushi's place, we'll sleep first and then go to the college.

Their chat really flourished — What does that Dandekar do now? And that Khandekar, what does she do? And that other bitch? And that one is married, is she, and that other bloke? — I couldn't tell how long this went on. But when I woke up they'd run through their list of names. Out on the street this old friend with his mouldy old bicycle only asked, How long are you staying? and went his way. Later on I would see this first true-blue Poonaite sometimes going on the same bicycle. And saying to me, How's "He" doing, go away.

Until we reached the college our gentleman was bursting with enthusiasm. He began to babble about Poona — how everything in Poona depends on one's circle of acquaintances. People from far away come to Poona and one has to manage introductions for them. One should never fight shy of offering them tea or something. Don't you think this is like our Sangvi, now. Take this pal of mine. His grandfather, he's a well known Sanskrit pundit. His father, you know that novelist don't you, that's him. Now, one can only get to meet such a person in Poona, where else? Moreover Poona is the centre of culture and history. Not far from here is the factory at Pimpri. In all my three years I was not able to go and see it. Do go and see it yourself. In it everything happens automatically — and so on, a good deal more. Until we reached the college.

Having been overawed by its appearance, my chest began to heave — I shall be nowhere in this place. Besides, great persons and politicians and literary writers, so many have been through this college. I mean to say its tradition is certainly very luminous. Here I can acquire all the gear required for the ship of life.

But as the queue slipped forward I began to feel increasingly disappointed. There were pretty, pretty girls in the queue too. Having seen their transparent clothes, etc., I began to feel scared. I thought — This clearly means that they have come here with better marks than me. My clothes are, after all, only the creations of Natu, our country tailor. Besides, already I have started to miss things about my home.

The college principal was saying a few words to each youngster. To me he said, Why are you taking the Arts? I said, Father said, Take Science. But I fought with him to take the Arts. I like arts. He said, Pay your money over there.

At night terrific sleep descended upon me. But ever since Nana, Maushi's husband, got home, he had refused to let me fall asleep. Even after dinner was over. He inquired about all sorts of things from our village. Then for a long while the talk revolved around me. Nana told me right out, Conduct yourself in such a way that you become something worthwhile later on. Study with an aim. I agreed with him on this and said, Yes.

Don't just say yes. You have to try hard. I said, Yes, once again.

It's exactly when you are so sleepy that someone waxes eloquent on philosophical thoughts. Still I was pretty well-be-haved. I sat up straight and tried to pay attention. My whole life was taking a crucial turn — and to think that I'd feel sleepy when all this was going on about my own aim in life.

When he announced that he was conveying all this on the basis of his own study up to the Intermediate class, Maushi even made some tea. I'd been up all of last night. Nobody cared a hang about that. My gentleman was smart so he had gone by himself to the pictures.

While I was wondering how long exactly one should stay up according to etiquette after one's tea was drunk, Nana said, What have you decided to study for your B.A. examination?

I said, I have not decided yet but languages I do like.

He said, This one should determine in advance. Listen to me, take history. Later for your M.A. also, pursue history. Because the professors of other subjects have to work too hard. On no account should you take languages. If you become a language man then every year you will have to read new books to keep up. But once you've done history, that'll last you for life. What can change in history?

This was another thing that I found illuminating.

At long last Maushi said, Now that's enough, all right? Let him sleep.

But I said, No, no, I am not sleepy.

After a little more time had passed, though, I suddenly paid attention again, at which time Nana was saying, Sleep now.

Then I slept.

Next day we had to get through many chores. If there are many such chores to do I normally feel excited all day. Our gentleman and I set off after lunch. Now for the first time I really saw Poona at close quarters. By the entrance of the Literary Academy we saw a man in trousers like breeches. This just had to be some great literateur, I thought, watching from our autorickshaw.

Having arrived at the hostel I took charge of my room.

Then wandering all over the city our gentleman and I bought a thousand things. A mattress, sheets, pillows, a mirror, hairoil, polish, powder, face cream, shoes, woollens,shirts, stove, strainer, pans, cup-and-saucer, needle-and-thread, brush, shaving things, so on. Our gentleman was buying away without so much as consulting me. He did know all about this. But all the same he'd got these things organized for me in every way imaginable. So for the next month or two he left me no chance at all to do any shopping myself. He even bought a badminton racquet for me. He said, One doesn't merely study at college. One must acquire a person-ality too.

In addition he made a great many purchases for himself. Indeed, I felt that he was merely using my preparation as an excuse, having come here to buy a rocking horse, umbrellas, a photo of Tilak,[2] etc.

In the evening, looking at his things, Nana said — Hey, why did you buy Tilak's picture? In our house there's one just like this one floating about somewhere. From a magazine. You could have framed that.

Then he asked Maushi for the magazine. In it was the same picture.

Nana said, Now isn't that so?

Then he gave away his picture of Tilak to me.

Put it up in your room. But don't take a 'drop' like Tilak from the examination in your very first year, see — he said.

Then generously saying that Maushi could do the rest of my organizing, our gentleman left. He must have received much approbation from Father at home.

Until classes started at the college, I stayed on at Maushi's. Each day I'd take a turn up to my hostel room, though, and return while contemplating what I was going to achieve in Poona.

Our college was spread out as extensively as our village. The hostel was huge and everyone had a room to himself. That really pleased me.

Not too far from the hostel begin ranks of hills. Further in fact one encounters a jungle the way it is in the mountains. Behind the hostel stood our messes. Around these the peaceful bungalows of some ancient and learned professors. Outside one of these bungalows was the plate of Professor J.K. Shah, and so on. In another lived our hostel warden named Paranjape. And besides, on the side of the hill in increasingly peaceful surroundings were the bungalows of even more scholarly professors, even the college principal himself. I saw a great big dog there.

One house had no name plate at all. So I asked someone standing there, Who lives here? He said, I do. I never did learn the name, after all.

Within about five minutes' distance from the hostel was the college, and so was the canteen. There I ate novel Madrasi dishes which we couldn't get in our village. One a day. And memorised their names. Only when I'd finished my omelette did I find out that it was not a vegetarian dish.

Beside the hostel, wide playing fields. And in the yard of the college were trees and bushes of many varieties.

At last college opened.

Right away, on the very first day when I returned from my bath, the hair oil bottle slipped from my hand and broke. Only at the bottom did some oil remain. The rest spilt on the floor. First I put the lower portion of the bottle safely aside. Dipping my hands then in the oil on the floor, again and again, I smeared it on my head generously. Even then a great deal of it went waste. Besides, at home the oil gets absorbed by the mud floor but here was a flagged stone floor. That's why my mind was more agitated. I rubbed some into my arms and legs also. When I left home, Mother did say — Now, however will you manage, My Little One?

Then I went to Madras Cafe and ate something. I was aware that a great deal of oil was dribbling off my head. All day I moved about the college like that. In the evening, having become depressed for some reason, I was lying down with a newspaper over my pillow. Just then someone knocked on my door. Wiping the oil off my forehead carefully, I opened the door. This chap was someone from my own class.

He said, Who are you?

Pandurang Sangvikar.

Me, Suresh Bapat. We are in the same class.

Yes.

I just thought I'd come by. Thought I might do the introduction.

Right. Will you have tea?

Certainly.

Where are you from?

Belgaum. My father's a magistrate.

How many brothers do you have?

We are six brothers.

And sisters?

Three sisters. What caste are you?

One should not bother with muddles of caste and such.

I don't believe in caste and all that. Just asked.

Those who say they don't believe in it try to take credit by saying so.

That is quite right.

But all this while Suresh was staring at my head. Finally he said, So your bottle broke, did it?

This is absolutely great.

Then we became friends.

After waking up in the morning, to lie about for a couple of hours is surely sentimental. I kept thinking of my house as a terrifying entity. Our house meant terrific racket, barking at each other, scampering, the coming and going of farm hands, the stove for ever burning, large rats creating a ruckus, on the terrace white, black, black-and-white, roly-poly red-eyed pigeons, so on and so forth.

Moreover, in the last days before I left home to come here Mother had voiced the most awful notions about me. Ever since my childhood I used to feel I'd become someone great. This thing, whatever it is, is rife in well-to-do homes in the countryside. What "great" means, of course, is never clearly defined.

That way I myself used to feel often that I must become great. I mean, in my childhood I used to feel that I should fight battles like Bheema[3] with a mace and annihilate all my enemies. Later, that I should make inventions like Thomas Alva Edison. Later still, that I might be able to create witty jokes like Gadkari, the playwright. While in primary school I'd feel I must become a school master and a "Sir" at the high school. However, that my wanting to become great was nothing at all I realized after getting to know two or three chaps at the hostel.

A friend called Tambe said to me, I write letters to my mother in verse.

Even before this I had scant respect for him. But after learning this my respect redoubled. His aspiration was to win the Nobel Prize. He'd even started to write a play. When he was late getting up in the morning he would come to my room brushing his teeth. Spitting out of the window, he'd state that he'd got up late because last night he'd finished a whole scene of his play, saying which he would leave.

Many people rise late. But his late rising was great indeed.

I never particularly asked to read his notebook. So he became quite fond of me. He used to say, Sangvikar, you're the true connoisseur. The rest only praise me. I frequently gave him tea.

His method of composition was as follows — the drafts would be written at night and they would be transferred into a fair book right through the day after being edited and improved. He would say, This way I'm sure to fail in the exam. I would ask him, which great authors have passed a B.A. anyhow? Gadkari? Khandekar?

One of the scenes of his play went thus —

Prabhakar: (Shuffling backwards) Sudha, answer this!

Sudha: But dear Prabha, you goose, my father was with me, and still you called out to me.

Prabhakar: (Moving forward) Is that so? I thought that you meant it from the heart when you called me an ape.

Even a scene or two of Shakespeare might have been written with just the same intensity. Later Tambe was bound to become great. But to write day and night with such commitment to oneself is doubtless greatness already.

On the wall of his room he'd written this line, so that he could read it as soon as he woke up —

Arise, awake, and stop not until thy aim is reached.[4]

Compared to Tambe's, my aim and my struggles for it were like nothing.

But another chap, Madhukar Deshmukh, was more a friend of mine than Tambe. When he first arrived in the hostel he came into a room right next to mine. At that time for a whole week his baggage lay packed the way he'd brought it. I asked, Do you wish to leave this room? Then the real reason turned out to be altogether different.

His father had said, Take Science. And he had been enrolled in Science. But he wanted to study the Arts. He said, I am still considering.

Then he determined that come what may, he would take the Arts. And then he opened his trunk and all that and arranged his room very neatly.

Until some resolution had been reached he felt suspended between two worlds. When I asked, What is your aim in life? He told me, One shouldn't ask such questions. When we go to the hill for a walk I'll tell you.

His aspiration — I mean to say, the moment I heard it I realized how inconsequential I was. To Establish Equality in the Whole World. A man who has such an aspiration *must* be tremendous. Right there on the hill he asked me what my aspiration was, so then I hemmed and hawed and told him I hadn't yet decided.

After that I too resolved, whatever my aim, never to say what it was.

Suppose one says, I would like to dismantle our house and build a new one. And on top of it place a tower clock. Meaning that everyone in our village would know what time it was by just leaning out of their windows — if they heard such aspirations, they'd laugh at them, won't they?

Madhu Deshmukh, though, used to tell me all his intimate matters — I shall learn to play the violin and conquer girls, he'd say right out. For this he attended violin classes daily. Madhu was my special friend. He told me many things, opening out his heart to me.

Once he came back in the afternoon, I heard his door open and pulled shut with great force. From my room I heard his books being flung down. Then he himself fell with a thud on his bed. At that the whole room shuddered. When these thudding sounds were heard time and time again, I was alarmed. Coming out of my room I called out, Madhya, open the door.

At which he did.

Whatever are you doing?

Then what he told me was great. He said, I have experienced pain. I'm trying to fall down on my bed with a suitably satisfying thud. But I can't seem to manage it.

At first I used to go to Maushi's place often. Later that frequency diminished. Maushi used to make up her face and dress up. Everybody in Poona dresses up, it's true. But it's not nice for one's own Maushi to dress up and strut about. Maushi tarts herself up every day and goes out promenading. Even though she is a mother of four children. This is really bad. Once with much hesitation I told Nana about this. From that time my relationship with Maushi soured. Nana said, When you come here, you get your dinner, don't you? That's enough, then.

Thereafter I visited only once in a while for a meal. I was new to Poona. I was bound to speak like that. The very first day when I went out for a walk in a nice part of town, I thought, There seem to be quite a few prostitutes in Poona. But even after behaviour like Maushi's if a woman's husband calls her his wife, why should anyone else say anything about it?

Another calamity would descend upon me regularly. My Mother's letters. She'd write, I think of you very much. Besides, all your four sisters too remember you. But I miss you most of all. Then I would send off a long reply. But, truth to tell, gradually, Mother's memory became fainter. And here novel things kept happening. So naturally one neglected old things. But having written a long, long letter I'd go to Madras Cafe and stuff myself on something or other.

By and by I began to smoke cigarettes. Not that I picked this up in the company of Suresh Bapat. I had smoked many times before. Now it had increased, that's all. Once when I was a child, I lit a match and began to smoke it like a cigarette. Then my Father beat me. So then I said, weeping the while, I am smoking a make-believe cigarette and yet you beat me. Then surely some day I shall smoke a real cigarette. Later when we were a bit older — having seen a hero in a film smoke a cigarette with panache when he'd been captured by a gang of robbers, and wanting to be sure to smoke a cigarette properly if ever we were captured by robbers — Eknath and I both finished a whole pack at a sitting. Because, after smoking two or three, who'd have taken the packet home? It'd be better to smoke it all and be done with it. So we smoked.

My real need for a cigarette arose when Father once wrote to me a no-nonsense letter. Before that, I'd smoke with Suresh just for fun. Father wrote, In three months you've had almost one thousand rupees. So let me know how you've been spending the money.

Thereafter arrived the money order with the message — According to your demand I am sending two hundred rupees, so make sure your study goes well.

This hurt me a lot. But I looked over the stubs of earlier money orders. Even there was the same message — *So*, study hard.

Meaning, the money was expressly given only so that I would study.

Actually, what has money to do with one's study? I don't throw it about much. Still, compared to others my expenses were considerable. That much is true. For one thing as soon as I get money I give tea to Khan bhayya, our hostel watch- man. Next, one anna each to as many beggars as I meet that day. On such days Suresh was bound to be with me. Because I treat Suresh, give him tea. When I start handing out cash to beggars, liberally, Suresh says — This ass, he's scattering money about, the beggar! When I ask him, Don't you feel anything for the beggars? he says. Of course. I feel bad. But until I finish my M.A. and Ph.D. I'll not bother about such matters. Till then, it's dad's money; later, our own.

Next I buy things from the second hand market. Then, because old books in mint condition were to be had for a pittance I started to buy them. Further along, eight or ten annas daily for cigarettes.

But at first I did not incur any wasteful expenses. One might say that the alms to beggars met that description. Still, a rupee or two a month wasn't much. Come to think of that, of course, so much money went in treating friends to tea, and so on. By contrast we ought to give beggars much more. Not that one feels pity for every beggar. But one goes about on the streets with as much as five or ten rupees in one's pocket — because it is better to have some ready cash. So if some poor man is asking for a paisa, then shouldn't one give him an anna?

Otherwise too, Rege, Jog, Chavan all extracted tea and such from me. These couple of chaps were from Poona. Genuine Poona chaps. Who sat on the back bench with me regularly. So they were nice chaps. Beyond this, I found no other good reason to offer them tea. On the contrary, they were Poona chaps! One might tolerate the Toughs of Nagpur or Rascals of Mumbai, but the Crooks of Poona — watch out for them, that's what my pensioner uncle'd said when I left home. The Toughs and Rascals might get you on some rare occasion. But Crooks positively infest our society. So one encounters them among one's regular circle of acquaintance too. This notion of my pensioner uncle was so right.

Rege, Chavan and the others used to say, Your hair is beautiful. Besides, you are bound to stand first in the class in the examination — they'd say that too. But not all of this merely because they wanted tea. Not merely in front of me. Even to others they would repeat the same sort of thing. Later on, that I played the flute well was also spread about by the same chaps. They would come to my room and right in my presence gobble up my sugar, ovaltine, milk, biscuits, etc. I am, you know, quite capable of establishing contact with a new culture from such close quarters, so why grudge them anything? I never did say a word to them. I thought, perhaps the poor chaps don't get these things at home. Let 'em eat. Still, the poor chaps do wear expensive clothes, I must say. Indeed, Jog would often ask for loans of money.

But once he made a thorough fool of me. He said, You performed a most important service the other day by giving me ten rupees. Come, I'll feed you. So saying, he took me to a cafe. And, after having paid the bill out of *my* ten rupees, he said — Here's the change, after paying the bill.

So then I said, Just see if I ever give you even a paisa again. Then he says, Don't. I'll find many others like you.

From that time, on this or that pretext I started to lose my temper with Jog. So what if he was one of the top thirty matriculates? I myself must have been among the first five hundred. Or Tambe might have been in the top five thousand. Every ass says that Jog has flair — even the Marathi professor himself once read his paper to the class. I'd made an issue of it, naturally. I said — Jog, your essays are beggarly. What you say is also shitty. You cannot really speak well. Your speech is always cluttered with some pompous lines from Tukaram[5] and cliches such as 'softer than wax,' etc.

He was badly offended by that. That way he was full of self-importance. Some days he'd come to me in the evening. The weather would be fine. The sun tender and the air beautiful. Who'd want to go for a walk at such a time? But Jog would say, Not coming? All right, then. I'll go along. *With oneself does one debate....* Or time and again, if someone started to utter platitudes such as — *Consider Truth to be Light* — and if that person was invariably this Jog himself, wouldn't one get really angry?

Once he said to me, You say "res-to-runt." That's wrong. The real original pronunciation is "restaran."

Heck! These three were crooks. You'd have to call them crooks. Mind you, once I conveyed my intention to go to dine with them at home — saying, I'd do one Sunday with each of you in turn — they even stopped passing by my door.

Once such riffraff among friends had been choked off there only remained Madhu Deshmukh, Tambe, Suresh Bapat, and one more chap called Ichalkaranjikar. All of them were nice.

Suresh and me — our friendship meant going for walks on the hills, kicking up our heels there, and not into crowds to muck about with people.

Ichalkaranjikar on the other hand was a low rascal. Being city-bred, he was well versed in city ways and etiquette. He'd call me savage but good. Why then our friendship did not last I cannot understand.

Our first introduction had been wonderful, though. During the first term he used to live in town with relations who were from Mumbai.

So then once in class when the teacher started to teach, yet again, the Consequences of the French Revolution, rising to his feet, Ichalkaranjikar said — Sir, this has been done before. Teach what comes next.

I was dozing right behind him.

Blazing with anger the teacher said, No, I am just beginning the topic today. Ichalkaranjikar said, Then look at my notes from the last class.

So then, in a moment sweeping his eye in red-hot anger over the whole class the teacher said, Who else says this has been done?

Nearly the whole class was dozing. So no one made out what was going on. But I caught on. With my head still resting on the bench I yelled — Yes, this has been taught.

I felt an unnecessary concern for Ichalkaranjikar. Mean to say, in front of me sat this well built fellow, that's why I was able to rest my head on the bench with impunity.

Then I felt scared that this teacher would ask to see my notes. And I hadn't brought my history notebook thinking — Why bother? But he asked some other chap instead. And then resumed teaching — Last time I had merely introduced this topic, now I narrate in detail.

Ichalkaranjikar turned around and said to me, Now you may go back to sleep.

I said, Then who will listen to this rubbish?

He said, The beggar doesn't even prepare before coming to class.

I sat up alert.

He asked, So, what's your surname?

I told him my first name, contrarily — Pandurang. Smiling, he said, In that case mine is Madhumilind. So then I laughed aloud.

He said, So, what happened?

His first name was awfully lyrical and all that.

Then he said, Where do you live?

I said, Hostel.

Then I am also coming to the hostel next term.

Then the hour finished. We spoke a little longer. His surname turned out to be Ichalkaranjikar.

Now this chap was really a merry old fellow. Whenever he was bored somewhere, his occupation would be to come to my room and have any old argument. He'd tell some story about Mumbai, and I'd repay him by telling some tale from Sangvi. Eventually tiring of this I'd tell him myself, Now quit. He used to live with relations quite far away. Yet he'd casually drop by my room at least once a day.

I went to Suresh's room. Now, there was a new calendar right over his bed. Of a naked woman. Sitting by a stream. And in her lap a swan. And so on. I said, One shouldn't display such titillating pictures in one's room.

He said. All people are naked beneath their clothes. Displaying pictures in the room makes no difference.

I said, That's true.

He said, And you? You don't take off your underpants even in the bathroom. You are a dirty fellow.

In his room was also a picture of his mother and father. I said,

Such pictures are obscene.

No mother, no father — ergo, NO ME!

That would have been wonderful. *They* are responsible for the cycle of our lives. We'll hold them responsible for everything.

Keep your opinion to yourself. I'll put up anything I like in my room.

This wrangle stopped right there. I got awfully angry. But after some days on the pretext that the frame broke he put it away in his trunk. My own bag was already packed, to go home for Diwali holidays.

In the holidays I went home.

Rendered accounts to Father. Listened to whatever he said. Diwali was over.

Then I set off for Poona.

When I came back, Ichalkaranjikar had already come into the hostel. Thereafter he wouldn't stop following me around. He'd show his uniqueness by wearing shirt, trousers, even shoes all in sparkling white. He also had his weight cards from the age of ten all neatly arranged.

Even his room was novel. On his bed he'd keep all the tea stuff— stove, milk, etc. And in the. mosquito net above, his notebooks and books, etc. This net would once in a way descend so low with its burden that it looked certain to burn over the stove. On the table — all the sports cups and medals, shields, that he'd won, starting from his school days. On the chair a very large table lamp. And the mattress, though, on the floor, in the Peshwa style.[6] So that if any chap came to class in stiffly ironed trousers we'd take him and sit him down on the mattress.

In company Ichalkaranjikar was, that way, quite well-mannered. So the tricks he otherwise played did work. Another of his tricks was to call just any chap to his room, and, having made only one cup of tea, drink it all by himself while chatting with the visitor. Subsequently, if one of his visitors, being offended, began to speak about Ichalkaranjikar's uncultured behaviour we would be immensely pleased and go and report this to Ichalkaranjikar.

But even he met his match in a great chap called Chakrapani. He'd made just the one cup of tea and poured it when Chakrapani said, apparently surprised — So, you *know* that I don't drink tea?

That tables had been turned thus we learned from Ichalkaranjikar himself.

He played one other sort of trick.

There was in the hostel an African boy from Uganda. He would always criticize us, call us names — that Indian people slept with their clothes on and that it was not hygienic. It's shameful, one must take off one's clothes to sleep. At least you educated Indians mustn't behave like this....

In the summer he would take off even his underwear to sleep. One night very late Ichalkaranjikar and four or five others — Suresh and so on — came to me. They said that they had all "viewed" the African. He's sleeping on his stomach. How funny he looks!

I took hold of the ventilator bars above his door and looked in but found the African asleep naked on his back, in the lovely glow of the night lamp. Because they had fooled me I started pummelling them. Then they all said, We too were fooled just like this by Ichalkaranjikar. We then fooled many others by showing them the same sight. Finally, looking in, Suresh said, Give me a clap! Now he's turned over! Then Ichalkaranjikar and I looked in, hanging on to the window bars. But he was still lying face down. Then we started walloping Suresh.

After this scuffle we learned that the African had woken up. But it wasn't possible for him to come out as he was right away. Meantime all of us ran away to our rooms and went to sleep.

Next morning the chap asked me, What was that riot at my door?

Cocoon

Then, when I had narrated the whole business to him, he laughed and said, What else will an Indian look at?

Ichalkaranjikar and the rest of us friends would tease a chap—Pradhan. He was a veritable ninny. One night I turned up the switch to put off his light. Meanwhile in the dark Ichalkaranjikar removed the light bulb and put it in his pocket.

Pradhan said, Sangvikar, put on the light. Turning the button up and down I said, Where, what? The light doesn't go on. Your fuse must have blown. Still Pradhan did suspect that the bulb might have been taken out. In the darkness as he fumbled to locate the bulb he got a shock.

Indeed, everyone would put a copper paisa in his bulb holder and then refix his bulb in the evening. After darkness had fallen he'd turn the switch but there would be no light. Then when he took off the bulb he'd find the paisa.

Then cursing us he would come into our rooms. But we would drive him out again. Until the wireman came he'd sit alone in the dark in his room. Once the fuse had been connected we'd all be ready for more horseplay in his room.

When he received ladus and such goodies from home we'd all immediately polish them off. Then he began to hide his box. Once we learned that he had received goodies from home but were unable to locate the box anywhere. So we found a key that would fit his lock. Once when he went out we opened the door and searched his room. So, where should he keep the box but under old newspapers with old clothes and shoes and the like on top of it. The goodies were finished right there. Again piling up the things the way they were and locking the door, we all kept mum. We thought, today or tomorrow Pradhan must scream at all of us. But Pradhan also kept mum as though nothing at all had happened.

All of us friends were, without exception, from the first-year class. Many in higher classes were bookworms. Besides, they'd impart serious information to us. So, with them we behaved politely.

Some of them were all right, though. They'd ask us — Has such and such an English lesson begun? Then they would say, Pay attention to this lesson. Some time during it Patwardhan will make his old crack saying "Will you take me" instead of "Will you make tea." Then laugh out loud on purpose. Our seniors told us the same thing.

After that we spread this around, about paying particular attention. At precisely the right time for the joke we set the classroom ringing with laughter. Probably the teacher also caught on to that. But once we were in the intermediate class ourselves, the next year's fresh lot did the same thing again, and so we felt that our labour had been wasted.

But I don't really approve of many people laughing together — such laughter in concert is as horrifying as howling.

In college, comic plays are unfailingly performed. And the entire theatre laughs. Even we ourselves don't mind that so much while we are watching the play. But once Suresh and I got bored and left the play and went out. Stood drinking tea at the stall outside where it was very quiet. Leaving aside the persons at the tea stall, there was not even a sparrow about. Then, at brief intervals, after an actor's or actress's thin voice was heard, the whole theatre would roar with laughter — Haw haw haw kho kho kho ho ho kho kho ho ho. We both found this terrifying.

Suresh and I were greatly in tune on such matters. If some girls approached us, he and I would either enter some shop and inquire about their rates, or on occasion even buy bread or some such thing.

Once in fact Suresh went into a barber's and came out with his top all shaved smooth. He said to me — You don't put oil on your hair. So you look terrible. Now, how do I look, because I don't *have* any hair! All in all, girls would stay away from me too.

But there was one thing about Suresh. Sometimes when we went wandering down some street in the evening, he'd stuff a bloody red tomato into his mouth and chew away at it while staring at girls — tomato after tomato.

Then, if we men and girls went together on some picnic or outing or something, Suresh and I would fall out to the edge of the group, naturally. Truth to tell, we became friends because of our habit of going to bed late. After midnight the cafes would close. Only he and I could manage to walk far away to the railway station to drink tea and then walk back.

Still, if there *were* girls, we *would* go on those pinics. On that pretext we got to see some Beauties of Nature. On an outing if one keeps a bit on one's guard one can protect one-self from girls pretty well.

Mean to say, a girl asked me, although we had never even met before — You go to music class. Why? So I said, I am learning the tabla.[7] You know, T A B L A. So why would that girl speak to me again?

Suresh and I would manage to entertain ourselves at a picnic by devising funny names for some of the girls. A girl whom we saw after we two had come back having drunk *neera*[8] juice, we called Neerali. Another was sloth-lazy. So she was Yawn. Yet another walked oh-so-delicately, therefore, She-of-the-ways. Another was *lalbund*, really red — so she was Bundi. Another, because she'd keep pulling forward a lock of hair, was Pluck-lock, etc.

But how long can one amuse oneself in this way? So, being bored, once we quietly avoided being seen and walked right up to the top of the caves at Karli. To see what lay beyond the caves. Above, though, was only a great pastureland. There was no one there. Just tall grass. Then we ran and ran up. And, because it was slippery, balancing ourselves and holding hands, we still managed to slide along further and further. And finally, rolling over and over, we got stuck in such a wet place that at first we didn't know where our chappals had got to. Grass so tall that you could communicate with each other only by calling out. Innumerable baby frogs. Somehow we managed to get right up to the pasture.

When we returned we appeared "romantic" to all the others. Someone gave us this fishpond — Baby Tonic Hasn't Really

Helped! But the fact was, many thorns had pierced our feet while we were coming down.

After we'd come back to the hostel, Ichalkaranjya came into my room as was his wont. Gathered all the news about our picnic. And he said, So then, now I shall give you one more fishpond — You sod, you are, naturally, Fishpandurang!

Pleased with his own joke he gave us tea.

Well, our friendship took shape, and all that. Even then, while swimming, Suresh never taught me how to dive. In Sangvi we only knew how to dunk ourselves in the water.

Here at the swimming pool I would just jump in from way up. And whack against the water flat out. My chest and forehead and thighs would grow red and burn.

Suresh would say, I shall never teach anyone anything at all. Let this carry on for eight or ten days. Then you'll manage naturally.

Once after wandering about the railway station for long we walked to the bund on the river. There, as we listened to the roaring of the water, the day dawned. The river was, of course, in terrific flood. Still, Suresh said, Do let's bathe right here in the river. Now, having lived in the city, time and again he would go crazy over such things. Saying — There's probably low water here, or here, or here — we walked a long way downriver. When the river opened out quite wide, we saw shallow water. Then he suddenly pushed me into the water fully clothed. But he himself only started swimming after he'd taken off his clothes. The water was warm. Climbing up on the bank I wrung out my clothes and slept on a rock.

When I woke up at last, quite far away Suresh too had gone to sleep nonchalantly. But it was afternoon by then. I was terribly confused, unable to understand it all, where we were exactly.... After a while I went towards him. That worthy was fast asleep. And that too on a rock in such a way that even if he stirred in his sleep just the least bit he'd fall into the river. Then suddenly I grabbed his arms and shoved him into the water. Even as he fell he woke up and started to yell. That I found extremely funny.

But he came up from under the water open-mouthed, fully clothed, and having swallowed a great deal of water. And jerking his limbs to clear the water, over and over. Coughing and spluttering, vomiting water, in terrific anger, he got out aiming to come at me. Then, with me running before and he after me — till we reached the bund. Even when we became frightfully tired, we kept running. Whenever I stopped, though, he too would run very slowly. It was impossible that I'd run faster. In this way, stumbling and struggling terrifically, we came back to the hostel.

However, Suresh said, When I fell into the water I lost my keys as well. In fact he may have lost them somewhere before also. Then he and I slept in my room.

All day long, and all night long, and again till next afternoon. Both of us awoke simultaneously. He said, We ought to be able to sleep like this for fifteen days at a stretch.

For that, we must not sleep for fifteen days at a stretch first! Eventually, one had to stay awake anyhow.

In all, though, we didn't spend the entire year in such activities. We all continued to study and pass our exams. Ichalkaranjikar, indeed, achieved many glories in the National Cadet Corps and sports. His picture too appeared in the college magazine. One of Tambe's poems also appeared. It conveyed the sense that the words he'd put together were not really his. This of course I liked somewhat. But the greatest thing of all, I mean to say, was the ending of this poem — O Reader, even if you had not read this poem, it would not have mattered to me, really. This, in the *shardoolavikridita*[9] measure, was great. In fact Tambe himself was a great chap. I began to encourage him to write plays.

Moreover, this year Madhu Deshmukh indulged in so many hassles, got involved in so many tangles, that only eight days before the exam did he return to his senses. Mean to say, when the Poona city civic elections came round, he was canvassing for eight whole days. Besides, even after his violin classes ended he continued to practise at home.

Aside from this he was the first among us to fall in love. Because his demeanour was bold. When his affair ended, he even managed to prepare for the exam better than the rest of us. Still, in one or two subjects he had to be promoted somehow. And his father said, When you have chosen the Arts on your own initiative, you are having to be pushed and shoved up in this way. Needless to say, all his other accomplishments were not worth retailing to his father. So he just said, No. I shall study well next year and show you that I can get good marks.

Already this year he was going bald. So he used to say to his father that after some time he wouldn't be able to harm even the hair on his head.

But all in all Madhu Deshmukh was a crazy chap. As he'd already finished falling in love, later he would threaten anyone who was about to fall in love — Go ahead, fall in love, you nut. Later on when you become a baldie like me, then you'll understand.

But it was not nice that he should pursue his affairs by borrowing money from me. Already as a punishment his father sent him less money. But when one chats with one's sweetheart in the canteen one is bound to need quantities of food. Therefore, more or less borrowing money from me, repeatedly, he brought the tally of his debt to fifty rupees. But as he was a friend, until he had finished his exam and was ready to go home I ignored the matter. In the end I myself didn't have enough money left to return home. I also starved and was obliged to survive on bhajis for two or three days. Then I did really pester him a great deal with demands for my money. He said, If you were going to behave like this why did you give me money in the first place?

I said, All this happened on account of your love affair.

Merely because he told me messy stuff about his love from A to Z — intimate details and all — did I condescend to spend those days on nothing but bhajis. The introduction between this girl and him, the tying of the love-knot, conflict, resolution — all occurred in the prescribed, the conventional manner. But one day at the time of paying the bill in a restaurant she said to him, Today I'm going to pay the bill. You never let me pay. Upon this, truly speaking, shouldn't he have said — You know Pandurang Sangvikar, don't you? I borrow money from him and pay these bills — and then let her pay the bill? Instead, Madhukar Chintaman Deshmukh, the Worthy Lover, replied — Dear, later, all your life you have to cook for me and feed me. Now, how would some "experienced" girl from college like this? She shivered all over, and only said, I *must* pay.

From that time on, saying — Now the exam has approached anyhow, and whatever happens happens for the best, and love is eternal...he got down to his study. All this I found rather comic. But hearing this and other such things about girls I began to feel great regard for them.

Mean to say, quite naturally, girls are endowed with luminous power. In contrast, men! I feel scared of girls. Because for one thing any girl can look at a man as though she would like to eat him up, swallow him whole. On the other hand... men. Therefore, even as the exam was going on, I thought some compassionate thoughts about the women in our class. These sixty or seventy girls. What'll become of them later? Some will end up here, some there. They will get married and find odd-bod husbands. And they themselves look so delicate. They will go through confinements. They will have babies. We will have nothing at all. If all mothers in the world imparted the right sort of education to their children, why would there be any wars in the world? But isn't all civilization in the hands of all mothers?

But mothers must not love children too much.

Finally, Madhu said, Keep an eye open for someone who'll buy my violin for ready cash.

After I had managed somehow for some days — merely sending postcards home to say, Yes, I am coming home — finally Madhu gave me my fifty rupees and I went home.

Returning home from college, and after the holiday was over returning *to* college — I found these already very romantic. But the things that my Maushi managed to accomplish in her life included, among others, finding out first which train I would be taking for home, being present there at the exact time, and sending down some goodies for those at home. Anyhow, she does not know what to do with herself at home. Having seen me into my train, she fancied that to wave at me and to promenade back and forth some eight or ten paces by the side of the train was very romantic. So when I started for home I'd feel like a small child. Besides, on reaching home, Father was as ready as ever to ask — Doesn't a chap who gets money for no labour, to stay in a hostel and that, doesn't he find any scholarships? Moreover, Mother cooks a variety of goodies, and insists on expressing her love by feeding one. That too, naturally.

In fact this kept happening every time. So all the fun went out of it. Nor could I pass all the time with friends who were also studying in various other cities. Then I'd go to the farm and quite pointlessly look at beauties of Nature and that. Later, slowly, I acquired the habit of reading also. Instead of reading sundry useless books, I began to read the great classics right from the start. This, I mean to say, I did with great determination. In addition, it was my occupation to reckon what I had achieved in the year that had just passed. And how I had advanced. And whenever I had words with Father — so what if I didn't study, I have accomplished this much; mean to say, I have learned to play the flute really well, etc. Besides I'd also resolve upon the things I'd like to accomplish in the coming year.

At first, before I left home I would touch Mother's feet — and Father's, if he happened to be before me — and then leave. Later on I started to avoid this. But this time, prior to leaving, I'd got through all that.

I departed with the resolve that this year I must really read something with depth in it. Then into the train came a gentleman

Cocoon

from Nasik. Because of him my resolve was reinforced.

I felt this bod was really great. Anything he said he would state firmly. So I felt that he must be a teacher. But we did not exchange any personal inquiries throughout the journey. We thrashed out many other matters instead.

About one thing, however, he bugged me. After he'd said whatever he wanted to say firmly, if you asked him for reasons for them he'd only say, Because it *is* that way.

He said, It is necessary for a unviersity to be opened in this region also. Reason? — Such is the requirement.

He said, And this university should be located at Nasik.

I said, Because you are from Nasik, right?

Then he said, No. The real reason is that, in every way, Nasik is a central location.

I said, Then so is Manmad.

He said, Manmad is, too. But Nasik it is that is appropriate in every way.

After some time, as I had read through N.C. Kelkar's life of Tilak in the holidays, I broached the topic of Tilak. So then —he too had read the life. So I couldn't say very much more.

He said, Agarkar is superior.

I resolved to read Agarkar's life this year. But still I kept arguing.

He said, Society is made up of individuals. Because individuals make up society. Take a simple example — Has there been another man as great as Agarkar? Take a simple instance — What did Tilak write during so many years of incarceration? *Geetarahasya,*[10] then. It took a whole year for me to decide even to read this huge work. And it isn't really correct that someone like me should read it in their old age. But, after spending so many years, Tilak only wrote *Geetarahasya* — while Agarkar translated Shakespeare's *Hamlet,* you see. You couldn't have read *Geetarahasya,* but you just might have read *Vikaravilasita,*[11] that's why I made this comparison.

But it really hurt me that I had actually read neither. I resolved that upon reaching Poona my reading must commence with these books.

In the morning getting off at some station along the way, the gentleman said to me, But you really did bother me a great deal. At one time a berth over there had become vacant. So I kept feeling that I ought to occupy it and sleep until morning. But you were such an eager listener, you know, that I thought....

After reaching Poona I began my reading. But such obstacles came in the way that this year, forget reading, I didn't even manage to study properly. Still, I did acquire a good deal of personality.

Madhumilind Ichalkaranjikar Saheb managed to get a room right next to mine that year. So I was bound to contract all his habits bar one.Under his influence I began to go to the cinema once in a way. He of course went to every Hindi film. He used to say that just as the Age of Shakespeare was the Age of drama, and that drama had captivated everyone big and small, so now this was the Age of Hindi Films. Just as in that age had lived Shakespeare and Kyd and Marlowe and Jonson and Beaumont and Fletcher and Burbage and so on — didn't our teacher say this just the other day? — so now live Naushad and Burman and Madhubala and Wahida Rehman and Bimal Roy and Lata Mangeshkar and Kishore Kumar[12] and so on and so forth.

This was correct from one point of view. Because even though there's not even a cinema house in our village, there is a great craze for films. And even Father frequently turns on Radio Ceylon to hear film songs. Now, since my eyesight itself had been spoilt, so according to what the doctor says I ought not to see many films. Still, convincing myself that this was the Age of the Cinema I started to go to the pictures frequently.

In a way Ichalkaranjikar was as rambunctious a gent as he was polite. But he felt that I was a friend. So I never abandoned him. From sports to reading detective novels he managed to do a thousand different things. Moreover, getting up at five in the morning he'd go for private tuition in the city at six o'clock, return by eight to the hostel, then having played tennis until lunchtime, and having had his lunch, go to college, and in the evening to NCC parades or the films, chatting in my room until he felt sleepy, until I had in fact driven him away . . . . . He would be asleep by ten or eleven at night. In addition, besides visiting his relations on Sunday, all day long he'd pester the heck out of me.

By way of mere entertainment he would express contrary opinions and carry on an argument. Aurangzeb[13] was greater than Shivaji.[14] Because if Aurangzeb hadn't happened to exist, what would have been the worth of Shivaji? Or, if I said that it was bad that Dr. Ambedkar[15] had started the wave of religious conversion, he'd be ready to say this — that Ambedkar could have really messed up politics, if he had wanted to, starting a conflict between upper and lower castes, by giving rise to communism, spreading it — what would you have done then? If such a thing goes on for hours and hours, who wouldn't get fed up?

But mainly he was a rascal. On the street if some lovers were walking hand in hand in a lovey-dovey way, Ichalkaranjikar would drag me before them. And then, taking my hand in his and walking in the same lovey-dovey manner, he would stare backwards at them. Then when they let their hands separate, he'd let go our hands too. I was so tall and he such a shorty, this looked terribly awkward.

If we happened to be sitting in a restaurant discussing something meaninglessly and loudly, and if— so as to listen to us, or just because he found no place elsewhere — someone sat next to us, Ichalkaranjikar would first drive them away and then go on with the useless discussion. For obtaining this result he had various tricks. "Get up from there, you are stinking badly" — saying this to him, while looking at me. Or if the man ordered something to eat, saying to me — Pandoba, no matter what I tried this morning, I was unable to shit. So you know that I did? — beginning in this fashion, he would force the other man to get up and leave, one way or another. Those who happened to be eating at our table would pick up their plates and go to another table.

On the whole he knew very well the weak spots in the etiquette of city folk. So I felt, Once I learn from these demonstrations of Ichalkaranjikar, then I needn't bother to learn too many other things. Therefore I should follow him implicitly.

In my childhood in my lane a horrible thing occurred once. From that time I learned that I ought not to have much to do with girls. A boy called Rama once took a really young girl into a cowshed, saying, I'll show you some fun. Then suddenly that girl started yelling and howling. Lots of women and children gathered there. The girl's mother beat Rama with her chappals. He hid in his house for the next ten or fifteen days.

One thing is good about a village — whatever you do, there are those who happen to see you. But those who happen to see you in the city don't even know you.

In general, though, this proves handy for chaps like Ichalkaranjikar.

But really, a girl's inner being would slip past anyone's imagination. Yet Ichalkaranjikar used to say that girls like a "solid" voice. Still, while I did have some sort of contact with girls for one reason or another, I wasn't able to make out any such clear sign of their preferences. His experience in this matter was terrific. These complications he used to confide only to me.

I used to say to him — On an average, how much would one have to spend per month per girl?

Then he'd say, Some girls take on one's own expenses, even.

Meaning, it is gratis? All that happens is gratis?

You are an ass, Pandya. Son, see — it is this way, some girls too must want boys.

This point was pretty fine too.

Besides, just by looking he could tell which girl was "loose." What he used to say was probably all untrue. Because, who's going to narrate such exploits truthfully?

Once when he went after a girl, first she called him naughty. Then he thought, This is a terribly innocent "brand new" virgin.

Later, confronting her on the street one day he said, Why did you call me naughty?

She said, Tomorrow I shall complain to the principal. Rascal!

I asked, But Ichalkaranjya, suppose she had really complained?

He said, So what, At most the principal would have hanged me. What else?

Later he jostled that girl in the street. At that time, stopping, she called him a savage and all that. He said to her, I do so much for you... & Co.

Then occurred their love. And then they were able to get along fine.

I said, But suppose she'd refused to speak to you? If she'd left without a word?

Then there are others, my friend. Don't ask silly questions. You go, like an ass, for walks on the hills. Move on the streets instead — then you will understand everything.

Once in fact he took a knife from me. It was a knife I'd originally brought along from home thinking that I might just as well keep it while travelling to Poona. I asked him, What's the knife for?

He said, to cut mangoes.

But in fact showing this knife to some girl as a threat, he took her by force to see a film. He said, Heck, in Poona one has to struggle so much, one way or another. In Mumbai whatever one desires is done in a day.

But one day I did quite thoroughly understand the real thing about Ichalkaranjikar. That because of such activities a girl had become pregnant. So then he laid a special responsibility on my shoulders — to convince his father that we were going for a tour to Kashmir.

Once when his father came to Poona I told him. His father said, One can only manage to see Kashmir etc. during one's student days. You chaps must go.

Then he forked out four hundred rupees.

That girl, though, came to Ichalkaranjikar's room every day.

He'd say, A silly pest like this does get on your back this way.

Then, when she'd had her operation somewhere, he said to her, You really are the limit.

I asked, When there were French Letters scattered all over your room, how could this happen?

So he said, You won't understand.

Later when the girl got married, at that time of course she too asked Ichalkaranjikar to the wedding.

I said, You were there even at the wedding. Whatever would she have felt that time?

Then he said, You so-and-so, what can she feel? Instead ask how embarrassed I was.

I thought, Shoot, it seems all right for girls. Let me also have a go.

But once, when I was all alone, writing a tutorial in a classroom, a girl shut the door from outside. I saw her at it myself.

Then the girl stood with her back to me so that I might see her through the glass pane.

Now whoever would beg such a stupid girl to open the door? So what else was there to do? Besides, this classroom was on an upper floor.

Then instead of asking that same girl to open the door, etc., sort of personally, I thought it better to get out of the window into the window of another room and thus out. So, placing my feet carefully on the sill — and meanwhile looking at two or three kids shouting below, I slithered and slipped across to the window of the next classroom.

I hoped to be able to get out via this classroom. But I'd barely stood in its window before I saw that a class was in progress there. Good thing that the professor didn't notice me. Then I sat on a bench listening to a chemistry lecture.

But I did not give in to that girl.

Submitting the tutorial I came to my room. But neither Suresh nor anyone else was there. Who should I talk to? So I wrote it all out —

Because of girls the spread of higher education has increased a little. And in general this is good for the progress of the University. All in all, in college the atmosphere is quite ripe for the establishment of Romance. Mean to say, in the college, the garden, flower plants and such settings, aphrodisiac and exciting, do create the right background. Moreover, it is far from the bustle of town life. Besides, the books prescribed for study at the first and second year are also Sakuntala,[16] *Shelley, Keats, and so on. The trouble is that each boy and girl has decided in advance How to Fall in Love. The way love proceeds in film and fiction, so it is in reality too. This is terrifying. There's no novelty in love any more. Now it is a good thing that I have got this down in writing. But when Ichlya returns I must tell him my glorious achievement.*

Ichalkaranjikar was enthusiastic about another thing. To get someone moving, to stir up activity, stimulate and organize people. He forced Suresh to enlist in the National Cadet Corps. He said, In the years to come the military needs of this country are bound to increase. Yet it is impossible that there will be a war. Therefore, if you wish to reduce anxiety on the counts of education-spouse employment, you'd better go into the army. Then for two days or so there were arguments in my own room between Suresh and Ichalkaranjikar and then Suresh enlisted into the National Cadet Corps. The argument was directed at me also. But I said, My Mother and Father are old now and I am their only son.

But he did encourage me to take on another weird enthusiasm.

That year right from the start he began to indulge in "affairs." In fact he must have got involved in hundreds of tangles with girls. From his pocket would emerge a thousand things like the knife which he had borrowed from me, some obscene photographs which some rascal had given him, chits and bits of paper of a great variety. Notices, bills, money, programme notes, and so on. Before going to bed he would carefully sort out these things. Mean to say, tear up notes from his girls and burn them, put all the coins together, put the money into his purse, throw away receipts, etc. As he accomplished these things he would become terribly serious and concentrate hard. He could not brook anyone coming into his room while he was doing this. Of course, he would let me watch it. But speech was taboo at that time.

Once when he had torn up some girl's note he couldn't find his box of matches. I said, Fetch one from my room. He went. Meantime, I hurriedly read the torn up bits of paper — Cycle... Nana... So what if it has been lost... towel... hammer — just then Ichalkaranjikar came back. And catching me by the scruff of the neck he threw me out. Thereafter he never let me into his room at these times.

I don't usually do such things. But suddenly I had become terrifically attracted by the idea of finding out what girls themselves might be writing. And that's why I had sneakily read those bits of paper. I wished my notion were true — that girls write something transparent and lovely and blue and loving.

Ichalkaranjikar drew up a great plan. He himself wished to become the General Secretary of the hostel. That is why in his "party" he wanted some five or six of his own chaps. Not that he asked me to stand for the election just for that reason. Because he also said to me, You must become the Secretary of the Debating Association of the college. Even when that brought him no benefit at all. And for that too he put in considerable effort.

He forced the chap who was going to oppose me to give up, first by threatening him and then by giving him tea. Thus I became Mess Secretary without opposition. He too became Secretary of another mess. By majority we then elected him General Secretary of the hostel.

He would of course have lost the college elections. So he entered the fray only for the hostel elections.

Now that the General Secretary was my friend, he gave me whatever department I asked for. Entertainment programmes

— that is to say the Variety. I was also Secretary for the hostel Annual, etc.

He said, Look here, Pandya, do take care, take on just what you can manage.

But I was full of excitement at the thought that I would "shine." I took all sorts of burdens upon myself. Suresh was clever. He wouldn't meddle with all this — Who's going to waste time checking accounts? And Madhu said, If someone like me had stood, he was bound to fall.

I stood for the college Debating position off my own bat. As I wanted to learn to speak at public meetings. The whole of last year I had never managed to go, really, to speak in a debate.

Actually, I did go once, fully prepared. And also entered my name to speak. But at the last moment my name was called and I didn't get up.

Then the chairman said, Has this gentleman given his name and then run away?

Then I myself answered, Yes.

Now this year I was in fact Debating Secretary myself. So, I thought, I'd feel some authority and learn to speak with self-confidence. This was an election I had actually won. Because in the college there were so many people from my district. Besides, via Ichalkaranjikar I obtained many votes from girls. Moreover I also got nearly all the four hundred votes of the hostel kids. In addition, last year during the annual gathering I'd played the Bhup raga[17] on my flute; all the kids had really crowded there to hear me play. So then I had promptly played the popular Hindi film song called *Bata batame rootho na*. It received a "once more" from the audience. The total effect of all this was that, of the two persons who opposed me, one obtained twenty votes and the other two hundred, while I got seven hundred.

When I had been elected some girls demanded tea and the like. So then I gave five rupees to Ichalkaranjikar and told him to take all those girls to the canteen.

He said, You must also come. Then I also went.

In fact last year some people had called me a silly goose.

They'd ask, Where has this "parcel" come from? They'd insult me. I showed them how I too could shine. When someone insulted me like that I'd go into Madras Cafe and, as I munched on something, I would ponder. Why am I not able to speak before a gathering of people? It is because I don't really attach much value to elocution, that's why. Or on occasion I'd feel, Rascals, how some of them shine in college! Since childhood I have lacked this training in shining. I did play a part in a play once. The school I went to was, of course, cheap. And me, the heir apparent of a country family. So this year I said, I must do something special.

Besides, last year at times I used to experience an over-whelming sense of inferiority. Mean to say, if you looked at any friend from Poona, he had at least one or two great relations. Someone's Mama would be working in Sassoon Hospital. Or another's sister would be the wife of a bank manager. Many girls in our class had poets, or great writers or professors as parents. Indeed, there were numerous great folk in Poona. So naturally there had to be a great number of their children, brothers, nephews and nieces and such in Poona. And one was bound to enounter all of these types because one lived in Poona. So the hurt of the fact that I had no great relation pricked me very sharply. Sometimes I would even say, Balshastri Jambhekar — the nineteenth century pioneer of journalism — belongs to my family!

But that was all done with now. This year I had thought I'd learn some more flute, but instead I forgot even the five or ten ragas from last year! This was a great loss. I'd thought I would do some reading yet I had merely looked at *Geetarahasya* in the library. Besides, my very good friends Tambe and Madhu Deshmukh also went off me. They began to consider *me* stupid. Suresh used to say, anyhow, Instead of merely eating and reading like worms at college, it's better to try all these things once. But in all this running about, don't you forget our walks. And do give us passes to your programmes, by the way.

Madhu Deshmukh became altogether an ideal chap this year, he started to study. He resolved to manage within the small amount of money his father sent from home. He started to wash his own clothes. He said, Heck, I too have worn laundered and ironed clothes. When you put them on, that day you feel stiff, awkward. Still, one does feel fresh in them. Once they have become soiled one feels low. Therefore, clothes washed every day are better, it's better to wash one's clothes every day — the mind then remains on an even keel.

But Madhu did help me in many things. Meaning — writing in his good hand the notices that were to go up at the college, checking the mess accounts and getting the bills ready at the end of each month, distributing them to all those who had their meals there, managing mess fund accounts, and so on. In return for all this, any time, I would feed him in the canteen. Besides, if the mess bill came to 35 rupees, 3 annas and 8 pice,[18] I'd say to him, Dash it, what is this hassle? Round it off to 35 rupees and 4 annas. You take 4 pice per bill for having done the work. Then he would mark up the bill to 35 rupees and 4 annas.

Moreover, having written *my* tutorials in different hands he'd submit them directly in the class. And he'd only tell me this later. Once, you see, he gave in my tutorial, having written it himself. And — thinking that I must also study a bit — I wrote another tutorial and submitted that to the teacher also. Then the teacher kept enquiring for a whole month who this Pandurang Sangvikar was. But since I wasn't even in the class at that time, how could that expose me?

At that time our annual general gathering was going on. Since I had decided that I'd start my study only after January I wasn't really paying attention in class. And if I did go to class at all, as I hadn't been there for eight or ten days before that, whatever was going on had little coherence for me. Besides, why should one listen to the same stuff for a whole year when one can finish reading it all within one month? If you look at it that way, why ever do we live in Poona to study for the whole year? This point is more fundamental. But it was necessary to sit in class for attendance. Still, one would feel terrific ennui all the same.

So I thought up a trick. That pleased Chavan, Tambe, Bhandardare, Deshpande, all the back-benchers — Write lines on a piece of paper from some well-known poem and send the paper round. Whoever created the best parody of those lines, I'd treat them to tea.

That is why many of the local students would sit at the back and do their darned best to parody the poems. Tambe, Madhu, and other such original poets sat in the front. But surprisingly, even if one only counted those who sat at the back, excluding these original chaps, still most of them seemed skilled in versification and parody. For instance, Deshpande parodied the famous line "Bring me a trumpet..." as follows — "Bring me a strumpet...." And having parodied so well, he was sure to get tea from me. The Mardhekar line "In a drum wet died the rats" I myself parodied pretty well. But how can one give tea to oneself ? So I gave tea to Bhandardare instead. He'd written — "The rats died in a wet drum." This I liked immensely. There was so much more like this.

One day this business got too noisy. The teacher asked us to leave the class. So then right from the back of the class I jumped out of the window. Later I heard that the teacher had called out — That's not the way to leave, go out by the door. It was quite a high jump too. I felt bad later on.

Truth to tell, the notions I used to have before about the erudition of teachers proved correct in only one or two cases.

One learned professor of Sanskrit would first recite a shloka19 in tune and then say, This shloka is beautiful, the next one is easy. He would then directly move on. He was good. Why would a genuine scholar analyse or explain a shloka?

Another learned professor taught Marathi. He was most awfully feeble. He felt no enthusiasm for teaching. He'd say, See, you chaps, you have come into the Intermediate class, haven't you? Now what's left that is worth teaching you in this poem, see? And so on. When a person who is supposed to teach instead starts to talk *about* teaching he is certainly very great.

Otherwise the nastiest was the gentleman who taught logic.

He'd teach so darn loudly that it was impossible even to doze in class.

Another had been a school master before. He'd progressed in his career by giving exams externally.[20] And having climbed slowly and gradually, he'd reached this position of eminence — where he was stuck. Because he was getting on in age. Otherwise, climbing on and on, who knows he might have become President of the UNO one day. He was so thoroughly organized that he would personally walk through rows of students to make sure that they were taking down what he was teaching. On the pretext that some student had no pen he would lend his own. Once one chap didn't even return his pen. So then prowling about the classroom he found a pen similar to his and seized it.

But let any teacher be what he may, as long as there was even one student in the class like Jog, one ought not to create a disturbance in the room. So I tweaked my ear by way of a reminder.

Unfortunately I discovered that the work I had contemplated by way of entertainment pieces or Variety for the hostel function meant that every week I also had to conduct some intellectual activity. Because our Mr. Warden said to me, Managing the Variety doesn't mean organizing a carnival. Once in a way each year you might do that. But speeches must be organized regularly.

In the rush of Variety programmes, I neglected the Debating Association. Because, after all, one had to be able to speak at least a few sentences properly at the inaugural meeting. Even the principal attends that. He would have thought, This creature is Debating Secretary, and he cannot even propose a proper vote of thanks. So I must of course learn matters like votes of thanks in the course of this Variety. Then in good time can be done the inaugural of the Debating Association. I will invite some great man and make a fluent speech. Mean to say, then nobody will criticize me for having made a late beginning. I must learn to give a speech first, though. Otherwise those who elected me would annihilate me with their laughter.

That is why I paid more concentrated attention to the Variety. Still, it was good that Madhu was managing the business of the mess. Otherwise I would have had to resign from it all.

The work of the entertainment programmes, that is to say of the guest- speeches, was really meant to be managed by me and also on behalf of the girls by a girl called Sathe. But this girl would only attend the programmes and propose the vote of thanks. Most often she wouldn't even come to the programmes. So then I began to ask Madhu or Ichalkaranjikar to give the vote of thanks.

I was learning slowly. For one thing — that I had begun to manage the quirks of the standard Poona speech. Still, by oversight my country accent would slip in somehow, and I'd feel bad. Yet I resolved firmly — I *will* propose the vote of thanks. Let whatever's to happen happen. So what if I mess up some of the idiom? In fact I hardly manage to recall the Marathi language itself at appropriate times, what to speak of village accents or the Poona accent? So, having girded up my loins, I started to rattle off some four or five sentences to accompany the presentation of garlands and bouquets and so on. I'd arrive having committed those sentences to memory. That's why everyone who had come there would feel that I hadn't become Debating Secretary for nothing.

When they had thus given their genuine approbation I felt, Now there is no reason why I ought not to conduct the inaugural of the Debating Association.

Then I went and booked a great woman sociologist of Poona to do the inauguration. Because she was the aunt of that Deshpande from our class, this worked out. Even though her subject was "Social Education and the Woman", she spoke well. Besides, she was such a famous writer the hall was packed full. That's why I forgot within five minutes the speech I had crammed for two whole hours.

Still, this great writer wasn't going to really give a speech as such, was she? She had brought a written essay along, she was reading that out. In addition, with a pen in her hand, she was making once in a way some small corrections as she read. She even explained the reason for this — that tomorrow she would send this essay off to some famous journal.

Then barely had the clapping ended before I was stumbling on stage. Now how would one describe this predicament? I stood there for a long time. But my fate was strong so the audience thought this was a joke. Because even then some people at the back were continuing to clap. That way I was able to collect myself together and begin.

In the middle of all this suddenly I recollected my Mother and so I became all confused.

Anyhow, I spoke thus — If every woman began to conduct herself like our guest for the day, why would there be any wars in the world?

At this everyone laughed. At this, I felt quite enthused. What I mean to say is, that I wish to express greater gratitude than the usual vote of thanks. So I thank her.

You might say that I had somehow bundled off this much of my speech, for I'd also managed to rattle off some lines of my memorised speech. Then everyone laughed at this too. Now shouldn't I too laugh and indicate that I had cracked a joke? But I became downhearted and slipped even further, and saying — Later, I'd also have to thank the Chairman for having come here today — I really destroyed myself. The Chairman was the principal himself!

So then I had to resolve that at no time must I let my self-control go. Thereafter, I shoved the work of the Debating Association on to an assistant girl called Lele and didn't even go there for a whole month. Because after this inaugural, in the presence of the very guest Lele had said to me, Was this the first time for you? You didn't speak too badly for that, you know.

This hurt me greatly. Why ever should she say a thing like that to me before everyone? Who knows how she herself speaks? But it can't be very good. Because after all she too has become a secretary. But suppose that she does speak well, why should this happen? It's only that from her childhood she's had training and I haven't. That's all. I will, with determination, teach her a lesson. Only then would I deserve the name Pandurang.

Having contemplated thus for a whole month, I resumed attendance at the meetings with the vengeful idea that I must speak better than this girl. Meantime, she'd organized a few debating meetings. Even I had gone to some of them. But I didn't participate, saying that I was not feeling well. Still, clearly, it was a prepared speech she gave. Rattling it off.

Later on at a suggestion from the principal and with him as the intermediary I arranged the appearance of a great Gandhian leader. For this occasion too a vast crowd of listeners had gathered. So once again I forgot the speech I had crammed. But I didn't lose my morale.

In a folly of pride right at the outset Lele went to make the speech of introduction. At that time a wonderfully funny thing occurred. That was also because of the great Gandhian leader. According to a suggestion made by the principal we had arranged an Indian style floor mattress to sit on, to suit the leader. Now, since this was not according to our routine table-and-chair affair, Lele was bound to slip somehow. She too had to speak sitting down at the mike kept low on the floor. The comedy occurred because of this very fact. She started — Today I stand before you to introduce to you a leader who works with great concern....

Yet, indeed, this worthy girl was sitting!

At this everyone laughed at her. For my part I laughed hugely. After a while it occurred to her why they had all laughed and she was really crestfallen. And when she realized that the "leader who performed his work with great concern" had also laughed, she lost all her pride in the act of introduction. Poor thing, she became quite red and came down. There's one good thing about me, I am so dark that I don't blush red.

Then even as the main speech was in progress, I prepared my own vote of thanks. Keeping in mind very carefully the error that Lele had committed, in turn I said, Now I have sat down to propose the vote of thanks!

Cocoon

Even at this there was a fountain of laughter.

Now it isn't really good Marathi to say "To sit down to give thanks." Many thought, however, that this was a pun at the expense of that Lele. Only then did I feel really happy — Ha, ha, haw.

In the throes of my joy I said to her, You'd prepared your speech like that, hadn't you? In that case you should have spoken while standing, with the mike in your hand.

So then she retorted, Nonsense.

Thereafter I started to attend every debating meeting.

At that time came a notice from the University, for non Hindi speakers. There was to be a Hindi elocution for them in Delhi. The University would receive from each college the names of one girl and one boy. After another selection, only two names would be sent up on behalf of the University, one boy and one girl.

The principal said, Select two carefully from our college.

We found a boy. But we couldn't find a girl.

Finally, Sathe suggested the name of a girl in the hostel. She said, She's from Jabalpur. She knows Hindi well.

I went to meet her.

I said, Aren't you from Jabalpur?

Yes.

Then, for a Hindi elocution competition, we have to select from our college a girl whose mother tongue is not Hindi. Can you speak well in Hindi?

In Hindi she asked, Why?

I also said in Hindi, matlab, I mean to say we have to send someone on behalf of the college.

After leaving school she hadn't done any elocution and such.

Still, I said, Do give your name. Do speak.

She said, Fine.

Only then did I remember, yeah, this was Rami.

— The monsoon. We'd gone on a picnic to some old fort. She had lagged behind, standing on a step. There were thousands of steps. All about her, grass. Below, only trees. Meaning, deep gorges.

Her chappals in her hand, heavy with caked mud. Even in class she used to be quiet. Never took any notes. Never took part in any nonsense. She was really good. I lingered behind. She was in front of me. The soles of her feet pink from walking, walking. But her walk was v-e-r-y slow. Then up at the fort occurred the usual tramping, games, eating, and so forth, among the rest of us.

For one of our programmes came a great gentleman guest. Only a few students had gathered. No girls at all.

I walked all over the hostels trying to gather more students to hear the lecture. I sent Sathe to the girls' hostel.

The great gentleman said, Let the audience gather. I'll wait.

Once Sathe went, she too just disappeared.

I myself then went to the girls' hostel. Having gathered some five or ten girls Sathe was coming along.

I said, The secretaries have this headache about a poor turnout.

Rami asked, Why must the secretaries feel that so sharply? I liked this.

Later she said, They've been calling your name for the whole week. Why don't you come to class?

Sathe said, He wastes all his time in these distractions.

Rami said, And what is that constant ruckus at the back of the class — it happens only when you are around.

I said, We write horrible parodies about girls and show them to each other. That's nothing new, is it?

Among those who spoke in the debates I wasn't the only one who was disorganized, cramped. There were people much riper than me. On the occasion of the debate on the "Question of the Minorities", in fact, one chap came to the dais and said just this much — I have not come prepared today. I have never seen a more genuine debater.

But whenever I got up to speak something very infuriating would happen. You see, my useless assistant Sathe and the fellow whom I had defeated in the election were in love. Those two had, in fact, aspired to become a pair of secretaries together. But I hadn't let that liaison materialize. Therefore, these two would sit in the back and make fun of me.

It is true that I realized that I was the Secretary of the College Debating Association, and that to improve matters was indeed in my own hands. Therefore, as soon as I could, early one morning I got up and went to meet the principal at his house and placed my thoughts thus before him —

It is the task of our Association to make debating prosper in the college. Therefore, Sir, *all* those who gather ought to say at least something. That way, all those who come there will slowly learn. Moreover, the number of those who come merely for entertainment, or for a turn about the college in the evening, will reduce and those who do speak will not be intimidated. What do you think of this idea, Sir?

He said, That you must decide on your own. But I do hear that this year the Debating Association is not going well.

Later, giving me tea, he said, How are your studies going?

When I put up a notice to the effect that everyone who attends must speak, the laughing lot dwindled. But the fifteen or twenty who gathered would all speak. What happened finally, in fact, was that only those who had a particular liking for debate would turn up. After this even that Leli began to think something of me.

But once a very terrible thing happened. At that time what came over all of us including me nobody knows.

Some eight or ten persons gathered to speak on the subject of "War and World Peace." To preside, there was Professor Shah. He initiated proceedings by placing before us the salient points of the subject and saying that arguments in keeping with these points alone would be useful, he asked *me* to speak first.

I began my speech. But from somewhere — was it from me, perhaps? — started this wave.

Once a sentence was over I'd start to laugh. Or all of us would start to laugh together.

Professor Shah was unable to discover the reason for this. Wondering if the speaker himself was making funny faces, he deliberately placed his chair to a side and watched. But how could all of us achieve the same effect?

For instance, I began — Today the world is caught in a terrible predicament.

At the thought that I had uttered the crummiest of platitudes I started to laugh at myself. Fine, but how would every speaker laugh at himself?

Later I said, In the *Upanishads*[21] is gathered the essence of all knowledge.

Laughter.

In them it is said — *Sarvetra sukhinah santu.*[22]

Laughter.

Unless all men foster emotional ties among nations, there is no way out for mankind.

Guffaws.

Nationalism is a sin.

Hoots.

Everyone including me laughed at all my sentences.

Later spoke four or five others. Still, after every couple of sentences the speaker himself would laugh and the listeners were of course ready to laugh. The speaker would pause after a couple of sentences only to laugh. And once he had stopped, those in front of him, thinking that he had paused to give them time to laugh, would start laughing in anticipation.

In the world there are two powerful nations, namely the USA and Russia. The great legacy which Gandhi... take Gautama Buddha himself... human beings alone have been given the power to think.... Now if the dominant mood of the house itself was of merriment at every statement, considering it merely comic, neither the speaker nor the listeners could help the situation, could they?

I wonder if everyone began to understand that any statement may be deemed absurd and that elocution meant the concatenation of such statements (except that it was our own fault that once in a way we *would* ourselves pause) — who knows?

Then at last the chairman said, kicking his chair over — I shall suggest to the principal that we close this Association, if this is what you gather here for.

Right there I started to try to convince him that we hadn't done this with any premeditation. That every person who had come to speak today may have descended to the comic level having realised that he was forcing himself to speak, that perhaps this was the case with each of us, perhaps that was why the mood was in such consonance, etc., etc.

But when the principal had finished taking me to task I said, All the effort I put in throughout the year has been wasted.

Later I placed the Association in Leli's hands and only went back once for the valedictory function.

Once I had to take Rami to the University for the trials of the elocution competition. There, even among the students of all the other colleges, Rami spoke effectively — bang bang bang.

When that was over, I said to her, Let's look for a taxi. She said, Let's walk instead, it will be like an evening stroll. So we walked.

How much would the taxi cost?

Perhaps a couple of rupees. The college gives expenses. Then we might as well go to the College of Agriculture and eat something there worth that much money.

But she only ate grapes. Then sugar cane juice. She returned the juice which had been served with ice in it.

She was selected. That is to say, she would be sent to Delhi. She said, My expenses to Delhi must be paid via Nagpur. I asked, Why via Nagpur?

She said, Just like that.

Then I found out from Sathe — that Rami has some mal- ady of the lungs; when she has an attack she gives herself an injection; lies about for hours and hours together. Now, going to Delhi from here by the western desert route would mean her lungs... that *would* be bad.

Thus the elocution business ended right there.

Even after that, though, I went to class only once in a while. Because there was, of course, the hostel Variety Entertainment.

Once a class was not held. Everyone scattered all over and began to while away time till the next class. I sat writing my tutorial. Five or six girls sat on right there in the classroom and began making a racket.

I said to Rami, Instead of this, why not sing a song? Then someone sang a Marathi song. The teacher from the next classroom came round and said, in English, 'Stop that'.

Then all of us came out of the classroom. Rami said, Anyhow, the song richly deserved this treatment.

I liked that.

I never shirked any work to do with the hostel programme, though.

Even here, however, I had to perform a particularly noisome task. Once in a way it would happen that the speaker would come and settle down and there would still be no audience, not a trace of it. Then one by one some would come and the meeting would take place. In such cases the job of gathering girls together was my lot. I'd have to make repeated visits to the hostel and say — Come on, come, how would we ever get on without you?

Even if there were only some eight or ten listeners, some speakers would still speak with deep involvement.

But most great writers and leaders of Poona don't really feel like putting forth their great thoughts unless there is a considerable audience. Fortunately, there were so very many great, really great personalities that they outstripped even the idealism of our warden and my own industriousness. We were indeed able to get hold of some new great personality for our weekly or bi-weekly programmes. On this pretext I got to know many great personages. I was able to exchange a few words with them. I got to know the houses of the great gentlemen whose names had otherwise been encountered only in books. I was able to see their bookshelves and the pictures on their walls.

All of them speak and behave politely. Those thrilling days passed very quickly. Indeed, those were the days for everyone to become enthralled. Even if there was a plain old flag-hoisting ceremony we would be overcome when some famous luminary tossed off a noble message. If some speaker said, This nation looks expectantly at highly educated young men like you, we would presume that it must be untrue that after B.A. one has to really struggle to get even a clerk's position.

But there's no dearth of personalities endowed with wisdom in Poona. Only there have to be takers for their wisdom.

Because of these meetings and contacts with this person, or the other one, etc., I absolutely forgot my earlier asinine self-imposed incarceration in my own room, my brooding over home or the future. My going to bed late, at any rate, remained unchanged. In the same period of time, night-time arguments and discussions in my room started to become really interesting. And of course our rambles over the hills also continued. Many times the whole night would pass that way. And in the morning we'd report directly to the P.T. ground.

Exhausted by lack of sleep at night and all this exercise, I'd go to sleep at nine or ten in the morning and somehow get up barely before the mess closed after lunch. On some nights would occur the pitiable situation that our chats would end by three or four in the morning, yet the night wouldn't end so it would be murder getting up in the morning after just two or three hours of sleep to go to P.T. At such times, I'd brush my teeth at night and go to sleep having changed into my P.T. uniform; and getting up just in time in the morning, I had only to put on my shoes to reach the playground in no time at all.

But I kept up my enthusiasm for causes, movements, and the like. Later on, in fact, there was no limit to such activities.

Then came the annual social gathering. On top of that I was in charge of the entertainment. Meantime, the prelim exams.

I had of course not sat for the quarterly exams. So when a letter went home from the college and I received one in turn from home,

I was able to manage with the excuse that I had been unwell. In the half-yearly, though, such subjects as I took I did manage to clear. Even about this a postcard might go home, so I myself wrote in advance — As my medium is now English, and also thanks to the Chief Minister of our state, Balasaheb Kher, who has excised English from the school curriculum, I had prepared only these subjects properly. The remaining subjects — later. Now what excuse might I give for not sitting the prelims? Or, should I study and clear the exams instead and thus be allowed to apply for the finals? My thinking on this matter, too, commenced at about the same time.

At night, there would be our debates, the hills, writing up the notices, a bit of the work of the mess; on the other hand, during the day I had to meet first this person and then that, go to the girls' hostel to find out who sings, who can dance well, make sure of these things, meet the girls, get them ready to perform, meet such and such a great writer, later fix the time of his programme, and so on, then report these things to Sathe — if I met her — all this, and again, go to fetch the writer chap, take him back, engage an autorickshaw, or taxi, push a bicycle, exchange namaskars,[23] have some of the notices typed, chat with the typist, give him tea, put up the notices in the mess, or on hostel boards, meet the principal to request permission to display notices on college bulletin boards, exchange a few words with him, pay the grocery bills, look at Shivaji's statue on the way back, order such vegetables as were required for the next day in the mess, look over the cook's accounts, find out who hadn't paid the bills, give them stiff warnings. Money, canteen — thousands of complications.

Someone might conclude that my daddy had sent me to college just so that I'd acquire a personality in this way, and all that. Ichalkaranjikar said, I am astonished that you can manage to do all this and that too with a smile and a quip. Suresh would say, All day this chap grazes here and there, quaffs tea and coffee, that's why his energy lasts.

Those days I hardly had time as I used to for spiritual contemplation and that. But if on some rare occasion I found a bit of time I could get some contemplation done. On such occasions I'd feel, Had I ever thought that I would be able to manage all that I am doing now? Long live ME! Hardly anyone else would have the same energy as me. I am indeed shining so much even in the Intermediate year, so how much more will I shine later on!

Mean to say, I am not exactly a nobody.

Once, two girls came to my room to give me information about a programme for our gathering. I was sitting in my room in my shorts and vest. The door was closed. When there was a knock on my door, I yelled, Ichlya, Surshya, why are you pestering me, you sods!

Then I kept quiet.

When there was a knock on the door once again, opening the door I said, Come in, you pimps....

And I was so completely annihilated by what I saw that I could only manage to splutter to the two girls, Come in, come in, come in. But the toughest thing was that they sat down on my bed and I sat, as I was, on the chair in my shorts. In shame, saying little, again looking down at my feet.

I gave them a notice that had to go up at the college. They left. Then I put on the pants that were on the bed and went to Madras Cafe, gobbled up something, and came back again.

I thought, This hostel is a real nuisance. One can't even change one's clothes in private. But then, why did I not, myself, say something like — Wait a bit, please, in dulcet tones, or on some pretext grab the pants? I must never hereafter place my clothes behind the bed. Whatever would they think, seeing my naked body like this?

But Ichlya said, In sum, the girlies are bound to be pleased with you from now on.

But next day when I went to college, as one of them reported to me that she had put up the notice I gave her, she was laughing.

Thus did I conclude the annual social gathering.

Now look here, Pandya, you are an ass. I had already told you that you should do only what you can manage. That one-act play, with expensive costumes representing several generations, why did you choose to stage it? And where was the need of so many gramophone records? Were they practising with all those records every day? If you'd brought only one each day, why would the rent have got so high? And a fifty rupee bill at the canteen at one go?

I was scared. The budget for the gathering had been 700 rupees. And I had incurred expenses over 800.

One chap said, Sangvikar has pocketed the cash. Then Ichalkaranjikar gave him a fistful. Son-of-a..., not one but two programmes of classical music were organized, you saw two plays. The programmes were grand. And throughout the year there were lectures. And still you dare say that?

With one whack this pest was taken care of.

I asked Ichalkaranjikar, Now what's going to happen?

He said, Meet Professor Paranjape. Tell him all.

I made all the accounts pukka and went to Paranjape. He was stark bare from waist up.

I said, I have some work with you.

Tell me if you can in a minute or two.

It's not much. I'll be through in ten or fifteen minutes.

See, my bath has already got cold.

Otherwise, why don't you have your bath, Sir, I'll wait here.

I have a class right afterwards. But what is this work?

My budget, the bills....

Then come tomorrow or the day after. What's the rush?

Sir, but the day after is the meeting.

Turning his back upon me he said, Come in the evening.

I went back to my room in a pother. All day long I was checking and rechecking the figures. Once in a way, if by mistake the total shrank, I'd be pleased. But when I looked for an error I was sure to find it.

I really felt most angry about this Ichalkaranjikar. Madhumilind Ichalkaranjikar. Now, *he* weighed a hundred and fifty pounds! The bugger never gave me an idea of the expenses. And today he was seen laughing in the company of a girl. I am caught, thus, between the blades of a pair of scissors.

A hundred rupees overspent — on top of that the accusation that I had pocketed it. Truth to tell, twenty or twenty-five rupees of my own money had been spent for this gathering. If in addition I had to make up the extra hundred, whatever was I to tell my folk at home? As though that Marubihag raga or whatever it is called.... She can sing only just about so-so. But she wouldn't come for less than two hundred and fifty. And that director chap, who polished off all the biscuits presented on the tray. Who knows perhaps he believed that one must eat all the biscuits kept before one?

In a way I too am to blame here and there. Deshpande had composed the orchestra piece pretty well, too. Still, why did every one of them demand coffee twice each day? But let that pass. But that slut.... She took the gramophone home to practise with. And she did bring back three broken records. All of them everywhere ready to sink me, the sods!

In the evening I put on some poor-old clothes and went to Paranjape's house. He was inside. I started to undo the laces of my shoes. Just then he said, I am about to go out right now. Come again later tonight or something.

I left my shoe laces open and descended the steps. Having caught the lace of one shoe under the sole of the other, I nearly flew ten feet ahead somehow managing to regain my balance. That's how I came to the door.

From behind me Paranjape said — Do close that door too. I closed the door, and then he closed the inner door too.

Again I sat till nightfall in Madras Cafe, smoking cigarettes.

Again and again I was looking over the accounts of expenditure. Classical singing, four hundred; drama, etc., two hundred; variety, one hundred; canteen, fifty; taxi, etc., twenty-five; of course, miscellaneous expenses apart. I even ate my dinner right there at the cafe and at about 8 o'clock I came out. On the way, there were hostel chaps and girls. Among them was the girl who'd called for coffee following each session of practice. The bill went up because of her. And what song did she set, after all? — "My friend, you ask for honey" — Bloody...

I went to Paranjape's.

Showed him all the accounts.

Something exactly like this happened once before, also — let's see, when was that? — hanh, it happened in the year 1938.

That's my year of birth, Sir.

Who was the secretary that year, I wonder? I met him just the other day, you see. Then after this he tried for quite some time to recall the name. I wondered, Why is this chap attempting to recall that fellow's name? The secretary of that time had also incurred extravagant expenses. So is he perhaps trying to recall the name so that I might make friends with that fellow?

At last he said, Hanh, it was Keskar.

After that any time I met a man whose name was Keskar, I felt like asking him, Were in you in this college? What had actually happened in the gathering in your time?

Eventually, coming to the point Paranjape said, At that time Keskar had paid the excess amount himself.

I said, But I shall not pay. As it is, twenty-five rupees or so of my own money has been spent for the gathering.

Your own money! And for the gathering? Why ever should you spend that? Now, look here, Sangvikar, it is fine that you spoke crazily like that with me. I am a different sort of man.

If you repeat such a thing to someone else, then he is bound to say there's something fishy in this. But I am not saying that.

Then he went into the house. And fetching a fistful of roasted peanuts in the shell he flung them before me and said, Have some, have some.

Then after that I proffered the accounts.

This hundred rupees, is that for the drama? How's that? P.L. Deshpande, ten rupees. Royalty. Just for a one-act play? Why wasn't it gratis? Fine, where's the receipt? Hanh. The second play, thirty rupees? Sathe's fine, receipt? Give it quickly. It's a must. Taxi, thirty rupees altogether? For whom? Why did you go about in taxis? That chap is not such a great director, is he now? Could have gone by bus. Fine, the other expenses of the drama — where are the bills? Drapery, fifty? Now look here, Sangvikar, if the budget had been ship-shape there would have been no questions asked. But once it has been overshot, you must also attach bus tickets in the accounts.

After having looked over everything in this manner, as he ate the nuts and at the same time criticizing — Pandurang Sangvikar, all this is very well, he said. But I will have to say that you are thoroughly impractical. Who asked you to indulge in all this nonsense in the Intermediate year? Let's see what happens in the meeting. I will certainly do something, of course.

Thank you, Sir.

Until now, out of politeness, I'd eaten only five or six nuts. But then gathering together all the scattered shells I said, Where shall I throw these shells?

With a laugh he said, Leave them where they are.

Again I put them back on the table very carefully as before.

Having returned to my room, I sat waiting for Ichalkaranjikar. But that worthy was bound to return late tonight. Meantime, I went to Suresh, Tambe, Madhu, everyone, to pass the time. All were absorbed in their study.

Madhu said, What's this new hassle since yesterday?

Nothing, really. The stupid figure of expenses goes on increasing. I've really had enough. Once this business is over, the day after tomorrow, I shall get down to my study.

Taking one look at my face Madhu burst into wild laughter. He said, Listen, old chap, if you have any sense, stop going from pillar to post. Pay up the hundred rupees yourself. And in peace start your study. There's hardly about two months left.

Then we had a crackling big argument. He said, Only low type of people get anywhere on the stage. They rise up like scum. Later on they settle down to the bottom like silt. You too are a third class chap. That's why you got into a dozen hassles this year.

I said, Nincompoops like you can't understand this. So how do you propose to make your name, eh?

Do you think, really, that you can manage all this? Your name is now known to a few people. What have you achieved beyond that?

However would you understand what I have achieved? Hey, you, there have been so many secretaries till now, like you. For instance, the secretary who shone ten years ago. Do you even know his name?

In the year 1938 it was a chap named Keskar. Dr. Paranjape still knows him.

Let it be Keskar or Pheskar, what you will. Get the budget right first.

I'll pay my own hundred rupees. I can manage that, you know.

If you do that, I shall say that it proves you have pocketed the money, you   fraud.

But all this noise rose to such a degree that two or three students from nearby rooms gathered there, complaining that they were being disturbed.

Madhu said, From today, you'd better manage your own mess accounts. I won't write your tutorials either. And so on.

Finally, a couple of chaps tried to shut us up. We had a roaring quarrel. Jagdale, the muscleman from next door, actually picked me up bodily and took me to my room. I was saying, Lemme go. That sod Ladi, he covered my mouth. Fifty or so students who were at work rushed out of their rooms. I said, I'll also become a muscleman and then show you all what's what next year.

Having thrown me into my room and bolted the door from outside, they all went away.

Later on I started yelling — My accounts are left in Madhya's room. They are important. Open the bolt.

After a little while someone quickly pushed the accounts under my door. The mess register which Madhu kept also came with that.

I said, Madhu, O Madhu, open the door.

In Jagdale's voice was heard — I'm not Madhu.

Then outside could be heard some voices and feet shuffling. Gradually, I could hear room after room close. Then all was quiet.

Having kept aside all the papers I started yelling suddenly — My cigarettes are with Madhu. With Madhu. You, Madhya Deshmuuuuuuukh! Bring me my cigarettes.

But no one paid attention to me. I lay there smoking the longer butts gathered from the corner of my room. Then in a drawer I found a whole long cigarette. I kept that for the last.

At twelve there was a sound from Ichalkaranjikar's room. Then I lit the whole cigarette and from the window side called out to him — Ichlya, open my room.

Right away he opened my room. Then taking all the accounts I pushed my way into his room. I started to tell him all that had happened today — about Paranjape and all that.

He'd taken off his trousers and in his brief loincloth he was brushing at them. Until he had again pulled on the used trousers and set right the confusion in his pocket, he said nothing at all.

Then lighting up a Berkeley cigarette he said, Hunh, what happened?

So, what I've been saying all this while meant nothing to you? Tell me again.

He said, You mean to say Paranjape did nothing at all? What does he mean by "He'll see?" See! Heck, tomorrow you must meet the principal.

Will you come with me?

Why should I come? I shan't come.

All this happened because of you. You yourself gallivanted about in a taxi, to fetch the classical singer and that. You are the

General Secretary. You ought to have given me an idea about this budget thing.

Then Ichalkaranjikar shoved me out of his room and told me, You are an ass. Now go to sleep.

Next day I got up early in the afternoon. Avoided talking to Ichalkaranjya all day. But on his own he came to me in the evening and said, I've met the vice- principal. Told him all. He said, It's all right. Now as a mark of respect go and meet him this evening. What, son?

Rubbing his hand over my stomach he said, It doesn't do to get scared, you son of a bitch.

That night I went to the house of the vice principal. His colossal Alsatian dog was sitting right outside. Taking a stand far away from him I started to think. The dog approached me and stood there laughing. A laughing Alsatian is really most terrifying. Then, when he turned his back on me for a bit I rang the bell. So once again the dog turned around and came at me grinning and laughing. Sir must've been watching all this from inside. Because when the dog finally put one of his paws on my hip he shouted immediately, Johnny, Johnny.

Mean to say his name was Johnny. Then the Alsatian sat quietly in his place in a corner and began staring at me with his grin in place.

Sir yelled once again from inside, Sit. This to me. After a short while he and his wife, together, like that, came out. His wife was looking at me with sympathy. Meaning, she must've learned about this budget business too. Ichalkaranjikar must have shot his mouth. Moreover, when she looks away I must... do up the button that has remained undone. At least while Sir is looking over the figures.

This bundle of papers with all the accounts had become so soiled from handling since yesterday, I felt awful. He didn't scrutinize every detail like Paranjape.

He said, You're still only in the Inter year and you are indulging in all these funny things? That is risky from your point of view.

Cocoon

I said, showing that I was quite consumed with regret and so on, I shan't participate in any such thing hereafter.

He said to his wife, This chap is in the Intermediate. He heads the college Debating Association. Besides, our annual was also organized by him. He did that well, anyhow. And you are also the mess secretary, aren't you?

The wife was saying, Hunh, hunh.

He said, See, so many people pass before our eyes. Some cannot even propose a vote of thanks properly. We see them later when they have become expert orators. Some take permanent stage fright and never come on again. Goodness alone knows where they vanish. I've been watching these things for the past twenty years — Regularly, each year the gathering, and other such programmes, sport, every new fellow who shines. I've had enough. Yet the funny thing is that I don't really want to let go of my vice principalship. Right, but how's your study going? The Inter results are pretty stiff. You know that, don't you?

I said, I've never neglected my study. I swot every night.

However, later on I did have to see him once again to obtain special permission to apply for the finals.

Coming back to the point I started to show him the bundle of accounts. Then he said, This sort of thing *will* happen. You are bound to keep all these bills in good order. Don't deny it. This does happen. What's there to check? Each year there's some such business. Tomorrow we shall see about getting the excess amount granted from the college office.

"We shall see." Again, we shall see. Then I didn't look at the roll of accounts even once prior to the meeting.

Until the time of the meeting I avoided Ichalkaranjikar. Not even a word. He's useless, the sod. Still, only he fought for me the next day. And of course that proved to be a disadvantage for me. For there were many of his enemies in the committee. I myself did little more than getting scared. The decision was, at first, that the Secretary should make up the deficit. For Sangvikar didn't have authority to overspend, did he?

Later, Professor Paranjape, the vice principal, etc., intervened saying, Let's do this — each year we take from every hostel student three rupees by way of entertainment fee. But we don't spent the entire amount of over twelve hundred every year. What's the harm in getting the college to pass payment of the extra hundred rupees?

Limaye said in a terrific temper, What will happen in that case is that each year the Gathering Secretaries will inflate bills and spend money beyond the budget. It'll become standard practice.

Ichalkaranjya said, How can that happen? How can there be another secretary like Pandurang Sangvikar?

Everyone appreciated this crack. Especially Sathe. She guffawed like a buffalo. Still, in general, after this there was an atmosphere of sympathy. I was really cheesed off.

Chaudhary made a suggestion as follows — That the college Debate is with Sangvikar; there, the expenses have been less than budgeted. Because this year he didn't organize any debates at all. So the budget provision can be transferred here.

This too, everyone thought, was another joke.

The vice principal said then, We cannot do that sort of thing.

Bhosale said, We could keep the mess shut for one day and that way recover hundred and fifty rupees or so. We could use that money.

Gupte was, of course, my veritable enemy. He said, Let four annas be collected from every hostel student. How many students are there?

Four hundred and eleven.

And how many girlies?

Sathe said, The exact number, well, about....

Let's suppose five hundred altogether. So then, five hundred into four, how many annas is that?

Ichalkaranjikar said, Chhut. Cut it out. Who's going to collect four annas from every student?

Obviously Sangvikar.

I'd really had enough. It'd be better to put an end to all this stuff. I have saved some sixty or seventy rupees. Let me ask for some more from home. Let me pay and be done with it. Who'd tolerate so much insult?

Finally the vice-principal and Professor Paranjape put their heads together and each whispered something in the other's ear. A long time had gone by. There was still the job of approving all the other expenditures. The vice principal then shut everyone up, put pressure on them —

I am approving Pandurang Sangvikar's accounts. The expenditure beyond his budget should be made up as follows. Every member of this committee should contribute four rupees. Of course that depends on everyone's willingness. The remainder the college will pay. Is this acceptable? Let's get on with it then.

But Limaye said, Suppose I am unable to pay four rupees? Ichalkaranjikar barked, angrily, Didn't you hear? The college'll make up the difference. Sit down.

Then everyone — except me — laughed. I was most frightfully agitated. I was feeling, Let's STOP this nonsense.

Limaye said, Me, I mean to say, of course I shall pay. It's not a question of the money. But... etc.

Present the next set of bills, get on with it. That's enough of that. Ichalkaranjikar — yours. Radio, carrom, attendant, fine. Next? Limaye? Mr. Limaye, "quick please." Hanh, snacks and the feast. Hanh, let's get on. Variety? Sangvikar? You did produce a great variety, at any rate. Everyone is sure to agree. Budget? Right? Twenty rupees less than the budgeted amount? Great, wonderful. Is that all?

I'd myself reduced the variety bill by paying 20 rupees out of pocket. At least here I'd managed the budget properly. What's more, so that everyone might feel I was honest I just had to do that. Everyone else's expenses, of course, matched their budgets exactly. The bastards gobble up the cash but their figures are immaculate. The pimps, very clever. I mean to say, real scoundrels.

Quick quick quick the clerk took signatures on all the bills and collected the papers together. He said to Professor Paranjape, Sir, my son's a little unwell at home. I really wanted to go home early. But I will take all these bills home today instead of taking them back to the office. I'll do all the accounting tomorrow and send the papers to the office the day after. Only Sangvikar's excess amount has to be drawn from the college. Will it do if that is done the day after tomorrow?

Professor Paranjape said, Fine. You go. But get this money sanctioned immediately and give it to Sangvikar. He will have bills to pay up.

Then the meeting ended. Ichalkaranjikar started to fight with each and every one. I myself quietly escaped from the college in the dark. I didn't even return for dinner. I roamed about a bit and only came back after I'd eaten outside. I stayed in Madras Cafe, smoking cigarette after cigarette.

I won't indulge in this sort of nonsense again. Whether I am unable to manage it or because I don't want to, say what you will. One comes into contact with all kinds of worthless people. One has to kowtow to them. Even when there's a flighty girl you have to treat her to tea so she might oblige you by singing, listen to her coy stuff, butter her up, tolerate assistance from asinine chaps and pay their canteen bills. In comparison that chap called Devi was better — the conductor chap needed three flautists for the orchestra, but there were only two among the hostellers. So this chap Devi says, I'll also come. Of course he could hardly play anything. He just sat there on the stage, the flute to his lips, uselessly, without playing. That did make the picture complete. After the orchestra had done playing, they all went to the canteen for tea. Then Ichalkaranjikar said to Devi — You sod, you just sat there, didn't you? All the rest will get cakes and tea but you will get only tea.

Still, sod it, Ichalkaranjikar, to enjoy all the fun, and me — this ass Sangvikar, was all the time pacing about backstage with the roll of programme sheets in hand, killing myself to make sure everything went on smoothly, the fun.

Still and all, this year the variety and organization of drama and all that, I can certainly say I have achieved something. I've got to know people, make their acquaintance. I got to know Rami quite well. I learned how to speak before a meeting. And so much more — that is to say, making new acquaintances, public speaking... and what else? A good deal more. Bit of this and bit of that. It'll be a good achievement, though, if I can avoid failure in the exam this year.

But if I hadn't done any of this I would have done so many interesting things with Suresh, Tambe, Madhu. We would have done so much wandering about. Gone to places, hiked in — or even without — company. I would have accomplished my aim about reading. Finished reading *Geetarahasya*. But what's the use of such thoughts now? First the exam.

Thereafter I started to go to class regularly. But most of the study was already nearly done. Some teachers in fact took their last classes. Once I sat in the front. Then one lecturer said to me, You are new, I suppose.

Left unfinished was the mess of the mess. The most annoying thing of all was that the mess cook would appear every evening with the account book. And of course I examined it. Each day he'd ask some such thing as — So what vegetable shall I cook tomorrow? I used to like lady-fingers. So I invariably said, Ramappa, cook lady-fingers every day. In fact the chaps once stuck an epigram to the mess notice board —

> *Vegie among vegies, eat lady-fingers*
> *Our love for Sangvikar forever lingers.*

But at last I had determined that there ought not to be any obstacle to my study. So I told Ramappa that thereafter he must not ask me about anything to do with the mess even when I ate there. Everything should go to Vaidya. This Vaidya was a poor old chap. Earlier he used to eat at different people's houses by rotation, on fixed days, as is our custom. I arranged for him to have free lunch every day and gave over to him the job of managing all the accounts.

Thus I managed to rid myself of the mess mess. I didn't have to break off relations with Ichalkaranjikar. For one thing, after the meeting was over, I hardly spent any time in his company. I spent the entire day at the library and this pest was thus effectively avoided. Ichlya in fact didn't even have an identity card to use in the library — one girl had made off with it for his photograph. Later he hadn't bothered to make another card. Girls *are* good. My work went well. But soon thereafter he was selected at Bangalore to become a military officer. Even before our exam he said "Ram Ram" to the hostel and went to live with some relation.

While going he gave me his tuition notebooks. He said, So, then, Pandurang Maharaj, I *have* caused you some trouble. But you just read these books. The exam questions are bound to come from these.

I threw the notebooks into a corner, carelessly. And besides he gave me a huge heap of books. Among them were many detective novels. All those I sold as waste paper. I kept only a *Life of Napoleon.*

The night before he left for Bangalore he came to me. He must have known that I would be in the library. From outside he began to yell and ullulate — Pandoba, Pandya, Pandu, Pandu, Pandu Sangvikar, Pandya Sangvikar, Hey Sangvikar, Pandu.... I saw him from the window. But I quickly slipped aside and didn't let him see me. He kept shouting until the library attendant drove him away. Then tiring of this he went away.

When I came back to the hostel in the evening, outside my door, a note for me —

Dear Pandu,

So I am off to Bangalore tomorrow. I'll let you know my address once I get there. Meet me tonight at my relation's. Or tomorrow morning at the coffee house. I am going to throw a party for some friends. So won't you come there?

Many girls will come there. So if you are not going to come there for that reason, I'll wait for you tonight till nine. So do come and have dinner.

Yours,
Madhumilind

I tore up that note. I thought, This military is a very good thing. Otherwise, whatever can you do with chaps like Ichalkaranjikar in civilian life?

Next day I was returning after lunch. At that time there was someone standing with his back to me at my room door. That was Ichalkaranjikar, for certain. With his back resting against the parapet of the balcony he was standing facing my room. Right away, I skeddadled, making my way from tree to tree, by a long route I left the college grounds. I had on only my pyjamas. No money in my pockets. In such a state where was I going to pass a whole hour? I could have bought lassi and cigarettes, etc. at Madras Cafe on credit. But Ichalkaranjya would have surely spotted me there. So I borrowed a rupee from Narayanappa of Madras Cafe and spent an hour reading any old newspaper in a cafe farther down the street. I read all the jokes in the *Weekly*. Drank lassi twice. Spent the rest of the rupee on cigarettes. Leafed through *Filmfare*. Perhaps Ichalkaranjya hadn't left yet. So stealthily I sneaked towards the hostel, but when I reached I saw that he wasn't there. Just then an attendant from the mess came to tell me, One Saheb had come to see you, he told me to tell you.

Then I went to the library. I wasn't able to study, though.

The exam was a mere month away. But I hadn't yet quite finished even some of the prescribed books. I finished these in such a rush that when I was done I couldn't even remember what was in any specific poem of Tambe or what exactly Cardinal Newman wished to say about the University. Then I became really jittery. So then in the company of Suresh, Madhu, Tambe and so on I sat discussing the examination. We reckoned that there were still twenty-seven days left and we had eight papers to study for, meaning that each paper must be done within three days' time. Only then might my existence acquire some meaning.

Then having come home to my room I sat up till 3 o'clock and made a master time-table. In between Suresh came for tea. He said, Instead, in the time needed to make a time-table, you could have finished Shakespeare. I've just finished mine.

I said to him, My time was wasted in all those activities. But how is it that you couldn't finish your study either?

He said, Do you mean to say that just because I was doing nothing else that I had to study? Do you mean to say one must do either drama and such or study — nothing else?

After he'd left I stayed up till morning and made another time-table for each paper datewise. First to third, Logic. Fourth to sixth, Second Logic. Seventh to ninth, English. And so on like that.

Just that morning arrived my money order. Father had written — When do you have your exams? I am sending you the final two hundred and fifty. So make sure that you study well.

I was terrified. Hundreds upon hundreds of rupees spent, and yet no certainty about the outcome of the exam.

It was month-end then. I would spend a couple of days lazing about and then work like a donkey. Then I laid in supplies of hair oil, kerosene, sugar, tea, soap, etc., enough for twenty or twenty-five days and spent a couple of days enjoying myself. As soon as the first date of my time-table arrived, I began my study like a zombie.

Some days I'd sleep only for three-four hours. I found the books most awfully verbose. So I bought cribs and learned them by rote. Looked through Ichalkaranjikar's English note-books once. At that time I felt, Forget these books-shooks. Actually it is because of these notebooks that the preparation for two of my papers went so well. Otherwise I was finished. Ichalkaranjikar the Great. All of a sudden I found confidence in myself.

Those were terrible days. At that time I felt great closeness with a chap near me. This was Joshi. He too was in Inter. But he had French. That's why I began to feel respect for him. Throughout the year he had studied systematically. Besides, in place of logic he had math. No matter which problem I asked him about from my room, he'd come right up to my room and give the answer. Every evening exactly at six he'd bathe with soap and ask me — So, how far's your annual "gathering" got? He'd say, I myself "gather" by going gobble-gobble at my study. Then at six he'd light his primus stove, pump it up and standing at my door, he'd ask, Do you like Shelley or do you prefer Keats?

I'd say, I haven't decided yet. I have yet to read them.

Then he would begin speaking about Shelley. But in a moment he'd bustle off saying, Dash it, the milk must have boiled over.

When I was just about to bring my mind back to my book, he'd re-enter my room and pouring his tea into a cup and sipping it, say — At this time you'd better make only such notes as you'd actually be able to read the night before your exam.

Sometimes he'd say, These dramas and gatherings are the curse of college life.

Or, What are you taking for your B.A.?

Meantime, refreshed mentally with the tea he had just finished he'd come to my room and say, I'll just take a wee walk.

Once in a away, to prevent this nuisance, I'd read with my door shut — then he would knock on the door — tuck tuck — and force me to open it. Then he'd say, It is so hot and your door is shut? One needs fresh air to study in. Gimme two annas?

Then he would go for his stroll. While returning he'd bring a two-anna loaf of bread for me also.

We'd go to dinner together. Even there he'd ask his just-so questions. Meaning—Yesterday you woke me up at four. Then I said, Let me get up after a bit. But then I fell asleep again. Like this. Every day.

He would study only until eleven. Before going to bed he was sure to walk by my room. I'd be busy, preoccupied with my struggles — for instance, whenever will this page finish, when *will* I finish writing this passage down, I'd better finish this today instead of tomorrow, should I have tea first or should I look at Viola's character first? And this chap would ask me, What, when are you going to bed? Or he would convey some news of hardly any import to either of us — Professor Paranjape is sick with the flu, you know? Or, that so-and-so was inquiring about you. Or that he'd met Rami. She said, How is it that Sangvikar is not seen anywhere these days? But before bed time he required only one thing from me — When are you going to bed? Wake me up before that, will you?

In the morning, with my eyes red-red-red I would wake him up. Then he'd say, What's the time?

This question was actually most annoying. Because if I told him it was 5 o'clock, he would still insist on looking at the watch under his pillow and say, Five, is it? Thank you. If it was 4 o'clock, he'd still look, and then say — Four, is it? Thank you.

Sometimes, after taking a turn about the playground I would sit down to study until morning. If I gave him tea once, he too would ask me to have tea just once, to return the favour. His calculating ways really got on my nerves. Who had offered tea yesterday? He or me? Then whose turn is it now to give tea today? Etc. But when I went to sleep in the morning, he would wake me up in time to have my lunch. So I never really lost my temper with him. because he was good. In my own gobble- gobble study I needed near me such a cool and humane gent really. Besides, as he woke me up from sleep he would seem to me fair like an angel. And when I woke him up — his eyes, so luminous, just like Mother's.

Those days were terrible. One evening, the mercury lamp near the hostel hadn't even been lit up yet. Although it was getting dark one could still sit by the window and read. But I stood outside in the balcony with my shoulder to a pillar. Most of the rooms were locked. There was a light in one room and it was open. Two or three chaps were discussing something about their study in a steady hum. That sound was terrifying. From the ventilators of a few rooms the square patches of light that showed were eerie. I was standing leaning against the pillar, like a cool, placid donkey, indolently rubbing my eyes. After reading so much there was sweet satisfaction. Still, leaning against a pillar, rubbing one's eyes — all this was terrifying.

Just then I saw Professor Shah's young son holding on to the bars of my back window. He shouted, Sangvikar, our exam is over!

And letting go of the bars he jumped down, whup, and ran away to his house.

I thought, All the same, I *will* pass.

Then the exam started. Rami said, Thank goodness you're seen at last, at least at the exam.

My eyes would ache after every paper. While I wrote I kept wondering, What the heck was the point I made on that other page? I *had* made a definite red mark at that point in my notes — that's silly, what does it mean that I don't remember? Just then, having remembered something quite different, I'd leave some space in my answerbook and go on with the new idea. In the last ten minutes of the exam I'd write any old stuff in these blank spaces and hand in my paper.

While writing the paper the only existence I had was in the paper and the bird-claw fingers with which I held my pen. Then the image occurred to me that perhaps it was my brain that was dripping drop by drop on to the writing paper. I even wrote up this image in my English essay.

The moment a paper was over I would come back to my hostel room and prepare for the next paper. Joshi would fetch me my bread. This was excellent.

Once, instead of going directly to my room, I took a turn about the playground behind the college. When I looked up my aching eyes were suddenly dazzled — such a terrifying pink glare in the sky. In the distance it had become pitch dark. I looked again, so as to adjust my eyes — why, there was a kite flying coolly, slowly. Way up, tiny. Because of the trouble with my eyes many times I'd lose sight of it. So I began to peer even more carefully. Way way up, holding its wings so level, how can a kite fly? It's cold up there at that height. As one gradually ascends above the mean sea level, the temperature gradually decreases. And yet, floating like that, holding the wings stiff, and that too all alone. Kites have the presence of God for their neighbourhood. Then I felt, I must not write exams hereafter in this fashion. I mustn't participate in anything at all hereafter.

The exam was done. I had a simmering hope that I'd pass. At least I had written more than Madhu, definitely.

Now I thought I'd spend a couple of days lying about in my room. But I wasn't able to do even this.

In a day or two, having demolished the mess accounts, we would close the mess and go home.

Awfully early next morning, having heard loud bangs on my door, I woke up angry, mad. It was the servant from the place where we bought groceries for the mess. He said, I've come from Gambhir Shet — the malik[24] sends for you most urgently.

I said, I'll come, and promptly went back to sleep.

Again at 11 o'clock the chap came to rattle my door. Angry, I got ready and went with him.

In the shop Gambhir Shet was sitting comfortably. As he always did. He sat me down before a bolster and gave me some cardamom to chew. Then he said, So, the exam only finished yesterday?

Yes, and just as I was hoping to take a bit of rest you started pestering me.

Look at that! Ramappa told me Sangvikar was busy with examinations. So that's why I've waited for the past ten-fifteen days. Examinations are the season of seasons for each college year. But let that be. The accounts? Those can wait, we can settle those any time at all. But, Saheb, we do appreciate prompt settlement of bills. Some others might collude with the cook and carry on underweighing and so on in the supplies. My business is not conducted like that.

Do you mean to say that I have kept your bills pending?

Until recently your dealings were all quite correct. But during the past two months....

Then crawling about on the floor he reached over my head and brought down a ledger from a box. There was, of course, a pencil already marking the place.

Cocoon

He said, Look. It's all correct until January. The February deposit was only one hundred rupees. Nothing at all in March.... Now shall I show you the daily accounts?

Having had enough, I said, Let sleeping dogs lie. Perhaps it has not been possible to make the payment. There's such a to-do at exam time. Perhaps we are behind in payment. Fine. Now, Shet, who was bringing you the cash?

Ramappa. From the start it was Ramappa. But you'd better look out, Saheb. We experience such tangles all the time. Not that there is any problem between you and me. But do take care, all the same.

Nothing funny is likely to happen, Shet. I had given the whole accounts job to a friend called Vaidya. He looks after all that. His exam too was approaching. May be there was some small hitch. I shall look into it all and bring the money tomorrow. Don't you worry.

Chhe, chhe, Of course I shall receive my payments. But you'd better look out for yourself. Such complications happen all the time.

On my way back, naturally, I saw the statue of Shivaji. This time, children from some school were paying their respects before it, holding up their hands in a namaskar.

I came to the college. I went right up to the stove in the mess kitchen to Ramappa. Sweating hugely, he was rolling chapatis.[25] I had always felt something very deeply about this dark-dark Ramappa. A sort of affection. That was my way. Tremendous affection about anything at all. Now the wrinkles on this Ramappa's face were beyond counting. All his body has been reduced to, you know, dry leaf, humus. While standing, his limbs would tremble. Even his short shirt was out of shape. But while cooking he'd wear his dirty dark sacred thread and struggle enormously. This shirt — it had first been flaunted about on the body of some handsome student and then come to belong to Ramappa. There was no account of his years — all was past, that's all. All his conscious years had been spent in this one mess building in the college. His whole existence had been picked and carded, battered like cotton by dirty plates, and bowls, and the smoky walls in front of the stove.

Some princely students, who fancied themselves, had even started a move this year to dismiss him because he looked sickening. But I and three or four others had opposed this nonsensical notion with determination. I even turned one of those chaps out of the mess on the pretext that his bill had been paid late. One of us in fact said that because the snot from Ramappa's nose had dripped into the amti[26] it was tasty today. We like Ramappa, he likes us.

This chap, as a child had been sent away with a man by his own parents so that he might find some way of feeding himself. Now, that child had started with washing dishes and had become a cook by his own ability. Nobody from his time was left here now. Some had indulged in fraud. Some had died. Even as he told us about his own wife dying, not a wrinkle had been disturbed on his face.

After noon or one o'clock the mess building would become desolate. Most of the servant folk would go into the city to have some fun. Some servants who had been suffocating in the company of white collared students would foregather and chatter on, their gossip interspersed with genuinely obscene swearing. Ramappa, though, was always sitting against the pillar of the mess. Always wrung out, drooping. He's sure to become a ghost and haunt this college! He has digested the terrible language of students who were driven crazy by the bother of exams. He managed his colossal stove well. He always stood politely in a corner as he asked for his salary. If one gave him money for Gambhir Shet's bill, he'd go right away with it to pay it and stand in the evening in the same way in the corner with the receipt. Having, in another, prosperous era, served so much rich ghee that it would stick to the plates, now he pities students who have to make do with imitation ghee. They used to eat ten chapatis then, now they have come down to three. He must have seen many a mess secretary. From those who ensured that the monthly bill wouldn't exceed thirty-five rupees, to those who hiked it up to fifty rupees, all sorts. Crooked, hypocritical, some like me compassionate. But Ramappa had never been the object of anyone's criticism. That's why he was contented.

Hundreds of students had eaten Ramappa's food. I used to make up dreams, that after some twenty odd years, somehow Ramappa'd still be alive and would still remember me. In the dream, even if he isn't able to recognize me, he still comes, wiping his hands on his dhoti and seems to recognize me a little at least.

The first large photograph of Ramappa I had taken this year. And hung it up.

This poor old man, with a dirty-dark dhoti on, he would cook for us hundred or so chaps. Dripping with sweat. That was the worst. That in return we should pay — cash! And he must labour so that we might eat. Eat! I hadn't been able to come to terms with this from the moment I came to the mess as secretary. Why only a cook, one feels the same about one's own mother. No one should labour so much by a stove just so that others may eat. What does it signify to those who eat? All they have to do is lift their tongue and shove the food up against their palate.

That is why, even though Dnyanu and Manu, the servants in our mess, complained to me many times about him, I said not a word to Ramappa. They would say, Saheb, Manu saw this with his own eyes. Ramappa hid a great big bag of dal behind the stove. Saheb, yesterday he went off with a whole panful of shrikhand.[27] I'd only say, Fine, I will take him to task. By and by, even Dnyanu-Manu stopped coming to me.

Bathed in sweat through and through, I went right into the kitchen. Ramappa gave me a pat[28] to sit on. Putting a lid on the vegetable pan he said, Examination over?

Ramappa, how much is the bill that we owe for the groceries?

Only yesterday did Gambhir Shet give me the message, I was going to come to you.... But you... the examination. So I said, not now, a little later.

Never mind. How much is still to be paid for the groceries? How much have you paid until now?

Whatever Vaidya saheb gave me I would take over and pay. I don't know anything else.

I sent the servant to fetch Vaidya. This Vaidya, the sod, was for ever in shorts and for no reason at all he contrived to look poor.

He said, Until February everything is clear. Only I haven't got the receipts. I have already given two hundred for March. There's some ten or twenty left with me.

Ramappa arrived, rushing and scuttling from inside.

I said, Ramappa, Vaidya says — The February bill's been paid. Ramappa said, How? Only one hundred. That's all I took to the grocer.

Vaidya said, struggling to get up, Hutt! Call Manu. I've given Ramappa the money in front of Manu on three occasions. Right here.

Manu growled, Saheb, don't mix me up in all this, hanh. We are poor servant folk. Our destiny is tied up to merely twenty rupees or so.

I said, Whatever is the truth, tell me. Was any money given in your presence?

But Manu wouldn't say. By now some other students had also started coming in to eat. Witnessing these goings on they were all happy.

Vaidya thought, The secretary does not trust me. He started to speak louder and louder. I pacified him and said, My man, you keep quiet. We are bound to find out who made off with the money. Don't you worry. Manu, do tell. You, Dnyanu, do you know anything?

Dnyanu said, Saheb, should I serve dinner now or do this sort of business? Now, Vaidya saheb used to give money in our presence, that is true, but which bill or which month or how much, how should we know? You tell me.

Meaning, this only left Ramappa. And only Vaidya. Yet, actually, perhaps I might be the only one left. Because Ramappa said, Whenever I take money to the shop I don't return without a receipt. If you like, confirm this with Gambhir Shet. All the receipts for money given by Vaidya I have handed over to him.

Vaidya went to his room and returned with a file that was chock full. Then I took out all the credit-debit accounts, sun-dry little bills, up to February and examined them.

All receipts up to January were just fine. There was only one for February. I said to Vaidya, Tell me, you mean to say after that you paid twice, a total of four hundred rupees? The receipts for that much Ramappa has not brought to you? Isn't that so?

I told him a thousand times to bring me back the receipts. But he'd say, Until you have paid up all the balance Gambhir Shet won't give any receipts.

Then why didn't you go yourself to check?

Me? Me — If I had nothing but accounts to do I would have gone. But my study? But right away I did come to your room. You said, Ramappa'll never do such a thing. Later, once, I had left a note in your room, to say that you should go to the shop yourself and check.

I said, it is correct that you had met me. But I didn't find any chit waiting for me. Vaidya, this will have bad consequences.

He said, Sangvikar, if I have mislaid even a paisa of mess funds I would not mind listening to you. I don't owe anything to the mess except that I get one meal a day. In the mess next door I have my evening meal and keep accounts there too. Ask that secretary. I haven't mislaid even a paisa. I did leave that note for you. Moreover, when I thought I'd tell you, when we met in the street, you never even acknowledged my namaskar.

This much, anyhow, was true. Because whenever I met Vaidya it was always — accounts, bills, Gambhir Shet, so much of the deposit for this month is still left; I'll now send so much out of the bill for that month tomorrow; some chaps *don't* pay their bills to me, would you ask them; Ramappa hasn't brought me the receipts yet, or he has, on and on and on.

I threatened Vaidya unhesitatingly, that I'd give him over to the police. And just by the way, I threatened Ramappa also. He began to touch my feet, pleading. But I pretended anger, etc., and went away.

Cocoon

In the evening I asked for my dinner in my room. Ramappa brought me my plate himself. And he waited in a corner, obsequiously, scared. I gave him a notice to be displayed on the board, to the effect that no one should deal with Vaidya any more. And that all remaining money was to be paid to the secretary.

After he left I checked all bills from January on. But there was nothing to be gained from that. Salt, chilli, wheat, rice, etc., groceries apart, there were a thousand other complications — four annas for repairs to the stove; soap; rent for a bicycle for Dnyanu to go to the vegetable market; incense sticks; milk.... Who was going to add up all that?

The figures for each month ran into three thousand or so. So once in a way I would feel that a misplaced sum of six or seven hundred was really nothing.

As I was looking this over, it had become evening already. In the evening Vaidya came with the ledger, register, etc. Giving me some twenty or twenty five rupees, all the balance he had with him, and a list of chaps who owed money still, he said, Sangvikar, honestly, I didn't take the money.

I said, Get out.

Thereafter, taking care of the money to be collected yet, the expenses of the current month, deposits — subtracting the deposits, and so on — all this went on till late into the night. Eventually I came to the conclusion that I would have a cash collection of about three thousand. Deposits yet to be refunded — Three thousand two hundred. Besides, Gambhir Shet, the fuel man's bill, and so on. So in the end how much was the shortfall, that is to say *my* deficit?

Just then I felt tremendously sleepy. All night long, figures — addition substraction, multiplication-division — all my forgotten arithmetic from the matriculation days was thus revised. It was almost morning already. So I slept.

When I woke up I found that it was only about ten o'clock. Just two or three hours' sleep. Further, in my brain still crowded figures, figures. When I saw all that mess spread on my table, I was reminded of the unfinished calculations. Still so many hassles left.

Cocoon

And a letter had also arrived from home — How did your exam go? When are you coming? Sumi, Mani, Mother and our wee Nali are all waiting for you. Start soon.

My departure was surely now delayed until this mess hassle was sorted out. For one thing, there were calculations to be done about how much balance was left with each member of the mess. Then subtracting that from the deposit, find out how much of the deposit was to be paid back to each. All this must be done first. I considered asking someone to come and help but I really couldn't, because they were all preparing to go home. Now I must gird my loins and sit tight through the day, with whatever courage may be left in me. But I'd better break the back of these hassles.

By evening I had arrived at this destination — All confusion apart, six hundred rupees, that was the sum unaccounted for somewhere. Vaidya must have pocketed six hundred. Six hundred.

I communicated all this nonsense to Suresh, Ladi, Joshi and Co. Ladi said, So your story has come back to square one. Suresh said, You ought to go to the police immediately. Joshi said, But what's the use? To go to the police, you will need permission from the principal.

Ladi said, Before that we shall bully that sodding Vaidya and extract the money from him.

Mahadevan said, in English, Either Vaidya and Ramappa have kept the money together. Or Ramappa has taken it all himself. And, if that is not the case, then Vaidya must have stolen it all by himself.

Ladi said, Whatever is this sodding Madrasi saying in English?

Suresh said, Keep an eye on him. Otherwise the pimp will go to Vaidya immediately.

Joshi said, Vaidya will not misappropriate so much money.

I said, Ramappa is certainly not involved in this.

Because he used to bring you tomatoes once in a way, that's why, isn't it? Suresh said.

Ladi said, Pandoba, you are dumb. Don't you ever again indulge in tangles like the annual gathering. No one here will pay your debt for you. Sod it, Six Hundred Rupees. That's not an easy matter. That means nearly a whole year's expenses for the likes of us.

Mahadevan said, Last year a mess secretary paid up one hundred from his own pocket. But in fact he had pocketed hundreds prior to that — so he paid up the hundred. This much was actually true.

Having driven away Mahadevan, we decided that we should bully Vaidya. And demand the money from him. Shut him up in his room and beat him up.

Then first Suresh and I went to his room. It was a terribly beggarly room. Lying down, Vaidya was reading a large messy bundle of papers. We ourselves shut the door. Then he struggled up. Said, Do sit down.

Suresh said, We've not come here to sit down, sonny. We've come to hammer you.

I said, Vaidya, I am asking you straight, before handing you over to the police, tell us what really happened. Then we won't do anything to you.

Vaidya broke into a heavy sweat. At first he said nothing at all. Having placed the papers that were in his hand meticulously on the table, he went into a corner and stood there, trembling.

Then he said, I tell you the truth. Sangvikar, this is Ramappa's work. Ramappa has cheated me too handily. I used to only collect money from the chaps. As soon as I had a couple of hundred with me, I'd hand it over to Ramappa. I really gave him 200 once, and just the other day I gave him 300. I had warned you. He is a crook. Besides, I felt it a risk, keeping all that money in my room here. Suppose someone had stolen it....

You pimp... I tell you one last time. Otherwise do you see this? Saying this, Suresh started to roll up his right sleeve.

I really didn't feel like beating him up. Meantime Ladi and Joshi too arrived. In Ladi's hand was a long-handled broom. Holding the broom end in his hand he directed the stick at Vaidya's chest and pinned him against a wall.

I said, Hey, wait Ladi. Vaidya, tell the truth. How much did you take, and how much Ramappa?

In no time at all Vaidya started weeping. Eventually, he yelled loudly, You are beating me? Even when I have done nothing? All together?

Then, suddenly brushing the broom aside he leapt towards the door.

Suresh grabbed him by the collar and aimed a slap at his face — Trying to run away, are you, you son-of-a-bitch?

Hand over the money. Hand it over!

This sight got Joshi's wind up. He said in English, "This is inhuman." He opened the door and he went out.

Just as we were about to shut the door again, Vaidya suddenly wrenched away from Suresh. He leapt right at the door and went out. Suresh went after him, all agitated. Then, because of all this scuffling, shouting and screaming, many chaps from rooms within earshot gathered there. Since they were all B. A. students they were Vaidya's friends.

Vaidya said, yowling, screaming, They are beating me.

They all put Vaidya behind them and surrounded Suresh. Ladi then relieved Suresh and he and Suresh together attempted to get hold of Vaidya. There was a great deal of fist work. I too participated. Mean to say, These chaps are doing so much for me so how can I just stand around watching?

Vaidya, though, got away. Running away from us he entered Professor Shah's bungalow. Then uttering threats about giving him up to the police, we too withdrew. We'd barely reached our rooms when Khan bhayya[29] arrived. He said, Shah saheb[30] is asking all of you to report to him.

Suresh said, Tell that Shah saheb, we shan't come.

But I just had to go. Sod it, what's happened is not good. Still, it is good that Vaidya went to Shah. If he'd gone to Professor Paranjape it would have been a tough thing. Shah is, that way, a fairly good bod. Once when the class gave over there was a rush of students on the left side of the staircase. So I started to descend along the right. Professor Shah was coming up. Taking hold of my elbow he had said, Come on up. Then, like that, we climbed up again. He said, You're a sensible student. Your name is Sangvikar, isn't it? Now, this is the way. So then I came down by the left-side stairs. At least one can talk to Professor Shah. With Paranjape one has to listen to insulting language and on top of that pay a fine of five rupees.

I went to Shah. He said, in English, 'What's this mess, Sangvikar? Are you off your — ?"

I began to narrate to him the entire history of the mess mess.

He said, You'd better finish quickly. At 8'o clock my students come for tuition.

I said, That is to say, there's still half an hour's time. The point is that the boys used to give money to Vaidya. This money has not reached Gambhir Shet.

He said, Don't forget there's the cook between. Then once again in English, "Don't forget that." I know Vaidya thoroughly. Then this again in English — And if you hand him over to the police, I shall give evidence from his side. Vaidya, (and again in English), "You can go now. Don't worry. I'll settle this."

Even then Vaidya wouldn't leave.

Shah said, There's no threat of the police. Sangvikar is not so (again in English) abnormal.

When Vaidya left, Shah started a sticky argument with me. He said, I have spent fifteen years... (mixing English off and on in his speech). Such cases occur frequently. But ninety per cent of the cases lead to the cooks. In 1942 there was a similar case of a secretary called Vishwambhar. It's the cooks who do all this. And if that is not the case, the secretary is crooked. The secretary is the one who "gobbles up" the cash. Once you are preoccupied with your study, they have a free hand. And you only find out after your examination. Well, it's not much profit, finding out then. Because at least in a small measure the secretary does make off with the money. Don't deny it. He ought to appropriate the money. Otherwise who'd bother to handle this business of two or three thousand per month in an honorary capacity? That apart, how much money do you have to make up? I can tell you that Vaidya has not taken any. It is not in him to do that. The poor chap is taking a B.A. He's made an awful effort for four years. Now if at such a juncture you trouble him I shall be very sorry. But just suppose, that either Vaidya has embezzled the money or the cook has made off with it, now what will the police or anyone else do? For one thing you have no proof. You know, the police need very solid proof.

Stopping his flowing rhetoric I said, The proof is that he has taken money from the chaps but he hasn't given it to the cook, though.

All very well. But you had put your signatures on receipt books two months in advance. Now there must be, even now, some receipts left over with your signatures? Isn't that true?

Yes, that's true.

Then what will you tell the police? Vaidya cannot be involved in any of this. But about Vaidya I have already told you. He is a good boy. Nor can you implicate the cook. These chaps are in fact crooks. They might, tomorrow, even beat you up on the streets. There is no proof good enough to go to the police with. But if you do register a complaint you will have to spend your summer holidays here. Endless bother. Besides, if the warden comes to know of this, he too will say that the secretary has taken the money. This happens every year. So if you are prepared to take my advice, I'll tell you one thing.

Mean to say, I must myself pay six hundred rupees, isn't that it?

Yes. See, it's the easy way out. What is your father's situation with regard to property?

The situation is fine at home. But he won't send money for this sort of thing.

Then you'd better decide how you wish to proceed.

I came back to my room. Suresh and Ladi were of course still there. They said, Nothing doing. We shall go to the police. What's he mean, ask for money from home!

I said — That's true. Whatever will I tell them at home? Once Mother lost four annas, coming back from a shop, and she went back looking for it all the way down to the shop again. And Father is, of course, constantly complaining about the regular money order. How can I send for six hundred more?

Then Suresh said, Come on you chaps. Heck, this bloke has started his Hamlet act again. *We* have to prepare for going home.

I said, I shall tell you in the morning just what we should do.

Suresh said, I suppose Your Honour will contemplate until then? Who is going to wait in the hostel till tomorrow morning? We have to return home tomorrow.

Then I went to Madras Cafe with all the calculations floating before my eyes. Sat smoking cigarettes. That night I contemplated a thousand things.

Returning to my room I wrote out a notice announcing the closure of the mess. Whatever supply of grain was still left I returned to Gambhir Shet the same night. Whatever else was left I gave to Ramappa. I put up a notice in the mess that tonight's was the last meal of all. All the members were to come and render their accounts.

That night there was a whole queue of members. My good neighbour Joshi found all this so very droll that he stopped studying, sat on my bed and took a holiday.

One chap would come, I'd examine his bill, deduct it from his deposit and return the balance to him. By then the next chap would be ready waiting. Then he would check his bill and pay it. He would go away with his deposit. Those who didn't come that day, were met only the next day. I cleared all their business. Some chaps seemed terribly hard up. Some who hadn't even paid their deposit said, Will it do if we paid our bill later on? I said, No, no, I want it right now. Some borrowed money to pay me. All in all, I had to pay out more money than I received. All the money I had with me I disbursed in those two days.

Then I was left — penniless. And six hundred rupees worth of bills still to pay. During those two days Gambhir Shet's man visited me many a time. Finally I got angry and said to him, Tell your Shet I will not go away from here even if I die. Then he didn't come back.

Once the movement of all those crummy students reduced and I was left by myself, then I really thought of Yama the god of death. What *have* I done here? What shall I do now?

I don't give any importance to money. I used to leave as much as two hundred rupees in my table drawer. Just about anybody came into my room. It was always unlocked. Someone might have taken a hundred or two. But in the bustle of my life I didn't ever know.

But now — who could I ask for this money? Of course I shall not send for this money from home. But no one else'll give me a loan of so much either. Besides, if I thought of repaying it next June, and suppose I myself failed the exam, why should my daddy send me to Poona again? I had done nothing right.

Then I resolved — this very night I shall run away somewhere and in fact even commit suicide.

Should I knife myself?

Then I took the knife out. Tested the blade on my finger. Only after I rubbed it a good deal did it draw some blood. The knife was blunt. Who'd stick a blunt knife into his stomach? Then I put the knife into my pocket and came to Nana Chowk.

I'd come here once before for some programme. At that time I had seen a sharpening machine here. The chap with the machine sharpened my knife. Then, testing the edge with my finger I said to him, Sharpen it better. Until then he hadn't even looked at me. Now he had in fact already started sharpening another very big knife. Taking a good look at the b-i-g knife I felt, That is a very lovely knife.

Then he pressed my knife against the wheel a few more times and gave it back to me. I took the knife and returned.

The crowds on the street seemed monstrous to me. These people are all asses. They purchase cloth... and stuff like that. Sods, worthless chaps.

I had not eaten the day before. Because I had only two rupees left with me. What will I do with the rest of that money? I might as well have a lip-smacking meal. I have been hungry since the morning anyhow. Thinking that this would be my ultimate meal I entered a good restaurant.

I studied the menu. I could ask for a one and a half rupee meal. But just above the meals in the menu I found bhajis.

And when the waiter approached me I told him to bring just the bhajis. Now that I am about to die, what's the use of a whole meal? Perhaps if I eat a meal I wouldn't feel like dying. This is all right. I haven't slept for two nights either. Still I'm not a bit sleepy. And although I am awfully hungry, I feel no cheer in this.

I ate the bhajis. I must at least have some tea now. I'll feel better. A bit.

Then the tea arrived. I didn't give the waiter a tip. Right there I bought three or four packets of Charminars[31] and started back.

On the way I saw a girl I knew. She was moving awfully slowly. I should take her to my room. If I tell her I wish to die she is sure to come. But instead I didn't even pause, just took a good look at her while going. And then came to my room.

I closed the door carefully. Closed the window too and opening the knife laid it on the table. Took off all my clothes. Put a fresh cigarette into my mouth. Just lay on the bed. Then I put on just my pants. Opening the door I made sure there was nobody nearby. Everyone had gone home. Only one room was without a lock on its door.

I took another fresh cigarette. And, having closed the door, shoving the pillow comfortably under my head, I lay back, thinking that that'd be my last cigarette.

I took another fresh cigarette. Actually I should have been joyful at that time. But I was needlessly angry. That cigarette finished. Again I took another. And lay back again, looking at the knife.

Cocoon

After that one was done, I took another cigarette. And took the knife into my hand. I tried its point on my stomach. Then having checked it by placing my hand on my chest I took the decision to stick the knife in just where there is the throb.

Then I put on my shirt. And taking the knife up in my hand I lay back again on the pillow.

Just then from the ventilator above the window entered a sparrow and away it went again.

Then after a while I rose and rubbed the knife so much on the floor that it lost all its edge. Then I threw the knife into my trunk — I am not going to commit suicide. Then smoked all the remaining cigarettes. And then fell into deep, deep, dark sleep.

When wakefulness came to me, everything was closed and dark. Is this tomorrow night or the night of the day after? After a while from the college could be heard the stroke of the gong — One. Is this half past twelve or half past one? Then after some more time again there was a single stroke. Then I fell asleep again.

Later when I woke up it was still dark. Is this another, still later night or what? But now I couldn't sleep any more. I got up. Put on the light. There were two or three letters and the milkman's bill under my door. I looked at them. In the letter from home it was written that they were really waiting for me eagerly.

Then from a room in front where there was a light on I borrowed some milk. That chap was immersed in his study. I asked him what day and date it was. Then asked for a cigarette. Then he said, I don't smoke. I then collected stubs from my room and smoked those. There were plenty of stubs, big and small, from yesterday and the day before.

I drank tea and commenced a substantial missive to Father. I wrote all about the mess. I resolved that hereafter I would do nothing else besides study. But when I wrote the figure — six hundred — it infuriated me. I erased that and wrote five hundred. Later I changed that to four hundred. That would still leave two hundred to be found. To be paid to Gambhir Shet.

Couldn't I ask him to wait for a couple of months longer? Why not? Even *his* daddy will wait. So I wrote to Father to send me four hundred rupees.

And again I lay on my bed tossing till morning.

This time I did exceedingly civilized speculation.

Other secretaries pocket hundreds of rupees and here I am asking for six hundred from home, to make up a loss. Six hundred! I used to behave so affectionately with those chaps in my mess. Even with Vaidya. With Dnyanu-Manu-Sadashiv— with everyone. All are crooks, the sods. Sadashiv was a dishwasher. I owed him some twenty-five rupees out of his wages. But just now I told him a lie, that he won't get any wages-fages, his money had already been paid. But until now I was really affectionate with everyone. Then there are those two chaps — they were poor. I used to give them enough food for two in one plate, sent to their room. In our mess I was allowing four chaps to eat four charity meals according to our traditional custom of "fixed days." There were others who didn't pay their bills. They would provide instead a description of poverty at home. So then I would not pester them about the bill even if they were as much as two months behind at a time. I was allowing several chaps to eat without paying a deposit. But all were sods, the crooks. Sod 'em, all human behings are crooks. When I have fallen upon such days no one has come to my assistance. Everyone's behaved according to rules and legality. One fellow actually told me, shamelessly — It was in fact your own "weakness" that you let us eat without a deposit... don't have any money right now, shall pay tomorrow. In great anger I grabbed his collar, so then he quickly abstracted money from his trunk and paid up. And he said, moreover, We didn't know you were such a cheapskate. What a cheapskate!

And to top it all, I mean to say, me of course! What a goose — what did I achieve this year? I did some reckoning. Whatever did I achieve? Achieve! Heck....

That very next morning I put the letter into the letter box. Not that everything thereafter went smoothly.

Later I even got a telegram to say that the money had been sent and that a letter also followed.

For those three or four days in the interim I was desperate with hunger and the craving for cigarettes.

Once I went to Maushi's so I might get a meal. But as I approached her house I felt, What will Maushi say, seeing my present condition? She will inform them at home. So then I sold some books for cash instead.

Once I begged four annas from Joshi and ate two large loaves of bread, one for each meal. There were no more cigarette stubs left in my room. My fingers were stained a deep yellow, being burned over and over again.

When I asked for another one or two annas, Joshi said, No. Then I did not go to anyone else.

Just then the money arrived.

I handed it all to Gambhir Shet, saying, You will get the rest of your money in June. Then he said, Fine. That was all, Fine.

When I went to the fuel man next, he said, There's no balance from you. Just the other day Ramappa brought it all.

That sum of forty rupees made a very tidy amount for my own expenses.

Returning from the fuel man I was just pedalling my bike along, rather distracted. On a turn my bike collided with a girl's. Now this is sticky. But who do I find when I look up? It was Bundi. She said, If you must speak to me, you can stop me properly, can't you?

I said, I wasn't minding....

She said, Where to? And still in Poona?

I said, There was a problem at the hostel mess.

She said, Yes, of course. You were secretary. Well, bye.

Thereafter I decided not to tell anyone about the mess mess. Not even Suresh. Because when I get caught everyone else thinks it's a good joke. Therefore if anyone did ask I began to tell them, Where... Oh, oh, nothing really. A bit of a bother, that's all.

As I left my room I told the warden that my Maushi was unwell, that's why I was tardy in returning home. Besides, in handing over charge of mess vessels and such we were a few bowls short. I had to go all over the place looking to see if they hadn't been left in some chaps' rooms.

When I reached home, Father said, Got my letter? I said, No. As soon as I got the money I started for home. The letter must have been on the way while I was coming home. He said, The letter said that I had purchased you. By paying four hundred rupees.

I said to myself, You think four hundred will do it, do you? There's still two hundred more to pay.

You don't even go to your Maushi. Your Nana is such a great Saheb. He earns three hundred rupees a month. You don't take his advice. Consider yourself smart. Even though you are our only son, you oughtn't to behave in this fashion. You are not a millionaire. A coin is like a round wheel that runs this world and yet you purchase your experience by being careless with hundreds.

These are the salient points of Father's yakking in the holidays.

Now, once a chap has been had, all this must of course apply. Whatever others say is proven correct once one has been thoroughly and properly deceived. One who is never deceived would never have to listen to others. Why should he? That's why I shan't allow myself to be deceived hereafter. Still, by the same token — that my daddy has purchased me — he can no longer be my father. He's my owner. I eat in his eating house.

THREE

A routine for how I should proceed, in case I failed the exam —
this I determined before the results.

Then, I passed.

This was one good thing that happened.

Long live Examination! That sodding Joshibuwa has failed. And
so has Madhu. And also Jagdale.

Then I set off for Poona for the Junior year.

Father said, Do exactly what Nana says. I shan't give you even
one cowrie more than 1000 rupees this year. If you like, take
away the thousand right now with you. And don't you bother
to come here in your holidays. Stay right there. Do whatever
study or swotting you have to do there. What's transpired is
more than enough.

I was going to accept the thousand rupees. But I thought,
Suppose someone makes off with the whole lot on the way? So
I said, Send it to Maushi. But that meant going to Maushi every
month for the money. So I was a little cheesed off.

This time I travelled directly on student concession, that is
to say, by passenger train, to Poona. It jogged along, dragging,
stopping at every station along the way. Right from the time the
train started I began, on the back of used paper that I'd brought

with me, to make a strict annual budget for the thousand rupees. Thus preoccupied I didn't really notice the boring journey. As each sheet of paper was scribbled over I'd chuck it out of the window.

The sheet disappeared, taking wonderful twists and turns, followed by the next sheet. I felt like buying cigarettes. But, so that the total expense of my travel should not exceed seven rupees, ticket included, until I reached Poona, I kept chewing on the pocketful of betel nut chunks I had brought from home.

The budget estimate was prepared with meticulous care. Two hundred — debt to repay. Meaning, the remaining sum of eight hundred must see me through nine or ten months of my college terms until the end of March.

Now place the eight hundred thus in a corner. Thus. Now, what are my normal, routine expenses? Let's list them. That's fine. No pictures, of course. End of cigarettes. Restaurants, no more. What's likely to be my miscellaneous expenditure?

End of tea for friends. That way I should manage in eight hundred.

Our train was so awful — the chaps who sat next to me at one station kept getting off after every two or three stations. Just as I arranged myself at some ease, stretching my limbs, some new person would get on. And he would inevitably sit on *my* bench. I even asked a chap who got in at Dehu Road, whether he wasn't going to get off at Pimpri.

So he said, Chhe, what's there in Pimpri for me? I'll get off right here at Chinchwad well before that. The train does stop at Chinchwad, doesn't it?

So then this year I must not go about everywhere like last year with five or ten rupees in my pocket. I must enter the city of Poona with no more than two annas in my pocket.

Otherwise, there's the hostel, of course. Why must I wander about? Just thirty rupees for my meals. I shall skip meals every Saturday and Sunday. Tea and that sort of thing, right here in my room. Only in the mornings. Only ten rupees for tea.

This'd be the only expense, and occasionally, cigarettes. Altogether at the very most five rupees. Less, but no more. So this would be my expense every month. Multiplied by nine. Over and above that, the fees. Meaning, this total comes to exactly eight hundred. But I have with me a total of one thousand. No, sod it. I quite forgot Gambhir Shet's two hundred. I chucked out the sheets of paper that had by now piled up in the corner. But that's fine. Eight hundred. Just eight hundred.

Because of Nana's bullying I took History. And besides, to go with it, Sociology. I kept wishing that I had taken languages.

Nana said, Now your father has left everything to me. I have more experience than you. You just study quietly.

Hereafter my desires and wishes have no value — that's how I had behaved. So there's nothing that I can do about this, at least openly. This is bloody awful.

On reaching the hostel I was given a corner room upstairs.

This room was terrible. In it, a couple of years ago, just before the exam, a chap had committed suicide, he'd taken potassium cyanide. Moreover, it had a wooden bedstead. Meaning, there were bound to be bedbugs. And besides, a corner room. So squirrels, rats and cats would all come there. I knew all this already. Moreover, from here, the taps and the bogs were all very far away. But when I looked at the room closely, it pleased me very much. Even though it had two windows, there was plenty of gloom in it. Through the window, in fact, I could touch the branches of a tree. Through the other I could see the whole of that lovely hill. Dark, dark hill. Above it, naturally blue skies; below, clumps of woods.

I fetched from Maushi two hundred rupees as my first instalment. I said, now I shan't need any more for two months. Out of that, I immediately gave one hundred to Gambhir Shet. I told him that I would pay the rest next month. He muttered and groaned. I said, I'm not going to cheat you out of it, am I? That's all right, then. But it will be bad for you if you take the matter to the warden. I am bound to pay you some time or other.

Next month, though, I didn't go to him at all. Next visit to Maushi was only in August. So how could I pay Gambhir Shet in July also? I only had one hundred rupees left with me. Somehow, cutting corners, I had to make do with this amount.

Now this Gambhir Shet seemed to me a monstrous chap. Who knows he might actually complain to the warden. But when would I ever pay up the debts in full? In trying to pay this debt, I got into some terrible habits. One of them was that of thrift in books-notebooks-paper. Another was, to eat so much at lunchtime that my habit of snacking here and there right into the evening (as in the year just past) was quite broken. Then once again in the evening I'd eat so much at dinner that I wouldn't feel hungry all night long. That's the reason why it would take a long time for me to have done with my meals. Then Koddam would say, So, how much longer are you going to hog?

I'd say, I eat rather slowly, old chap.

Perhaps you do eat slowly. But how about eating less, as well?

This Koddam was a new chap this year. There were many new friends. But at first I found it difficult to be without the old friends. Suresh — and others like me who only studied the last fifteen days prior to the exam — had passed. And those who had swotted all year long, deeply, profoundly and all that, those poor friends had, alas, failed.

I got a letter from Madhu. In it was some fundamental analysis of the exam system and the like. Now he was a teacher in a school in Mumbai. He'd written that he would stay with me in March for the exam.

After he failed, Tambe just stayed at home.

I never knew what Joshi did afterwards.

Suresh, Koddam and I became friends right from the beginning.

In addition, a new fellow called Patil came to our hostel. I was his only friend. He had no other friendships. But if Koddam or

Suresh happened to be in my room, he would talk with them.

Patil and I met in the bathroom. Our bathrooms were all side by side in a row outside the hostel buildings. At the bottom of every partition was a bit of open space. The upper part of anyone standing in the bath would of course be seen above the partition. And his feet would also show below. Once as I was bathing a tiny sliver of soap slid towards me from the next stall. And after it came a hand struggling to grab it and retreated again. The soap was indeed pretty thin. So naturally it would slip. Next came the washing soap and again the hand. But this time the hand wasn't able to reach the soap.

This used to happen to all of us. But if we shoved a hand to the other side   the chap next door would invariably pour boiling hot water on it.

But I didn't do that. I picked up the soap wafer and gave it to the fellow there from over the partition. The chap on the other side was Patil.

He said, I'm done with this shirt. So I won't let the soap slide over there again. Thank you.

After that he used his soap more carefully.

Patil's subject was Economics. He was a very decent sort of chap. He never took tea or anything. This of course proved profitable for me.

Koddam, Patil and I — we were some three or four friends. Indeed, we were such good friends that the hostel chaps used to say, they would even let each other use their underwear, but they wouldn't part with a saucerful of tea for a stranger.

This really hurt me. I'd fed hundreds of chaps before. But I didn't ever tell these chaps that. Because they would have merely laughed it away.

Patil's room was just the bare room. The cabinet in the wall held only his comb and a bottle of hair oil. Just that. By the door — a pair of Kolhapuri[1] country chappals. On the peg — two of his shirts, one washed, the other to be washed. A towel, that was washed every day. So it was always damp. On the table — only a pocket dictionary and a great heap of rough yellow paper. In the table drawer — some letters and a few coins. That was it.

But of course one saw all this stuff only when Patil was in his room. Once he left, most of his stuff would be on him. It would go to the college. Only his cot remained in the room. On his bed instead of a mattress was a thick, rough blanket. He'd draw this over himself in winter, while he slept on a bedsheet, which later he used to cover himself during the summer, when the blanket in turn served as a bedspread.

There was little more in Koddam's room either. Indeed there was just one more thing. His father's jacket, which he wore all the time. In fact in winter — even while he slept or went to the bogs or the bath.

He used to say, I do not wish that my son — I hope I *will* have a son — to wear this coat, that's why I am wearing it out.

The hostel boys would say, But did it belong to your father or was it *his* father's before him?

At that he would say, Oh, I never had a grandfather at all.

Whenever anyone took the micky out of him, Koddam would carry the moment off by making some return crack. Always at his own expense.

In all probability he was able to compose himself in such situations because of that jacket. Whenever he had to say something, poking both hands into the jacket pockets was enough. Then whoever wished to rib him could try. Koddam would stand tall.

He used to say — Whoever has his hand in the pocket is in the racket.

No matter what Koddam says with his hands in his pockets, he really socks it to them.

Koddam was used to keeping his personality intact in any sort of awkward predicament. At college, really, everyone ought to know how to manage this. One stupid chap tries to show off his "personality" by carrying a tennis racquet all the time and wearing tennis shoes; another by carrying English novels all the time; a third by means of a set of white clothes. But Koddam managed it all with just his jacket.

That way Suresh was part of our group only because of me. And also because of his habit of tight-fistedness. But since he was unable to get tea in my room any more as he used to, now he'd visit just once a day.

I met Mehta without any special effort on my part. Once I was returning with a loaf of bread. Meanwhile someone called out to me.

Pandurang.

When I looked round I saw a girl, a relation, and her husband.

She had married only during the last holidays, when I had met her husband. Now, we had just spoken about this and that, but as for my feelings — I was jolly angry. I had only one anna in my pocket. Now, at least these two and me — that means I must have a total of three annas. What should I do now? Chhe. This is terrible. I haven't even invited them to have tea. So now they will invite me. Sure. But — really — they are *my* guests in Poona. Now, whatever shall I do?

Just then I saw Mehta coming from the opposite side.

I asked these folk to wait for a moment and reached Mehta on the run. We'd actually known that we were hostellers together. I said, I've just left my wallet in my room. Now I have met these relations. Please, give me a rupee or so. I'll return it to you immediately, just as soon as I come back to my room.

Mehta promptly gave me a rupee. I took it in such a way that the relations would not notice the transaction.

Then I returned to my relations. Now, how could I suddenly suggest that we have tea? I chatted on for five or ten minutes longer. Then I took them to a restaurant. If I hadn't met Mehta then, my penniless state would have been exposed.

Mehta was an awfully rich chap. In his room were three or

four bath gowns. And fifteen or so woollen trousers hanging in a row. I had only the four tailored the last year. But two or three brothers of his were Collectors[2] in the government. His dad was a merchant or something in Colombo. His mother was — obese. And his sisters beautiful. All this I found out from his photo album. He had many hobbies related to his camera. For his B.A. he had taken Philosophy. Mehta considered Dr. Radhakrishnan[3] his guru, because Radhakrishnan had once stayed with his uncle. At that time Mehta himself was also living with his uncle in Ahmedabad. Then Radhakrishnan was supposed to have said to Mehta, Your reading seems formidable.

Mehta used to tell me a thousand things about English literature. Indeed, he really had a certain kind of gravity about him. In his opinion, Freud, Lawrence and Huxley were great literary figures. On this matter he asked me my opinion. I was embarrassed.

In fact my association with Mehta was really limited to my teaching him Marathi. He himself said, Let's sit every evening, over tea, I will learn Marathi.

I really liked this pedagogic method — "over tea." With biscuits and Gujarati snacks too. But I did teach him Marathi in just two months — later I told him to go directly to *Shyamchi Ai.*[4] He took two days and read this novel.

Then he said, This book is "sentimental."

I said, May be. But it is good.

He said, It may be good, but it isn't great.

I said, For instance?

He said, Now look at D. H. Lawrence. That's a "great" writer.

Whereupon I sat in the library for a whole week and read Lawrence. Mehta on the other hand would actually buy books. So he was able to read at night. In the library I finished two or three novels somehow. And once I had a discussion with him. I said, You might say that Lawrence is "new." That is, "modern", but he's not really "great" or anything.

He said, Chhe, chhe. Now take Forster. Is there no difference between Lawrence and Forster?

At this I was annoyed. Mean to say, he will just keep on dropping new names. And now I'd have to read Forster just for discussion's sake. By then he'd be ready to cite the example of Huxley — how far might this not go?

I therefore argued like an ass and had a scrap with Mehta. The epilogue of my argument was — Gujarati people are useless.

He said, That's all right.

Then the Marathi lessons also ended. That is why his pronunciation of Marathi remained bookish, as it were.

Truth to tell, my life had become that of a moribund chap.

Not nearly enough cash. Every night my bedtime thoughts would be — How much more do I owe Gambhir Shet still? How much do I have left with me? Should I go to Maushi's next week or the week after? Am I spending just the right amount every day or not?...

Mehta, now, would read Aurobindo Ghosh[5] at bed time.

Suresh and Koddam, etc., would supply ever new jokes about Sardarjis.

This was all last year's lingering foolishness. But who could I share this with? "Shining!" Dash it. All it meant was earning some fishponds and going about strutting thus among people. Keeping in touch with dozens of people. Shit. And of course I didn't have the habit of living thriftily.

All in all, that I was an ass was beyond doubt.

In our history class there was a chap called Verma who literally shone! He was a number one shiner. Mean to say, he'd play the guitar or something in his fancy clothes, on the stage. And he was the Sports Secretary, etc. And a number one smartass. He would spend the money obtained from home immediately and then, borrowing money from anybody at all he'd take girls around.

And what of the cheap girls in Poona, anyhow? They got nothing at all from their families, one presumes. Once they had paid up their college fees, all they had to do was to come from the city and go back to it. That is to say, a practically gratis sort of education. And of course they'd welcome a chap like Verma and gladly wrap him around their little fingers.

In short Verma was a goony sort of creature — hour after hour he could be seen hanging about with girls, gassing about — "churning jaggery", as we might say.

My association with him was limited to the classroom. Not that he ever really bothered me. At any rate unlike others, he didn't ask — What was taught yesterday? I wasn't able to come to class, you see.

But once he did come to my room and asked to borrow five rupees — in great style. I mean to say, in English — I'll return it in a day or two, he said!

A whole month went by, yet the gallant wouldn't so much as mention my money. Hitherto I had of course met hundreds of such people. But at this time, even if I had just an anna coming from someone I was unable to sleep just thinking that it was mine. Finally I was down to only about eight annas or so. That's why I became really agitated.

Patwardhan said, Now forget your five rupees. Even *my* money's stuck with Verma. He's sunk so many chaps' money like this.

Toni said, Sangvikar, you sod, don't you fret about your fiver. Don't you know what sort of a chap Verma is? He will pay, some day.

Patwardhan said, Sod it, in our class there's Toni the rascal on one side and then his pal that Verma on the other. Sangvikar, you'd better snatch Verma's black jacket from him.

I only asked Verma one final time.

He said, in English, Tomorrow, sure.

After two or three days, I hadn't quite exhausted my eight annas. I could still buy a local postcard. For five rupees this wouldn't be too much to spend. I took Verma's address from the college office. And I wrote him the following on that open card —

Sod it, Verma, you untrustworthy chap.
Return my money right away. It's been too many days.
Or else, better think carefully.

After two or three days, in the very next history class, Verma threw a five rupee note on my bench and said, in English, Fuck it, you sod. For five measly rupees you write a letter home? Idiot. Take it.

Greatly offended, I said, Verma, you'd better hand it to me properly.

Toni said, Sangvikar, you've behaved like an ass. If you'd only told me the other day I myself would have given you five rupees.

Patwardhan placed the note, which had meantime fallen down, in my pocket. He said, Sangvikar, see what Tonya is saying, son-of-a-bitch. Tonya giving you five rupees...!

Toni yelled, Patwardhan, you Konkani[6] pimp, who asked you to open your mouth in the middle of this?

Patwardhan got up like a jack-in-the-box, saying, Bastard, you convert,[7] he's my friend. I *will* speak.

Then these two grabbed each other's collars. I got Patwardhan away. Verma stopped Toni. The girls in the class found the whole affair amusing.

Toni said, Patwardhan, do you know? Sangvikar's letter fell into Verma's daddo's hands. The letter only said, "Return the money." His daddo thought it was a lot of money.

Verma said (naturally in English), Nonsense.

Toni said, We have our own understanding with Sangvikar.

We'll borrow ten from him again if we want to.

At that Toni and Patwardhan began to hurl horrible curses at each other.

Verma said to me, Both these chaps are daft. But Sangvikar, now do one thing. Father threatened me, that I'd better bring it in writing from the chap who wrote, that it *was* only five rupees.

Otherwise — don't come home! Father said, in fact, if that chap is willing, to bring him to our house.

Damn your father, I said in English. I won't come.

Verma said, Please, won't you at least write....

Oh, I can't spare time now. I'll do it in the recess.

But in the recess I went off somewhere. Heck, who's going to wait for chaps like this?

Later, when I returned to class, Verma was not in the room. But I learned that he had some sports meeting to attend. So he'd gone there.

Then all of a sudden I felt pity for Verma. Not too much, though. So I just scribbled a note and gave it to Suresh —

Verma's Father, Your son borrowed just five rupees.
I have got it back. So.

Suresh said, I'll give it to Verma... if I meet him.

After class I happened to meet Verma myself. I said, The note's with Suresh Bapat.

Where will I find Bapat now?

Why're you asking me? I shan't write that note again. You find Suresh.

Verma went off to locate Suresh.

In the joy of having got back my five rupees, after class I left for the market   to have a haircut.

On the way — Suresh.

What, Surshya, how're you here?

Coming from the cinema. But — hey, sonny... here, take your note. After you handed me it, I felt like going to the pictures. Take it.

Suresh flung the chit at me. I in turn flung it far away. He said, Where are you off to?

To this cinema here.

Now, just as you scheme to proceed to the market so you can get a cheap haircut, that's when you are bound to meet such pals asking you pat, Where to?

Later, Suresh went back to the hostel. Verma was still looking for him.

Cocoon

Suresh said, I did have the note with me. But just now as I was coming I met Sangvikar. I gave it back to him. If you'd met me before that I'd have given it to you.

Verma said (of course in English!), What nonsense. What a stupid.... Right, but where's Sangvikar now?

Gone to Hindvijay cinema. He'll be back by nine o'clock or so.

Thinking he might meet me in the interval Verma came to the cinema. He hunted for me high and low in the interval. Then thinking that perhaps I'd not come out, he waited till the film was over. But how was he likely to meet me there?

Finally, at ten he came to the hostel. And in my happiness — not only because my five rupees had been returned but also that he had been dangling till nearly midnight — I wrote for him once again the entire history of this episode.

After he had left, laughing horribly with Suresh, I said — The sod. Shines in the college, does he!

At least once I really must hammer this cat. Three days in a row now she has drunk up my milk. Climbs from that tree into my room. When I open the door I often see her running away by the window.

So then one day I tried a little trick. I closed one window in advance. Kept the other slightly ajar. Tied a cord to one flap of the window and let it out through the door. And then, through the chink in the door I watched, waiting for the time when the cat would come in.

It had a fixed time, the sod. I buy just half of a quarter of one seer[8] of milk. She can't stand even that. She drinks it up with her eyes closed — today we shall teach her a lesson.

After a while the window rattled. The cat climbed down from the window, off the tree branch. Then at leisure into the room. Directly to the milk.

At that instant I closed the window. Opening the door I entered. I shut the door after me.

The cat flung herself at the window, started to struggle.

I managed to hit her with a flung chappal. She jumped down. Meantime, keeping the cord taut I closed the window properly.

Now what shall I whack her with? The belt about my waist is best. I tied the belt thoroughly to my right hand and pulled out the trunk from under my bed. I started to lash out, cut after cut with the belt — phut, phut, and so on.

Hissing at me — phiss... phiss — the cat attempted to slink further and further inside. Under the bed in a corner there was a heap of waste paper and finally she went behind that. I too crouched down lower and lower with the belt and let the so-and-so have it. Till I myself perspired profusely. Until she should know better than to enter my room.

Once in a way she'd catch at the belt with her paw. The more she did that the more I lost my temper. I carried on my phut... phut... phut.

One hard blow in fact caught her in the eye. That really frightened her.

Once indeed she caught and held in her teeth the very belt with which I was hitting her. Mean to say, now that rather expensive belt was done for.

So in a fit of anger I yanked at the belt so hard that she was dragged out from under the bed, the belt between her teeth.

At that time I really gave her a terrific kick in the back. She let go of the belt and lashed at my foot. Blood.

But she herself yowled and went straight to the corner pile of paper and hid behind it. Now I couldn't quite use the belt.

Then I found another smart ruse

I put a panful of water on the stove. I'd pour boiling water from over the bed precisely into that corner, then the sod must come out.

But now my foot was burning badly, smarting. And I was worn out. Besides, hammering on my door, Patil had already shouted once — Whatever is going on, Sangvikar?

By now the water was boiling.

Now, as I pour the water the so-and-so would have cause to remember for ever. But when she comes out I shall hold her tight jammed in the door. That way — a permanent lesson.

Then I opened the door just a little, no more than would allow the cat to barely get through. I turned off the stove and with mighty thick pads of paper I picked up the pan.

The cat was listening to the noise of the stove. Meaning — what the dickens had she been feeling all this while? Did she really think that I might be making tea for her?

Here, you sod, have some tea! Saying this, from above on the bed, I emptied the pan over the corner and jumped with a thud to the floor by the door. Now to squeeze her in the door. Her head out and her tail in the room. In addition I'd deliver a smacking big kick from behind and then let her go.

The cat yowled and howled as she ran from under the bed. Then she saw the door was open. With a leap she tried to leave by the door.

I banged the door shut. Hard.

The cat got away, though. And having caught my own fingers in the door I screeched madly.

Two or three nails of my left hand turned black and blue. For the next fifteen days they throbbed with pain....

I had to do everything with my right hand.

Patil said, Sangvikar, suppose it had grabbed you by the throat?

Maushi said, Now you appear, after two whole months? I took one hundred and fifty rupees.

I went straight to Gambhir Shet and paid him a hundred. On the 15th of August — Independence Day — I paid off my entire debt. Now, FREE. However, with the remaining fifty rupees I must manage for another month and a half. That won't suffice. But I'll borrow some twenty or twenty-five from Koddam. Then after another month and a half or so ask Maushi for forty or so more. 'Nuff. Meaning, for some more time I must live in penury.

Not a bit of enthusiasm, no verve, no freshness. Just as I thought I might do a bit of reading, the six monthly exam came round. This History. I really cannot manage History. I am bound to fail. I told Nana this. In a sort of pitiful appeal. He said — Do what you like.

Having met the principal about a change, I made half a dozen trips to the University and changed my subjects.

Right away, then, the six-monthly. Now I took both Marathi and English. In fifteen days I managed to do a surprising amount of study.

Otherwise, that blooming History, that daft branch of learning! To make a career of such a subject is daft, indeed. Mean to say, they found a stone inscription and all that, I believe, that's why they found out about Asoka.[9] When they lack interim proofs these chaps make all sorts of presumptuous conclusions. Where does the history of America begin? — After Columbus I believe! Meaning, let all that about the Red Indians go. And whatever is found in excavations — with that alone does history grow. Otherwise they begin with the time the Aryans came to India. And, one *can* make guesses about the clothing and stuff like that, but about the minds of people of that time, where does one find out about that? And if they do not find anything in excavations, then whatever they know today is the WHOLE truth. In general, History is pretty daft.

Suresh had Marathi from the start. When I first sat in the Marathi classes, having given up History, Suresh yelled — Jay, jay! Bravo!

Nana let them know at home about this.

From home came Father's letter, You are an ass. If you must read the *Dnyaneshwari*,[10] why go to college for that?

Don't we read it at home too?

This pleased me a little. At least he considers *Dnyaneshwari* part of the study of Marathi. If he had come to know that for our study we also had Keshavsut, Mardhekar, and N.S. Phadke,[11] he would have straight come here and said — Pack your things and come home!

But I escaped that.

I finished the study for the exam smartly in just fifteen days.

But Surshya started a novel thing, real nuisance. Whenever and wherever we were — say, on the hills for a walk, or in the classroom or in my room, everywhere Surshya's favourite topic was — My giving up of History. Needless to say, I would lend him a hand.

We'd fancy ourselves historians of the nine-thousandth century of the Christian Era and speak about the bygone twentieth century —

...And, at that time there used to be Centres of Higher Learning called Universities. Now you will say, What the dickens is this thing? So then, in Universities would go on study of some subjects. Now what does study mean? So, then, even a language called Marathi would be studied.

The people of those times used to take Exercise. We shall tell you in brief what Exercise means. Now for instance, Exercise means that thing by which people's bodies became tough. Indeed, some of them would do, for instance, squats, others would run, for days on end for no reason whatsoever.

Furthermore, these people would consider themselves either Hindu or Musalman. Every person used to know who his own father was. These people used to relieve themselves in closed toilets. That is to say, they used to do many things in such a way that others might not see them.

In the Twentieth Century, people used to even "marry." Now you will ask, what does this Marriage mean? So then, Marriage was such a thing that a man could only marry a woman. During these Marriages would be played loud band music. Moreover, large crowds would gather. This actually means that the same woman would cook the food for her married man and wait for the time when he would return home.

Now, you will query, Where did he go? About that, now, some research is going on.

However, on the basis of information currently available, Mahamahopadhyaya Girijashankar Martand avers that they would study in Universities all the year round. What would that be for? Now that was for a thing called Examination in which everyone used to gather together and provide answers for some questions.

All Gentlemen would sit their Examinations properly.

When, five years ago, the Mahamahopadhyaya[12] placed this view before the public, at that time everyone thought that he was out of his mind. However, now his view has come to be generally accepted.

Only recently the Mahamahopadhyaya has done some further research. According to it, it has been found that, in the Universities there used to be a subject of study called Algebra. In this subject we have not been able to quite understand the odd matters studied. All the same, assuming that "a" is 5 and "b" is 4, then a - b = 1. That's the sort of thing that went on. This is given only by way of example. In the same way, replacing letters with vast numbers, calculations would go on until they filled up whole notebooks.

Furthermore, those people would say that after twelve o'clock it was one o'clock. Or after thirty-one days of July were over, instead of counting the thirty-second day of July, those people would consider it the first day of August.

Now you may ask, what is that thirty-one? Who is thirty-two? What is the muddle July-August ? Well, researches into this matter are going on.

But, you will ask, how could these people assume that any particular number meant such and such a thing? The answer to that is, they were clever people. Right from childhood they would force their children into school, and teach them Tables up to thirty and this education in the Meaning of Signs was already accomplished by the age of eight or ten years, then these children would on their own learn larger signs by means of the smaller signs, quite of their own accord.

These people also used to undertake something which they called Travel — sitting, some fifty odd bods of them together, in a bus. All the same, they did not even get to know each other.

These people put on Clothing and earned Money.

Now you will ask, what does Money mean? Now, things known as Money have been found in Excavations. In addition, these people used to make Poems. It was the custom to expect everyone to know how to read and write. There was a phenomenon called the Book. There were hundreds of thousands of Books. But every day all over the world so many Books would come out that even the Learned Persons of each Language themselves were not able to read all those Books — Now, this opinion of the Mahamahopadhyaya is foolish. Whoever would write so many Books!

These people were ill equipped to exist, to such an extent that they had annihilated, with their Guns and merely for entertainment, great big Godlike creatures, White Tigers, Lions, Elephants and Whales.

Now you will ask, what does Gun mean? And what is Elephant? These you must see in museums. But what this God-Fish or Whale was no one is yet able to say.

Suresh would start some sentence. Then I would utter the next — this blethering would go on until both of us were thoroughly tired of it. Or else it would start when we became fed up with all other things.

When for eight, ten days at a time I had no money at all, I would discover some new form of recreation. A chap called Kalya was just one such discovery. He was a body builder type of student from Satara. He used to narrate thousands of tales about wrestling —

The other day, that champion wrestler Dudhnath was made to bite the dust — by a scion of our own Satara, don't you know....

Having once started like that he would go on — who used what hold and who was then brought down to the mat.... Once in a way, by way of example, he would make some chap stand before him and demonstrate different holds elaborately.

Once he started to show me sword-play. But he wasn't able to proceed with his bare hands. Then he took off his pajamas, and standing only in his briefs, pajama in hand twirling round and round, swishing about swiftly — he showed all the moves.

His squat, dark, ringingly solid image would look very comic. He could not manage English at all. But if someone said something extrasmart in English to him, he would demolish them by using difficult and choice English words.

Then coming to my room he would say, Sod it, who'd dare mess about with me in English? I just "frogged" that so-and-so, you know.

"To frog" somebody or something was his keynote — This wrestler from Satara frogged that Punjabi Musalman rival... I will frog the exams... that girl should be frogged... yesterday we had shira[13] in the mess, I really frogged that sweet shira.

Everything about Kalya was — unique.

But I wouldn't be able to meet Kalya every day. When the three cigarettes — my daily quota — had been smoked, there would be little else to look forward to for the rest of the day. Then I'd go to the library and read a novel or so. Or go to the Vetal Hill[14] with Suresh. Read, regularly, all the new and ancient notices in the college. And, of course, I'd attend class punctiliously.

One day when there was a student strike, for the United Maharashtra Movement or something, there were only Professor Gune and me in the classroom. Then Gune Sir and I discussed a thousand different things.

He said, Do you desire that Samyukta Maharashtra should come about?

I said, Of course I do.

All in all, though, I just had to keep doing something. One may not have money — but one must per force resort to something or other.

That way Rami was just great. Of late I hadn't spoken to her for days and days. The moment the class was over I promptly returned to my room. For my room, though, I feel — tremeeeeeeendous affection. Even if I merely lay about staring at the hill it would become evening before I knew it. But Rami was great. No nonsense in the class with notes and such. And she is never, of course, in the library. Nor in any games. Nor at any meeting-feeting. And of evenings I just don't go out at all, so how would I run into her?

I once made a terrific resolution. I observed mauna, total, absolute silence. Didn't speak to anyone at all for eight days in a row. At the time of attendance in class, I would merely stand up. No saying "Yes, sir." In eight days I read a frightful amount in my room. I even read the next year's textbooks, having brought them from the library.

But then once Suresh came into my room. He had taken a bet with everyone that he would make Sangvikar speak. This of course I learned later. Surshya started —

Everyone was able to read and write in those bygone days. The most developed people in the Twentieth Century were the people of Hindustan. For in Europe every single person was able to read and write, whereas in India only ten or fifteen in a hundred could do so.

I said nothing at all.

Surshya went on —

However, by and by even Hindustan declined and the percentage of literates began to grow. Besides, they used to believe that Human beings had Minds. Still, till the end they were unable to say what this Mind was. In that time there were numerous, persons who spent their entire life reading hundreds of Books. The title of such persons was "the Learned Ones."

Upon this, unable to bear his dull prattle, I immediately broke into speech —

But during the same period of time there were also some good people. They used to live in the Montane regions of Orissa and Bengal. They used to worship stones.

Surshya shouted — I've won the bet!

Then thereafter I gave up my mauna.

Once, even though he was quite reluctant, I took Patil up the Parvati Hill. It had already rained that day. And there was every chance of more rain.

Patil said, capitulating, All right, let's go. But we must come back early, okay?

I held his hand and made the steep climb at one go.

Patil began to pant awfully hard. But I felt exhilarated.

Let's stop here for a bit. Let us sit here for a while, do, said Patil.

Still I dragged and pulled him, right up to the collapsed wall at the top of the hill.

I was, most pleasurably, sitting on the fallen wall and with the cool, cool wet breeze blowing over me, enjoying the beautiful view beyond.

Finally, darkness fell. And it also began to rain a bit.

Patil said, Let's get going now.

On the way down, I deliberately avoided the steps and started to hop skip and jump down rocks along awkward paths. Patil came after me carefully minding his step. I would suddenly stop on the way. Once he reached me, then I'd proceed, jumping. Now the rain began to fall in real earnest. And we came down on some very strange road, indeed.

Beside me Patil was shivering in his rainsoaked clothes. But being soaked had enthused me no end.

Patil said, Let's go back by bus. I'm feeling cold.

I said, Better still, let's spend the bus money on bhel.[15] And then walk as we eat it.

Then as we ate the bhel we walked and walked and walked till at last we did reach the hostel. I went to have my dinner right away. Patil said, I shan't eat today.

That night Patil ran a terrific fever. I learned this in the morning.

Cocoon

I felt most awful. If he hadn't been up to that much, why did I have to bully him so ruthlessly?

Next day Patil's temperature rose even higher. He lay down all day with his country blanket over him.

I fetched the hostel doctor. For two days I nursed him. Brought his dinner to the room fed him coffee at my own expense, and went to the doctor regularly for his medicine. Even as he was saying No, no, I put my mattress on his cot. And I slept on the bare mat. At night I lay reading in his room and administering his medicine regularly.

When he got a bit better I determined never to force myself on anyone in that way. This wandering wherever I pleased, getting soaked through, roaming about, behaving any old way, doing all sorts of eccentric things — all this only with Suresh. Since childhood I'd gone my own bizzare way. Perhaps another person would not be familiar with this sort of behaviour. How could I presume that another could behave just like me? Not even a stone resembles another exactly. So no human being is going to be like another. One must con-duct oneself with this in mind.

Come to think of it, there's not so much similarity between Suresh and me either, is there? Only you are exactly like yourself. At least Suresh and I resemble one another a great deal. One must find out first whether another person is at all like oneself.

That's why (heck, girls!) all the contacts I had with girls last year turned out to be good because of all the activities I was involved in. Mean to say, right to the end I kept my own character, my honour intact. I came across so many girls, but I didn't misbehave, ever. But even as entertainment I found girls a nuisance, generally.

I just thought, why should one struggle and strain so much? For one thing, I never did encounter a genuine girl. I have heard, though, that there are such girls.

One girl I did used to like. On one of our pleasure trips she insisted on playing on the gramophone the Marathi song —

The moth claims the flame,
Why do you then blame the flame?

— again and again, and she kept looking about her quite overcome with emotion.

But I said, Phyattt.

I had also liked another.

She once said, You really did play the flute well.

I said, Phyattt.

Then there was a third one. She in fact never spoke a word.

I said, Phyattt.

Girls have to be the ones to initiate things.

Rami is the only really good one.

But even Rami is a bit distant.

Everyone at college considers things true when they in fact know they are false. At the hostel every year they successfully carry out the ceremony of Rakshabandhan.[16] On this occasion the girls are supposed to tie the "brotherly" thread on the chaps' wrists. I did go last year. Girls and the chaps all gather in one place. The girls tie the rakhis. And, exploiting this opportunity, the furtive cooing of romance too carries on for two or three hours at a time. This is terrifying.

I met Rami by chance and she said, Why didn't you attend the Rakshabandhan ceremony yesterday?

Meaning, Rami herself must have gone there. At least she should not attend such occasions. But who am I to treat her in a proprietorial manner? How can one person act in a possessive way towards another? But then, did she by any chance go there hoping that she and I would meet? Or did she broach the subject today just because she merely needed something to say? These days my clothes are pretty unkempt and I actually look impoverished. So anyone says anything they fancy to me.

Meantime Madhu Deshmukh visited Poona and naturally stayed with me. And in fact he wouldn't just go back.

He said, One feels so happy here. A.... ha! Sod it... Mumbai is such a bore. Living by teaching school. A man may become anything else but he mustn't become a school master. Just to contemplate one person presuming to teach another...that is itself such a horrifying notion.

Looking out of the window he would say, A.....ha! How lovely. That hill. How many many times we have sat there. That gulmohar tree.[17] How many memories come crowding in.

Then he recalled his sweetheart. He said, Do you ever meet her?

I said, I see her regularly at the college. Once she did ask where you were.

Madhu said, Then what did you tell her?

Why should I say anything at all? And why should she ask either? Then finally in a huff Madhu left for Mumbai.

When someone from my past went off like that I became listless. My cigarette expenses went up. I'd feel, I didn't belong to this place, to that hill. Did I? I too will be gone from here in the same way. Lying in the room day and night like this, one gets accustomed to the usual sunlight from the window, the predictable tree, the same old angles, etc. From this same room must have gone away other students like me. The college is sixty or seventy years old. Up until the Flood, hundreds will have lived here and gone. There's to be no trace of them. Of me either. But those minds that are attached to places, always trapped like this.

While one is thinking such thoughts the sun-like moon-light outside seems terribly gruesome. And the lamps that are lit in all these four hundred rooms — even more gruesome. All those who are studying are, all, all quite impermanent. They live in colleges for four years like ghosts and then — depart. And this room of mine, all closed up.

Then I had a dream which I hadn't had for many many days. First, a dark-dark screen. The planetary boluses that revolve and revolve. Stars, all whirling at tremendous speeds. But everything is as though it has been charted out. Nothing collides with another. When they do, though, everything would be over with a bang, the way the counters are broken on a carrom board, the game's over.

And a hideous magician has put his spell on all of us and left us on a planet. All of us students. All teachers. All servants. The whole city. Having converted us first into twisted and warped ghosts. The magician has also possessed us and then let us go. Amongst us we can only make signs and gestures. We cannot really speak to each other.

Then suddenly someone slayed this magician. And promptly, promptly all the ghosts came out of their monstrous shapes. The castle of the magician also broke up. Everything became thin air. Then our planet twirled and whirled and began to wander here and there. Now, amongst all these innumerable stars where might this planet drift that has come out of the magician's spell, with no control over itself? At this great speed. It must burst into oh so many shards.

And the numerous dissonant voices coming from so many rooms — so grim, oppressive. This closed room. Given to me on contract for one year. Once the exam is over, tie up your things and get going. Why, this is so far only the Junior year. Meaning, I still have another year left. But it will be some other room next. And what after that, anyhow? Sangvi is not here, it is far away. That too is my place. Once, in my childhood, a singer had sung a song to the sound of a tambourine in our village fair —

Once the journey's done, the two brothers clash
The soul is no kin to the body, no
The soul is no kin to the body.

Either this is false, or else attachment is. One wouldn't be in this quandary unless one of them was false. But there are always two things. Only one of them true. Otherwise, why are there bars on the windows? This room doesn't belong to my old daddy.

I told Suresh these my thoughts about the room.
He said, Listen, I'll tell you a joke.

Cocoon

Once a chap came out of the blue to my room and knocking on my door — tuck tuck — he forced his way in. He said, Excuse me. This is my old room. A....ha! This very room. What days those were! This is the very window. This the same, selfsame tree outside. My table too used to stand just like this, by the window. A...ha! The very cot. Mine was just like this. This used to be my cupboard. In this cupboard I used to keep my clothes. A....ha! And just like this, here inside — A stark naked girl!

Surshya's jokes are tough. Goodness alone knows where he doesn't obtain them from.

The time before darkness falls in the evening is most terrifying. Monstrously terrifying. No movement. Even the children of teachers behind our hostel create a mayhem that is terrifying. The dark refuses to fall speedily. You mustn't lie about in your room like this at such a time. You'll go crazy. Go for a walk and then — eat. Hog. That is the sure antidote to the listlessness of the evening. This solution, hogging, I used to employ after I'd done a lot of thinking — What is going to happen to me later? After I have left this college? These chaps, all my friends, where oh where will they go? Who among them will become great? Who will get on in life? Who will fall by the wayside? Was it predetermined by someone three years ago that I would be precisely here, in this very room with these my friends; that I would arrive, live, laugh, read, sleep, all on this very space small as a needle point on the Earth? After our wee little school chums have grown up, this new lot of friends by the dozen have grown close to me, speak to me — whatever can be the reason for all this?

On account of all these thoughts I began to lose my glow. I could not even talk properly with the few friends I had. One of the reasons for all this cogitation was that Kalya the bodybuilder wouldn't meet me regularly. Nor would I regularly sit in the library, reading. Surshya and I wouldn't go every Sunday to Sinhagad.[18] And the biggest reason was that my room has two large, very large windows, and what is more — both of them insist on showing me the outside world. If there is moonlight one might lie about, regardless. And look at birds in the tree. Look at the hill as one smoked a cigarette. I know all the events and mysteries from the time of year when this tree has only bare branches left, to the time when it fruits. Lie at ease looking at it in self-absorbed contemplation. The tree from one window — and through the other, the sky.

Moreover, inequality is bound to persist in this world. And there is of course the maker and governor of all, Lord of all Lords. But everyone must possess at least a little money. Otherwise, slowly, we shall all become communists.

Evenings, Patil saunters about, purposelessly, in his rolling gait, taking long, long strides on the verandah.

Shaunak splits each cigarette into two and makes use of it twice.

I wait for dinner, and in the meantime I gossip with Khan bhayya — He says, Hindu and Musalman, both religions are achha. But man it is who is crooked, not religion.

As one of his daily meals Shekhar invariably eats just tea and bread.

Even though there are thousands of bedbugs in his room, Naidu doesn't tell the true reason why he refuses to sprinkle bug poison — that he has no money to buy it. He says, Because there are bugs in my room, no one comes to have a natter. That's good, because my study goes well.

In Koddam's room on the wall hungs a dirty old calendar. On it in scrunched up space he scrawls whatever he may have spent each day. In this record you will only find annas and pice; in the space for rupees, a big zero everywhere. One chap asked, Why then did you draw the column for rupees in the first place? So he said, The rupee expenses go into a secret ledger. I don't want any complications, in case the income tax officer....

When in anyone's room he hears the noise of a stove, Dhainje goes in, and telling tales and cracks from his village, extracts tea. How terrifying all this is. Some may possess money, some others may not. But of all these friends' situation I had not the foggiest notion during these last two years. They must have been like

Cocoon

this always. Only I couldn't really get to know them. Therefore that time — all friends were spendthrifts. From large families. If we got bored, there was the cinema, or Madras Cafe, records, restaurants, we'd go and munch peanuts in the park here, or guff bhel in another park elsewhere. In the evening we'd have no appetite. We'd barely eat one chappati in the mess, having first removed its half-baked edges. We'd leave our rice unfinished, rise after eating just the curds, then take some friend to the canteen — in such mean financial states passed the last two years — and now I am smothered under this monstrous heap of thoughts, feel frightened for no apparent reason at all.

The other day Koddam was given some scholarship because of his caste. I read his name on the notice board. Everyone came to know, this way, that he was from a backward caste. Why should anyone refer to such things, so I didn't say anything to Koddam. He mustn't be hurt for such stupid reasons, that's why.

But Koddam himself came to me, a fortnight or so after, yelling in triumph, Long live Caste! I got a scholarship. Sangvikar, Patil, I got the money today. Come, today I will give you a "party."

Suresh, me, Patil and Koddam — we all went to Madras Cafe. There sat Mehta. Now he too would have to be included. Koddam had fixed only one rupee as his budget. Finally — five people can be accommodated, one batatawada[19] per head and tea. We'd finished eating the wadas, and Koddam was about to order tea when Mehta said, I don't want tea.

Koddam was scared. But taking a hint Mehta added, Koddam, I know this is your party, but I shall also treat everyone. basundi[20] — Five basundis. Later, Koddam's tea.

Mehta's bill was almost two rupees. Koddam's, one rupee. All Koddam's happiness vanished. Sod it, why should such things happen?

I was not to go home this year for the Diwali holidays. I decided to read right here. I knew, of course, that I would get terribly bored in the holidays. So I decided — Stay up all night, sleep all day long. The moment the six-monthly exam was done I began this routine.

Once when I was stiff all over from having read into the morning I turned out the light and went straight to the hill.

Ahead of me were two girls. Perhaps they came every day. But I myself never took this well trodden path. One of them was Rami.

I said to her, Hallo. Semiramis. Does it provide you exercise, this wandering over the hills of a morning?

A little.

I said, How did your exam go?

No'bad.

Where are you from? I believe I have forgotten. Now let's see — it was Jabalpur, wasn't it?

'balpur.

Going home in the holidays?

Yes.

When are you going?

...'morrow.

Drat it. This one speaks only a word at a time. This is tough. And she has this trick of always speaking mincingly. That is special, though. Mean to say, instead of saying Jabalpur, '...Balpur'. Instead of saying Satara she says '...Tara'. Instead of uttering Day-after-tomorrow, she says — '...morrow'. Lovely!

On Diwali day, I became very disturbed. There was no one else in the hostel. During the holidays there had been some foreign chaps. They too had now gone away somewhere on a tour. At any rate, because of their presence around me, my English improved considerably during these holidays. What's a tea straining thing called in English? What are globs from the nose called in English? I found out many such valuable words. Where else would one obtain such knowledge except at a college?

When the holiday was over a chap from Sangvi brought a large tin of Diwali goodies from home. I kept this under wraps. For a month thereafter every morning before my tea I'd eat just one laddu.[21] The shev-chivda[22] and such lasted many days. At last Suresh spied this through a chink in my door and out of the blue I was raided by some twenty or twenty-five chaps. And whatever was still left was demolished in just five minutes.

A terrifying property of hostel chaps was this sort of gang behaviour. I wasn't myself to suffer much from this. But with minimal use of the brain anyone would have understood why — Four hundred odd persons of the same age, brought together for a span of years having broken ties with their hearth and home. Each one with a different personality. So, without forming gangs, activities like looting, hold-ups or horse-play would be impossible. Their favourite pastime was when a group was in the mood — to behave as they pleased without caring a hang for anything at all, torturing and teasing unsuspecting chaps.

Now, Mahadevan was a gentlemanly chap. Since it was what he wore at home, when he was in the hostel he would wear only a lungi.[23] Once someone found out that under his lungi he wore nothing. Not even a loincloth. Then everyone pestered him no end tugging at his lungi. Once in fact a chap undid the lungi. Then he began to wear a loincloth.

Now why is this so? Someone may not, perhaps, like certain things. Or perhaps there are chaps who cannot afford to wear a thousand articles of clothing.

In comparison to some of these chaps, Ichalkaranjikar was a gem. Of course he too indulged in horseplay. But nothing so monstrous. Besides, he wouldn't pursue this business of "shining", of vying with others and all that. He always did this and that in the manner of a python. Whatever he did, he did for himself. Not like this for a gang. Ichlya the great. But all these chaps, sods, gather together in a group, guffaw together like pigs, have a go at their victims. Even Suresh was one of them.

Take Subhash. He was an awfully clever chap who had been in a mental hospital. After some digging, someone obtained the information about his joining the hostel only in the second term. According to his doctor's advice, instead of writing the exam, he had stayed at home until after Diwali. He was going to write his exam this year. You could spot the signs of his mental disturbance in his speech. He would suddenly spit as he spoke. He would move five or six paces forward and turn right back. Hunting for the place where he had spat before he'd spit there once again. And then, move on right ahead. Now, hostels provide plenty of leisure to observe these things.

When all this became known, Suresh and some other rogues perpetrated many tricks upon him. One of them was of course to bolt his door from outside when he was in his room.

Once they bolted him in the bog. Then in a great fit of anger he pushed so hard that he broke down the door. Then Professor Paranjape fined him ten rupees. No one, naturally, knew who had shot the bolt from outside. That someone did is certain.

Paranjape said to him, I am fining you because, having realised that you have to pay up, they will pity you and stop bothering you, the mischief-makers.

When such things occurred every day, each one worse than the last, even someone like me would go crazy. So what of Subhash, who was vulnerable to start with?

Gradually, Mehta, Suresh and others became friends with Subhash. That is to say, Subhash himself decided to be wise and began to behave politely with them. Even though Subhash had surrendered, the gang hadn't had enough. In little odd ways of course they made fun of Subhash every day. They would take him to a restaurant with them and eat heartily at his expense. One by one they would make off so Subhash was left to pay the bill. As soon as Subhash went into the bathroom, they would snatch all his clothes from above the partition and take them away. Then he'd shout and scream and beg them to return at least his pajamas. Once he made such a racket that Professor Shah came from his house in a foul temper. He ordered Subhash to come out. Subhash shut up at once. I was there myself at the time. I came out and told Shah everything. What else could Shah do but curse the rowdy students? Then I gave Subhash my towel for a wrap. Thus, half naked, Subhash went back to his room without a murmur of protest.

Subhash used to go to bed well before eleven. But until he'd actually begun to nod with sleep, Suresh and other looters would linger in his room, nattering. If he really got fussed, they'd say — We shall just sit here till four in the morning!

Subhash had really lost weight from anxiety. Whatever was he to do?

Once they all sat about in his room till eleven at night. Then all of a sudden they left. Subhash went to sleep right away.

But they had all foregathered. They all set their watches to read five o'clock in the morning. Those who were still awake in rooms nearby were also told about their plot and they too adjusted their watches to show five o'clock.

Then they kicked on Subhash's door bang-bang-bang, woke him up, and entered his room and turned on the light.

Subhash said, Hey, what is this? You don't even let me sleep in peace. This is too much.

Modak said, How late you do sleep. You sod! You went to bed at eleven. It's six or seven hours since then.

Gore said, Hey, our Mehta is off to Colombo. He's had a telegram from his father. Let's go and see him off on the Madras Express.

There can't be any Madras Express at this time. And how do you say six or seven hours have passed? It's only half past twelve. Now go away. You can tease, but surely there should be a limit. Now get going.

Suresh said, Have you gone batty? It is five, you pimp. Throw away your watch. It's just a box for your paan lime.[24] It is after five o'clock. Get up, UP!

Subhash examined everyone's watches. In one it was five o'clock. In another ten after five. In another, indeed, it was half past five.

To make sure that they were not merely pulling his leg he went to the rooms of two or three other chaps to look at their watches. It was, indeed, five o'clock.

There was one thing about Subhash, that he took care not to let on that he'd been crazy. At such times, then, he didn't even dare trust himself. He too felt, vaguely, vaguely, that perhaps it was five after all.

Then they dragged him to the tap. He said, Do I have to come?

Modak said, Whatever do you mean? You are Mehta's closest pal. Even if we didn't go it would hardly matter. You must go.

Subash was flattered and overcome. So he happily agreed at this point.

Then all of them went off to Mehta. He was in fact coolly reading until this time. But of course, he was ready with his tie, jacket, etc.

With his suitcase, Mehta started off. They all made for the taxi which was already waiting. Only Subhash and Mehta went in the taxi. The rest said, We'll follow on our bikes. But of course they came right back. And, having changed again, they sat about blethering.

After half an hour or so, Mehta returned alone in a taxi.

He said, Sod it, I had to do more work than you chaps.

Where is Subhash?

I've left him waiting at a rendezvous at the station. I gave him one anna and told him to buy a platform ticket for himself and the moment he left I grabbed a taxi.

Wah, wah, Mehta! Well done! — they all said and went to their rooms and back to sleep.

Later, Subhash came by himself to the hostel. They were all asleep. Only I was reading. He came straight to my room.

He said, What's the time?

Two o'clock.

I've walked back all the way from the railway station. I wish I had money in my pocket. But why do these chaps do all these things? Now what am I to do about them?

Having heard the entire story from him, I said, I have a knife, first you take out Modak and shove the knife into his gut. Murder them all. Even Suresh.

Thinking I must be an ass, Subhash went out of my room, fuming at all these chaps. Then until he nearly broke them down, he banged and banged on their doors and woke each one of them up in turn. He gave Modak a tight slap. Modak said to him, Subhash, have you gone crazy, or what? Who woke you up? Who took you to the railway station?

Then Subhash grabbed Mehta's collar.

Mehta said, You didn't happen to see all this in a dream, did you? We were all already in bed by 12 o'clock.

Then Subhash came into my room once again.

In a fit of anger, I said, Why do you keep coming to me again and again? Get out. They are your pals. What the deuce can I tell you?

Crestfallen, he said, Shall I clear out tomorrow?

Suddenly I felt pity for him. I went with him to where all of them were standing. I said, Modkya, Mehta, you are all donkeys. Whatever have you all determined to do with this chap?

Modak said, You go to your room. Sodding Pandu.

I got mad, and first hurling four curses at him I said, You pimp, I shall take out your stuffing tomorrow. If I don't have you thrown out of the hostel, my name is not Pandu.

Just then Kalya, Patil and others woke up and came out rubbing their eyes. When he learned of today's affair, Kalya nearly blew his top. He said to Modak, Modkya, you are too full of yourself, you son-of-a.... If you bother Subhash from tomorrow I'll break your leg, you clod.

Modak yelled, I know, I know, Kalya....

SHUT UP, Kalya shouted. Say one word more and I throw you downstairs.

Indeed, Kalya shouted in such a terrifying manner that they all stood speechless. Then they all went away without another word. Only Suresh stayed on, because he was my friend.

I said to Suresh, Isn't it monstrous to trouble someone like Subhash?

He said, That's true. But we are toughening him up. He cannot survive if he stays this way.

Be that as it may. This is inhuman.

May be. But this business is better than "shining" on the stage.

All in all, this sort of thing is mixed up in the very blood of such savage chaps. They only know how to torture someone. What can I do about it? But what's the use of my quarrelling with Suresh either? I must still maintain my friendship with him.

Thereafter for some days no one badgered Subhash. He really managed to study well. But Subhash eventually left the hostel, following a nasty event.

For Suresh and all indulged in one more secret mischief. As he was a bright chap, a girl from his class used to treat Subhash well. In fact Subhash scarcely knew a thing of matters like love and such. But Modak and some others placed in his room a phoney love letter in the name of that girl. In it was the message — Meet me tomorrow evening at seven.

Subhash thought it a genuine message. He dressed carefully and set off for the rendezvous. After him went all these chaps. Subhash was in fact anxious about whether they hadn't sneakily read this note in his room.

At the appointed place, they all waited with Subhash. The hour named came and went.

All of them started to tease Subhash — So, Subhash, who are you waiting for? Etc.

Subhash said, Get out of here.

Subhash thought, with all these chaps here why would she come? She might even have gone back. Perhaps with this thought in mind he suddenly picked up a big rock and hit Thakre on the head with it.

Thakre thrashed about and fell unconscious. The doctor arrived. All of them beat up Subhash thoroughly. Thakre was in the hospital for a week or so.

Professor Paranjape made a visit to the hostel. They all told him that Subhash had once been insane and was still a bit crazy. I was standing by. But Paranjape didn't ask me anything. And I did not volunteer anything either.

Paranjape asked Subhash to leave the hostel. Later came Subhash's relations from the city. I helped him pack his gear. Patil brought a taxi. All those who had made his life hell were watching from the balcony, furtively, like thieves.

Subhash left. While going he only said, Bye Sangvikar.

Later I met Paranjape. For an hour I narrated to him all that had transpired. Paranjape said, All that may be true. But the hostel is not a mental hospital, is it?

I said to Paranjape, in English, You don't have any sense.

In that case, is the hostel a place to harass someone till he turns crazy? You are an ass.

Actually, I said all this in my mind, really. All the same it was true enough to be voiced so emphatically.

Even as some chap is half drowning, struggling for his life as he tumbles under water and attempts to surface, while those who are standing on the shore again dunk him under, clapping and laughing, even so is the hostel a monstrous place, isn't it?

At that time I classified human beings into two categories — those who harass and those who are harassed. In these two categories must fit all the people in the entire universe. That was my very own discovery.

I wasn't going home during the Christmas holidays either. But out of the blue one day a lorry from our place came to our hostel. The driver came to my room, having hunted all over for it. He said, Your buffalo is going to calve within the week. Your mother has called you home right away to taste the fresh milkcake. We are starting tonight.

I hadn't been home even at Diwali. So my Mother had felt really sad. Moreover, in two or three years now I had not tasted homemade milkcake. Besides, I was in a spot about how to spend my holiday. I made quick preparations. And in that lorry I returned home.

I had looked so crushed that Mother felt terrible. I said, Mother, I've paid up two hundred rupees of that debt. And then there's only the mess food. Not even a cup of tea between times. So what will I be, if not withered like this?

Mother said, You are a ninny, My Little One. Spend all the money that's left with Maushi. I will let her know. When you go I shall give you a hundred that I have. You must drink three quarters of milk every day. Stop staying up all night. But you are awfully impractical. When you do spend, you require three thousand per year. Otherwise, you manage with just forty a month. Spend all that money right away. Then send a letter home. You dunce, all this here belongs to you. You should ask for the money as your right. But hereafter do write up all your expenses in a book. That will come in handy to fling at Father's face in the holidays, at least as a pretence — Do this much for me, please.

As I left home there was just this one thought in my mind — Some day I shall conduct myself in such a way that Mother will feel happy on account of me.

When I returned to Poona, I splurged.

Gave Maushi Mother's chit and took all the remaining money from her. Made some new clothes. I started to buy a lot of books. Gone was all the footsore trudging to the vegetable market for cheap haircuts. Plenty of milk in the room. Plenty of food and that. Grapes every day. But because Mother had told me to, I made it a pukka habit to write in a diary every expense I had incurred each day. I purchased this diary for a jolly princely sum of four rupees. On the first page I inscribed —

Mother as well as Motherland are superior even to Heaven.

But I did not abandon my simple friends. Nor did I develop fresh friendships with useless rich chaps. Koddam, Patil, Dhainje, Kalya all became even closer friends than before. I immediately narrated the history of my penniless state, and how hereafter I was going to have it cushy. These are my genuine friends. In July, at a word from me, Koddam had loaned me thirty rupees. Even when he had needed it himself. Every once in a while Patil would treat me to sugar cane juice when we went out. I fetched from the market all sorts of fruits and things, worth as much as fifteen rupees. And the four or five of us made short work of that. Joy, oh joy everywhere, my dear!

Five is hardly an age to die. The whole point would be, Why was a child born in the first place if it was to die at five?

I felt enormous sorrow when my five year old sister died. If Granny had died in my home at that time, and Mani after I'd got used to such thoughts, I might not have felt such sorrow so sharply. But in the history of our house in the past forty years the first person to die after Grandpa was Mani. During my entire existence of twenty years this was the only person to die in my house. My sorrow was infinite.

I was here in Poona at that time. It was so much worse. Even my friends understood that I was bereaved. But I didn't tell anyone that Mani'd died. So they started to tell me, Old Boy, the rings of sorrow turn and turn and suddenly begin to revolve round one with tremendous velocity. There isn't always a reason.

But there was a reason for this my sorrow. In fact sorrow with a reason isn't real at all. But this much is true — it really does eat you up inside.

After me, there were four sisters, one after another.

Even till I was quite big, if they didn't buy me a new shirt or something like that — I used to stamp and thump and say, I am the only son and still you don't pamper me!

Then Father would say, Don't you think you have obliged us. We shall have more sons.

From then until recently I have only had sisters. I have remained the only son.

Now, the way my sisters were treated at home — in the true-blue Hindu way. They were not to ask insistently for anything; the older sisters ought to do the younger ones' hair; wash their bottoms; do whatever chores Mother asked them to do. On and on and on.

Having become the progeny of parents, then sisters must do sisterly chores, brothers must educate brothers, older brothers should arrange to get their younger sisters married — this is monstrous. In our home too, so many such monstrosities. Then it naturally followed that Sumi should not visit our home after she was married. All the same, I hardly liked that Manutai passed away.

She was such a quiet person — in work, in her talk, her walk, in her singing, in her going to school.

Mother would say, She has no brains. If somewhere a lantern glass shattered as it was being cleaned, no matter who else might be scouring it, Mother would say, Manye, just you wait, you brat! Then Mani would say from somewhere inside the house altogether different, It's not me, Aaee.[25] I am sweeping. If someone tipped over the milk pan Mother would say, from wherever she was, That has to be Mani.

Since at each confinement yet another girl arrived, my Grandma got tired of looking after Mother and baby when Mani was born. Because, with Mother confined, Grandma had to manage all the chores in the house on top of looking after the two. She would scrub the infant Mani with a vengeance. Once, having forgotten to mix cold water with the hot bathwater, she laid the baby face down on her own legs to wash her. When she realised that the water was too hot, she thought, Who is going to put her in her

Cocoon

cradle again, change the water and lay her on my legs again? Forget it. Then Mani screamed and howled and Mother rushed out of the house. Having tested the water with her fingers, weeping, she said to Granny, You get up, I shall wash her. At that Grandma dashed Mani to the floor saying, A mother of daughters oughtn't to be so stuck up!

Yet even Mother was not overly fond of Mani. When she was still in the womb, Mother would feel — ija, bija, tija,[26] I shall be third time lucky. This third one will be a son. But Mani was born instead. So Father too looked at Mani askance.

That year there was a terrible epidemic of smallpox that killed some fifty children in our village, among them, Mani.

When I heard about our farm watchman's child I was really scared. Even when that boy grew very ill, his mother'd had to go to work. Anyway, why waste a day just sitting by his bedside, she thought, and left him in the care of her tiny daughter. In the afternoon the boy felt he was burning so horribly that he struggled out of the hut and jumped into a well.

But Mani died in her bed.

Precisely when Granny was all ready to go on her customary winter pilgrimage in the month of Kartik,[27] Mani started to burn with a raging fever.

Mother said to Grandma, Must you go this year too? This little one is still feeding at my breast. In the village all sorts of untoward things are happening. Won't you go next time, for the monsoon pilgrimage? Now take care of Mani.

Grandma unpacked in a fit of rage and said to our neighbour — You go alone. I am willing to give up my religious rites for her daughter's sake. The girl hardly has a touch of fever and this one feels I must dance attendance on the child. Why the deuce would the small pox Devi[28] bother to visit them?

Mother said, weeping, Go if you wish to. But don't, for goodness sake, invoke the name of the dread pox. I shall look after my infant and also manage the rest. But rein in that tongue!

Grandma didn't go. Because she happened to invoke the name, the fever in fact turned out to be the dreadful pox, according to the superstition. Mani turned a flaming red.

Children from our neighbour's house stopped coming to ours. Only the two women remained in the house. And even they, sulking, would hardly speak to each other. If Mother asked, for instance, Has this water been warmed? Grandma wouldn't utter a word in reply. And if Grandma said, Make the bhakris for the farmhands' dinner, Mother wouldn't make them.

Just at that time my Father took it into his head to demolish our filthy old house and build a new one on the site. That year all of a sudden cotton had found a good market and Father'd made a packet of money. He said, I shall build such an edifice, three floors, and on top of that a fourth, the terrace. There won't be another like it in this village.

Mother said, I won't let you demolish the house until little Mani feels better.

This got Father mad.

Now I have engaged labour and the mason and you come up with this stupid idea. Mani should recover in a fortnight or so. But within that time the cost of labour and the mason's wages will shoot up. Another couple of chaps in the village are also planning to build new houses. We'd better engage the labour right away.

Mother said, Get out of my sight.

This made Father really angry with Mother. Only in the evenings would he ask after Mani. Grandma and he would argue together angrily. Occasionally he'd fetch the doctor. That's all.

I would get letters from Father to the effect that our cotton had fetched a good price this year. That the election was over. That the flat roof of our old house had been dug up. Soon the floor below would also be pulled down and then work on the new house would really start. That the honour and prosperity of the whole family depended on me. So and so's son had gone to Germany. That I should just go ahead and study. So on and so forth.

I was really working here. And suddenly came his letter —
Mani died of smallpox. Don't you take it to heart too much.

I was so shaken I thought, How can anyone just die like that?

Last holidays, that Mani, who had, with a broad smile, brought
me my forgotten comb as I was leaving home. Now when I go
home on holiday I won't ever see her. What on Earth does this
mean? And then I became unimaginably numb.

Soon after that a long letter came from Mother. Really detailed.

In the end she'd written, As I write this letter, I remember how
it all happened, and the events of the past fifteen days and I burst
into tears repeatedly. The end of my sari is drenched with tears.
But don't grieve too much. You still have three sisters.

The blisters on Mani's body had become large as lemons.
Grandma looked after her, fussing and fuming all the while.
For the sake of little Nali, Mother wouldn't go too close to
Mani. She'd only look at her from afar. But seeing Mother,
Mani would raise both her arms and say, Hold me, hold me.
But Mother wouldn't.

When the blisters ripened and swelled, however, Mother
began to sit beside Mani's bed. They weren't allowing anyone
else in the family to go near Mani. So that she would not worry
her blisters, small, long bags of cloth had been tied tightly at her
wrists, covering her hands. Even through these she'd scratch them
and break them open. So both her shoulders were stained with
blood. Then, angrily, Grandma tied her arms down tight to the
sides of her bed.

Then she said, Untie my hands.

So then Mother once asked her, What do you want? Water?

But Mani did not reply.

Mother said, Mane, speak, speak. Tomorrow you won't be
able to speak. Talk to me today.

But she didn't talk to Mother at all.

Grandma said, Manutai, what shall I tell your big brother to
bring for you from Poona?

So she said, Red sari.

Red sari!

When she uttered this, just at that moment, what might I have been doing here, exactly? Was I in my room or on the hill? Or was I laughing with my friends, or looking at the hill through the window? She must have been thinking of me. Red sari.

This is what she'd ask me for during every holiday. And each time I'd say, Next time, sure.

Then because I was going to bring her a sari, she'd do so many chores for me. If she refused to scratch my back I'd say, You want that red sari, don't you?

Slowly she'd begun to lose her voice. There must have been blisters all over, blisters in her throat as well. Blisters had erupted in her eyes so her pupils had already become white.

Mother said, Manutai, what *do* you want?

Mani said, Free my hands. Fire, I am burning all over, O Mother!

Then she couldn't even open her mouth. A drink poured into it wouldn't go down. Already her eyes were lost.

From the far side of her bed Mother would call, Manu....

And, her hands tied like Jesus Christ's, stretching her white eyes wide, wide, she'd look precisely in that direction.

Then from beside her head Mother would call to her, Manutai.....

Mani would raise her head, straining to look at her.

Grandma said, She can still hear.

And two days later, without so much as washing or laving her body, they buried her outside the village. And with her they buried everything that had touched her bed. The schoolbag, her bedsheet — everything.

Then for two or three days I blazed with rage. I couldn't make out against what, though.

I said, I'll murder Father. I'll kill Grandma. Then I'll set fire to that whole house. I'll burn all their cadavers in that house. Spare only Mother. O to die thus.

They buried Mani, buried her, buried her, buried her. I was ablaze with my emotions. That's not a fib.

I bought a flame-yellow sari such as little girls wear. Cut it up into shreds. Then I lit them up one by one. In that blaze I burned my hands. Then — I emptied my inkpot on the floor and cooled my burning hands in the ink. Staining my hands again and again I marked paw prints all over — on the pillow, mattress, table, books and notebooks, the door, window, on the walls.

Then I gave all the milk in the pan to a pariah puppy.

I said, I'll take revenge for this. I'll spend a hundred rupees every month. I'll demand two hundred a month.

I went alone to the Vetal Hill. Sometimes I ran around like a madman. Sometimes I just sat. At night I walked along many many streets in Poona.

When a policeman halted me, I told him, My sister died.

I really took this to heart. Maushi came over to my room with her son. And what's more, she said, consoling me, Who is going to live for ever? Then she said, Come and stay with us for a week.

I said to myself, Why just for a week? Why not ten years? In India in every house young children have always died. So it is true that no one should be too preoccupied with death. But it isn't possible to give up, just give up such thoughts either. Those who're still living are at least bound to think about death.

All the same, Maushi forced me to go home with her. In just a day or two I got bored and came back to my room. Because, at her place, they all handled me with special care since I had suffered pain. In my room I could do as I pleased.

All this happened naturally. Without contrivance. I began to find interest in nothing, meaning in nothing. As I walked with Mehta among the city crowds in the evening I dwelt on thoughts of death constantly. If someone in the street refused to give way to me it would make me angry. I'd stand outside my room in the balcony. As the movement of the hostel chaps reduced it would all become quiet. The swathe of moonlight that had fallen on the rooms opposite would gradually slip down farther and then fall over the ground as well. Then it would creep right up to my feet. And continue to crawl upwards until I was able to see the moon. Then the moon would go down behind the roofs of the rooms opposite me and then there'd be darkness everywhere. So many such nights. Someone would come and say, Come on, don't stand there all night like a ghost.

Now after this, at home, everyone started to like my remaining three sisters.

Of them Sumi got married soon after and only two were left. At the time of this wedding everyone in the family was rejoicing jubilantly. Even Mother. When I heard Mother laughing away loudly I'd feel like asking her — And what of Mani's death?

But after Mani died I didn't write home at all. When letters from Mother started to arrive frequently I wrote to her, Stop sending letters.

So in response to that Mother wrote a long, long letter.

After that there was a college trip to the caves at Ajanta. I thought I might feel a little better for seeing Ajanta.

Ajanta.

That enormous solid stone semi-circle. In front a water fall that eternally descended with a roar. All day its music echoing in my mind. And me, peering into cave after cave there.

In one cave a vast and tall statue of Buddha. Crosslegged. Buddha looking straight out of the door of the cave. Whatever is he looking at? He is very, very disturbed, bruised, hurt. His eyelids seem half closed. I stare unthinkingly at those half open Mongol eyelids. With the five fingers of his right hand upraised, he is counting the fingers of his left hand. There're ten fingers to the hands. He measured the vast enormity of all creation and destruction with these fingers. I look up once again. Such a great statue cannot be taken in from one angle of vision. One must shift one's viewpoint again and again. On the stony visage, gentle ripples of delicate expressions. A most poignant helplessness sweeps over me with giant wings. And having lifted me up in its claws, it takes me up, up and away. Way, way up. And then suddenly drops me from above. I must crash down somewhere. Before me this image. On its face a suffering beyond measure — Indeed, immeasurable. This suffering at once expansive and infinitesimal cannot be grasped between one's fingertips. It is a sorrow that whirls round and round. Even to drink of sorrow one needs to cup palms of sorrow. It is impossible to measure this desert-vast sorrow by my cowrie-sized sorrow. Mine are circumscribed little woes. How can I perceive this face through the narrow chink of my pain? I crash down into the abysmal sorrow on that stone face. Now the circumference of my pain too becomes immeasurable.

I said, Have pity on me. *And pity from you more dear than from any other.* But this Buddha will not show compassion for me. His compassion is not for me.

This eternal blaze like an atom bomb is frozen in its gut.

To the next cave. A similar, enormous, sublime image deep in its centre. A similar one again in the third cave. The same in each cave. One goes to look, stealing up, cautiously, like a small child. An image of Buddha, who is smiling, blissful. The hair on his head done in ringlets of stone curls, round whorls. Vast forehead. And those finely worked lips that once whispered the greatest mantra in the world. This image has one hand raised to bless whoever looks at it. It is, really, a blessing for the scavenger who is dog-tired after plying the swishing broom all his life. For those who live out their lives and die in the dust. For the mother who wanders from door to door for a handful of mustard seed.

Up, up the inside stone stairs in the cave. Above, there are large cool viharas,[29] for prayer and meditation. Everywhere a tranquil, deep darkness. Once upon a time I was searching for a box of matches. But I couldn't find the box in the dark. Then I shouted for a box. Flinging away anything else that I found, I searched for the box all over. Mani came in through the door softly. I only heard her footfalls. I asked, Who is it? She said, Me. Then she started looking for the box of matches for me. In the dark she stumbled over a trunk and fell right down. When I ran over and groped about to pick her up and put her on her feet again, she'd already got up on her own and gone away. One cannot become darkness in the dark. All things desert one, except oneself.

In the cave before me, there's only darkness. Even if I go a thousand miles, walking on and on, the cave won't end. It is so deep, full of darkness. I am wandering here and there inside it, but in fact there is nothing here.

In the next cave too, just about the same sort of darkness. But to the left, from a casement enters a little light. And right there, on a head-high, wide, stone bed sleeps the Buddha. On stone. With his stony right arm for a pillow, he sleeps on peacefully. This is eternal slumber. Above, on the wall, below all round the bed, are many gods watching this Mahanirvana.[30] Perhaps he was tired of this Earth. That's why he is departing with a smiling visage. How many storms his veins have encountered during his lifetime. Does he not feel the slightest burden with this death? Look how he sleeps peacefully, on his right side, with the right arm under his head, the other laid straight along his thigh. Yet this too is death. In the end he too was a mortal human being. Yet he alone understood the weak vertebra in life's slithering, creeping sorrow. Otherwise, this laying down of the body is like everyone else.

Everywhere else in Ajanta his image is in an upright posture — seeing it horizontal like this, a barely noticeable edge of suffering cuts me to the quick. Large drops of blood well over and begin to drip along the cut. My benumbed tongue begins to lick at the cut. And this Buddha, on the other hand — he has attained a state beyond laughter and tears, with that enormous body. The saplings of his ahimsa[31] never really flourished thereafter. It was all a waste. When one comes out of the cave again, one sees silvery sunlight. To the Buddha, sleeping inside in the dark, this is of little consequence.

And this clash between two bulls, the tails of both raised and coiled by their ferocity. Shoulders like water pots, dew-laps hanging so large. Neither is likely to retreat. And the Buddha meeting Yashodhara.[32] She is seen standing here, within her eyes the many long years that have passed since that midnight when Prince Gautama[33] left the royal palace. Today he is holding a begging bowl, as a mendicant bhikku[34] before the door. Fooling herself — that Gautama must still be Gautama, her dear husband, that he could not have become the Buddha — she is standing by her door. And he, standing so high, towering like a tree. Meaning, Buddha has now become a Mahatma — a Great Soul. And such a tiny Yashodhara, at the door, with her darling Rahul.[35] Fascinated, awed. A slight darkening shadows her eyes. Because around the visage of the enormously tall Buddha is a luminous halo, and around that the deep dazzling blue firmament. Such a detached heart for a father. Such a composed heart for a husband. Now he's nobody's kin. And the pearl string on Yashodhara's forehead has slipped down somewhat. So she looks utterly rustic. Bent a little at the waist, she stands there, watching. There is no limit to our losing ourselves in this mordant universe of feeling. Here, though, it is only just sport for the day.

And as we were returning from Ajanta a chap said, That was a wonderful outing. Another, winking an eye in my direction, said — All the same, there were some pretty boring chaps with us.

And I was saying to myself, Whatever bundle of dharma[36] she had, she bundled it all together and departed. And of course shed all her suffering, before going away, for us to remember. That is the only thing she has not destroyed, a durable bond between herself and us. All else, all her inscription on Earth she has quite erased. She had just started to attend regular school. They used to shove her out of the house even before it was seven o'clock. She'd barely mastered the alphabet. And she was able to read only those lessons that had been drilled. So she must have seen only so much of the writing on the wall. In her pocket she had the marble seeds to play with. The frock that had clung to her skin. She renounced all this. Now she must be stepping along the long dark night. The night that disowns everything. When I enter that path, she will have advanced so far, so far ahead. That means I can never catch up with her. Saying, What is past is past, now perhaps something fresh. With her, too, passed away her little womb. She has curtailed a terribly long column in the national census. Now she is not bothered by any of this. She experiences no constraints now. No bounds. There is a shore which can only be reached once. What dharma could she have carried with her? She had brought with her only her karma[37] when she came. On her way out, there's only that dark journey. Her journey is verily her own. She is now free of all else. Free of this, free of that. Colour-free. Flesh-free. Mind-free. Perception-free. She is even freedom-free. Only her almost erased, misty mind-image with me.

The remaining days passed somehow, anyhow. When the holiday started, I went home.

Then I arrived home.

Everyone said, You've become thin.

I felt better.

Now there wasn't any image or trace of our old house — a crisp new structure. Everything had changed. Now I shall have to ask all the time — Where's this, where's that? On top of that, this is the longest holiday of the year. Three whole months.

The moment she saw me — Mother's expected, howling lament.

When anyone has died — this inevitable lament in a certain key, almost in verse. This is, really, a specially annoying feature of our summer. Each year someone in the environs of our house is bound to have died. There's neither work nor particular chore to be done in the country in the summer. That is why, as they have been unable to do during the whole year, relatives visit the houses of those who have died. All the women round about, too, then gather together and wail musically. Sometimes, on one side one hears the crackle-bang of a wedding while on the other side loud, loud howling. Summer is great.

Mother lamented for a considerable time. Neighbours collected. There was exchange of wisdom, from several viewpoints. I took part, wiping away a tear or two.

When the memory of the dead has begun to fade it is terrible to revive it. The dying of a person means his absolute disappearance. Meaning, we too must also obliterate him or her. Yet the stain cannot be obliterated. This much is true.

Later, throughout the holiday, Mother was relating memories of Mani. This fifteen day affair will last her her whole life. A life-long irritation for me. One can do whatever one wants for oneself. But to keep narrating things to another is to create irritants for them. But narrators love to narrate. And listeners must suffer them.

I kept feeling that our new house was a horrifying phenomenon. Father's built this tomb on her dead body, after Mani died. In all this, all the time I felt that the old house had been better after all. There was a gloom in the old house. Everywhere densely packed stuff. And the presence of neighbours. Now this is like a fortress. As children we could walk to our neigbour's houses in a jiffy, our filled dinner plates in hand. Now no more mud walls. Underfoot, a flagged floor. My sisters' hobby of decorating the floor with rangoli[38] — gone.

Grandma said, That house broke my back. Forever plastering floors, mopping. Now your mother can live in comfort.

Mother said, I too have spent twenty-five years in it. Now nothing more for me. This is for the bride to come.

New bride? Heck! My bride.

Father said, The upstairs room is for you.

First I went and inspected the room upstairs. This house was a horror. A really high room. Bright, bright light here, windows, a breeze. What a room! The earlier house was good. You could see everyone. Some people eating, some asleep, some in the washroom, some by the mudstove. No one comes up to this second floor, though. So then I was free to smoke.

Then I waited, expecting Father to say something about the cigarettes. Of course he will bring it up. Then I shall burst, say anything I feel like. I'll gather together all my year-long fury and answer back. I'd say, I'm just waiting for the moment when you croak finally.

But even after he learned about the cigarettes, he said nothing at all. Mean to say, once he actually put in my drawer a pack that was on my table. I noticed that. Only once did he say — Stand a little away from me when you speak. I cannot stand the stink of cigarettes.

Three months — morning, afternoon, evening, dark. Three whole months like this. But they passed.

Every evening, sitting on the roof terrace, I'd just indulge in this — not far, the village panchayat was building a high, raised tank for the new water system. A labourer from below would hand up a hodful of lime. The first hand on the ladder would pass it up to the second one above. He to the next one above him. In this way would pass, from hand to hand, the same hod over the heads of some twenty-five labourers.

Even as the first load was about to reach the top, from below would start another three or four, right up the middle. Towards the end of the construction of the tank there would be a whole long vertical line of labourers, ten hodsful going up all at the same time, and descending again.

Once the tank was done, I'd sit watching the fun of the pigeons on the terrace. But that didn't promise to be as interesting as the construction of the tank.

During these three months, from the start, I had grown disgusted with my village. There were several college-going chaps in the village. But they returned home much later. Until then, once in a way some half-educated chaps like Lalaji would drop in at my place, and fools like Sotmya, always with a wad of paan in his gob. Even their talk was asinine. It was but natural that Lakhu Shet had failed to make a go of being a lawyer. I began to avoid him particularly. But after all of the others had finished their exams, by May, there was a bit of fun.

It was at this time that I determined — Now this will be my senior year. And then B.A. After that, I'd find a job no matter where, and leave all this behind. Enough of this coming home in the holidays and again going back afterwards. Now Father had begun to place before me, deliberately, matters like how much money he had put by, what he hoped to do after buying which piece of land.... I said — Now I don't have any wish to take your money, you. So that I might look after you in your dotage you are fussing so much. If there'd been another son, he might have participated in all this non-sense. I won't even step into this place any more.

For one thing, all these people are selfish. I can't get along with them. Mean to say — take any farmer who spends his lifetime contemplating how to extract whatever little cash he can from some source, and how to squeeze seventeen annas into every rupee of sixteen annas. If one earns a fixed salary, one knows one would earn only so much during the next fifteen years, for instance. But with these folk — this year, six thousand, next year ten thousand, and the year after, by dint of some more striving, it will become fifteen thousand. So who'd want to spend his whole life indulging in such non-sense?

Besides, everyone has to marry. And of course have at least one son. Even if little infants die these people don't care a hang. And the aged folk, somehow hanging on just this side of death. If young girls die, that's even better, a dowry saved. If boys die, their brothers are overjoyed — so much less to share of their land and property. In a city there are no such complications about property. Old pensioners have bungalows there. And hospitals for children. No nagging problems about land. A rented house. As it is, birth onwards there is nothing that one can call one's own in the whole world. Even one's house belongs to a landlord. Only the vacant space in the house belongs to oneself. All else is ephemeral. No complications like buffaloes to milk. Buy bottled milk and drink it up.

In a city there's no one to ask you, What is this you are doing? One is no one's relation. And those things which slowly become routine in the city, seem novel to these village folk here. Now, only the unlettered people of the city attach any importance to good clothes or passing an M.A. But here everyone gives these things great importance, everyone. Here, the entire village comes to know about it if the minister is coming. And if someone's son passes with a first rank, everyone is tickled. And they never tire of quoting his example to their own children. If someone is going abroad they hold meetings and felicitate him. And everyone attends such meetings. He is regarded as being godlike. One starts boasting that his son earns four hundred a month. But all his life the thought festers within that so-and-so's son gets a thousand, so in comparison this amounts to nothing really. These are selfish people who hover about money like a cartwheel round its hub. And — such and such a chap's bananas sold for two hundred thousand, yet while he himself made only some thirty or forty thousand profit. On the other hand that chap managed fifty thousand out of his cotton, without stirring from this place — such are their topics of conversation about achievement.

Besides, every morning they must have their tea. That's a legacy of the city, actually. Goodness alone knows what these chaps used to drink before tea entered our country. Moreover, whoever sends his children to the city to study gains status among these folk. And the more gold you give away at your daughter's wedding, the greater your reputation. And when they treat you with respect, they are false, and when they insult you, they do so by battering you with their shoes. This is a settlement of useless people. I cannot survive here. For if you start moving in the company of the "respectable" people of this village, your value too will rise. But if you go with simple folk, even the simple folk will consider you to be of no account. Besides, in the city one's likely to find a dozen friends who share one's likes and dislikes. You'll find none here. Here, if you must have company, you will have to fall into line.

Once Father and I had a crackling quarrel. He said, You'd better dress properly. Move about with chaps your own age; go about our village with your hair stylishly combed. Whoever will say, looking at you, that you're my son?

Then for an hour without pause I talked back, addressing him as thou. So much, that he looked quite crestfallen. Until Mother dragged me away from there. For a month after that he didn't speak to me. Once, in front of some guests, he spoke, for the sake of propriety — Come, let's eat. I said, Either you sit with these people, or I will.

Then in June at the time of my departure, Mother gave me a talking to — Don't you realise how hurt he is by your behaviour? Because of you, throughout these holidays he couldn't stand this house.

When I left Father gave me lots of money. A couple of hundred would've been enough, but in his umbrageous affection he parted with more. He said — Look after yourself. Fine, now I am the only son, see? If I'd had other brothers, the same father would have treated me like an enemy. Fine, then.

Then I set off for Poona.

All things considered, Suresh was really my friend. He alone counted as a more or less good friend. It's good to have such persons on one's side.

There would be no exam or anything for the Junior class this year. Only one at the end of the two years, after Senior. That was quite far off, we thought. This year from the beginning we did a good deal of tramping about. Our favourite hobbies meant going to Fort Sinhagad in the rainy season; and also going to the Vetal Hill. Even during the Senior year this went on.

Actually, we had of course been several times to Fort Sinhagad — with outings of other boys and girls. You can hardly call that visiting Sinhagad, can you? This year we went to Sinhagad so many more times. Still, each time there would be some new mix up.

The first time, we set off on bicycles. With packages of bread and chivda and that. I even carried a knife, thinking I might just as well carry it. But, not far from Parvati hill, Suresh's bike had a puncture. And so we came right back.

The chaps at the hostel said, So you've seen Sinhagad, eh? Suresh said, We could've started again after fixing the puncture, of course. But hereafter, we won't take our bikes.

Next time we left on foot. But in the late afternoon we were still on our way. Then, having bathed in the dam water at Khadakwasla, we returned, again on foot.

Once again the chaps at the hostel — So, have you done Sinhagad?

Next Saturday, of course our bikes were ready again. Having nattered till three in the morning, we began to feel sleepy. So then — if we slept at all, it was only natural that we should wake up only in the afternoon on Sunday. So, without going to bed at all, we set off at four in the morning.

Even before the sun came up, we were at the foot of the fort. Having pedalled hard, we were dreadfully tired. Sleep nearly overcame us. So, then, who'd want to climb up along the steps, one step at a time? We tried a direct slope up the mountain and arrived straight at the top.

Suresh said, it is still early. We're not going to look over the fort all day, are we? Heck, I am most terribly sleepy.

I too was feeling groggy. But I said, Let's walk around first. Then let us return home early.

He said, It's fine for you. You will stay awake for the next fortnight without a break. It's the end of my capacity to stay awake. I shall sleep here. Saying this, that bod flung himself down in the grass. I was cheesed off. By myself then, for a long time, I sat on a tower somewhere, looking at the lovely prospect. The tinkle of springs is great. Indeed, nature as such is greater than man.

Then I myself fell asleep.

In between, someone woke me up. When I blinked to see who it was, the bod who had woken me up said, It's all right, really. Go back to sleep.

I got mad and said, Meaning what?

There were some fifty or sixty other people there, picnickers, boys and girls. The bod who woke me must be their teacher.

One chap said, We thought you were a corpse. Go back to sleep now.

Two or three girls tittered.

Hot with anger, I flung myself down again. When I got up later I saw it was already evening. It was pouring with rain. It'd be a relief to know that it was still today's evening.

Aflutter with fear, I ran, ran all the way to where Suresh had been sleeping. But where exactly he had flopped down I forgot. I hollered for him many times. Perhaps he was still lying among the tall grasses, so I began to step carefully.

Darkness had begun to fall. I thought, not having found me, tired of looking for me, he might even have gone down.

I started to descend along the slope. Everything had become slippery, really. So I slipped and fell down a thousand times. But I was in the grip of such a state of anxiety that I had to put one foot down after another.

Along the way, I climbed up a hill and looked to see if Suresh could be spied either behind or in front of me. There was an iron post there. I went up it like a monkey. From there I could see all the world around and about, swirling and turning. In the near-darkness all vegetation began to appear terribly green. White runnels of water along the way were making a constant noise. What an ass Suresh is for sure. He must have gone away by himself. He's really capable of being such a goon.

Then in the sheer dark I placed my feet wherever they might fall and came down to the base of the fort. What do I see there — both our bicycles. Meaning, Suresh must still be up there. The silly ass must still be asleep.

I ordered something to eat at an eating place. Now the night really advanced. I ate my food, wondering all the while whether a snake or something might not have bitten him in the grass.

Even when I had done eating, that worthy hadn't returned. And now I only had the matches, the cigarettes were with Suresh. I'd had enough. So I again slept right there.

After quite a long while Suresh woke me up. And *he* was smoking as he came down.

I said, Gimme a fag first.

He said, This is the last one. All gone. I got one lit up at the fort. The matches were with you. So, lighting one from another, I finished 'em all. Now I shall eat here. Sleep till then.

But Suresh won't even let me sleep, would he? He himself had just come back refreshed, having slept all day long. He started nattering —

Later, after having completed their acquisition of knowledge, these people used to enter Service.

Now, you might say, What is this novel thing called Service, then? So then Service signified, going somewhere at ten or eleven in the morning, each and every day of one's existence, and sitting at the same work always, and then returning home at five or six in the evening. However, each person slept at his own home.

On Saturday-Sunday, these people would venture out into the midst of Nature.

Now, what is Nature? Nature would commence a mile or two outside the city. Most persons granted the appellation of Poet would wander about amidst Nature. Now you will ask, what is this Poet?

At last his guffing was over. Then we returned to Poona, pushing our bikes as madly as we could. Along the way, Suresh went on nattering. We reached the hostel at one after midnight. Thereafter, Suresh camped in my room, of course, and started off again —

These people read regularly. Even Poems.

Now you will ask, what does Poem mean? So, then, only Poets would make Poems. Not to write like all other people, in long lines, but to dispose alphabets along shortened lines — that is a Poem. But this anarchism was indulged in by a very few persons. For who had the time to indulge in this? Therefore, not even one in a hundred engaged in the enterprise of Poetry....

Finally, I slept. Goodness alone knew when he went away.

We went once again to Sinhagad properly. Walked about a lot here and there.

Looking at the samadhi[39] of Tanaji, the tomb of the Maratha warrior who sacrificed his life in conquering this fort, Suresh laughed explosively.

He said, Let the beauty of nature and all that go to hell. *This* is the real joke.

At the same place we ate the bread and such that we had brought along. We sat on till it was evening, on a tower, conducted a profound discussion. Finally — How to climb, like fools, down all those steps — we discussed that. Then we concluded, We don't need the problem of the steps at all. We'll descend round that bend we see before us. We shall slip and slither down if required. But that way we shall descend directly, and be sure to have some fun.

Slipping and sliding, descending by zigzag paths, we came down quite a way. Just then there was a hammering shower of rain. And we got thoroughly drenched. That increased the slipperiness of the slopes even more. For a long time afterwards, we were descending thus, tumbling over and over again.

On the way in a puddle we saw large crabs. Suresh caught one or two. But he let them go afterwards.

We'd tumble into very deep pits. But it was all grass so we were never hurt anywhere.

Suddenly, once, we saw a baby snake, twining round and round itself, to no purpose. Quite fast, really. Suresh put a quick foot on it and crunched it flat.

Surshya, its ma or someone will come after you. You haven't yet seen a really large snake.

I do want to see one at least once, anyhow. Let us see what it looks like.

But a snake does not bite when you can see it clearly. We only come to know of it once it has bitten.

How dare a snake bite me! What harm have we done him?

Then we sat on at that place for quite some time. We'd already covered much of the way. Otherwise, coming down by the steps, we would still be higher up somewhere. We were not really getting tired of the place, still we got up and left.

Thereafter we began to encounter large, really deep pits. If there was grass at the bottom, we'd jump in directly. But if that wasn't convenient, we'd descend by the support of tree roots and branches and creepers. There was so much moss on the branches and roots that before one slipped from our hands we had to make sure of holding the next. Our feet too would slip from under us. Finally, once, we had no option left and losing our balance we fell, tumbled over and over into a pit. That is how it went.

But this was better all the same than running down hundreds of steps off balance, like a doddering old man.

The rain too took interest in us once again. And now, we started to feel quite cold. Yet inside our clothes we were soaked through in perspiration.

Then we came to a ledge which sloped downwards and below it was the most enormous deep gorge.

Standing on the edge of the gorge Suresh said, What sort of a pit is it? Better call it a small valley. Let's leap into it.

But I could not summon enough courage to leap. Moreover, by then it was almost evening. Only the twitter of some birds here and there. Suresh said, Let's get it over with. If the rain worsens, it'll get tight for us. We have descended half-way anyhow. And I cannot see any other shelves or cliffs like this anywhere ahead, at any rate. If we slither down straight we shall reach the base, surely. This is probably the last ravine to cross.

No convenient tree branches, you see?

You just watch how I come down.

Surshya, enough of this now. Let's go back up and come down sensibly by the steps. Besides, the bottom of this valley is quite narrow. And I can see another deep valley over there in front. See those vultures, going straight down from above. This runnel also falls steeply below its sloping course. If you jump even a bit too hard, you are bound to tumble down right over the edge of that terrible cliff.

It doesn't matter if I die. I have many brothers. I *shall* go down.

Then first he let both his legs down, holding on only by his hands, and said — There's not even a rock to support my feet. Only a hump of mushy moss.

Suresh, Surshya, let's go back up straight.

Pandya, How do you propose to go back up now? How do you think you will climb up those ten-fifteen pits above us? Come on, we can get down with the support of roots, but to climb up that way will be too tough. Better instead to let whatever is to happen happen. We'll go down this way.

I had begun to feel afraid, somehow, that Surshya might wish to commit suicide, perhaps. For quite a while now he has been loping ahead regardless, like a new-born calf. He slips. Bangs into things.

Heedlessly throws himself over cliffs, collapses at the bottom, and looking up at me, he laughs like a monster. But there's no remedy now. Now even going back up again is really tough. Vast upslopes and grass and snakes and pools and crabs.

Stand here Pandu, hold tightly on to that branch above. I got hold of the branch above me securely and stood up. He grabbed my ankle in one hand and holding a rock by the other hand he went down sliding — srrrrrr. I thought, if Surshya drags too hard at my ankle I am sure to fall over this rock on my head. But if that begins to happen, then I shall keep hold of this moss-wet branch, entrench my other foot and just won't let myself come down. I yelled, Suresh, my foot is going. Even this branch is slipping out of my hand.

But I could see below me only his head and his shirt, wet, torn and soiled, on his shoulders. Now with all the weight of his body on my ankle, he let go his other hand. I wasn't able to take all this terrifying weight. I yelled — Have you found a foothold somewhere or not?

Suresh said nothing at all. But he did let go of my ankle. And just by leaning against the slope he slipped and slid all the way down. Once in between he also took a leap. And, way below, he landed on his back. Then he tumbled and rolled down further, down, down. Like a bundle of rags he disappeared into a pool down there. I thought, Now he is surely done for. But he was out of the water in the pool in no time at all and lying down on the ground belly up. Looking up at me he exclaimed, A... ha!

Where shall I descend from, here or there? — in this dithering I let a lot of time go by. Having got up, standing on the edge of that cliff below, Suresh was searching for a way down from there. Then he came back quickly a little towards me and said, Hey, there's a lovely way from here. Come on down, quick.

It took me ten times longer to come down. I did not leap like him. I jumped by holding myself off a branch. I got hold of it in two places quite securely and started to hang free with a swing.

Now there was nothing under my feet. I knew not where I ought to lean next. Just then that branch also broke. So then I let go and fell on a long, long stretch of the slope. Just as I had already slipped down quite a way, like on a slide, and was about to leap forward so I could come down with a nice whack, Suresh advanced towards me. So I smacked into his body. Both of us crashed down.

He said, Your bones — gosh, they hurt me so much.

And my pants tore, of course. Also, having banged my elbow hard, I did not know for quite some time whether I had an elbow any more. I thought, Now my arm is paralysed for ever. But then it soon began to ache, it was all right, really. It began to ache really monstrously.

Then I drank water from a spring. And lay down at full stretch. Suresh too was stretched out. We were both panting. Still, we lay there quietly. Now frogs began to croak. The darkness really began to thicken. The cicadas began churring.

I said, Let's go.

Where?

Down.

There's nothing below. This is a long, mile-high spur. How do you know?

I've already explored it.

Why then didn't you tell me before?

Because if I had told you that you'd never have come down here. Then I would have been here all alone. I was afraid. Now the two of us can manage together somehow.

You are lousy — saying this, I ran all the way to the cliff. Above me Suresh was yelling, Don't run. If you slip you will be shattered to bits.

Gingerly, I advanced to the edge of the cliff. We had come down at a most terrifying place. The slope, shelving inwards, became invisible beneath my feet. Far below, again, there was another giant slide, all the way to those fields away down there. If we jump down, with the littlest of effort our bodies will reach there with a bang, dashing down to the base. But the cliff was leaning over most frighteningly.

And Suresh was still lying over there, calmly, his arm over his head.

I said, Suppose the mother of the baby snake you killed turns up now — what will you do?

Then he got up, in genuine fright. He said, We must do something right away, while we can still see a little about us. It will be really tough spending the night at this place.

The deep gorge was in fact very strange. On one side poked out a high cliff. On two sides, hills rose steeply. And a waterfall on the fourth side, rushing down with a deep, hollow sound. From the cliff could be seen only the tops of some trees. And now even they had begun to resemble ghosts and phantoms.

Then, sweating profusely, the two of us rolled a boulder down to the cliff we'd just descended. It was a huge rock. We placed it carefully just at the bottom of the vertical slope. Way up there was a hollow. Once we reached that it would be fine.

Then we could go back up the way we'd come.

At such times, the most terrifying tricks were sure to occur to Suresh. If there was anyone with a head in the whole world, it was Suresh. He said, You sit on my shoulders, with your legs round my neck. Then I'll climb up on this boulder. You do the rest carefully.

So then — me on Suresh's shoulders. Now, if I were to lose balance, or if his foot slipped off that boulder, it'd be me that would come down hard to perish. So I began to make every move most cautiously.

First Suresh squatted on the rock. With me atop him, he gradually rose upright. Then with terrific grit he grunted up at me. So then I looked up. Right above my head projected outwards the tip of an enormous rock. Grabbing hold of it with both hands, and placing first one foot on his shoulder, then settling the other, I straightened up slowly.

Then with one hand I clawed at the protruding long tip of that rock. I made sure of another handhold on another rock. Dangling from the rock above, then, I managed to put a bit of my bum on another projecting ledge of rock — Suresh was, of course, tottering beneath me. The sooner I took my foot off his shoulder the better. But I wasn't quite able to perch securely on that rock.

Suresh was, all this while, looking up, I suppose. Because he'd say, Don't scrabble about with your hands up there too much. My eyes are full of dust already. Can you find anywhere firm up there?

I said, No. There's a long root. But that's too high up.

He said, Let's come down then.

Letting go both my hands from those rocks, I slid all the way down.

Suresh asked, Can you hold my weight?

I said, Perhaps I'll lose my balance.

Then do this — go up with your back to the rock. Then you can sit on that pointed rock. You should find going up easier.

So, once again, I was on his shoulders, this time back to front. As before, I came up to the protruding rock. Feeling about behind me with my hands for the rock, I settled my bum on it.

Suresh, wait a bit now. I can't even see where that root is.

Never mind, you have managed to sit there now. Put your feet on the rock you are sitting on and relieve me first. Then I'll guide you.

I extracted first one leg and placed it carefully under my behind. I let the other dangle below. And I also had hold of the rock above me with one hand anyway.

The moment he was relieved, Suresh stepped backward some distance and yelled, Now to your left above there is a hollow. But somehow you'll have to stand up first. You are lounging as if in a chair!

Then I raised my other leg to where I was sitting. Lodged my feet firmly and swiftly placed my left hand into the cleft above me.

Suresh said, Excellent. Now throw your shoes down. Otherwise you will slip.

Somehow, by rubbing them against a rock, I managed to take off my shoes and chuck them down. Immediately Suresh threw them back high up into some grass. Then he threw up his own shoes. And our bag also.

Now I was hunkered down on that rock, with my hand stuck into a hole.

Surshya, what now?

Now, get up with a snap towards the right — I mean your right — there's the long root, grab that. Be careful.

First I craned my neck and so caught a fleeting glimpse of that root. Then, with the utmost power my legs could provide, I suddenly lunged up at that root. And having stretched upright, I began to dangle by that root. Now my toes were barely on the rock and my hands round the root.

But it was all mossy and I kept slipping all the time. Still, having twisted my hand into a loop of the root, with all my weight hanging by it, I quickly set my foot into the hollow above. Then my other foot. Then, held another root with the other hand. Meantime my middle kept swinging in the air for the longest time. I yelled, Shall I let go this root and grab the grass?

Why ask me? Go just a little bit higher now, and it will be over.

Then transferring all my weight to one hand, I grabbed a fistful of grass. Then freeing my first hand I grabbed another fistful.

Then holding on to the grass I climbed all the way, hand over hand. My arms were trembling terrifically. My thighs of course were altogether — bust. With a final effort I somehow picked up my feet, took a step or two. And, having once glanced up at the fort above, I suddenly felt faint and collapsed into the grass. Then, in sighing satisfaction I lay on my back and closed my eyes.

Suresh was yelling from below — Pandya, Pandu. How shall I come up?

I was, you know, like stunned. When I finally came to, I heard his shouts — Pandu, are you still there or have you gone?

I snapped, as though in a sort of anger. I shouted, The way I got up is bad. I shall take a look from above. We might find another way.

Then I walked back and forth a good deal up there. The easiest way was where some water was cascading over many steplike stones. Besides, there was also a tree above.

Surshya, come from this side. But you'll have water splashing all over you.

Meanwhile, all on his own, Suresh had pushed the boulder we'd used before, right to the bottom of this waterfall. Then bearing the brunt of the water splashing all over him, he climbed quite a long way up. As I guided him from above he kept climbing according to my directions. Later I gave him a hand and pulled him up.

He said, however, As I was climbing, what were you yelling all the time? In the noise of the water I wasn't able to hear anything at all.

We lay there in the grass and ate the bread we had carried in our bag. We had really given up thinking about how we were to get back to the top again.

The darkness of night grew intense. Just the thought of climbing all those pits and slopes above us, made us roar with laughter.

Just then some three or four people came out of the distance, shouting Ho...ho.... At first we took fright. But when they had come close they asked, Did you see a buffalo hereabouts?

We said, No.

One said, At such a time, what are you doing here? Have you lost your way down from the fort?

We said, Yes.

They said, You are strange folk. What about creepy-crawlies, then — don't you understand what time of day it is?

Then directing us through the grass stretches they left us on a trail.

Go straight now, you'll see this joins the way down by the steps. And then they went ahead.

By the time we approached the steps it had become even more dense dark than before. Without saying a word, then, and with great effort, we cycled on and on towards Poona.

Suresh didn't like outings to ancient caves and such. He had finished looking at the Karli caves in five minutes. And then he said, Enough of this praise of mere rocks. Let's go and see what lies above these caves.

Now when I looked at the Bhaja caves, myself, I kept feeling bad, watching the noisy water fall from just above the caves — I said, One can't understand what our government does do. Because of this water this beautiful cave will break up after a few years.

Then Suresh said, But after some years the Earth itself will break up. What can the government do about that? The government is all right. Instead, if these caves and such, and the Taj Mahal and all that were to disintegrate quickly it will be better.

How can you say that? Such beautiful caves and...

That's all very well. But already the caves have grown cracks. Even with repair they are not going to last for ever. It is folly to wish to make anything permanent. Truth to tell, those who carved these caves ought to have demolished them as soon as they'd finished carving. For one thing, such things were fine for people of that age. Old books, old buildings, old ragas and all such ancient things were made by people for their own ages. Not for ours. Whatever is happening today, that is alone truly ours.

How so? Today I feel these caves belong to our age.

Go ahead. Nothing wrong in that. But we ought to let things perish as they grow old. Don't get so sentimental. Your relationship with these caves will endure, at best, only for the day. Before today, whether they existed or not was all one to you.

No, not just for today. I shall come again and again to look at them. Or even with my eyes closed I shall be able to see these carvings as though they were alive.

For how long? Only until your death, surely? At best? What'll become of you and them thereafter? Mainly, what will become of the caves after you are gone? Or, even while you are alive, you are not going to remember them for months together. That means that from your point of view they don't even really exist. So it's much better to see whatever the day provides and leave it at that. Come then, let's go and stand in the waterfall.

Suresh always goes to such extremes.

We knew the hills behind the hostel far better than we did our study books. If we returned from the hills to discover that our room keys had been lost somewhere up there, we would both know just where we might have dropped them. Many times we'd go alone and wander over the hills. By way of exercise. And when we were bored. But after the First Year and Inter, there was no fun left in these hills that lay nearby. This year we started to venture further into the interior. During our Senior year, in fact, whenever we went up we only went to the Vetal Hill. It was a great thing, this hill. Sometimes whole days, even an entire night would pass on the hills thus. To the Vetal Hill Suresh and I'd go together. For a solitary person this hill is pretty frightening. And what's more, it is the highest among all the hills around Poona.

It wasn't so much fun going to the Vetal during the day. All the while one was obliged to see Poona city lying around it. So one didn't quite get the satisfaction of having wandered over a mountain. In the dark it was like climbing up to some island high above land.

One afternoon, though, we saw something wondrous. As we roamed, we found some gunja creepers.[40] Underneath, a carpet of red, red gunja seeds. And crackling sunshine. Dried grass. We ate a great quantity of sweet gunja leaves. And brought back pocketsful of gunja seeds.

It was of course great fun on moonlit nights. One full moon night, we went up intending to sleep the night there with another four-five friends from the hostel. We'd brought only some sheets to cover ourselves. On the plain of grass at the top, with the moonlight spilling over, we had tremendous fun. But early in the morning all of us woke up because of the cold. We had to return to the hostel shivering in the early morning cold. Afterwards, baths in scalding hot water.

Desolate. Even in broad daylight sometimes, though, we saw men who ran moonshine stills. But they never had anything to say to us.

Sometimes at night on some hill in the distance we would see firelight. We took it to be the fire of some illegal still. But once we forgot to take a box of matches with us, so to get a light for our cigarettes we walked up to the top of a hill towards a fire. Just as we topped the slope, however, the fire-light disappeared.

Then we began to pay a good deal of attention to this mystery of the fires. After many days again one night we saw a fire. Stealthily, under cover of the trees we went towards it. But once again after we had gone round a bend or two in the path, we couldn't spot the fire anywhere.

Then we returned to our path again — and once again there was the fire.

I said, Forget this fire nonsense, Surshya. It must be some sort of sorcery.

He said, You are a country bumpkin.

You mean to say there are no such things as ghosts, or what?

There may be, and again there may not be. But to maintain that there are — what evidence do you have?

Look at this fire thing, for instance.

How can a fire be ghostly? It must have been lit in some cranny of the hill. From here we can see right into it, so we see the flames. When we go up there, we don't see it.

Surshya, the fire's not always in the same place. Sometimes it is on the plateau of the hill, and at others far away over there on the grassy plains.

You can see it now, can't you? Let us go. Let's go as the crow flies towards the fire. Let it get as late as it might.

I said, No.

Later, after some days, we were able to see something that resembled a torch, far away, going back and forth. The rest was dead dark. So there was no way to tell whether it might have been a lantern.

Suresh said, We could have gone, but the light can be seen only intermittently. We can't tell where it disappears afterwards.

I said, But why must we bother? Let us go right up to the Vetal Temple and descend from there. Let it be whatever it is, no matter whose.

For a long time after that we didn't see any fires at all. On dark nights we would deliberately go looking for fires. We always thought, Now we shall see one. But for many days we saw nothing. Yet our visits there were a minor thrill or, anyhow, stirred our minds up a little, that's all.

One dark night we sat in the Vetal Temple for a long time. It was bitter cold. But we didn't feel like getting up. At last we came down from the hill. And, while it was still night, shivering, we reached the road. There we were accosted by policemen.

One of the policemen asked us something in a growling voice.

Suresh said, in English, Shut up.

That policemen said, Even if you want to curse our mother or father we wouldn't mind that. But we won't tolerate this "shut up" nonsense. You'd better come to the police chowky.[41]

I said, Look here, sir, we are college students. We live in hostels. We'd got fed up with study so we went up on the hill.

Another policemen said, College students! Sod it. Do college students look so wretched? Such clothes. Come you pimps, to the chowky. We won't let you go.

Suresh too swore horribly at the policemen. They really had a verbal dust-up. Then we spent the whole night at the police station.

There, with his nattering, Suresh really tried the patience of two or three policemen. Turn by turn we kept it up all night long –

Every Government used to have a Police department.

Now, you might ask, who is this Government? What does Police mean?

Now, that gentleman, who in the public street went about openly in a pair of shorts, with a stave in his hand, and caught thieves for you — that was a Policeman.

It appears that Policemen must have been born out of an inherent desire for law-and-order in the Nation. Because, why else would anyone do the work of catching thieves, in shorts at that, and on a measly income of eighty or ninety rupees a month?

Now, what does Government mean? Every Nation used to have a Government.

Some eight or ten ancient persons would come together, and for a salary they would look after the balance sheet of the Nation.

Once in a way, two or three Governments would come into conflict.

This did not mean that the Oldies themselves came to blows. First having created some quarrel out of nothing, the Oldies would send altogether different younger men to their National borders to fight, while they themselves watched the fun from their rooftops.

The policemen said, By God! these sodding sons-of-bitches haven't let eyelid meet eyelid all night.

In the morning the police inspector said, That itself should have given you sufficient proof that these have to be college chaps.

In the morning the police took us directly to the college principal's bungalow. Many boys and girls in the college saw us, and having given us a warning, the principal sent the police back.

Rami asked, Is this true?

What is there to be true or false in this?

So late at night? And wherever is this Vetal Hill? Is that the one over there? Not that one? Then is it that one with the pointy top that I can see? Good heavens....

Then Rami asked Suresh also and reassured herself. She said to him, Suppose a snake or something were to bite you?

Later she contrived to meet me and said, You mustn't tramp about like a silly goose.

Then, wide eyed, she listened to all the strange experiences we'd had on Vetal Hill. She said, They keep us girls imprisoned. The girls' hostel is a cattle pound, really. One girl returns late at night and climbs over the wall into the hostel.

But we don't tell anyone about that. Can I come with you some day? Just to see? Ummm? When?

You won't be able to manage. It is too steep. And, besides, your lungs?

On that she said nothing at all.

I had erred. I must not again speak about her lungs.

Where the Vetal Hill ends, there begins the lousy hill of Chatushrungi. A further curse is that as you climb this hill you begin to pant, that's how steep and stupid this hill is. But we, of course, used to climb up from the Chatushrungi side anyhow. And come down on the Khadakwasla side. Once we reached the top of Chatushrungi everything was cheerful again.

Once, just as we were climbing Chatushrungi, Suresh asked, Isn't this the no-moon night of the month?

I said, Who knows? We have never climbed the Vetal Hill in the evening. We always go late in the night. We can't see the moon in the evening can we? Still, there probably is no moon tonight anyhow.

He said, Then today we are bound to see a fire.

But we didn't see fires anywhere. The darkness, though, was very close. Yet there was enough light to see the path by starlight. Up in the sky, stars were very thickly strewn. From afar the Vetal silhouette was clearly visible. Even the temple could be seen, faintly.

Then, while we were still below the hill we spotted a dim light in the temple.

And when we came up we discovered that someone had lit a votive lamp. This large, round, wick-in-oil lamp carved out of stone — we had noticed it several times. Yet we had never imagined that anyone would fill it to the brim and actually light it.

I said, We always come here late at night. The lamp must go out by then. Today we have come much earlier, that's why we are able to see it lit. Today, there was also a coconut. We broke that coconut, and having left one piece near the image, we ate the remaining flesh. What's wrong with that? Vetal is ours. I, at any rate, do give credence to such gods.

Thereafter, whenever we went there in the evening, that lamp would be lit. Besides, it was quite evidently lit just before we arrived there. Because the oil would still be brimming in it.

But who lit the lamp? Or did it light itself? But then, this before the god — a sliced lemon, turmeric, gulal,[42] kumkum[43] — who brings these?

Then we began to sit there keeping watch from before the daylight faded. On such days, even after it had become dark no one would come to light the lamp. And if we thought that it lit itself, it never did so before us.

Suresh said, Someone is performing black magic.

Then we thought of a trick. Suresh stood by the lamp. I came down the hill and ran up the neighbouring hill at some distance. This hill was well hidden by trees and underbrush. But I stood in a place from which I could see Suresh clearly. He made signs to me with his hand. Accordingly I moved a little to the left, a bit higher up, and so on, and so I fixed a place. I kept a marker stone there and came back to the temple. I said, I've marked the place. Tomorrow, without any anxiety we shall be able to see who lights the lamp, from our hiding place.

Then every evening thereafter we'd sit by our marker to spy on who it was that lit the lamp.

The first four or five days, sitting there like soundless lost souls, staring at the temple was a waste of time. Because, as we stared even without blinking nothing would happen. Then neglecting our task, or nattering about our favourite topic of history and enjoying ourselves, quite forgetting the lamp, when suddenly we looked again towards the temple, the lamp would have been lit!

Then we would scamper across the grass-land at the bottom and up to the temple on the hill. And then look in — the lamp, oil filled to the brim, signs of puja, of the god, and sometimes a coconut — all done quietly. If we came out, scurried around the temple, peering into the grass about and staring into the grasslands below — we found that everything was desolate. Evening dark, that's all. If someone were to hide somewhere in it, who was to know? But we used to search assiduously. In fact this quest had entered Suresh's brain and driven him crazy. But I would say, Why must we poke our noses into such questions?

Once we were late arriving. The lamp had of course been lit. We ate the coconut.

Descending from the temple, Suresh turned to look back. He said, Did you see that? Just now the lamp was alight. Now it can't be seen. Has it gone out?

I said, it's not visible, that much is right. Why? There is a tree and some grass between. Besides, we've come down quite a distance. That's why it can't be seen from here.

He said, Why is it dark in the temple, then?

Once Surshya has taken some fad into his head, he really does go after it, like crazy.

And so we climbed up half the hill once again. True, the lamp was no longer alight. Perhaps a puff of air had blown it out, or something. But why doesn't it always go out like that, then?

Right. Why does it not go out every time? Get the matchbox.

Suresh lit the lamp. There was plenty of oil in it still. Turning up the wick he lit his cigarette right off it. I began to become suspicious — there is profound darkness behind the image of the god, what if someone is hiding there? But being afraid, I didn't tell Suresh about this. He's mad. If I tell him, he'll go there to look.

Then we started to come down.

When we turned around to look again, once again darkness in the temple.

I said, The wick was sufficiently long, wasn't it?

Suresh said, O'course.

So then we waited right there, to see whether someone was going to relight the lamp. But utter darkness still. How would we know who came or went?

Finally Suresh started to go back up again. I said, Don't. What's it got to do with us? Come along.

But Suresh was not one to listen to anyone. I waited a longway below the temple. He entered and struck a match.

And then, wailing shrilly he ran towards me. I too started to run — What happened, Surshya, whatever happened?

But he began to run dementedly. Even after we reached the grasslands below he went on running. Not a word out of him, of course. Finally, with his left hand pressed over his right, he stood still.

I said, What happened? Did something bite you? Light a match. Look at the hand.

I lit a match and in its light looked — on his hand were two or three deep scratches. But no blood or anything. He was really terrified. He said, As I was about to strike the match and touch it to the wick, just then — something fell on my hand with a whack.

He thought that it might have been a bat.

All these nights we'd never looked to see what was hanging on the tree over the temple. Perhaps there were ghosts clinging up there.

After that we gave up the pursuit of Vetal. Then followed some bright moonlight nights. The lighting of the lamp also ceased. We were both quite convinced now that it was a desolate place. And on top of it, at night time. What if, as we tried one thing, something altogether different were to occur, no one was going to run there to help us. Poona city lay far away in the valley. No one would know a thing about us.

Thereafter we'd only glance at the Vetal Hill as we walked to the bathroom and back.

Cocoon

Until the half-yearly exam of our Senior year nothing new occurred. Always the full, pendant clouds; the gulmohar with its blooming flowers. The grass had been green almost until just the other day. Almost till yesterday, fell the scurrying monsoon rain. And even the rain this year had been very heavy. All the four monsoon months, across the windows the warp and weft of rain. And all these days, nothing at all cast a shadow on us.

Only at Diwali did I go home for a holiday. But even there I continued to study like a typhoon. Mother would say, My Little One, won't you sit with us for at least a half hour or so?

Professor Gune said, Sangvikar, your papers are excellent. I have given you seventy marks. But you *are* careless. Now this time it will be a university exam, better keep that in mind.

He himself told me, Do drop in at my place, I shall help you.

I started going to Gune's place once in a way. His name, his reputation was pretty widespread. That's why I cultivated a close relationship with him.

Gune sir had one house in Mumbai. And one in Poona. He would say, If I give up the Mumbai flat, and after a few years if the college management were to transfer me back to Mumbai once again, where else am I going to find another luxurious place like that? And who is going to take the trouble to look for it?

I'd say, These days accommodation has become a very difficult problem in the cities.

All his belongings were in two sets. Two radios, two photos of his parents, pots and pans, mud-stoves, furniture, somebooks, primus stoves — all the Mumbai things in Mumbai, and the Poona stuff here. Earlier, he'd lived in Mumbai for three years. At that time, the Poona house had remained closed.

During the holidays he would go to Mumbai and write books of criticism and such. But two strong boxes of books would go with him whenever he came or went to and from Mumbai. Likewise his clothes. Among his books there was everything from *How to Win Friends and Influence People* to encyclopaedias. As soon as new books arrived in the bookshop, the shopkeeper would send a pile of them to him. One table was reserved for such books sent on approval. The books he liked he'd buy. The shopkeeper would carry away the rest. Because of Gune I got to see so many new books.

In Mumbai there was a trusted woman servant of the Gunes' who had a key to their house there. Whenever he had to stay there, he'd let her know that she should sweep the house, etc. If he was going to stay for a month or so during the holidays, Gune's wife would write a letter to that effect to her a few days in advance. Then the servant would mop and dust the whole house, make it clean for them. She'd buy a milk card. Organize a young boy to do some of the house work. Stock soap, oil, fuel, etc., all ready. All the tins filled with necessary grain. The furniture all dusted and wiped clean.

When Gune and his wife got off at Dadar station in Mumbai, the servant would be ready outside their second class carriage. She would have organised everything, so that after reaching home they would only have to cook their dinner.

When Gune narrated all this to me as he sat in his easy chair after dinner, I felt most peculiar. Mean to say, I understood fully how secure this bod was. But he had no children and he fed just about anyone. And at least in the field of literature he had a name. Visiting his house enhanced my own value in the college.

To his house would come many a great person of Poona. Gune would elaborate his most recent and new thoughts on literature. Then people would ask him, Doctor, why don't you present these thoughts in the form of a book?

But he and I got along because, I think, I used to ask him many questions and force him to think. I had read the entire Marathi section in our library during the past year. Some books were just about so so. I had only leafed through those.

But Gune gave me a list of fifty well-known and great books in Marathi. He said, You had better read these right away. I'd already read thirty of them. The other twenty I finished, after some eight days of hard reading. Gune said, Sabhash![44]

Often, before going to his place, I'd prepare some opinion that would be exactly the reverse of his. Then I would argue with him. In presenting my opinions I would need to gather together all sorts of examples. I had to read a number of new and old journals, and two-bit, no-account poets, etc. A good deal of my time was spent in all this. But such striving for something was better, I thought, than conducting meaningless speculation in my own room. Forget study. Let me not get a first class in the exam, what use were mere marks going to be in one's life?

Once Gune said, It is a good thing that Aristotle's *Poetics* has been rendered in Marathi.

I took the book that he held and looked at the name. I asked, Who is this G.V. Karandikar? Is that the doctor in Budhwarpeth? He comes to my Maushi's.

He said, No, no! This is "Vinda" Karandikar.

I said, How strange that he has one name for his poetry and such a funny name here.

Gune said, A poet is genetically eccentric. "Vinda" sounds a little like a woman's name, so one can achieve the aim of getting men interested in reading poetry in this day and age by means of such names. At least when they see such names, people read their poems.

Gune was right about that.

Once he said, Gadgil is the greatest short story writer in Marathi.

I said, Greatest in Marathi?

He said, He's equal even to English story writers.

Whenever anything English turned up I would get cheesed off. Still, I went on talking — To start with, the short story is a no-account genre.

Gune said emphatically, Don't talk nonsense. The intensity and subtlety that you find in the short story cannot be found in any other literary form.

This view Gune had already propounded in one of his books.

I said, The short story is the form that runs the monthlies. There is nothing special about it beyond that. If there are no stories, who'd ever read magazines?

Gune said, That is precisely the greatness of the short story.

I said, That's right. The daily papers carry sensational items of news. That is why people read papers. It's the same thing.

Then he cited the instance of Chekhov. Whenever something English etc. appears I am bound to suffer defeat.

But I did triumph once.

I asked Gune, How is it that you have not written any important book on poetry as yet?

Then he said, I shall write one soon.

Then there was another thing about Gune — many well-known writers and poets etc. of Mumbai and Poona would visit his house. If I was at his place on such occasions, he'd point me out and introduce me — This is a bright student of mine. But once, after he had said this, a writer did not even look at me properly. This was an insult to Gune himself. That chap must've thought that I did not even *look* particularly bright. So I determined to participate vigorously in their discussion.

That writer was saying, Of late English poets have made greater progress than poets in other languages.

I'd drunk my tea quickly and was ready. I quickly inserted my beak into the argument saying, When you say other poets, who do you mean?

He said, I mean, compared to French poets and such.

I said, Perhaps they have, compared to French poets. But what are the means by which we might know whether they have progressed in comparison to Chinese or Japanese poets?

Cocoon

Then the writer felt insecure. He said, I actually spoke only about the language that I myself know.

Do you know French, then?

Not like that. But via English — now, it's enough to know the sense of a poem, really.

How can that be? If you were to turn a song from one language into another would you know its sense?

Songs are a different category. I am speaking about poems. With Gune.

But the best of poems are songs, actually. A novel is a failed epic; a short story is a failed story. Such a poem in fact means today's failed song, nothing else.

This opinion of yours is an extreme, really. In poetry are found the minutest of minute movements of the human mind.

One says that about modern poetry. That is why you critics are able to hunt for poets' minds in modern poetry and write volume after volume of criticism. Are you in a position to write even one book about the minds of bygone poets?

What can you say about the mind of Dnyaneshwar? After all, in the *Dnyaneshwari* we don't find the poet's mind. That is why — while teaching the *Dnyaneshwari* just saying such and such is its sense... such and such part is beautiful — beyond that ... what more can be said...

Just then I recalled that this year Gune himself was teaching our class the *Dnyaneshwari*. So I became somewhat confused.

Even this writer was not bad, really. The dunces who came to Gune's — each surpassed the other. Gune was well read even in English poetry. Many who discussed things with him invariably argued about how many cantos Ezra Pound had written in all.

But the most peculiar of them was a chap called Govinda. He was Ph.Ding under Gune. He used to write poems and ensure that they would be published only in superfine journals and such. And as we both liked literature, you see, we became friendly. But

I had to give him tea, always. Besides, he only smoked superior brands of cigarettes.

One night we went out for a cup of tea. Now, suddenly pointing to his chappals Govinda said, Look Sangvikar, see which pair this left one comes from, and the right one is from a different pair, see? Whatever will happen once I have become a professor?

I said, You are a poet, after all. These things must happen.

Soon thereafter a teacher from our college was incapacitated in an accident. So, in that emergency, Govinda was given a temporary position on the faculty. Gune and Govinda operated on the basis of... mutual influence. Some relation of Govinda was a friend of Gune's. From that time my opinion about Gune turned sour.

Govinda began to ensure that everywhere he would be called "professor." But I continued to behave with him as before. Go to the canteen with him for tea.

Once he said, In colleges teachers do not behave well with students. Mean to say, have you seen another "professor" who takes tea with students? And so on.

I said, Only you.

But Govinda would do all the nursing for the professor who was unwell after the accident. If he took a turn for the worse, he'd even sleep in his house. Give him his medicine and all that. Take him out for walks in the evening.

Once I said, Govinda, why do you take so much trouble for that silly old man? Just so your job will last?

Govinda lost his shirt. He said, Don't talk like a ninny. I feel such affection for him you have no idea. I do all this out of sheer affection.

I said, That's fine, then.

"Professor" Govinda was a heck of a man.

In the end Gune's relationship with me ripped apart. As we were arguing once, on and on and on, without losing our tempers, he said calmly enough — Your reading is inadequate, and your chattering excessive.

Peeved, I returned all the books I'd borrowed from him.

Goodbye! These people are really bogus. Learned Doctor Gune, M.A., Ph.d. And what about his Ph.d. thesis, then?

He said, Literary writers are superior to ordinary human folk. Now I have myself seen many people who're great and yet haven't written a single line. Only fifteen per cent can read and write, so does that mean that there is no greatness in the remainder of humanity? Just suppose — if Lakshmibai,[45] who wrote the great memoirs, had been illiterate, would that have made her inferior to Nehru? Only because both wrote autobiographies we know something of them.

Then Gune said, Have you read the book by that French somebody?

Let that be. I should've known from the start that Gune is only Gune and yet writes books of criticism. Now I can perhaps concentrate on studying for my exam. This isn't a bad thing to have happened, anyhow.

So then I began my study. Once the nagging Gune business was over, I resumed my daily after-dinner walks to the hills behind the hostel, from which I would return only after dark. Deliberately by out of the way tracks, leaving the road. Stubbing my toes, circling round and about, and down.

Once in the library Rami said, Which work of criticism did you read for *Macbeth*?

I've read many.

Won't you tell me about one of them, at least, please?

No.

All right. But why not?

Read them yourself.

I haven't asked your advice about that, have I?

I next met Rami on the hill. But her slow, slow walk, a drag, really. I got tired of that and went on ahead.

I said, This is a drag. I shall run up and back. You wait here. Then we can go back down together.

Fine.

That's to say, she said this as she pronounces all things — 'Hine'. Lovely, of course. When I came back and looked for her, she wasn't there.

One morning, instead of going to bed, I went straight up the hill. When I was coming down I saw her sitting under a tree. Even so early in the morning she looked so tired. I continued to stand there.

She said, I too feel like running like that, you know, skipping about all over the place! But I can't. My lungs. Trouble. Medicines every day. I'm really tired of it all.

I knew this already. But she still told me. She really is great. Even otherwise, she's always by herself. There was no glow on her face. Her looks aren't bad at all. And her skin, really gorgeous. And she is as tall as me.

Then she said, You are not obliged to walk with me. I shall go alone.

I said, Not as compulsion — I just felt like going with you.

She said, No. You go.

I didn't go.

But she said, You must go.

So I did.

I met Rami again in the street.

When are you going to return that book?

It just refuses to end. It's wonderful.

This is her usual trick. The book I gave her — I had given it to her because it was wonderful. So even if she was unable to finish reading it, she'd still say in so many words that it was wonderful.

I asked, Where are you off to?

I need some bread. Come along with me then.

Along the way, on the pretext of referring to *Macbeth*, I brought up the subject of life and death. She said, How many plays did Shakespeare write in all?

I said, My younger sister died. No one should die at such young age.

She said, The right age to die is this. Ours.

Then the days passed very quickly. I had not really managed to do any special study for the exam yet. I could hardly bear to hold books prescribed for exam. In such a state of mind, if Suresh said, Let's go to Vetal Hill, I was in a mood to do just that.

By the time I turned out my light and went to his room, he was ready. As he was putting on his tattered shoes he said, I was about to throw away these shoes. But this is good, one final use for them before the exam.

Outside, we ate something in a restaurant. After we had gone past all street lamps, everything was deathly dark. Then we came to some woods. Our brains, heated by the summer days and our study, now cooled in no time. As we walked, the dry leaves underfoot rustled loudly. Until we reached the Chatushrungi Hill, Suresh kept up a rattle about study, teachers, this book or that, the exams, and so on. Avoiding the stone steps, we decided to make our first halt at the top by the temple, climbing from the university side. Then Suresh began the bhunkus, his habitual goony nonsense — whether there is a genuine need for universities, and how people are photographed with a sort of plank on their heads when they take their degrees.

Later he said, In such darkness, or in a breeze, smoking a cigarette is useless. We smoke because we can see the smoke. What do you think? If cigarettes gave off no smoke, would you still smoke?

I said, A lot depends on being able to see. People drink tea. The reason is its soft rosy hue. If tea had been yellow, or purple, we would hardly have drunk it.

Then he said, I haven't yet done my work for the poetics exam. Sod it, perhaps one can tolerate even poetry, somehow. But how can you be serious about seventy different bogus ideas *about* poetry from seventeen different people?

We reached the top by the Chatushrungi temple. Then, leaving the temple behind, we both rested for a while, panting, against a black rock above. It was difficult to utter even a word. But even then, just a word or two at a time, Suresh still kept yakking. In front of us, all over the city — bright illumination. Indeed, where what was, all the streets — all could be seen quite clearly.

Then having observed that I was not talking, Suresh went on —

There was one thing about these people, that they would designate those people who were already advanced as 'tribals' and then teach them books, and hygiene and such. There were two continents that from the start belonged to the Red Indians. Some indigent people of Europe, having colonised them, slowly exterminated all Red Indians, claimed all rights of ownership. Then, inventing machine after machine, the Nation of these new American creatures did all sorts of peculiar things all over the place. But the Red Indians were the truly advanced folk.

Now, you might ask, what is a Nation? So then, these Nations used to exist in Maps. Now you will ask, who or what is this Map? Now a Map is a piece of paper. There used to be all sorts of doodles on these papers. They would call the people living on this side of a line Hindustani, and those on the other side they would call Pakistani.

As to change the subject I said, Can you smell the fragrance of the champak?[46] A...ha! Look at those champak trees. Just gorgeous great bunches of flowers all over the trees.

But Suresh carried on —

Now, from ten to seventeen ought to total seven by rights. But in their opinion, ten to seventeen makes eight.

I said, That's really enough, you sod.

Then Suresh brought up another horrible topic. He said, Do you know how male and female camels do it?

Fed up with this, I said, Heck, you never change, do you. There is some fun in hearing such things the first time. Why again and again?

Then he told me many other erotic jokes and made me laugh monstrously. I said, Let's go on then.

We started walking. Then because of the hundreds of lights behind us along those distant streets, we cast faint shadows before us. We climbed up, and up, until we came right to the flat top of the hill and then descended to a sheet of rock on the other side. Now — the lights of Poona behind us all disappeared. But the sky behind the hill went on glowing.

Scattered, bald trees. Right above us, a crescent of the moon. It looked funny, like a hod. Suresh always called the moon Chandrika — Little Luna. Even on a full moon night he would say, Look at her — Chandrika is up.

He said, All things really ought to be feminine gender. The she-words we use for fly, ant, and so on are so lovely. But the he-words like crow, rat are terrible. Are you actually able to make out whether it is a female crow or Mistress Rat? Then why should we unthinkingly say he-crow?

Then, even when we had tired ourselves out walking, we did not sit down anywhere. Now, leaving the direct path we started footing our way across the grass plain. The dry grass actually lay level with the ground. We had not come this way for such a long time. So we thought everything had changed. When one walks over grass in shoes, one feels so hugely proud of oneself. But the sound the dried grass makes as one walks is really quite pleasant. So much, in fact, that Suresh's nattering ceased on its own.

The moon rose in the sky. Looking at her shape, I reckoned that it must be exactly the sixth or seventh night of the lunar phase.

Then the grass patch ended. We found another vast sheet of rock. So clear was the dark that we sat down arms stretched behind us to support our weight.

From there we could barely see the Vetal Hill away in the distance. We sat there for a long time. The moonlight was so gentle that between it and darkness there was no real difference. This is wilderness. In the tamasha,[47] wilderness such as this is described thus — "Not a creeping ant, nor any sign of man." Like that. Folk theatre like tamasha is a great thing. Tonight, in the dense wilderness. One does not feel like talking. One loses all one's faith in oneself. If one is entirely alone, all by oneself, only then might one survive, such deep, dead silence. If one were to sit on a rock, all by oneself, then one might contemplate something profound, such a deep, deep night. If there are two on a rock, then all things lose their meaning.

The fact is, minus these two chaps, everything else is one. That oneness, and these two before it, as though with swords drawn — that is how far apart these two happen to be.

If one is alone, one might vanish, merging into that oneness. Two, however, have two separate minds. But that is not why they feel apart. The two have distinct bodies, which make the two believe that they are distinct selves.

With one's eyes open, finally one sees — everything outside is all one.

Stars are not all really white. Some are green. Some blue. Some pink. One star is ink dark.

And we cannot see the erased part of the moon even from this great height.

This Earth is light enough to pick up. A ball. But a colourful ball. Changes its colours like a chameleon in each season.

And these two begin to appear, gradually, like monkeys, sitting there. Looking out with twinkling ape-eyes. This seems very comic.

After all, two men cannot come as close to each other as they might like to. They cannot enter each other. Anatomy has stalemated that game.

There is nowhere a tender part in a man's body. From his head to his toenails, all hard. Then the back flows. The gut collects. And the brain vaporizes.

Do you see that tree before you? Who taught it to stand, balancing so well, forever digging itself in and living, just so? No hassle with mother or father.

Cocoon

My Mother took care of my eldest sister's confinement. How disgusting! These trees remain here, just as they are, having dug in their feet. In fact, the part of a tree we see above ground is not the tree at all. The tree above is merely the guts, lungs and such. The true, genuine tree is underground.

What does man have that is thus rooted in the ground?

Man has lost that, in his pursuit... to fill his stomach. Can you maintain that this Earth will never part company with us? Someone has flung us down from above, to no purpose, so that we might live here like tenants. This body is rented. A hundred-year lease. If you indulge in any funny business, you will have to vacate the house. You remember that, don't you?

A tree's dressed in a skin by the Earth. Pulling it out is as difficult as plucking a hair off one's thigh. Therefore, don't you ever pluck out any sapling rudely, crudely. Pull it up slowly, with care. Watch how its delicate relations — with the Earth inside, that are burgeoning — how they gradually, slowly let go, part. Watch that.

There's absolutely nothing in the soles of your feet to match that. So you come, from your room to this Vetal Hill. Effortlessly placing one foot after another. Trampling the grass. Picking up your leg behind you each time as you step out, without impediment.

That's how you reach thus far.

From here, the aircraft of any superior spirit, some Gandharva[48] or Kinnara[49] can quite easily pick you up and...away, fly off.

Even if you go round the whole Earth in this manner you will still fail to find any kinship between you and it. That is why when you take the ever-moving fish from water and dump them into a basket they stare about them, goggling, mute with agony. That is why a flock of birds of the wild, as it whirs and whirls and leaves behind it forest after forest, hasn't the least idea about where to go, they're unable to find home. Your haven is your body. Better live within it.

You sow your seeds without letting yourself come in contact with this Earth. And they too sprout without that contact.

Your parts may be decorated with ornaments, all of them except one. That one organ is decorated only by another organ which means that you attach yourself to one another only for decoration.

I have never found a girl that would really please me.

Not me either.

If you'd been a girl, I would not have let you go.

Do kiss my hand.

Give it here.

Yuck![50] No, not that one. Give your right hand.

That's just it. Suresh is always pursuing the other extreme. He would dampen the heat of the moment just like that. He fills again a state of great emptiness that has come about. He has perhaps only barely glimpsed the meaning of emptiness, from the shore, you might say. He has never flung himself right into it.

Now along the regular path, straight to the temple where a light burned inside. Bright-white light. Today, even after we reached the top the light did not vanish.

We could see some human shapes inside the temple and I was afraid.

Suresh said, Would it be better not to go in at all?

I said, Let's look from a distance.

But are these human beings or not? Suppose they are ghosts? But why would ghosts sit still? And why would they kindle a holy fire?

And suppose they are mantriks?[51] They might turn us into dogs and then not care.

Then let us not go.

Let's take a detour and go to the other side.

When we descended into the grassland, Suresh said, In the final analysis, whether it's you or me, what are we going to achieve? There is nothing about us that is in the least unique or special.

If we must achieve something, it must be something — the way the yogis do — that would hold us in its magic right through life. Right to the end, that is.

We ought to be able to talk to any other beings also besides humans.

In the grass, far far away, a vast banyan tree. Terrifying, even to look at. We had never knowingly quite gone that far, leaving our path. Its shape caused a thrill of pleasurable terror. We looked at it from a distance. We could see at its base some vermilion coloured stones, smeared with cinnabar — even from far away.

Vast girth, beneath it, dry clumps of dried up grass. All around it the pasture, dry, and a long, long empty slope. But this one great blotch, the banyan, deep dark, we could see that from far away.

Under the banyan a deep dark darkness. If one tried, with wide wide open eyes, one could perhaps see — then some few bushes, or something. Or are those great boulders?

Let us sit under that tree.

Let's not.

Just for a while. What's the risk here?

Of course. Whatever may not lie under such a deep-sealed tree? It may be anything at all.

All right. But let's sweep round that way first at least. You do this — you approach from the right. I shall approach from the left. We shall meet on the far side of the tree.

But suppose we don't meet anywhere on that side at all?

You go by the left, then.

You go first.

As I went from the right, skipping by bushes, avoiding the banyan's aerial roots, sure enough I collided against a great big boulder. A rock all smeared in cinnabar. A monstrous fear filled me but I stood still. No cry escaped my mouth. Then again gathering my wits about me, groping about with my hands, bending, crouching really low, I went forward. Again I stood still.

From there — what I could see under the banyan was tremendous. A faint belt of moonshine, as though etched all around it. But where was Suresh? Suresh! I wouldn't be able to see him even if he were to come close. But he echoes my call. He too must have been standing like me, looking outward.

Come here.

I then detected his white shirt from a distance. He was shifting about, coming towards me.

Just then, suddenly, from between us, a horse shot up with a really loud clatter, and terrifying neigh. Brushing against the stilt roots of the banyan, his skin rasped. Under the banyan into the tall grass, his hooves hammering, the horse disappeared into the distance.

And from under the banyan and then out — Suresh and me, bursting into great sweat, the roots flapping against ourfaces. Both soaked through. We started scrambling, running in any old direction. We ended up at the very edge of the mountain.

This was absolutely the wrong direction. We were lost. We kept feeling all the time that the black horse was galloping all around us.

Then we turned in the opposite direction. We couldn't see Poona. Where *is* the city? Then in a third direction. Still the same dark night as before. In this way we walked and walked and walked endlessly.

This mountain wasn't as small as we used to think. The orb of the moon had now turned a dull red. The only real light came from the stars. We wandered a great deal through the grass, trying to locate trees we knew. Even Vetal Hill eluded our eyes. All over the place, always, always, sandal trees.

The city couldn't be seen at all. Where were we to descend from?

We trudged. And trudged. And in one place, lay unmoving for a long while in the grass. Like lost souls. Neither spoke. Once we had both become calm, we got up and started walking again. Now we had to concentrate as we walked.

Then we came up a long slope, through a long valley covered in bleached parched grass, trampling dried tree leaves.

We looked once again. Now shone all around a thousand lights of the city. Some bright, shiny. Some dull. And red-and-green

214   *Cocoon*

fluorescent ads, winking on-and-off. Far off, at the railway station, thick clumps of twinkling lights. And, spread over the mobile and immobile universe, from where we were, to the end were spilt... heaps of darkness. Now in the distance barely discernible, the Vetal Hill. We were so far above it. All the way to the bottom, dim shapes of hills, appearing massed in mad formations. And we, standing before millions of bright, resplendent lights.

We ran all the way down to the river and sat with our feet dangling in the water before drinking our fill and dunking our heads right up to our necks.

Then back on the road. An Irani had just opened his restaurant. We spent all our money there.

I started to study intensely. Only six weeks or so left now. Book after book was going by. I still couldn't seem to manage to put behind enough study.

From my room this year I was unable to fully appreciate the spread of nature outside. Only far in the distance, right at the base of a hill, stood a clump of trees. The rest — all rock and the dry mean soil of Poona. Right at the base of that hill, though, some fifty or so large, quite large trees. And right in their midst, I could also see a small two-storeyed house. If I took off my glasses, I couldn't see the house. If I looked carefully, I could even see a window open in it.

I felt, the bod who lived in that house had to be great. I determined to explore the house among the trees. At least — if there was no dog there — I would approach it closely any-how. So I determined.

Once I did go in that direction. But I could not quite spot the thick grove anywhere. So, after many days, I took aim, as it were, from beneath my window, and set off. But in my path were other houses and huts. So I lost my way again.

Then I decided to go up to the hill first to spy out that house. I went to the hilltop. Our hostel I could see from there. So I came down, having marked the direction carefully. The trees were not really as thick as I'd thought. They just looked like that from a distance. But as I walked on I encountered tall trees. These, then, were the trees. Of course they stood in a thick clump. So I entered. Then I saw a quite long, broad house. But there was a lock on its door.

Thinking that the bod may have gone somewhere for a walk, I sat down beside the hedge outside. But the man didn't turn up. I imagined this gentleman wearing long, comic moustaches. At last even after darkness had fallen, there was no sign of life there.

Then I came back.

Thereafter I'd only look carefully at the house among the trees as I sat studying. I never did manage to go there again.

Instead, the exam approached.

Having got up early in the afternoon I would go to the library and, after eating something in Madras Cafe, return to the library until dinner time. After dinner once again at the library till eleven at night. Then back in my room for some more reading. Once in a way, before Madras Cafe closed, take a turn that way and eat something there. Back to the room. Study again until two o'clock or so. And again, after drinking some tea, study into the morning.

As the exam loomed near, the burden of study increased.

I'd quite forgotten whatever I'd read before. I read through all of it again. I didn't manage to study as vigorously as I should have. So I'd be irritable. Suresh said, Our exam hours are in the morning. You'd better get into the habit of getting up — in other words, going to bed — early.

Then I stopped drinking tea two or even three times during the night, and started to lie down around midnight or one o'clock. But I would lie still in bed, wide awake, until day-break. Sleep simply eluded me. Then sometimes I would get angry and suddenly sit up in bed, go out directly and bathe before dashing off to the library. Irritated, I would read through book after book. In such a dizzy mental state, it was impossible to take down necessary passages from those books. Even more difficult to remember anything. No question of learning by rote, naturally. Then I would lay aside my study books and just read any junk. Time would pass quite nicely that way. Once in a way, having dozed off right in my chair, I'd wake up really refreshed. Then I'd feel, now if I spend the entire day. this way I'm sure to fall asleep at night. But not a chance. Sleep — only in the morning. So then I resumed my late rising.

In this manner, at a time I spent even two nights in a row without sleep. Still no use. No sleep from morning right through the day. Even when I lay in bed at ten or eleven at night, I could not sleep. That is to say, the whole night would be wasted. In my brain would play useless ideas — What do little babies feel when they are dying; what after the B.A.; what was that that Gune used to say; why does that married girl come to Govinda's place, she's there even at night; Govinda has done his M.A. but his reading does not match mine; how many books have I read this year; but how can one cram that into the exam paper; I haven't even touched the grammar yet; I'll have to mug up all that; Gune is a fool; Govinda is an ass; all these chaps, black marketeers in the field of education, the sods; moreover, Gune writes his criticism and Govinda composes poems; the other day Dnyaneshwar came to Poona and said to me, college life is sheer paradise, if God grants me a boon I shall ask for this room in the hostel; heck — even.

Suresh hasn't managed to study properly; but I have read so much more than he has; but I must get done the study for these two or three papers in quick time; then why should I not start on them tomorrow; but no; next week I shall finish the other five papers, and then clobber these three; and my writing must be cleaned up too; sod it, there are a hundred such things if there is one; until next week I shall study for this paper; from the sixteenth for the next; up to the twentieth, *Macbeth*; then criticism on it; but I shall have to make notes; I think I can make short work of it in the final week; by then I should be in the habit of sleeping early; then get up early in the morning and, ratatatatat, learn by heart all this stuff; a fortnight before the exam, just cramming; for the rest, the exam is just like shaving; it's going to pass quickly; but what *is* the time; this clock is tick-tocking away; that's why I am unable to sleep; heck — I'd better chuck the clock into my trunk; shall I get up and chuck it in right now; but no; once I rise I shan't be able to sleep again; sod it, that mercury lamp outside is a nuisance; the room's all lit up; how can I sleep; if I shut the window, it gets warm; it's not so bad in the winter; once you are wrapped in a cover, then you're all alone; it's four o'clock already; every sod has started to get up; how jarringly their alarms ring; how can one sleep in such racket; now this means that I shall not go to sleep until five; that means I shall get up only at noon!

That is how it always went. Then early in the morning in my bed I would flap my arms and legs, turn this way and that, bang my head against the pillow.

Sod it, I've picked up this habit from Suresh. That useless bum. And he himself manages to get up and start work. Before, until three in the morning he would stay in my room nattering. Arguing about some vast, grand subjects. And I only said the other day that those who strike work are stupid; the workers in the city and employees in the post office are able to strike work because inconveniencing everyone is a successful form of blackmail. But the outcastes Mahar and Mang folk in the villages don't even get a proper meal. Who is going to give them proper wages? But actually they don't even get work, so how can they ask for more?

So then, having heard me out, Surshya says — Pandu, all this only after the exam.

Sod that Suresh Bapat. He'd copied question papers from the past two or three years. I said, I can't make out your writing. If you read this out, I shall copy.

So he says, Tonight I have to finish reading all of *Rukminiswayamvara*[52] including its detailed meaning.

Fine, how about tomorrow, then?

Not tomorrow either. If you wish to, you can copy them from the library. But isn't it too late now? Should you be concentrating on the exam or on these questions?

Other chaps from my class were much worse. Ask them anything about the exam, and they'd say, Why the heck were you sitting in the library throughout the year — why do you come to us now?

Or if I pointed to some genuine errors of a writer, and asked someone what the teacher had said about them, these worthies would say — You used to sit in the class just listening. Why didn't you take notes then? Now who's going to hunt for such things?

They are all no-good sods.

And then it would be bright morning.

If I slept then, I would get up only in the afternoon. Suppose this were to happen during the exam? So then I would rise and directly proceed to brush my teeth. And all day long I would be in a daze. Scowling. The other chaps on the other hand, were now in great spirits. And me, I was pretty nearly done in. Even Rami had started to come to the library to study.

In fact, the final crackling big scrap Suresh and I had was about the subject of my fragile sleep.

Having had a couple of wide-awake nights before, that night I was so dog-tired that I went to bed quite early.

But something woke me up. On checking I saw that it was just eleven at night. Great! Meaning, I had been able to sleep early. If I hadn't been woken up like this, I would have got up only in the morning. After so many years, at last, I would have got up in the morning. But this silly old hostel is the limit, really. Out there, in the corridor, someone was kicking at a door — dun dun dun. That thunderous noise! That must be what broke through my sleep.

So in a gust of rage I came out. Suresh was kicking at the door of Modak's room next to mine — dun dun dun!

I said, Surshya, I had fallen asleep. You shattered my rest. So he replied arrogantly, What can I do about that?

At least now go back to your room.

I shan't go until I have got back my dictionary from Modak. He borrowed it four days ago. He's still not returned it. I must have it, right now.

There was a dubious silence inside Modak's dark room.

Next Suresh said, I've kicked the door so many times but he still won't open it. How can he sleep so much? Wake him up. I'll take my dictionary and go away.

I said, Take mine and go.

Yours is an Oxford dictionary. It gives wrong meanings. I want my own dictionary.

Then, really cheesed off I summoned Khan bhayya from downstairs. He was an incredibly kindhearted man. He said, partly in Urdu, You are all saheb people. You cannot keep each other quiet. So how can I do anything? And he went off.

Then I said nothing to Suresh at all. His racket went on for quite a long time — bang, bang, bang. I had lost my sleep, anyhow.

I stayed awake until it was eight in the morning and then went directly to lodge a complaint about Suresh with Warden Paranjape.

Suresh was fined five rupees.

From Paranjape's bungalow Suresh came straight to my room. He said, Because of you I'll have to pay up five rupees, for no reason at all. Can you loan me five rupees?

I said, Shut up.

He said, Do you know why I was banging on that door yesterday? Modak was not alone in his room, you see. That Vijay too was sleeping with him. You know, that sissy from the first year. I had a suspicion from the start. But yesterday I really did catch them, that's why I was so burning mad. But this is all right. I shall pay five rupees. But at least in the end I did find out what sort of a chap you are.

Then I drove him out of my room and shut the door with a bang.

After that row with Suresh, I began to feel even more shut in. Not a friend left. All of them busy with their study. I used to

Cocoon

maintain a relationship with friends only so I could go to them for a while, for entertainment. And then return to my room to study. After dinner, a few minutes would pass in Suresh's room in banter so one felt a little better. Even that was now gone.

All the same, I did not manage to study well enough to appease my own mind. Truth to tell, this nonsense about sleeping early — I was really anxious about that. Otherwise, come what may I would've stayed up all night to study. How dare study fail me then! In eight days — I mean eight nights — I would have mugged up everything. On exam days I could always have got up in time with the help of someone else quite easily.

But right at the wrong time, in the rush to study, I was conducting my experiments with sleep! And wasting my time. So study got sidelined after all.

I tried every remedy on Earth — splashing my head with cool water; soaking my feet in hot water; lying down in bed immediately afterwards; swallowing plenty of milk just before lying down; going to bed with a cover, still wet from the bath; not going to bed at all for two nights at a stretch, then going to bed early on the third night; or wandering all over the place the whole day so, bone-tired, I might sleep at night. I did everything that the doctor ordered. But nothing at all happened. I did not take sleeping pills, though. I have not touched medicines all my life, not even now. So I determined. But because of all these trials I had terrific fever for four or five days.

I lay in the college infirmary for a whole week. The doctor did not even let a newspaper come into my hands. I spent those nights and days just staring at the ceiling. But I must say I did sleep a lot. I ought not to have eaten so many green mangoes. That was fine when I was just a boy. Now, if I ate at one go all the raw mangoes I can buy for eight annas, I'd quite naturally fall ill. The sun too had been really hot. Suddenly on the street I'd seen deep, deep green tart mangoes. I really made a pig of myself.

I spent my time in the hospital charting out how I had expended all the four years in this holy college, from the day I first came to Poona — took a really thorough account of that subject.

After I felt better my study went on. Only fifteen days left for the exam. My complicated sleep patterns went on. In the morning my mind would be what it should have been in the evening. And in the evening — like morning. But in the evening I would feel really fresh, while the rest of the world was down in the dumps. This was really an injustice perpetrated by the world on the likes of me.

Two days for the exam. Then at last I realized that that was quite enough of my sleep nonsense. The very first paper was *Macbeth*. I didn't even know yet where exactly any of the speeches occur. This 'context' question is a bogus question, and that too compulsory! Now I must really study a bit. Forgetting all that I had read all these days, at least the night before each paper I should look over whatever was necessary for that exam. Panduranga! You have really gone beyond all bounds!

I began to shove and cram all my study matter into my head. Suppose right when I must sleep I am in fact unable to sleep? — Instead of thinking such thoughts, it'd be better to study at least now. Because next morning at eleven — the exam. Just at the wrong time in the morning I'd feel sleepy. Khan bhayya would wake me up at eight. Then, getting through everything including my bath in ten minutes, I would quickly read this book, look over that page, skim the pages of the other notebook, run my eyes over all the marks I'd made the night before — in this manner, just five minutes before eleven, this soldier would march with a banging inside his skull, to go and write the exam.

In my childhood, before starting for an exam, I used to check and recheck my ink bottle, pen, blotting paper, and so on. Then Mother would say, My Little One, you must take along what is inside your head, really, mustn't you?

That was nice. Now, for instance, I'd have to write my papers mainly giving short shrift to my head.

As I wrote my papers, my brain would be really irritated. I would recall nothing accurately. I'd feel, I'd read so much, so much — and yet in fact here I am, unable to write a thing — this thought would run through my mind ceaselessly. It was a terrible thought. Still I filled my answer books.

Besides, in one paper I wrote such independent thoughts, such stuff that the person marking that paper would simply have to give me great marks. Because that day I had managed to sleep pretty well. I wrote — This Ketkar is a *Konkanastha* brahman. Such intelligent people ought not to get involved with art. Had he written treatises, he would have been admired. More than he is now for his novels. Moreover, I also remembered many instances of his cleverness from his novels. And I also made use from time to time of Hemingway and other novelists about whom I had heard in professor Gune's house.

I became greatly enthusiastic.

I felt doubly enthusiastic after I got acquainted with a young man, an external candidate who had come to write this exam. How can I call him youthful? He had children and all that. The bod actually seemed too much of a gentleman to bother to write exams and such after having got married.

After the first paper he placed a foot on my bench and said, You stuffed quite a few supplements, while I was worried about how to fill up the only supplement I had taken.

He was bald. This chap was Khanolkar. Besides, he really entertained me thoroughly. After every paper he'd force me to have tea with him, but make his inquiries about study in all humility. He'd say, I can only manage my exam tomorrow if you guide me to the right path.

Khanolkar was a mild, poor old sort of chap. But even when he said something simple, pedestrian, I would find it comic. And then when he said something about study I would laugh uproariously. Pure entertainment. Mean to say, he would ask — You see, the poet and professor Madhav Julian was thrown out of Furgusson College. I think I have read his resignation letter in English somewhere.

Or, Was the family of Rajkavi Tambe really poor?

Or, Did this bloke Matthew Arnold have a monopoly on solving the most intractable questions in the world?

Or, That chap called George Eliot — was he any relation to T.S.Eliot?

At his every question I'd laugh until all my tiredness evaporated. The irrtation in my brain would dissipate altogether.

He once said, Look, I am not quite ready for my criticism paper. Do tell me something. I have read a little, actually. But to be able to read one book one needs to read two or three others. Nor does the matter end there. One says this, another says that. This has tended to grow like Rama's fabulous tail![53] So I gave it up.

All in all, having just finished a paper, I would find this stuff pretty enjoyable.

Khanolkar once said, Yesterday, our baby scattered all my notes. In trying to put them together I lost my temper so badly, I slapped her smartly. After that she screamed for a long time. Then even more noise from my wife in her attempt to pacify the baby. I didn't study well. But I have written a pretty good exam today, anyhow.

This was really funny. For instance, that babies and all should be playing around one. And there is a wife too. And one is studying — this is tremendously funny.

About grammar he said, I've only done cases properly.

I asked, And figures of speech?

Khanolkar asked, "Figures?" What on Earth is this new thing?

Then I explained all the figures to him pretty neatly.

He said, Sod it, isn't this the giddy limit? You mean "vulgarity" and "exaggeration" too count as "figures?" Really? But with your help I've just done the preparation for one more question. Do keep explaining things to me like this, please do.

Once, holding his question paper before me that had odd, most peculiar marks on it he said, In our course we have the varieties of poetry, where was the Epic in all that? How did they ask a question about it, then?

I said, Epic actually means narrative poetry, you see.

Then he said, What then is the Long Poem?

Khanolkar's handwriting was beautiful.

He said — When he saw my handwriting and clean language, our headmaster would say, again and again, You must sit for the B.A. But if you must, study Marathi as your subject. You'll get good marks. He would say, See, you will manage it. One doesn't really have to study Marathi, does one? Even girls pass. That's why I am taking these exams. Let's see what happens. But you have helped me a lot. To take an exam privately means leaving matters to fate. And all the hassles at home, plus my job.

The other high old time during the exam was provided by Rami. Having handed in her paper, she'd use sign language to ask me — How was it? I'd raise both my arms. Then after we had come out if we discussed the paper she would say, No post-mortem, please. Let's drink some tea.

But with me would be that chap Khanolkar. So I would say no to her. Then we would continue to stand there for a bit longer, talking.

Rami noticed this so she more than once said on her own, Khanolkar, why don't you come too?

Rami really liked drinking tea in the canteen with someone. Then she'd go off with some girl. Khanolkar and I would go to the canteen after the rush there had reduced. Till then we'd stand right outside laughing explosively. I used to laugh like a tempest at those times. At anything at all. He would talk, and I'd be ever ready to laugh. My cramped brain would loosen up at once because of him. So naturally I laughed.

This is also why I naturally liked him better than Rami. Because, after every paper, he'd tell me what had befallen him the night before. He would narrate the reason why he hadn't been able to study well, and yet how he had written something at least. Sometimes, with his finger pointing at something in the question paper, he would query — Was that in the syllabus?

But once Rami really insisted. Naturally Khanolkar too came with us. Afterwards, when Rami had left, he said, Do forgive me. I would not have come between the two of you. But I wanted to ask a little about tomorrow's paper.

I said, What do you mean, Khanolkar saheb? What do you mean by 'coming between the two of us'?

He said, I mean to say, you two, and all that...

Í said, You are really the limit, Khanolkar. Do you think we're in love or something? There's nothing of that sort, see? Do come.

Once he told us an anecdote about his in-laws. So even Rami was pleased. Khanolkar said, My father-in-law and mother-in-law have both come to visit us. Yesterday. They are staying for a week or so.

I said, That means your exam is done for!

Khanolkar said, No, no, I'm going to insist that they stay until the exam is over. My father-in-law is very nice. He wakes me up at night whenever I need to be woken. My mother-in-law looks after the brats. So now at last I'm able to study really well. As it is I can barely manage to carry on reading till eleven or twelve at night. And once I sleep, nothing doing till next morning. Actually, a couple of hours' sleep is enough. But once you get up you have to convince yourself that you've had enough sleep and then you can get down to work.

This was wonderful. Unlike me. I had wasted the whole of the last month in my hassles with sleep.

Once when our paper was over, I didn't see Khanolkar at all. I was waiting at the door of the exam hall for him. Yes, in fact, someone had got up and gone away in the middle of the paper. That must have been Khanolkar. Poor fellow. It seems his balloon has burst. Then I felt terrible. All his effort, struggling with his job, family, household and all that, his in-laws, such terrific burden to manage, all gone to waste.

Just then Rami approached. She said, Who are you waiting for?

I suppose she thought that I stopped here every day and waited just for her. But I said, so that she shouldn't feel bad, Who else?

So then, Why won't you come and have tea with me?

Why not? What paper did you have today?

Sociology.

How was it? Did you answer all questions? I find the time given isn't adequate for me. Even today I left out two questions.

No post-mortem. Tea?

Come.

Rami really wrote her papers with a bang. But me — this year I'd spent altogether as much as two thousand two hundred rupees, and all I had done was behave like an ass.

It was like this. On Sunday evening, the thunderclouds gathered. Tomorrow, Monday. The last two papers. The day after, I would leave. How would I ever get a chance to go about this place again? Besides, during the last few days I had been battered increasingly by my emotions. The sky was brimming with lovely clouds. All day long I'd been maddened by perspiration, the broiling sun, the books and notes for the next day's papers. Now suddenly everything began to feel cool, thrillingly cool.

Then I went up the hill and sat down.

Seeing those clouds, I thought — Now back in my village it would be the sowing season; everyone would be preparing their seeds and things. I hadn't been at a sowing for years. At sowing time everything looks gorgeous. As for the sights of the city! City people only see what insects can. Just what they eat. Everything reckoned by its cost. Mean to say, every day one eats rice and chapati, where *do* these come from — well, from the grocer's shop. That's all. Now, what a tremendous difference between having wheat from the grocer's and getting it straight from the soil. These folk here don't even know what soil means. There's no kinship between the soil and them. They bury the soil under tar-topped roads and, moreover, walk on the roads in shoes. And live within cement walls.

As I was meditating in this fashion and wondering whether I should start for home on Tuesday or at greater leisure on Wednesday, a terrific drumbeat of a windstorm began. A tempestuous gale. And from time to time, cold drops of rain.

Putting my meditation aside, I ran all the way down from the hill. Well did I know all the short cuts there, to run like that. But the rain began to fall like a big blow. Because of the elemental stir, dust went into my eyes despite my glasses. Even leafless trees were keeling over before that powerful wind. And how can one take shelter under them, then? The good neem tree was too far away. So with long, leaping strides, I came directly to the hostel instead. But the rain was coming down so swiftly that already there were runnels of water in the ground. I was soaked through in no time. Why so much flutter to save my woollen trousers? They were bound to get soaked, no matter what. My shirt was already drenched. Then I decided to proceed more slowly. Already I was sticky with perspiration. So anyway I was going to have a bath.

But as I approached the hostel, a strange thing happened. The rain, falling thickly, had obscured our vast building with its minuscule windows. It could be seen a bit more clearly when the showers changed direction with the gusts of wind. And once again, in the swerving and straightening showers, would descend drips from the eaves and the thudding spatter of drops from the roof of the building, and the whole hostel would suddenly become indistinct once again.

At that time I experienced a sort of vision. In that dark terrifying moment of the evening I felt that I was a spirit. Anyhow, we *are* all spirits. Is there any sign indicating anybody's presence hereabouts? No. How I've learned by heart this whole place in the course of four years! Very few of those who entered the hostel with me are still here. Here, now, meticulously avoiding stones and such impediments in the dark, I ride my bicycle to and fro. That's how thoroughly one's internalized this place. All those friends from that time — where have they gone? How many faces! Many, so many. I can recite for you a thousand names without a moment's stumbling. This is that chap, that one is this. This one that.... That fellow had stone-gray eyes, the other one was coal-dark, that chap — tall. This one from such-and-such a town, that one from that class. Thousands of events. Thousands of bodies.

I've meddled in so many encounters. Hundreds. Even the making of tea by a group of us that had gathered together — that too now seems like a happening. As many days, nights, afternoons, evenings — so many happenings. Even fumblingly locking my room and rushing to college for a class was also a happening.

I've behaved here as if all of this belonged to me. And now I must leave it all and go away. For no reason at all. Why can't I live here all my life? Why is it that a contract terminates? This library, all these buildings about me — the college buildings over there — into these buildings have vanished four whole years. My years. This way they gulp down millions of years from thousands of people's lives. Nothing remains with us. If we struggle to recall all that happened here in this place, then might one drink in the space. These trees, these rooms, these windows, the hills, the grasslands behind the Vetal Hill, and the red gunja there — the relation with all these is sundered the moment one leaves this place. When relations are formed, one doesn't know that they must later break. This place can, however, break off from us. Because our feet are not rooted in this soil. And that's why, in the first place, we are able to establish the link between our years and this place. We walk on our feet and keep intact the tally of the old places over which we walked. This is really pathetic.

It is only space that is eternal. What of years, once we die they too are ended. But one can return to a place if one becomes a spirit. I've got soaked in this rain. But beyond this, what or who am I?

Will this place vanish right now in an earthquake conjured up by my own incantations? Will grass sprout here, all these buildings having been swallowed up? NO. In that case my mind is a futile exercise, my existence itself is unreal. In the book of this space I count for nothing at all.

This will be so throughout my life — nothing that is mine has any value.

Later I entered my own room like a stranger. Donned dry clothes. All the dregs of sugar, tea, all the milk that was left I dumped into a pan and made some tea. All night long I pretended to look over my work for the final two papers.

In my last paper I answered just about two questions, stopped writing, and then stretching out my legs, just sat there idly. Everyone else was scribbling away. Asses. When the bell rang, I was out.

This is the last of Rami. In the canteen. Never did see that bald bod Khanolkar again. Did he not take any papers after that?

No.

Your're sure to bag a good first, aren't you?

Yes.

What hereafter? M.A.?

Yes.

Where will you go now?

Sangvi.

What's happened to you? Wasn't the paper good? Didn't you write well? How many questions did you answer?

Post-mortem.

What will you be after the M.A.? Lecturer?

I shall just sit at home.

Yes. Of course! It's fine for you. Only we have problems. No idea what we shall do later and where.

This is the real Rami. Very pale, white. Hardly any bosom like a woman. Inside her, those rotten lungs. Her blue, unfocussed, glintless eyes, like a statue's. Tired after writing, with those clean nails, drinking her tea with the fingers of both hands pressed about the cup. I said nothing at all.

Really, what is to become of her? That way, afterwards, really long after, whatever does happen to anybody? I've come to know what happens to everyone of us hereafter. But how can I call it knowing? Who can profit from such knowing? What's the use to Rami of my knowing this? Suppose Rami asks now — Let's set up house together. What then?

Then I would be without an answer. Nothing is at last left in my grasp. At any rate, nothing that may be any good.

I was packing my stuff. It was my custom to sell all my old notebooks to the junkman. Now this great heap will have to be kept carefully until next year. And, besides, I shall have to go to Maushi's house to dump it. But must I appear for the B.A. exam again? Yet if not, what else should I do?

What I did has not been good. What will Father say now? And Mother? And the folk in my village? Next year, it won't be *Macbeth*. I made all those futile notes. What a lovely answer I wrote on *Macbeth*. I too had the experience of sleeplessness, just like him. Now dump all this as junk.

Just then Suresh arrived there.

I went on packing, didn't say a word.

He said, You did write all the papers well — dun-a-dun — didn't you? Aren't you going to bag the prize?

I said nothing.

Sod it, what is this, Sangvikar? I am leaving today. I'll treat you to the pictures today. Then let me stand you a great dinner somewhere. Or, dinner first and then the pictures afterwards?

I don't want a thing.

We scrapped, it was my mistake. Yes. I made a mistake. Hit me with anything. But where do you think we might meet hereafter? I am not going to study anymore. One of my relations has a firm. There he...

What are you telling me all this for?

Then Suresh departed.

Come to think of it, people like Suresh are good. So long as Suresh is with me, he is of course good.

No matter if he's no more with me.

I left for home.

I did something on arrival. I had kept some childhood me mentos carefully in a cupboard at home, I threw them all out. Long ago, when Mother'd gone to the fields, I would spread my game of marbles all over the house. Sometimes I'd play a game with cowries. There were tops too. As I was absorbed in my game, Mother would return and hide under the stairs watching me. I had carefully preserved all these, for no special reason really. I threw all of that out. I only kept, again for no particular reason, one stone marble and one large dev cowrie.[54] I felt, Let them remain.

When the ground got all hot the whole day long it was sure to rain in the evening. A little grass began to sprout here and there all over the place. In one place, which had been absolutely bare until last evening, a visibly cool green sheen showed itself today.

I was myself in a different sort of anxiety. Father did not lose his temper any more, that was just terrible. Only once did he say, When I was your age, you were already born. And as for you, what is to happen to your future, we can of course see.

Mother said, Little One, if you feel better here, then forget education. As long as you feel happy that's enough.

This, as Mother said, was right.

But I wasn't happy here either. I had to listen to nonsense every day about my getting up late. Just lying about all day long. Reading a little. Yet listening to the radio all the time. All day long, all night long I would be twisting the knobs of the radio. Songs, classical music, light songs, women's forum, stories from films, English programmes — whatever happened to be playing.

Father said, It doesn't look nice in the village to have such a grown up son at home. You had better go back there. And if you don't find a room elsewhere, go and stay with Maushi. I said, I shall go only just before my exam.

Father said, No.

Then for fifteen days I refused to speak to Father.

Even Mother had had enough of my irritability. I would fret and grate, grouse and grumble about the simplest of things. She said, I'll do whatever *I* can, but I can't do too much. You'd better go. You are best here only during the holidays.

So I left home.

Four

Anyway, writing down my expenses every night was by now a long time habit. I said, It'd be better to write a diary instead. At least that would break the habit of writing accounts. But I did not manage to write in the diary every day. I did maintain one for a whole year, all the same.   Whatever else I did during this whole year, I myself can barely remember now. Still, if I'm to tell you about this year, it is, for instance, this diary.

July 1

I am fed up with these round days. I'd rather have square days, and on the way, have each corner flapping handkerchiefs. Let the dark make the path on the wasteland like Mother. Only the fringes of the day had been wet by June. The feet, as though sown into the ground. June. *A:doramatapovanadigamanam.*[1] At the end of all — m.

July 2

If one makes a resolve something is bound to come off. I got up as early as six o'clock this morning. But I felt, whatever am I going to do all day? Whole day long. Hole day. Go the whole hog day. Then I slept.

Cocoon

July 3

A row of lamps. Rowful of poles. Body in motion. What occasion, which song, roll it inside you. Don't tell a thing, sing. Everything sinks, day by day. Stop for a moment to synchronise the tones of the many things you saw this day.

July 4

I sculpt the time measured by my own ego. Let statues of my form and figure be sculpted out of every moment. Ever since I was in the cradle, sculpting on the ceiling overhead. All the epigraphs, etched, now effaced line by line. That is how I went on chanting. Whatever was uttered became sticks. And whacked into my back. The millionaires of triumph are others. I am the lord of the unreal.

July 5

Shateshu jayate shurah — one among a hundred alone is born a brave man.

July 6

Our buffalo at home died, calving. She must have remembered me as she lay dying. I used to fling before her the whole load of grass that was brought home.

July 7

Forgetting the pain of the other extremity, she was trying to tell me something. But her lips never reached my ears. This is a daily ritual. So it prevails over me even today.

July 8

The longest tale anyone can tell would cover less than one hundred years, at any rate. So why bother to tell tales?

July 15

Who is going to write this stuff every day? In a way, all bum-kum.

July 16

Lost the second umbrella also. It'll hardly do if one has to buy a new umbrella every week. The last one I'd forgotten somewhere. But this one, someone actually really *stole*. There's no dearth of small-time crooks in Poona. I shan't now buy a third umbrella. It would be best to steal someone's.

July 20
I returned dripping, soaked through. The books too got wet.

July 22
Bought an umbrella. This time second-hand. Because I might just lose it. But this one will stay with me for ever.

July 25
What does Madhu understand of all this? — Now I get one hundred and fifty rupees; when, in future, will I get two hundred — he lives on this sort of reckoning. When he left home in the morning he said, You can indulge in all these pranks because you get money from home.

July 28
Madhu had come. When he went back, he had barely enough money for his fare. I gave him ten rupees and felt great pity. The money I give does not belong to me, does it? That is Father's.

July 29
Finally I did say to him — Dear friend, you do have a bicycle. So as soon as you have mounted it, the bike will start moving. Then he actually got on his bike and left.

July 30
How can I feel so much fatigue upon rising from sleep? Who squeezes out my body so much at night?

July 31
Took an autorikshaw, so I'd reach faster. It stalled on the way. Then I had to walk after all.

August 1
There are very few secrets about any man. Every man sleeps, eats, drinks, starts pissing as soon as he is born. Who teaches him all this? One who is born has a father and a mother, he inhales and he exhales. So that means there are hardly any secret things left.

August 2
Bundi ladus. Rava ladus. L...

Cocoon

August 3

Having pegged their nets all over in the ether, her senses are lying in wait.

August 4

Old friends and older acquaintances. Someone got married, another found a job. When the boluses of the moment fly off into orbit, the pegs here do not break. They won't vanish with the mere blood-and-bone-and-flesh, flinging away their stinking skins, they won't survive it.

August 5

No matter how many swaytrees³ are emptied into it, the mud-jar does not fill.

August 6

She looked pretty so I spoke to her. Otherwise what is one going to say to a girl for a whole hour?

August 7

One visit, twenty rupees.

August 8

So many calamities have descended on me, still I haven't acquired sword-and-shield from the bazaar.

August 10

I'll forget all the organs supported by my feet, pour venom into my stomach and wipe out the patch. I'll consume wish-pies. I'm existing by covering myself with my own hide. Everything is mine alone. The seed — only that from the sire. Still, it's necessary to extend one's line. I'll overcome wish-thighs. I'll sire new sires. More kin, greater sin, that's the thing. Consuming, or defending, it's all in the hands. Pyre and fire, the offspring will look at that. Unfortunately, our ancestors were not gifted with sterility. That's why this turn and return — all because of manly sires!

August 11

Having written literature, these chaps believe they have become immortal. Immortal Cycle Mart! Sod it. Meaning, even after the sun has cooled and the Earth has broken into fragments, still their names will remain immortal.

August 15
As I began to mend the torn sleeves of my shirt, I saw the cadavers of all my old shirts. Then I flung this cadaver out of the window. Below, the floating river.

August 16
The fate-line on the left palm is missing in the right palm.

August 17
Why did he have to meet me? I told him, I am writing the M.A. exam.

August 20
Pleasure the size of a peanut, a hedge stretching like a field, music spread over like a railway station, Poona like a simile, on a yawn-sized sheet of paper an organic homily.

August 22
My eyesight's getting poorer. Need glasses of higher power. To become totally blind is the perfect stage. The forms of all things become amorphous. The forms that were once perceived easily on account of touch and hearing, they come apart here. It is then the same as twiddling with the bellybutton of an alligator in a great river of red-hot gold. Once one has seen the remainder at the end of a sum, how much farther would the zigzag motion of futile anxieties stretch? Well, then, only as far as the last digit.

August 25
I have started my study.

August 26
Cobra's eggs. Swan's eggs. Eagle's eggs.

August 30
Study only at night. During the day, reading just this and that in the library.

August 31
Some reading does get done. Time does pass.

September 1
A, B, C, D have to Eternal Fire Gone.

September 2
Says Shri Chakradhar[4] in his *sutra* —
> *Within the tiny banyan seed is the whole banyan tree with all its branches and twigs, leaves and fruits.*

Greater:
> *One's own country needs to be forsaken:*
> *One's own village needs to be forsaken:*
> *The relation of relations particularly needs to be forsaken.*

September 5
Every night we fall asleep, we forget brothers, sisters, mother and father, Mama, Maushi — all. And even as we get up our flesh clothes our minds with all these raiments. Otherwise, our souls are naked. There is no kinship in the dark.

September 10
Writers write just because paper is so cheap. Readers read. If each sheet cost one hundred thousand — tell me, who would ever write? Even then, the rich would buy paper. And, still, the generous rich person would also sell it. But who would buy?

September 11
Even the mud took prints of my feet today. Quite rightly the dice of this very body have triumphed over this very mind.

September 12
If there are numberless roarers, still one might hear them out all alone. But for me, all the others are one.

September 13
The old books in the syllabus have changed. But the new prescriptions are even more horrible. I did read' them all once. Now what *am* I going to write about them in the exam?

September 14
It isn't so easy, is it? To read the script of not-even-so-much moist compassion. To read the non-script falling off the leaves, off the ground, drip drip drip? To watch the rainy season through the

lightest of glass. Is that easy? The pageantry of showers inscribes not itself on the mind. Never wiped off — he/she/it whoever dares deny the life of the drops, I shall only tell — You would swell and swank and give up the vow So you'll soak and sink and croak in the lake below.

September 15
I wish to take some rest today.

September 25
The shores of the brows of some Dravidian eyes. Winds that wash the seas. Brimming palms that drink up the Earth.

September 27
And of course I'm not prepared to associate with anyone, am I? My old friends have all gone away. Gone outside somewhere. If they'd been here today I wouldn't have had to worry about whom to spend my time with. I give these new chaps treats — food and that. But they don't mix with me as they should. They say, You are a nuisance.

September 30
What is the profit — tiforp — of sitting for this supplementary exam in October? Anyhow I'd have to spend the next six months at home. That's why it is better not to sit at all.

October 5
Enthusiasm, ardour, verve, energy, strength, power, vigour, vitality — whoever discovered these words?

October 7
   One should just read on one's own. Without even the shadow of another.

October 10
These two look all right. I knew them before too. But they can be seen all the time in that restaurant, so nowadays I too sit with them. Both are really something special. One is a Sikh. He is, actually, enormous.

November 10
It's all the same here and at home. Here in the city, or there — people are all the same, sod 'em.

November 11

He runs a vegetable business at Kamathipura in Mumbai, the red- light place. Earlier he worked in the mess. He recognized me. Sells a hundred rupees' worth of vegetables every day. He said — At first, you know, early on, I did have some difficulty, but I did manage to settle down. Once actually a crooked vendor threatened to murder him. This chap said, I am not scared of murder. I sleep right here in my place on the pavement. Have a go. But I wasn't murdered, was I? Sod it. Just suppose someone had actually shoved a knife into him while he slept? But all said and done, these sodding chaps are dare-devils really.

November 15

This is the final visit. Let whatever has to happen to me happen. But I shan't fork out 20 rupees to you every visit. I'd rather buy books instead. Or rather eat, even.

November 16

A raja in the sheershasana, the headstand — that is really something.

November 17

Hey, what film did you see? The Greatest Bhunkus on Earth, I said.

November 20

Really heavy cramming.

November 21

Study.

November 25

Study.

November 21

I've really started on grammar with a bang. I chanted all the syllabic metres. It was great fun.

November 28

There might be somebody who'd speak only in case-endings, and another who would refuse to attach tenses to verbs.

December 4
Again the same thing.

December 5
The same.

December 7
The same.

December 10
Still three or four months to go before the exam. Let's see, by and by.

December 12
When you check out ten, you might find one that's all right. But if you only think of looking for two goofies, you are sure to find ten.

December 14
Three months have gone by. I've been reading newspapers with interest. But in the end this is just like the drained-out feeling one gets as one rises from a card game. Nothing particular has been gained. Once in a rare way, somewhere, there's a war, then for months on end, negotiations, who said what, what some bogus leaders were saying, and so on —just this. Actually, it's better to ask someone to narrate whatever happened, after an interval of every five or ten years.

December 15
I can't quite manage this rote learning. Let anyone say what they will. But of course there's no one left to say anything. It was better before, when Father used to yell and shout. I have grown up, for sure. All the same, I don't do anything at all.

December 20
I woke up at noon today. The same routine as always. Drank some tea and then read an entire magazine, including the ads in it. Then went out and had some lunch. Sat in the library till four, reading. The *Leelacharitra*[5] is great. Shri Chakradhar would sit looking at an elephant he had made out of banana peel, this is great indeed. I too must sit staring at something like that. But

I am sure to get bored. I must read all about the Mahanubhava people one after another. I scoured through all the shops in Poona yesterday. But no *Leelacharitra*. How rottenly these chaps do their business. Had some tea at four and came to my room. When my cigarettes were over, I made another trip downstairs. This is a nuisance, really. I ought to stock four hundred packets at once. But then I might smoke them all in just one day. Now my throat is already ruined. I am tired of fags. One must instantly stop whatever one gets tired of. But there's nothing else to do. I ought to have tried before to get a job in some school or something. At least time would have passed that way. But I only get up at eleven, how could I manage school? In the evening, having roamed all the streets in the cantonment, and watched the people who lie about all over the railway waiting room, back again, footing it, via the Sangam[6] and so to the Jangli Maharaj temple. The bells there were going BANG BANG BANG. I too entered the temple, on impulse. Then had my dinner and went round to those two chaps. There they were, yes. At the same table.

December 25
Did nothing at all.

December 26
Did nothing at all. Chatting at night in the restaurant.

December 28
Sunday. Sat about all day in the restaurant, listening to the radio. Today they played almost all the film songs that I like. My head became numb, like.

December 30
The bad thing about these two chaps is that they yak too much about books. How much can anybody say about books, after all? But it is good at any rate that, with this, they also speak of other things. Now, tonight, I shall sleep only after finishing that book.

December 31
Met Bhandardare.[7] I said, What, Old Chap, still doing parodies, I hope. He said, See, now I have set up a family. Now forget literature and all that. Now

My unfair love's breast for my pillow below.

Bhandardare the Great!

January 5

Those two have not been seen for a week or so. I get bored sitting there by myself. Then I returned, cursing them.

January 6

They weren't there today either, sod 'em. But what's the use of losing one's shirt like this over others? It's my own mistake that I leave my life hanging so much by others'. If there are people of congenial views, that becomes a problem, really. Yet time passes smoothly if one is among like-minded people. But this is not good. So what if I don't meet anyone? I must sort out things and manage my own time.

January 7

This too I shall manage some day, and that as well. Like the street will come to my lips the favourite line. I dare not swallow fire, but is that any reason for rejecting anyone? Are they going to start burning one as though one is a sati?[8] They do let one live on, don't they? So why need one curse anyone? But as long as that restaurant remains there, these two will also be there. Always.

January 8

That's why I grow ghostly hands. That's why I write a letter like this to Mother.

Janurary 10

He had such terrific fever. But he still wouldn't say anything to anyone. As I was casually starting to clap hands with him I felt him burning — that's how I discovered it. Otherwise, all his movements and talk, just as usual.

January 12

We must have beggars. There isn't a sense of completeness without them. Sodding luxury-loving people can't even bear to see the beggars in the streets. Nor are they content to say— move along — to the beggars that there are. Now, I had no money today, that's a different matter. But I am not ashamed to see a beggar.

And a beggar who regularly sings to a one-string fiddle, really great. What is that song, anyhow? —

This eyeless one has lost his stick,
By chance have we met the weak and the sick!

Great.

January 13

Until just the other day I used to say, So what if I got gypped in the exam, I have achieved this and that. Achieving. Sod it, achieve what? I'd better shut right up about achieving. Nobody can achieve anything, really. One must leave everything that has been achieved behind on this Earth. But at least one does achieve — money, job, some weight in society, etc., some worth among a few, a wife and all that. But by gum I have not achieved a thing like that. So what have I achieved, then — achieved? It's better not to achieve.

January 15

Was that the orbiting of invisible stars? I put on the light in fright and lay down until daybreak. It's part of my fate that I must wear this millstone of sleeplessness.

January 20

ə a : i i : u u : e ə i o ə u um aha.

January 22

Public, lick, lotus, scrotus, immutable, mutable, table.

January 25

Just suppose that you *had* passed the exam last year. So what? Then M.A. So, after that? Later at the very most some other such higher degree, etc. Then? Then a job? Then marriage? Marriage and all that, and kids? Then prestige in society, etc. Next? What next? Nothing next. It is better you exist like this. At least some such thing you have already come to understand. One time or other, later, you will have to do all these things. Even Lord Shri Krishna himself says so. But one must first comprehend that, if nothing is accomplished before that, one finds a great big hellhole out of which one can't climb. From that point of view, you are better off, really, as you are.

January 26

In the end Govinda did become a pukka lecturer. One lecturer died the other day. Gune of course argued that it was a time of emergency and all that, and naturally got Govinda appointed. Met him today. He said — How awful I felt, Sangvikar, when sir passed away. I said, No more, sod it. The boss is dead, Long Live Govinda. His existence has acquired meaning, the poor thing.

February 1

February has arrived. I must really push on hard with my study.

February 10

I just can't see the end of this study.

February 15

Can't seem to get this study done. Besides, this month has twenty eight days.

February 16

He writes, This life is meant to be lived. Now who on Earth would say it is meant for a walking tour, anyhow? Let whoever wants to write, write. I mustn't pay heed to that.

February 17

Right here, below, he was looking for a rupee note, which he had lost. Two or three others gathered, and joined the search. I was there too. Then one said, Take a good look in your pocket. Then it turned out that the note was inside his pocket, safe. That chap seemed jolly honest. He said, immediately, Yes, yes, it's in the pocket.

February 20

Bought five new volumes of poetry. One or two poems are all right. Occasionly, a few lines seem penetrating. I copied those.

February 21

I have two hundred rupees left. Still, I have written asking that another two hundred should be sent.

February 22

Sod it, the Short Essay, alias the Light, Personal Essay. What is one to say in the exam? I really ought to have taken the exam last year.

Every book this year is a punishment. But these punishments are simple enough. If death is inflicted upon me, by hanging, relief! Not that sort of punishment here. There's no death sentence in exams. Only rigorous imprisonment. Write once again. New, ever new books. No death.

February 23

I'd met her before at Gune's. New critic. Today she sat yakking with me about some useless things. She writes pointless criticism in journals. All the time, Literature is not this, Literature is not that, and, In literature one must preserve allegiance to felt experience. Sod it. what the heck is 'literature' anyway? IS it just a single thing? The novel, poetry, drama, all dumped into a sack amount to literature. The business of critics is astonishing. *She* gave me tea. But I did the listening part.

February 28

March already. Gotta start study. Must. If you *won't* you *are* a fool. Must stop chatting with those two in the restaurant until late at night. All the same they are not always to be found there. A long and idle wait for those two until I get headaches. Cup of tea after cup of tea. Packet after packet of fags.

March 1

I really must do something. I must suddenly achieve something and shed the ash that covers my flesh. Otherwise, it will be proof that I possess no intelligence.

March 5

At the height of the midday sun the branches of trees nodded, yes... no. I am going to accept the reality of everything once again. Beginning, middle, end — the lot.

March 7

Every lover must kill his beloved and having made a drum out of her hide, sing love songs to its beat. Otherwise, plain love is good enough.

March 8

In the city each one lives for some objective. Let the bus arrive a shade late, sod 'em, all begin to shuffle and shift and complain,

Cocoon

curse the administration — these people are the limit. All the more so in Poona. This is not so as yet in the villages, that is great. There, even if the motor arrives two hours late, no harm done. And these people, covered in powder and cream, waiting for their bus, taking their place in the queue in good order.

March 10

Are these books fit for a B.A.? Bachelor of Arts.

March 11

I did meet Dr. Gune. Do drop in, he says.

March 12

Are you a fool? You still don't take things seriously. The whole year is gone, and yet.

March 13

I must stop this magazine. They print anything at all, sod'em. This time there's an out and out erotic story. And that too written in a phoney artistic intricate roundabout style for no good reason. In the modern style and all that. But then, what's wrong with magazines with pictures of naked women? At least they do not drum up their commitment to high art. I'll continue to subscribe to this weekly, though. If nothing else, in it appears a list of donors to the Saney Guruji Fund. It is there that I learned where Suresh is these days. Suresh. Let him be where he might.

March 15

If one must write a novel, it has to be like this! Just as fat, and as hollow. But if there is romance in it, it is such a bore. And what is the conclusion, pray? That the gallant hero and the heroine marry. What are his other fifty novels like? I must see this chap, once, really. His bungalow is on my way. It's all right that I'd read it for my exam. Still, there must be those who'd read it just for pleasure.

March 16

If anyone must write poetry, it is this worthy! He must have listed all sorts of emotions before starting his composition. Verbs he only dumps somewhere in the middle of some of the lines. The rest is endless sentence after sentence. And aren't his lines bloody long — from this side of the page to the other. It reads like a novel. Sheer nuisance. Nuisance. Sod it, this is like living in a necropolis. Last year when no such book was on the course, I didn't take the exam, wretched bright spark that I am.

March 20

Those two came over to my room. Why you don't come to the cafe now, they said. I said, And what about those days when you don't come and I get bored stiff sitting all alone? Upon this they thumped each other and said, Forget all that. Then in English, "Do visit us." I am not free now, for these things. I might have gone every day, otherwise. But I have made it a habit to live just for myself. Even if everyone else were to die, I ought to be able to survive. But how to convey this to these two chaps? Today, at least, because they insisted, I sat there till 11 o'clock. After many days, chatting like this. That's why I didn't feel bad afterwards about the time wasted. But I must not waste nights like this.

March 25

My study is almost done. Once in a way I also memorise things. But I can't manage too much of that. Through the window of the house next door I see all sorts of unmentionable silhouettes. It does not feel bad, while one is watching them. But it isn't nice really. The landlord says, last month there was too big a bill for electricity. You study at night and sleep during the day. That passes, though, because the landlord's son is a friend of mine. But it is not nice

March 30

After eight more days, the exam. This year, once the mucky exam is over, I shall feel liberated. At any rate, I guess, for the M.A. one doesn't have to study such muck.

April 15

What does it mean when someone becomes a B.A.? It means, for four college years, just a few months before each exam, he studies for a total of five or six months. What do the rest of the months signify? Just sit in the classroom. Fall in love. Make notes, keep them ready for the fortnight just before the exam. All humbug. But four days had hardly passed after my exam began when I lost patience and let the stuffing come out of myself. That was quite wrong, I agree. My papers hadn't gone badly until today. But my brain seems to whirl, it's gone crazy. Don't feel like reading anything. Tomorrow, my hand will refuse to move when I write. Better go to sleep now, and when I get up in the morning, I'll go and see *Suddenly Last Summer* at Alka cinema. No more complications.

April 16

I *am* an ass. For no reason at all, extended my anxiety again by a year. So what if the prescribed books are useless. It is true one is bound to feel bored just looking at these books, but one doesn't have to feel affection for their writers, does one? One can scrawl any old stuff for twenty or twenty-five pages about them. That's easy. How can there be only likeable books in Marathi and English? Ass. Ass. Ass.

April 17

It'd make more sense to get into the spirit of study just a month before the exam, but I won't have that, not me. This — what? — this can be written easily. This author is a fool, of course — why take any trouble over him? — and so on. And my interest in a thousand distracting matters. When the exam was only a fortnight away I went to a music concert, because it was a rare performance. When I heard two or three ragas, my mind became quite ecstatic. But when I returned at dawn, all over the street —just this mist, spilling over. Who needs a mist on such an occasion? But there it was. So thick that even street lamps looked dim. Sod it. And I had felt at that time, that music is the language of the soul. Soul. Sod it. Soul, the veritable soul. Time and time again, questions about death. Nothing very special really, but the same predictable thoughts. At least during exams one ought to put aside such asinine reckoning. I could have spent whole days after the exam, contemplating death over a cup of tea. Ass. And the Poona folk are keen on Acquisition of Knowledge. Even the discourses of J. Krishnamurti[9] I heard exactly at that time. Unfailingly. For eight days. Actually such discourses too simply must occur in the summer. At exam time. I spent the entire Diwali holiday just lying about in my room; wandering about here and there like a loafer. But at those times no special programmes would be organized. Just had to come to this stupid Poona, hadn't I. Goodness knows how many more years I shall have to stay here.

April 20

It must have been predetermined that all this would happen to me. Now why this futile headscratching? Instead, I'd better go to *Suddenly Last Summer* again tomorrow morning, and to *Legend of the Lost* in the evening. At least those six hours would pass thus. I'd better spend the rest of the time outside also, thinking about what I might do hereafter. What hereafter? After. What is after? There's nothing after. But thinking about this is for tomorrow, sitting down properly for the task.

April 22

Moropant — 1729 to 1794
Soren Kierkegaard — 1813 to 1855
Fyodor Mikhailovich Dostoevsky — 1821 to 1881
Friedrich Nietzsche — 15 October 1844 to 25 August 1900
Hari Narayan Apte — 8 March 1864 to 3 March 1919
Our Grandpa — 1868 to 1918
Those two chaps —
The first one — 7 February 1935 to date
The brother of the second — 5 May 1936 to date
Self—5 May 1938 to date.

April 25

As yet nothing has been communicated to those at home. The exam is still going on. But why wait here any longer? Better go home. Where else can I go? In the end, home is mine.

Then via Sangvi I came to Mumbai. In this world everyone must have at least one friend or so in Mumbai. Moreover, such a friend must be also well-off. Whenever he came to Poona, Madhu would say to me, Why don't you come to Mumbai, so what if you lack particular reason? I used to think that since he stayed with me, he *would* say this as a formality. But that was not the case.

From Sangvi I wrote to him, that my situation was thus. His reply came immediately — Somehow I should collect enough money for my fare and get down at Byculla station. Rest when we meet.

I took all the money I had and travelled directly to Byculla.

He had written, At ten I shall meet you under the clock. If I am not able to manage, come to my school, which you can tell by such and such signs.

When I reached it was only 8 o'clock. Mumbai appeared to be bustling with enthusiasm in the morning. So I felt bad. But, on the same bench on which I sat waiting for Madhu, a porter lay down, his feet towards me. Then I shuffled and shifted towards one end. So then the porter stretched his legs out further and began to slumber in comfort. Then I rose. Seeing that the whole bench was free, the porter really spread his legs out freely.

Madhu did come at ten.
He said, Do you see this girl eating the blood-red ice-fruit? She shoves the whole stick into her mouth. And then takes it out again. A... ha!
I said, Find me a job.
He asked, You think this is Sangvi, do you?
Madhu showed me his school. Said, Now you do what you like until 5 o'clock.
I said, Meaning? Whatever can I do?
He said, Whatever.

I wandered about Mumbai.

One pan-seller was beating his brother, angrily — four annas less in one rupee? Four annas? I brought you to Mumbai — just a useless addition to Mumbai crowds, and he went on beating him him mercilessly.

One bootblack also gulled me.

Feeling sheepish, therefore, I came back to the school and sat there in the teachers' room until 5 o'clock. There, quite grown up women were chatting with each other — No one else is such a naughty girl as you! One woman teacher was saying to another. But one or two of them were beautiful.

At five Madhu and I came to his room at Mahalakshmi. I said, Madhu, I shan't accept money from my family. I shall sit for the exam quite properly this year, work at least until March and also study.

He said, Leave aside study. First think about getting a job. You see my condition, don't you? It's two years since I left the Inter class. I am working on the basis of my Hindi teaching certificate. But I cannot manage B.A. level Hindi externally. So, either work, or else accept money from your family and write the exam properly.

But his advice was all wrong. I said, You see if you can find a job for me. I don't want anything else.

You'll get a job. But then you'll not manage the exam.

I'll manage. I've already finished my study. It's just that I didn't want to sit for the exam. Do you want to find me a job or not?

In that case you should take even more money from home. See, a B.A.-failed chap does not earn much. Don't get wrong-headed notions.

That was all that happened that day. Then I gave up pursuing Madhu for a job.

Next day, dressing with some care, I went to one of our heavyweight relations. He was my Mother's cousin. That is, her second cousin, quite a close uncle, you might say. This Mama of mine could easily find jobs for just about anyone. So he was sure to find me one too. But I had to think things through as to why I needed this job, to convince him.

Mami, his wife, was of course at home. She said, Why didn't you come here to stay?

I said, I was going to come straight here, but my friend pressed me really hard.

I thought, I might as well open the topic of a job with her. That way, when Mama returned in the evening it might go easier.

I said, When will Mama come back?

She said, He comes home at six.

From just this much she must've gathered that I had come for a job. But she said, Do you have some business with him?

So I too said, Not really. Just asked.

In the afternoon she asked a young chap my age to come by and sit with me. This chap's face was so cruel that I thought, This chap too must be unemployed. I asked, What do you do?

I don't do anything at all.

Then he voiced his view about the entire world — It is not as though one finds satisfaction in doing a job and earning money. It is better to wander about without. Take all the scolding your father dishes out in the evenings. And while away the whole day reading the newspaper.

He said, further, I don't read a lot. But whatever I do read I read rather intensely.

He had read all of Tolstoy.

Then, so as to initiate some discussion, I said, I have read only *War and Peace*.

That must have been the abridged edition.

Then, you mean to say you have read all of his novels whole?
Of course.

Thereafter I didn't say much to him. But to read in that fashion one must be either unemployed or probably a most persevering person.

Cocoon

In the evening, Mama came home.

But even after dinner was over I didn't know how to broach the topic of a job.

So he thought I must be intending to sleep there and they got everything ready for me to stay over. Now I knew I wouldn't be able to get up until ten next morning. So it'd be better to relieve him right now — so, a little scared, I mentioned the point.

At this time the entire discussion took place in low tones. First Mama said, You, and a job? What for?

I said, I am tired of gobbling up money without earning it. I want the experience.

Well, this noble spirit is not such a good idea. It's fine in America but in our country even the really down-and-out people can hardly find work. So why should someone like you struggle? Actually, you should spend your money in comfort. Write your exams seven times, if one try isn't enough. Go abroad — instead, what is this crazy idea you have invented?

I said, I want a job. From the first of next month.

At last he said, But why are you in such a rush? I shall find a job which will make the least demands on you. Everything is possible for me. Just wait for another month.

Then he quizzed me, thoroughly — Morning job, or evening? At the harbour or in the port office? etc. And he also said, Next month you'll have to come there once. My assistant interviews candidates. Then next month, or at any rate no later than the month after, come and join us permanently. Will you now go to Poona in the meantime?

Then at 10 o'clock I returned to Madhu's, and told him everything. I was going to get a job. I was to work till March and then write a solid exam in April. That night, I carefully worked out a schedule for the entire year.

When I woke up, Madhu had long been gone. This day too I spent wandering about. I wanted to go to one or two other relations also, but thought, Why go at this awkward time in the afternoon? So I went to J.J. Hospital instead to meet a doctor from our village.

Long after I'd become really tired footing it around many of the hospital department, at last I traced his presence and stated his name. I was allowed into a ward. Inside, the sick were lying quietly on cots. When I had proceeded quite far I saw the doctor. Along with two or three other doctors he was attending on a patient lying on his back. Besides, it was so sweltering in there that I came right out again.

There was a bench outside. I flopped down on it, with my legs stretched out before me.

To my left there was a long queue. One at a time, people moved forward and slipped a chit into a window. There was no way to tell who was on the other side or what he might be doing. After a long while from inside would emerge fifteen or twenty little packets or a bottle or some such thing, through the hole in the window. Then the next in line would move ahead. My watchful eye was also on the doctor's door on the right. Someone would come out. And the door would swing backwards and forwards before it finally shut slowly. But our doctor wouldn't come out.

Looking alternately at the queue and the door without pause made my eyes ache.

Still, it was good that the hall had a high ceiling, very long and wide. Constant little whisperings. The shuffling of feet and sounds of shoes made the hall so dreadful that I felt — How would it sound if I were to shout koooooooook? Because of this insensitive hiss-whisper, perhaps all the patients inside would surely die.

Besides, that queue, bent zigzag, remained just as long as it ever was. Of course one by one people in the queue were leaving. And yet I couldn't make out where new ones were coming in from.

Some time later I happened to focus on a thin bony quiet girl of about ten or twelve. That is how I found out that the queue was at least definitely moving forward.

That girl became lost in a crook of the zigzag queue.

Then later for a long time her loose schoolgirl frock alone could be seen. Now after some eight or ten people had gone by, it would be her turn. But behind her the queue was as long as ever.

But, naturally, this girl hadn't come all by herself. Constantly her father or uncle or whoever it was would approach her, say a few words and move aside, sit on a bench before me, do this or that in some other place, look at photos and such on the walls and would again come by her and go away. This chap, her father or uncle or whoever, was dark like her and handsome. Both their clothes were really cheap. He wore very well polished, splayed, old shoes, while on her feet, beneath thin straight legs sticking out below her frock, were plastic chappals. In the man's hand was something like a fat register or file, or something.

As one by one the people went forward the girl advanced beyond the turn in the zigzag — on her cheek and neck I saw a distinct, continuous four-inch long patch of leucoderma. Then I did not take my eyes off that girl.

Shuffling, shuffling forward, gradually she came close to me on my left, just two steps away from me. Standing up straight. Interested in nothing at all.

Now her father or uncle or whoever stationed himself beside her constantly. I continued to watch everything from my proximity. She came really close to the window. Then, shoving her aside, in her place stood her father.

That girl stood at attention on the other side of the queue.

Now it was this chap's turn. He handed in a chit through the window. She was still standing by. Only once did she move her hand and scratch her nose, once again letting her arm slide downwards.

Taking the packets given from inside the man stood before me. He wrapped them in a hankie and signalled to the girl on the other side. She broke through the queue and came across to our side.

Then they began to walk away.

Just then out of the file or register the man held, slipped a sheet of paper. And swaying and swinging from side to side, it fell to the floor. He hadn't noticed this. I quickly gathered my legs in. In the meantime the girl had bent down gently, retrieved the paper and handed it back to the man. Then she went out of the hall after him.

Once she was gone I couldn't bear to look at that queue. The whole queue stood as packed as ever. Not even by the smallest sign could one distinguish a single individual. I felt so drained that it was just as well that I didn't meet my doctor friend. Still I just took a peek inside — standing by a table, I saw three or four doctors chatting. Having noticed me, our doctor said, Hallo. Then in English, "Meet my friends."

Then he took me to the doctor's clean canteen and made me eat and drink my fill. He said, If you'd like it, I also have some brandy.

After that I came back to Madhu's. Madhu and I went out to the sea for a walk. It must be absolutely gorgeous to commit suicide in this sea. Madhu said, Then fish would probably eat you up. Still, as one dies, it must be more beautiful to die in water than in the air.

We sat for a long time. Then Madhu had to take a tuition. I returned directly by train to his room.

There weren't too many people in the train. Beside me sat a greasy sort of chap. From his bag he took out a new bottle of attar. After having stared carefully at the label, colour of the bottle, etc., he began to glare at me as though he disap- proved of my staring at him. Then he broke the seal, put a little attar on his hankie and closed the bottle again. Sniffing at the hankie, he again made as if to look at me. Once again he opened the bottle, tipped it over his thumb. And stretching his thumb towards me he rubbed a bit of the attar on the back of my hand. He said —

It's quite good. Then he got off at the next station.

Later I saw, in the wallet of the chap in shorts sitting across from me, a photo of a beautiful actress.

Cocoon

I got off at Mahalakshmi. Right outside a chap with a topi said to me, Do you have five-ten paise? I only registered this after I had gone past him. I turned back, counting the loose change in my pocket. Taking out four annas I started to look for the man under the topi. But in the crowd there wasn't a single topiwala. I took a look outside also. There was no one there really.

I bought some bhel with the four annas. Eating it as I walked, I returned to Madhu's room. And lying down in bed I thought, There's no vital force in my life.

I am only just starting to appreciate the importance of money. I had always been peeved about it. I went about — in this twentieth century — when I had money. But I've never man-aged without it. Therefore, I *shall* work this year. But there's as yet two or three months to go before the job comes along. Whatever shall I do until then? I shall go to Poona. But what about money until then? That is the question.

I'll need at least a hundred and fifty or so. I shall certainly not stay with Maushi. One hundred and fifty. Madhu would not have so much money to spare. I am going to a relation tomorrow, so I'd better ask for it there.

As soon as he returned, Madhu went to bed. He only said, Where did you eat?

I said, In Fort.

I got up only late in the afternoon the next day. Didn't know what I should do. I'd not had a bath since coming here. The tap ran dry here quite early in the morning.

Using some water from the bucket Madhu had filled I washed my face, etc. And in the bright sunshine I went to Mahalakshmi. As it happened, at that time no train was scheduled to appear. It was very hot. Behind me the tea stall man stood with his back to me. I finished my tea and put the money for it in the saucer. Even that cup and saucer he retrieved by twisting his arm out behind him. A crippled old woman was begging in a shrill sort of voice. She was just about under my feet. Someone might think that this was part of a theatrical performance.

After quite some time I saw a train approaching from afar. I got ready to board it. But it went on without stopping — khadad khadad. The people standing in it went right by us, watching this performance of the cripple and me. And then, only the cripple woman and I were left.

I asked my relation for some money. Fortunately, because it was Saturday, I found him at home. I was going to ask for a hundred and fifty. But then I suddenly blurted out — I want four hundred. Right away he took out the money and gave it to me. Immediately, telling him that I'd already had dinner, I came back to Madhu's.

On the way I had a big meal.

Madhu still hadn't returned to the room. Anyhow, I was only sleeping at Madhu's, these past two or three nights. As soon as he came back at night he'd fall asleep. I'd begun to hate Madhu. He'd said, On Saturday and Sunday we shall go out a lot. It was still two hours short of his arrival. I packed my trunk. Without even writing a note or anything for Madhu, I locked the room and slipped his key inside, and set off for Poona.

After some six weeks or so, I would say Ram Ram to Poona too, so I was very pleased. Poona is no paradise but a few peo-ple do consider it so. But in these two months I studied like the Shaitan[10] himself. Once I got stuck in that job in Mumbai, I may not be able to study much. It would be better to get everything done now. So

Cocoon

I bought a copy of the syllabus and all the new books immediately. Read them through the nights in two weeks. Whatever notes I needed to make I made in the library during the day.

And yet there was no letter forthcoming from Mumbai. I began to get anxious.

At last came two letters.

The first — from home. Asking, Is this, your address, correct? You left home ill-advisedly. You don't understand how in our heart of hearts we love you. The past two months have been awful for us. So that no one should come to know about this in our village, we have been silent, quietly waiting for your letter. When we got a letter from Mama saheb, at least we knew you were all right. But why did you go to him for a job? Why do you need that kind of work? Have we ever grumbled about giving you money? But you really oughtn't to have taken money from the Ingles. We've already sent back their four hundred. Let us know if you need more money yourself. This *is* your address, isn't it? We wore ourselves out sending long, long letters to you at different addresses. That's why this letter is so short.

Then, next, a letter from Mama — I had located a job for you. However, your father has, instead, found fault with me, and he insists that I am not to involve you in jobs and such.

Then for a whole month I did nothing at all.

Besides, between then and then, unexpectedly, I ran into Nana and Maushi in the street. Right there, in the broad public street they bestowed recriminations upon me. When did you come to Poona? they said. Where are you staying? You can't even manage to drop in at our place, can you? And here your father and mother have been writing us long, long letters, persistently blaming us, saying, that we didn't look after you well enough. Even though you were in Poona, they say, you didn't instruct our son to behave in the proper way. Now look, you aren't a baby, are you, to carry on like this? You are a fool. It doesn't matter at all if you don't come to us. The house is for those who wish to come there, and the door is always open for those who wish to leave. You are a vagabond. Such a son hadn't been born in our clan for the past fifty-six generations. And, besides, you go about with a packet of cigarettes in your pocket.

Mean to say, my job idea remained dangling in mid-air. I'm not going to be able to do anything out of the way. Go where I might, my home gets in the way. My feet are pretty thoroughly stuck in our home. I'm the only son.

Then I started to go to the doctor regularly. Started taking injections. The doctor said, Inside one year I shall make you all right. But you must take regular treatment. I started to take daily doses of medicine. After coming down from the doctor's clinic, I would go into a high class restaurant and sit there listening to recorded music and eating any old thing. Giving waiters whopping big tips. I thought — What the heck does anything matter? Just as long as one's being is comfortable, there the matter ends.

But it was odd, strange, this flaunting avowal of my happiness. For one thing, I never did get over my habit of going to bed late. And moreover I was doing all this for others. What I might do for myself I never did quite discover, in spite of much pondering.

So what else could I do? This is a miserable country — there's nothing for the youth here to do. Everything is decrepit. And even the youth here are like me. Now, if one could quickly progress to old age there might be some sort of happiness. If I get sucked into youth and suchlike muddles, there's sure to be a problem. Mean to say, I did have to be born in this very country, didn't I?

What's more, this whole Earth itself is wretched. There's a set code, from time immemorial, that youth here must achieve something. But no matter what you do or get, you are only left with old age for profit in the end.

In the last holidays I had thought, Now I shall stop all this nonsense. It's best to get right outside anything. Now, when one feels suffocated, one must get out.

But actually, let all this go into cold storage. Face the stupid university degree business for the rest of the year again.

But I spent the whole year in comfort. Never really studied. Did whatever, whatsoever I felt like doing. Wandering about, roaming around, sitting in restaurants for four, five hours at a time, going to the pictures whenever I felt like it, making forays to hill stations — Mahabaleshwar, Matheran, and such — alone or with somebody like Pai.

This Pai — my new friend. Stays at the same lodge, right next to me. Earns three hundred a month. And spends it all. Dresses properly and all that. Eats and drinks on time, singing lessons every day, and ready to go out with me on a jaunt any time at all. There's nothing wrong in that. He behaves like a friend with me, doesn't he? Enough, then. If our entire society were made of such people no one would become a nuisance to anyone else.

On the debit side, however, there was one thing about Pai that rather irked me. He *would* womanise. I never said a thing about this to him. I never knocked on his door when it was closed. If, when I was climbing up the stairs, some girl was coming down with him, at any odd time of night, I never observed her carefully. Just said hallo to Pai and went right up to my own room.

Every day Pai would have a new girl with him. Once, even a pretty respectable girl who had been my classmate.

Just once I really did lose my temper with Pai.

I came back to my room at ten that night. Opened the door. Just then Pai climbed up the stairs. Behind him, close — two girls. Both rather young, good looking. Pai came towards me, but they stayed there on the stairs.

Pai said, Sangvikar, please do me a favour. You see the one in the red skirt — no, not the one with the bobbed hair, the other one — take her to your room and just sit with her. I shall take only the other one.

Whatever do you mean, Mr. Pai?

Hey, the one in the bob is willing to come along. But the other one says, What shall I do meanwhile? That's why, you — keep her for a time in your room. Do *something*!

No. Sorry, Pai.

And entering my room I shut the door. Those two were staring at us in great curiosity. I thus let Pai's quarry get away. Pai had managed to get these two schoolgirls after great effort. But they were so skittish that they were not willing to part from each other.

Later that night Pai said to me, Sangvikar, you were right, too. But I still say you are a card!

Bundi was a woman in the real sense. Complexion, face, fingers, eyes, bosom, neck, all of it woman. Really, the bounteous one.

She herself said, I know you... and so on. We'd first met at such and such a place... now that Deshpande is in Delhi...how highly he speaks of you, great, and so on.

I said, Deshpande is a ninny.

She said, Exactly!

She herself asked, Where are you off to?

I said, Now, having perused the *Dnyaneshwari* for such a long time, surely one must have some tea.

I merely had to ask and she instantly came with me.

One thing about her, ceaseless chattering. I thought, she just needed someone to listen to her, that's why she chased me. On many occasions she has caught me sitting by myself in the canteen. But, still, she was a bit much, really.

In sum, all the same, because of her I managed not to get bored. She had such great stores of ever new stories, yes! What some political leader had uttered the other day; then some private stuff concerning him. What someone thought of such and such a book. And a good many visits to the cinema, too. From her brothers she would get passes to cinemas. Sometimes, when she had two, she'd say to me, Come along. Then yours truly would say — I've seen it already. And then I would rush to make sure I saw the film.

Bundi told me about one film being very good. She said, You have got to see it. About children from one house. Possessed by ghosts. Who do all sorts of marvellous things. Their governess ferrets out the ghosts. On a terrace she first sees a faintly visible ghost. With a jacket on, and a square face. Up above there are numerous birds, and beyond them — blazing sun. Her eyes are dazzled. The figure of the ghost, most blurred. Then, when the woman runs up to the terrace, what does she see — only hundreds of pigeons and their hum. This shot is surpassingly lovely. You must see it.

I went and saw that film. But I sat there watching out most carefully for the shot of the appearance of the ghost she had described to me. And, really — the description she had given me, terrific.

I met Bundi later. But she said nothing about that film.

This time the latest —

Sangvikar, yesterday, see, a funny thing happened. I mean, she said, our landlord's pet monkey Nanya is usually tethered. I started to go to college. On an impulse I held out my bicycle key to him. So then he quickly flapped his hand over and grabbed the key, and he swallowed it. I thought, Now the key's gone. Now who is going to walk all the way to the college? Babu picked up my bike and took it to the key-wala. When the landlord came home, we fought with him over the monkey. He said, First fetch a loaf of bread. Then, holding the loaf out to him he said — Nanya, the key! Quickly then Nanya took the key out of some place in his mouth, put it on the ground and ate the bread. Now we have two bicycle keys!

Bundi was really fond of telling such strange tales.

Once she said, I've brought two cinema passes. Today we really must go together.

I said, No.

She said, Then at least for a long walk, or something?

I said, No.

Turning her head to a side coyly, she said — The weather is so lovely today.

I said, Yes.

So, let's go, shall we?

I was watching all her shenanigans. I lit a fresh cigarette. She said softly in my ear, Now enough of that.

She said softly in my ear, Now enough of that. Then holding the cigarette carefully, I inflicted a nice little burn on her hand.

Rubbing at the ash stuck to it with her other hand, she said Shhh... Brute!

All those around us were of course watching all this. I thought, Now she's sure to hit me. But wordlessly she picked up the key from the table and went away.

After that I came to my room. Everything had become an unbearable burden. Bundi was really good. But I was, myself, terribly — this thing. The tales of Bundi were done.

Among other things my main hobby this year was to insult — phut-a-phut — my old friends whenever I met them, to blast them off. All these old friends were bums. One old friend began telling me happily that he'd found a job. He said, Come, I'll treat you to tea. I said, No, I don't want tea and that. What do you think his work was at the office — to check whether entries from one ledger had been properly transferred to another or not. If the transfer was correct, to initial the page and proceed to examine the next page in just the same way. So what if such chaps happen to be old friends?

I said to another, Come to my room. Then we shall talk. Actually, I don't particularly want you to come, but I just said that, a formality, you know.

Because of all this, ceased forever my meetings with no account people who asked me — What are you doing nowadays? At best, one could just do namaskar and go one's own way. No more.

Pai is friend enough for me. Which is your home town? Your language? What have you studied, are you a student, what are you going to do afterwards, what has some scope for employment these days — none of this nonsense. This is the genuine, sweet life of the city. At the lodge — we live side by side, don't we? So we should stay friends. Who needs other useless complications?

In contrast, if I meet Tambe, he bugs the heck out of me by recalling old memories. Once in a way he also shows me his poems. Takes me to his room and reads them to me. Also reads out to me his diary in which anything at all may be qualified by the adjective "immortal." That "immortal" evening.

I remember that "immortal" hostel. Those "immortal" nights there.

Sod it. It's actually after listening to his diary that I gave up writing in my own. Sod it — the stringing of petty words on a line, like narcissistic staring in the mirror, recalling and reviving every night, whatever happened during the day.

But I live with it all. At least I must tolerate Tambe's stuff. I can't flick off Tambe like the others. In fact Suresh was better. But only in comparison. Never a letter even after that. Didn't even meet me when he came to Poona. That's good, really. However, he did meet Tambe. But not by a word did he ask Tambe about me.

It is our misfortune that people keep boys of the same age all together somewhere in a college, wash their hands off them, and let them survive how they might. Then it is certain that, later, one would meet that silly Desai, as a friend, in the street — who says, I wish to become an M.A.-LL.B. And Deshpande, who used to invite me home to dinner and then conduct a fundamental discussion on literature, is bound to ask me over again whenever he happened to pop into Poona. Those two chaps in the cafe did better than this. They sat with me till 11 o'clock at night, when friends were becoming increasingly scarce. Of the two, that Sardarji was simply super. Long live Kapoor!

But all this went on only until February. As I was already fed up with all this tramping and roaming about, I set to work on my studies. I thought — How many times am I to write the same exam? I shall try this year too, if possible, take all the papers at once. I mustn't think too much about the exam.If one thinks in advance about such things one feels trapped.Therefore, better not get into the old traps of time-tables, and decisions about when to finish studying for which paper — none of that. Push on just the way one can manage. There is a rock in one's hand, isn't there? Then one is bound to drop it some time or other. So what's the point in moving back and forth — That's one of Father's pet remarks. Let me grab hold of that rock, then see what I can do.

One night, some time before the exam, I memorised the whole answer to a question. So, terribly fed up, I left my room. There was of course greater boredom outside in the dark. On the radio, in the restaurant was playing an intermi- nable film song, one that covers both sides of a disk. First, She would say — Don't you go, leaving me all alone. Or some such thing. Then He would say — Don't you go, leaving me all alone. Then they'd both sing together — Don't you go leaving me all alone. Or some such thing. Then I came back quickly to my room, lay down and started reading.

In my matriculation year Mother would make tea for me. I felt like re-living that. Mother makes lovely tea. The old house then was really wonderful. At eleven or twelve at night, done with her first spell of deep sleep, she'd get up to make tea for me. And, many a time, even while the tea was still on the mud stove she would nod off again. I'd find that really funny. Meantime I would wash my tumbler and put it before her. That's how I studied for my matric.

Just then I felt a drugged sleep come over me. I hardly had time to lift my finger out of the book.

The lamp kept burning all night. I doused it only after getting up in the morning. Then, seeing how lovely the atmosphere was I fell back into blissful slumber.

This time I didn't struggle too much for the exam. I'd write something for three hours, my mind at peace. I didn't estimate, after returning to the lodge, how many marks I might get.No postmortem. No Rami. Even though I tried, this time I didn't find anyone like Khanolkar in the exam. Perhaps such gentlemen rarely sit for such exams. But I really had been fortunate that time. By good fortune, my seat happened to be right in the middle of the hall this year.

Before this, I used to find my seat in all sorts of peculiar places. Once it was right in the front of the row, in a corner. Before me stood a huge big wall. To my right too there was a wall. I had thought — Do I have to bang my head against this wall before me?

Once my seat was on a bench placed sideways by the window. So then as early as four o'clock the sun would stream in all over me. And of course, the exam was naturally in hot April. My whole brain felt it would crack. If I asked them to shut the window, it'd block the ventilation. Steaming perspiration all over, then. Besides, just at this time, as I was writing my own paper I felt that a chap to my left facing me was staring at me all the time, because of the glare of the sun on his glasses. But why would he stare at me, abandoning his own paper? Busy with thoughts such as these I hadn't got down to writing my paper well to the end of the fixed hour. I would suddenly dart a glance at him, at which times he would be quietly writing in his paper. But, in sum, I couldn't concentrate.

As a matter of fact, last time, there was in front of me the seat of a rolypoly married girl. Perhaps during those days of the exam, she didn't find time to wash her hair and such, or perhaps her husband hadn't even noticed this, so from her bushy hair would waft up a monstrously strong hairy stink.

But this time I was placed in the middle of the four straight up and down rows. No stink from anyone, nor a wall before me. Still, it was really terribly hot. That's why, I actually took off my own shirt and wrote my afternoon papers clad only in my undershirt.

Later someone did laugh at this. But all these chaps were inexperienced novices. Who was to know who's who? Besides, even in the Ajanta caves Pulakeshi or some such emperor can actually be seen sitting bare-bellied with even some foreign emissaries in his durbar. Who would write exams with their shirt tucked into their trousers in the hot April afternoon? Let those who would, do so.

Then when the exam was quite done, I put an end to this saturnine spell that had dogged me for years by saying — This is the last exam, let me pass or not pass, but this shall be the last. Now I shall spend the whole of my remaining existence at home. Won't even think of Poona. And so I left Poona. Forever. For home.

FIVE

I came home.

Drawing littlest Nali close to him Father said, If in this one's place we'd had a boy, our hearts wouldn't have got tangled in a son like you, a home-wrecker.

Mother said, Our house feeds fifteen, twenty people quite easily. A son of my own womb is hardly a burden. But I don't wish to put up with your irritable temper.

Grandma said, Pandoba, I can't quite reckon how many years you've been studying. What have you become, now you're back? The farmhands said, Now this year will be spent at home, will it?

I thought, The less heed I pay to my home the better for me.

If someone in our village made mocking inquiries, I would tell them — There one must eat rice and chapati every day. I can't manage without bhakri myself.

Or — Those people live even on the second or third floor, sod'em. Who'd live in that sort of a city?

Seeing that I was sitting sort of numbly, sometimes Mother would say, What does this mean, that our guest is sitting alone there, and you are sitting here?

What will I do, sitting there?

Then Mother — Ask him something about his place. Argue about something. Or — Do your nails. Have you noticed how long they've grown?

During that time a wireman from our village, on a job elsewhere, got stuck to a wire and died. He was a very good man. So the contractor delivered his dead body all the way here, to Sangvi.

Father said, See that? Who's going to do this much for you?

In fact, he said further, Even if you were multiplied by twelve thousand, still the sum of the last six or seven years comes to zero.

Nali had just been admitted in school. She was used to unhampered living before, so she found going to school quite terrifying. Then, frightened, she'd still get ready to go to school.

Besides, a couple of nasty girls in her class would also bother her. The teacher did nothing to them.

At first, I performed the duty of taking her to school. Outside the school there's a platform around a neem tree. I would stand there, and once she had entered the school, I would come back.

Once, the girls were still going in. So she stopped with me by the platform. I was standing still. She sat down. Then she took out the slate from her satchel, then her book, which she placed on the slate. Holding the bag by its two bottom corners, she shook the bag out. The pencils that fell out she placed on her book. And having spread the empty bag beside her, she patted it as she said, Now sit down.

As I sat down I said, So, Nalinibai, what's your plan for the day?

Meantime she popped into her mouth a dried apricot she'd had in her pocket and said, School's not quite filled up yet. Let's sit here, you and me. Then, when the bell rings, you can go back. I'll go in.

I said, Yes, sister dear, but that's a very short while.

Then, looking about her idly, she finished her apricot. Putting down the nut from it, she began looking for a stone. I said, You can't break it properly. Give it here.

Then I banged a stone on the nut — wham! We couldn't quite make out where the nut bounced off to. Then I started looking for the seed.

She said, Dada,[1] you can never find a nut that's bounced off like that. Wait, I'll give you another.

Then, even as she looked about her all over, she drew out another apricot from her pocket and ate it in a jiffy, as her eyes bugged out wide. And then put into my hand the slurpy wet nut.

This time, holding the nut between two fingers, again I hit it with a stone, wham. But the bang was really quite hard and the seed within was crushed to bits.

Then she picked it up bit by bit, putting each piece directly on her tongue. That made me feel quite bad.

I said, Do you have any more apricots?

She said, There's one more.

I said, Give it here. Now I shall break it neatly.

But she said, Not now. I'll save it for my recess.

Then she refilled her satchel carefully and disappeared through the school gate, running a little, walking the rest of the way.

I thought — Dear girl, there's no escape from this. Better get used to it. For many many years to come, no escape from this for you.

That is Nali.

Just senior to her is Jai. She has a loose tongue. She and I can't really get along. Once it started to rain, so at the time when school gave over I waited with an umbrella for her by the school gate. But I couldn't see her anywhere. So after a while I came back home. So then there she was, in her underwear, wringing out her soaked clothes and putting them up to dry. I said, Where were you, you goose?

She said, Useless uppity. I did see you. But I deliberately took a detour. All the girls would've said — So now your Dada has to hold your umbrella over you, has he?

Her patent strong words are — Useless Uppity. If I ask, Do you concentrate properly at school, or do you natter away? — You are useless uppity. If Mother says, Brush your teeth first, won't you? — Mother is useless uppity. And thus she'd go to the washroom. If Grandma says, This one is really spoilt, then — Granny's also useless uppity.

Older than her was Mani.

Older than Mani, Sumi. She's married and now lives at Nagpur. One good thing about her is that, she'd never come home, ever.

But once in a way she writes fat, long, long letters. For some time her letters would mean — Life is very tough here, it really stretches us and causes us great difficulty, because we can't even find a servant and if we do, he turns out to be a cunning fox.

At last, once her husband found a silly old handyman somewhere. You might think he was nearly daft. He wouldn't do any work properly. If he meant to pour oil from the tin into a bottle, he'd put the funnel upside down over the bot-tle and pour the oil through the nozzle. While stacking up the tiffin carrier[2] he'd place the topmost box at the bottom. Once, when he went to fetch ghee he even forgot to take a container for it. So he brought it back in his cap. And then, as things proceeded this way, on and on, after four or five months, he took four hundred rupees from the table, a watch and a jacket, and ran away.

I was older than Sumi.

Father had started all sorts of antics. I refer to elections Once, in an election, the opposing party was very strong. So his friends said to him, You must distribute a barrel of liquor. Then you will see how we gain strength for certain.

Father said, That I won't be able to manage. Besides, we are varkaris,[3] liquor is taboo for us.

So then, when the votes were counted, Father's share was really very small. He'd just escaped losing his deposit. And the other party won by a huge margin. Right there and then, in the presence of aeveryone, Father said — That chap was bound to be elected.

Didn't I say so? Why spend on liquor just to save one's deposit?

And he listens to kirtanas[4] regularly on the radio, Wednesdays and Sundays. But let that pass. Yet once when a kirtana about ahimsa was playing, I'd had enough and finally said — Whoever can quite manage to live perfectly by the principle of ahimsa?

He yelled, You don't need to spend money just to listen to it, do you?

And then he turned the volume higher still and went back to listening.

Once he said, When will you learn to milk the buffalo? Come, I'll teach you.

I rubbed some butter on the teats of the buffalo. But even though I tugged and pulled at them — not a drop oozed out.

Finally getting up I said, Chhhe, this feels just too mushy-mashy.

On this, Father — Hey you, one has to practise first on a buffalo.

Once some part of an oil engine on our farm was stolen. We tried hard to find out who, or how. Shortly thereafter a new one was bought and fitted to the motor to pump water.

At this time a stranger came to our door and said, Mahajan,[5] I will get back your stolen stuff. I should be able to manage that for a couple of hundred rupees or so.

Having thought a good deal over this, Father said — We've bought a new part. And for that already we've had to spend five hundred. You keep the stolen part yourself. Just don't steal the new one also thats enough. Then, Go. Treat him to some tea.

I took him out and gave him tea in Sunat's teashop.

Thereafter, there occurred many thefts near our farm. But nothing on our farm was stolen again.

At that time we used to send our peanuts for shelling to the mill of a Marwadi.[6] Suddenly he went bankrupt and many farmers from our place found their money locked up with him. Then all of them conducted a regular raid on his mill and appropriated all the goods and chattels they found there.

Father ignored all sorts of other things there but grabbed a huge safe-like cupboard. He hired a truck and brought it and dumped it at home.

Gratified, he said to the others, You sods, are you going to construct a canejuice press out of the mill-wheel which you've brought, what? You ought to look for an article like this one.

On the front of the cupboard was a massive built-in mirror. Besides, inside there were many shelves. We started keeping our clothes and jewellery in it.

Father would say, Does it look best here, or in that corner?

Every day before he went out he would put on his cap, first checking his reflection in it. Only then would he leave.

However, this lasted only about eight days or so. Because, after that, he came to know a secret piece of information — that the cupboard had already been made over to the Marwadi's wife. So he would do better to return it before he was served a summons.

Then Father had to empty it in a hurry, hire a truck once again and overnight deposit it in the Marwadi's mill.

In any sort of cabal or scheme in the village, everyone calls my Father first. Because he only speaks ambiguously.

Mean to say, if one chap had gypped another, Father would say to both, You'd better see for yourselves whatever....

If there is a brawl over the boundary of a field, he roars out —You sods, for a bit of ground you break heads, do you? Far better to use them and cultivate profitably whatever land you have and buy other lands.

Of all the things about him this was what I liked somewhat.

Until only just the other day, there used to be a crowd at our house of those who borrowed money at interest. But since the departure of our trusted hand Jhagdu, that had ceased.

Take a hundred today and bring back a hundred and twenty five next month — a word-of-mouth transaction. But of course there were always needy people. Often genuinely needy chaps would bow before Father, but he wouldn't give them money.

He used to say, I only do this as a matter of charity to others.

If someone took more than two months to return the money, Jhagdu would take care of him.

Once this servant was gone, Father sustained sharp losses. Such a servant, so loyal to the master, but so wicked to other people — and yet Jhagdu had been ruined by a mere caprice in number lottery.

At a time Jhagdu would consume as many as eight bhakris. Mother would say to his face, You are really my foe.

Even if he just stood in someone's doorway, the money would promptly come from within.

But, really, Jhagdu himself was not interested in anything. With the single exception of tamasha, of course. No matter where in our neighbourhood villages there was a tamasha show, he would drop everything else and go there.

He did have a father and a mother, but he still lived in our cattle shed.

Moreover, he was in charge of our stud bull, Budhya — permission for his use had, of course, to come from Father.

Often people would bring their cows in heat. They'd tie them up in our front yard to a post and say to Father, This one needs to be serviced.

During my childhood, in the presence of Mother and my sisters, I'd find the whole thing most awfully lewd.

For servicing their cows —two seers of jowar from those people and further thirty rupees a month from Father — that was what Jhagdu managed his living with. But the entire sum of cash he'd invest in a number lottery and manage with the gains from the stud-bull.

But unexpectedly, in one speculation, he won one-and a-half thousand rupees. Then Father said, Have I forced you to do anything until this day? But you really must not speculate with this money now. Spend just one hundred. I shall lend out the rest of your money at interest. In a couple of years, I'll return the entire enhanced capital to you.

Once again, Jhagdu lost the hundred in the lottery.Later, when the remainder had grown to almost four thousand rupees, Father said, So what if that parcel of land is a site on the hillside? Don't we too have fields there? Buy it. At least bajri[7] will grow there.

Then Jhagdu really worked on that field. All our village people began to think well of him. Now as a landlord with six acres of land, a bride was offered to him. The marriage took place. Even a child was born. And then ail of a sudden Jhagdu just disappeared somewhere.

Some said that in the tamasha of the famous dancing girls Jheli and Phuli he sings songs about Krishna and the milkmaids. Some said they'd met him at the Jejuri fair.

Then, there was left his field. His parents said to Father, Make over this field to us.

Father said, The field belongs to Jhagdu's wife. Once her daughter has grown up we shall transfer it to her.

The parents said, That brat isn't even Jhagdu's offspring. Jhagdu's wife said, Of course she is.

Then Father put a notice in the newspaper to call Jhagdu back. But he didn't return even after a whole year. Why would he bother to read the newspaper? But he doesn't care a hang for his field, that much is certain.

Then, according to tenancy law, Father had the land registered in his own name.

He said, In the purchase of this field, actually only some fifteen hundred rupees of Jhagdu's money figures. Let him come back whenever he likes — then four thousand will be due to him from me.

All this had been going on for some time when I took the B.A. exam a second time.

Later, only the other day I went to Atya's at Indore. Then she said, Hey, remember that Jhagdu who was at our place — once a little while ago he had come to my house. She said, He belongs

Cocoon

to our village-soil, after all. So I fed him. But he didn't appear to be happy. As he was leaving he put as much as five rupees in my little one's hand, for sweets. I said, Why so much? He said, Baiji,[8] yesterday I made a big kill in the game. He didn't come by again. I too didn't invite him again.

Then, to look for Jhagdu I began to walk about through gamblers' dens in the open space outside town near the Devi temple. Looked in at all the dens. But I couldn't see Jhagdu anywhere.

Looking at my clothes, everyone there would make signs to the others. Because I was asking around whether anyone had seen a chap called Jhagdu, a big built solid chap from Sangvi village.

One said, Bhai[9] saheb, you don't really think any Deviwala will really help you in this, do you? If you really wish to grab him, you must do so when you spot him yourself.

I said, Sir, I am not a policeman. We have four thousand rupees that belong to him, which he has left behind. That must be returned to him.

But still no trace of Jhagdu. When I came back I told his wife that he'd been in Indore. So she said, Then you might as well have carried my chappal to hammer him.

To be frank, there were several such blokes in our village, now not a trace of them can be found. Those who leave Sangvi once, never return. And our Sangvi people say, Those who come to Sangvi, never leave Sangvi.

In an open field outside the village was Sunat babu's teashop — the only one here. Because, for one thing, if someone else did start one it wouldn't run, or if it does, Sunat babu is sure to deliver the threat that come night he would uproot it and fling it away.

Because he just used to loaf about the village, he had, under duress, been made to sign up in the military in 1935. He fought in the Indian National Army in Burma and still had half a dozen INA medals from that time. He'd wear them on special occasions, mean to say, elections and such.

His teashop would really run only on account of the tipplers and habitual gamblers. But Sunat would tell them that drink is bad, and so is gambling. The man who plays with numbers, having had a drink first — that man is also bad. If you really want to throw money away, you should go to Burhanpur, he'd profess.

He would visit Burhanpur himself. As soon as he'd managed to put by a hundred or so. During Sunat's absence his son Ragho would take charge of running the teashop at the rent of ten rupees a month, which would be promptly recovered on Sunat's return from Burhanpur.

Then his son Ragho himself would go to Burhanpur, but not return early. Because, even if he had, he wouldn't always have the opportunity to manage the teashop. That depended upon Sunat's putting by one hundred rupees first.

That way, these two, father and son, had a good relationship. Mean to say, before leaving for Burhanpur, Sunat would lend him two or three rupees by way of temporary advance.

Once when Ragho went to Burhanpur, he did not come back to Sangvi at all.

Here, having managed to put by one hundred rupees, Sunat had become so impatient to go he thought that he could barely manage to hold on for another week even.

But even after his saving went up to two hundred rupees, there was still no sign of Ragho.

Then in a fit of anger Sunat shut the shop, locked it, and went away.

There in Burhanpur, Sunat came to know that when a while ago, some riots had taken place, Ragho had been mistaken for a Musalman and killed.

Sunat said, Sods.... These descendants of Mohammad. But let that be. That way, even I am a Hindu in name only. But how did my son come to be thought a Musalman?

Then he came to know that, during the upheaval, all Musalmans had gathered in one house, and he had happened to be there.

Then, having made friends with those who had taken shelter in that house, Sunat found out that once, as Ragho had been hovering

Cocoon

about a Musalman woman, he'd fought with another Hindu customer. At that time, Ragho had declared, like a Musalman in Urdu, This is my wife. Then all those who'd gathered there had seconded Ragho's claim and resolved the quarrel.

Then Sunat went to that woman. And declaring before her people that he was a son of the Indian National Army, he fought with them, and took possession of that woman.

With his pockets full of money, the high reputation of Sangvi, and tales about the War in Burma, he said to her in Urdu — Now you are my daughter-in-law. Come with me.

He came back to our village with this woman, Jaitul.

The daughter-in-law and father-in-law might have in fact cohabited forever in Sangvi. But in the meantime, some other chap had raised another teashop in the open space outside the village.

Sunat said, Now I have a daughter-in-law. Otherwise, I would have fought with him and brought his place down.

There was hardly sufficient custom in our village for two teashops. Besides, Jaitul was actually so beautiful that drinkers and gamblers started contending with Sunat for her. But Sunat would pretend to her that he was a reputable person in our village. So now that his usual devil-may-care rashness had left him, he couldn't silence his rivals. And so his shop began to lose custom.

Then some people reported to me that first Jaitul had run away. Others said, In fact both of them ran off together.

However, Sunat didn't leave without admonishing us — Sangvi does not know the true worth of a man.

There's one thing that's not so bad about the open space outside our village — no such problems as majorities and minorities there. Mean to say, not every drunk and gambler but nearly everyone goes to the same teashop and eats paan from the same shop, Balu's.

Here the village panchayat has put up a lantern. Not, of course, for the convenience of these folk. In fact if some government chap visits, we have to ensure that he knows that it is placed on the way to the toilet.

Once four American farmers paid a visit to our village, to see it.

If some such visitors are expected, no one gathers in that place.

Then the whole area is all cleaned up.

So, then, these Americans came. Then they too asked why there was this lamp post so far away from everything else.

Since I was educated I had to go with them and the crowds that followed them around the village. As we were going down a lane, a drunk was trying with all his might to open the door of a house. But the door refused to yield. The visitors stopped to watch this unusual affair.

Finally, a woman from within the house said, You fool, why are you pushing the door in instead of pulling it out towards you?

At last when the door opened he entered.

One of the Americans said, It really is good that prohibition is operative in your state.

Some of us took these visitors far away to the bogs.

As we were going one of them said, This is really not okay.

But when we were returning, the other three said, This is not hygienic.

Lakhu Shet said, Then send us some aid for that from there.

All this, of course, in English. But I said to myself in Marathi — So what if they are American, they too are farmers.

Because, later on also they made all sorts of inquiries. Took some photos. They said, There are so many of you educated people here, yet you don't have any dramatic or literary activity? But we said, Only radio and that. Because there was

no fun in presenting to them our Lahanu and Dhulkya.

Dhulkya is a Nath.[10] All day long he grazes cattle. He has a mountainous buffalo bull. He says, This bull is my field-and-farm. Dhulkya's income comes from this bull — and the rest, that is, corn flour, for which he moves from house to house every morning singing devotional songs. From him one could gather ever new stories about Gorakh Nath. If he finds me at our place some mornings, I give him extra meal. So he tells me new things, always fresh things. That is to say —

If you stay short, you'll suck milk,
If you grow tall, you'll lick mud.
you know, pared to your wife.

Or —

The sun and moon have fallen asleep
O where have they gone to sleep?

Or he would narrate some such tale as follows, that would go on for five or six hours at a time —

There was once a farmer. He couldn't have any children. He tried all ways. But no child was born. His wife said, Go to the Brahman himself and find some way. Then he went to the Brahman — Maharaj, I cannot have children. What shall I do? The Brahman said, Come tomorrow with a present for me. I shall study the Shastra meanwhile. Then he went home. The wife asked, What did he say? The farmer said, He will tell me tomorrow. (This recurs hereafter as the burden of the tale.) *Next day the farmer went to the Brahman. Placing some money before him he said, What do the scriptures say? The Brahman said, You must build a temple and worship there. Then the farmer came home.* (Then his wife asked & Co.) *The farmer built a temple and began to worship there. But still no child was born. Then the wife said, Go once again to the Brahman and ask him properly.* (This too is repeated each time.) *Then the farmer came to the Brahman* (and said, and all that). *The Brahman said, You goose, which deity did you install there? The farmer said, There's only the temple. The Brahman said, Come back tomorrow with a present. I shall check with the scriptures.* (This too keeps recurring.) *Then* (Wife asked, etc., and Next day, & Co.) *the Brahman said, The fittest deity among all deities for childless people wanting male offspring is Tulasi,*[11] *Install a Tulasi plant in the temple and worship her regularly. Then the farmer installed Tulasi in the temple and began her puja. Still no child* was born. Once at night when his wife went there to light the lamp she saw a mouse gnawing at the Tulasi. Then she said to her husband, *Go and find out exactly what the scriptures say about this.* Then (the farmer again..., etc. The Brahman and his present, etc. Then the wife said & Co. Then the farmer etc. next day.) *the Brahman said, Hereafter, you should bring the present on the first day when you come. So this thing can conclude quickly. The farmer said, Yes. But what do the scriptures say? The Brahman said, Hey, the God of Gods is the mouse, really. Indeed, he is the mount of Lord Vinayaka. Feed him, give him drink. Then the farmer left all the grain in his house uncovered. The place was soon teeming with mice. But once there came a cat and having caught a mouse it went away.* (Then the wife said, etc. Then went the farmer to the Brahman, etc.) *Then, striking his forehead with his palm the Brahman said, You goose, the real God among Gods is the cat, you see. Worship it. Feed it milk. Then the farmer started to give the cat his cow's milk. Still no child would be born. But once a dog came running there and grabbed the cat by the scruff of its neck. The wife said, God, O Hare, how can we have a child this way? You should go again and check what the scriptures say. Then the Brahman said, Dear Farmer, this affair is stretching on and on, and still you don't comprehend the real God. See, if you really think about it the true God among Gods is the dog, of course. The dog is actually Khanderao, the great god. Serve this dog. Then the farmer began to offer the dog milk and curds. But, you see, what happened once was that the farmer's wife had made a bundle of bhakris to take to the field, and gone to fill water at the well before leaving. Meantime Khanderao made short work of the bhakris. When she came back she found that the bhakris had gone. The dog had gobbled them up. And her husband would be there in the field, hungry. How can she relight the mud stove and bake fresh bhakris? Then she lost her temper and flung the water pot at the dog and the dog dropped dead. Then, in great fear, she started holding — Whatever have I done! I have killed the god himself. So then, taking all her clothes off, she sat in a corner, howling. Meanwhile, the farmer, mad with hunger and angry, returned home with a stick. The wife was now whimpering in the house stark naked.* (Then, narration of the whole incident, etc. Then, once again to the Brahman, etc.) *The Brahman said, Listen, old chap, for a sonless person the god of gods is of course his wife. Worship her.*

Then the farmer came back home. Here his wife was hiding naked. The farmer brought camphor and incense sticks and that. And he went to his wife. Now the wife dared not ask any questions. She didn't ask what the scriptures said. She just sat there, shivering. Then the farmer put her to bed as she was. Applied red gulal powder all over her body. All the way from the parting in her hair, her forehead, her nose, her mouth, her navel, her cleft, right down to the toes of her feet he covered her in red powder. Offered her the camphor. Stuck some incense sticks into her hole and lit them, and folding his hands together he started to say, Hey Mother, you are the real Devi. If you are pleased, I shall get whatever I wish for. He started to worship his wife like this every day. So, in the end, who really turned out to be the true god of the sonless chap?

A tale or two of this sort.

Further, some time in the middle of the story, other variations and deflections — the farmer forgets the money he's to offer, and the wife recalls all that has passed, taking all the time in the world to do so. And, once in a way, Dhulkya himself says — Now the rest of the tale, tomorrow.

Once in a way, I also attend Lahanu bhagat's[12] oral recitals of vahi[13] songs, tambourine and all that, in the Maharwada[14] outside the village. On moonless nights. These performances last all night. That's one good thing.

You can't see the Sacred Mount Meru[15] between Earth and Sky
You can't have a wee bird small as a mustard seed, in a moment
O, Listen! The City of Kaundinyapur
Where King Shashangar ruled ho ho ji!

And then right into the morning — the tale of Raja Shashangar.

Occasionally, by the time the son of the Queen Bhujawanti, (in the story) starts to fall in love with her, it is already morning, and Lahanu says — Now the rest on the next moonless night. Now I must take the goats to the hills.

Once in a way I hand over a rupee for tea for all those who have come together for this. Jaggery worth ten annas; tea-dust worth six annas; and goat's milk — after drinking such tea, one finds even more energy to sing and hear vahi verses. A chap like me really likes this sort of vahi song —

A hut of grass is held up by a pole
The kite hovers in the sky, in God's neighbourhood.

But Lahanu's own favourite song is the description of Kanod devi —

In the land of my Kanod, my beloved Goddess
Is the grove of turmeric, my! The grove of turmeric
Its shadow so deep and dense,
Mother lost her heart to it,
In the land of my Kanod, my beloved Goddess,
Is the grove of kumkum, my! The grove of kumkum,
And its shadow so deep and dense
Mother lost her heart to it...

Then, as per the pattern in the song, whole groves of gulal, and dates, and almonds.

Sometimes Dhuklya says, Compared to what I know, Lahanu knows nothing at all.

Lahanu says, Let's have it out, then.

Then Dhulkya says, But I shall not cross your devi. If you want to sit together, we must sit here, within the village gates.

Then Lahanu says, If you want it, come to the Maharwada.

But once all of us persisted and arranged a contest outside the village gate. So then Dhulkya really lost face. Dhulkya's vahi songs are too classical and all that. The people felt that there was stuff only in Lahanu's singing. Besides, Lahanu sings to the tambourine. In the end Dhulkya brought out a most powerful vahi —

Lo, the mother and her daughter always squabble like rival
wives, ho...
Mother turns out the daughter from her home
And retains the son-in-law, ho ho re ji...

All the people were very pleased. But Lahanu parried with great ease —

Ho... the betel leaf, and fine lime on it
Childbearing wife, and her husband is the suckling
She put him in a wicker basket, carried him to the field
ho ho re ji
And first kicked him and then suckled him at her breast
ho ho re ji...

In the final analysis, though; even all this stuff is really dated. Little comes up that is fresh, new. I feel sometimes, all their tales and vahis from the Maharwada must exhaust themselves some day. What next, then? Mean to say, thereafter only the radio.

But one thing about Dhulkya's buffalo bull has been left out. The other day at the Bull Festival, some nomadic Bharadi people arrived and camped outside our village. Ever since childhood I have had this curiosity — Why do Bharadis wander about the village at night, wrapped in a blanket, lantern in hand? Grandma used to say — They are the thieves of thieves. At any old time of night, when these chaps go about singing the same line of the same verse over and over in a heavy broken voice — are they keeping guard over the village, or what? Goodness knows —

Hey... 'n hey... Vanji's[16] oxen have... returned again... hey....

Such lines are awful enough. On top of that their singing is terrifying too, and wrapped in a blanket, glimpsed in one's sleep at three or four in the morning — the Bharadis are really too much. Of late they only come by once in a way. But during my childhood, they were all over the place. Their own area of origin is somewhere among the Satpura[17] mountains. But nearly eight or nine months in a year they are on the move. Their camp means — big strong women, smooth-dark children, chickens, donkeys, ponies and a whole storm of dogs.

Once, some time ago, for a payment of ten rupees, they killed the entire rabid and mangy population of our village curs. Their own dogs entered all the lanes and byways from one direction.

With every group of five or six was a Bharadi with a long stave. Once they had driven our curs to one side of the village, their dogs fell upon them. Only four or five of the Bharadis' dogs died in this skirmish. One of their dogs was also badly bitten by another rabid dog. Therefore they really walloped it with staves and flattened it.

After that for some time everything seemed so quiet in our village. Because, otherwise it had become impossible to sleep.One cur would bark aloud something from one side. From another side would come a reply from some two or three others. Then there gathered some ten more from this side, and converging they'd hit a horrible keynote and yowl for a long time. When we were young we would fall asleep in the dread belief that when village dogs howl they are witnessing the death-god Yama taking away the souls of dead people. But what of the fact that as grown-ups we quite lost sleep altogether?

Now then, with these Bharadis was a smallish bright, white buffalo bull. All four of its hooves would be tied to pegs. These Bharadis and Dhulkya had a little war of words. Mean to say, Dhulkya said, Since the Bharadis' runt has come here, my own business is down. A Bharadi retorted, Dear chap, this bull is not some ordinary little thing, it is of Mandsaur stock. The buffalo cows of your village won't forget him. So some two or three of our chaps said, Let's have it out on the coming Bull Festival day. Dhulkya's bull was — vast. And the Bharadis' was a really young 'un, but once in a temper he was terrible. Besides, it had tough strong legs and really sharp horns. And on his forehead were long, long tufts.

On the festival day the announcement was made. The Bharadis and Dhulkya went all over the village and said to the people — Come... Come on....

Dhulkya brought his elephantine bull, with its shiny dark skin, and red eyes, with red gulal powder flung on its forehead, and so on, with much pomp and clatter at the head of a procession. The people of our village said, Let someone get ready to collect the dung of the Bharadis' white calf.

But when the Bharadis released that tough little bull who had been standing far away in the dry river bed, it was felt that this little bull-calf wouldn't exactly be a washout.

Dhulkya didn't allow the gamblers to bet that day. All the cash had been placed in the prize-money.

Two or three of us friends had climbed a tree. So then our man Popat said to me from down below, you know, sort of jocularly — Well, Pandu Tatya, frightened, are you?

But a drunk went close to Dhulkya's bull and, thumping the bull's back, said — Wah wah! Some three or four chaps dragged him back saying, Do you long for death? Still he kept trying to advance.

Both the bulls approached each other, flinging sand around with their pawing.

We were all expecting that right away there would be a broken bone or two.

But goodness knows what Dhulkya's bull felt — for he merely sniffed the little bull's forehead, turned tail and ran away — bhrrrrr.

So our climbing into the tree amounted to nothing. Dhulkya ran after his bull and everyone laughed at him all day long. No one had seen a fight like this anywhere else.

On that same occasion our man Popat told us many rather knowing stories about buffalo bulls. He said, our milch buffalo ran away from our house. And then she got stuck in a deep mudhole. There wasn't much water in it. But the mud was really deep. Now, how to bring her out, the silly fool? Somehow we went in and tied ropes to her. But they slipped off, some even broke and still the buffalo wouldn't come out. We shoved her calf before her. But she wouldn't emerge, would she! Still, she had to be taken out right away. Mean to say, we were worried about our milk for the evening, see? Then someone devised a trick. He led a great big bull into the hole. The bull had barely proceeded towards her when the cow and bull both came out.

After a pause he said, But because she was giving milk, she ran away. It would have been a problem if she hadn't been in milk!

Popat narrates everything in a most fundamental sort of way. Once I asked him, Why is it that days are long in summer time and short in the winter?

So then he answered — Right from the start that's been the science of it.

There's another rather special man in our village. He's mad. He's been given the name 'Jayhind'. In his hand there's always a neat bouquet of flowers and leaves. Jayhind has a house, but he wanders about here somewhere by the open space outside the village.

There was a messy episode in the prime of his youth, just when he was about my age —

Normally he didn't go out after dark. But one moonless night, it was really as dark as death. He got delayed somewhere in the taluka[18] town. The people there didn't invite him to stay the night. And neither did he ask them himself, saying, Why bother?

At night as he was coming along by the bamboo grove he found that he couldn't see the road. Overhead, deep wawdi rattle trees. And no road in front. So he started looking for the road.

Already it was a notoriously frightening place. Then, as he was looking for the road, he came right up to the edge of a well.

There he saw a person standing on the parapet wall of the well.

That was the ghost.

It said, Your father snatched my horse away from me, you'd better bring it back.

So then he didn't return to his house at all. When he was found wandering about among the fields, he was brought home, burning with fever.

He asked his mother, Did my father have a horse?

The mother said, Yes.

And that finished him.

Then he started roaming on the grazing lands and among fields. His wife or mother would locate him somehow and bring him back, feed him, and once again he would go rambling off.

The soles of his feet split and bled unhealed. His mother died one day, even as she was staring at him in concern.

Then one day the people in his neighbourhood bought a horse and gave it to him. Having performed a puja for it, Jayhind took him and went to the haunted well.

The ghost was of course at the well.

It said, That's not my horse. Because, the moment you let it go you'll see it will run off.

The horse did get loose and galloped off wildly, goodness knows where.

Then Jayhind asked the ghost, How can I find your horse?

The ghost said, Ask your father about it.

Then he started looking for the place where his father had been cremated. Frightened, his wife also started to enquire of this and that person in the village. He himself never spoke to anybody but his wife. Someone told them, His ashes have been thrown into the Tapti river, they are lost now.

Now who on Earth would know just where his father had been cremated in the cremation ground?

But in the end his wife's folk brought a Kaikadi[19] bhagat.

This bhagat said, I shall stop all this nonsense of his.

Then, in an all-night sitting the bhagat took Jayhind for a real ride grabbed all his gold and cash from him. And said, On a moonless night I shall make everything all right for you.

On such a night Jayhind and the bhagat went to the haunted well.

The bhagat said, Climb down into the well.

Frightened, Jayhind said, The ghost is in the well!

The bhagat said, When I say climb down, you climb down. Then this chap leapt in.

The bhagat said, Now dive into the water and bring out seven pebbles that lie in the soil far below.

So this chap threw up seven pebbles.

The bhagat said, I shall charm each pebble and throw it in and I shall leave. If the ghost comes, tell him — Either eat these pebbles or else drink up the well.

Then after each pebble had been chucked in the well the bhagat went away.

What transpired after that there's no means of telling.

Jayhind told one person only this — When the ghost came I was asleep. To another, Jayhind said, I myself swore at the ghost and forced it to come. And it said, *I* am your father. After I had died, why did you people let my horse starve to death?

But in the morning when people came to look for him, there was very little water in the well and he was standing at the bottom. Then he was hoisted up. After that he never bothered anybody. But his wife ran away. There's nothing in his house now. Once in a way he goes in and, having swept it where rats have hollowed it here and there, he leaves.

This and that person began to report to Father that I'd started to keep company with not-so-nice people in the village.

Father replied, He's not an ignoramus. He knows what's what. But to me he said — Be with anyone you like. But if you create the least little bit of mess anywhere I shall whack the daylights out of you in front of everyone.

He took care to tell everyone who had no particular occupation, and also our farm hands, and those I went about with, that if they taught me bad habits, they'd better consider what he would do to them.

So some of the tough, intelligent ones really stopped mixing with me. Later, whenever the talk began to get really colourful, these chaps would say to me — Shet, this is not your sort of company. You'd better go back home. So I was furious with Father. Day after day is passing by in my life, as in the life of some dumb creature. So what should I do, sitting at home?

During the past year, my Father has tried all sorts of stuff, wanting to teach me the affairs of the world a little and also to

Cocoon

acquire some paramartha, some higher merit for himself. The tasks assigned to me I carried out properly at least at first. But all the same, I really cannot perform meticulously and continuously any old chore given to me.

One of these things is — our store for sulphate. Father goes to Nagpur before the summer and brings back lorry loads of sulphate. And my work is to keep a note of how many sacks were brought, how many still remain. During the monsoon, when demand for sulphate starts, for a few days one gets no respite at all. Father would instruct me regarding whom to give it to on credit and to whom at one-and-half-rate. The people from the neighbouring villages themselves come with their carts to carry away the sulphate. Every person pays me cash and tells me how many sacks he wants. When his cart arrives, it is my work to open the store and get our hand to fetch the sacks, enter the number of sacks gone, and render accounts every evening to Father.

In fact, in this business, there's oodles of money to be made. But it has become the unwritten law in our village that only Father should do this. Because for the more important people of our village, we sell sulphate at the lower Nagpur rate. Some others say, Why get involved in so much hassle, we don't have a son like his at home. Some say, Why create hostility?

But in the end one chap did reveal the fact that Father sold sulphate to him at one and a half times the real rate. Now let me see how that man does this business any longer, he said.

Then, going to Nagpur before Father, he made an agreement with the wholesale merchant. As a first instalment, he started with two lorry loads from Nagpur. He himself sat with the driver of the rear lorry. On the way, two chaps got into the first lorry somewhere, saying that they'd get off on the way further along.

After they had already put behind about half the distance, the fore lorry was stopped in the bed of a stream, right at the hour of noon. Even when the other lorry driver honked his horn loudly, the front lorry remained stationary.

Then his driver said to our man, Go see what they are doing.

The man got down and went towards the lorry in front. Then

two or three chaps got down from that lorry, knives in hand, and said to him — This stuff is ours.

Without uttering a word, this chap then returned empty-handed to our village.

Someone said, Why did he have to take such a big bite if he wasn't able to chew it? Some said, my Father surely had a hand in this.

But why should I worry about that? For many days after that the police inquiry went on. Besides, in the meantime, that chap also received a letter from the merchant in Nagpur asking when he was going to carry away the remaining instalments of sulphate. After this incident, that man once again began buying his sulphate from us.

Our taluka has quite a good cooperative bank. Its elections are won either by our village or by the eight or ten neighbouring villages put together. The people of our village collected five hundred shares each. For a hundred rupees per head. Nowhere else do the collective votes amount to this much. That's why if someone from our village stands for the post of Director he is bound to be elected. For a while now, some neighbouring villages had formed a coalition of some kind and decided that they wouldn't let the uppishness of Sangvi continue. Otherwise, the victory of our village was certain.

For the past three or four years Father has been Director. If you really think about it, apart from winning the election, there's no other profit in being Director. Yes, there *is* one other benefit, however, that every Saturday, on the pretext of taking him to a meeting, the bank sends its car for him. Besides, the Director gets a room in the taluka town for his use throughout the year. The key to that room is with Father. Whenever someone respectable from our village goes to the pictures or to shop, he can spend the night in the Director's room. That's why there is constant coming and going at our place of those who come to ask for the key. I give that key and tell them to bring it back the next day. Actually the room can hold, somehow or other, four or five people. But sometimes, on bazaar days, as many as twenty chaps from Sangvi sleep there. If someone from another village wants to be accomodated at night, all these chaps say to him, You'd better try harder in the next election.

In addition, on Saturday afternoons, there are always some five or six chaps waiting at our place. When the car arrives, Father, with his swagger umbrella, and rolling gait walks up to it and he then calls to some two or three men standing by, who then climb in and sit by his side. The rest sit in a gaggle beside the driver. Once in a way this driver, Baidu, gets rather sore about it, and getting down from the car he says, You drive the car yourselves.

Then Father says to each chap one at a time, You get down. And you, what do you have to do there, eh? All right, you stay. And you? To the cinema? Which picture is showing? Marathi, is it? You stay, then. And you — then you'd better do your shopping next Saturday. Come on, then. Baidu, better get the car moving. All these fellows will give you tea. Hey, all of us *are* the Cooperative Bank. Let's start now.

Then, next day, cracking jokes and teasing them in like manner, Father returns after his meeting with his umbrella in the same way.

Once in a while the car just doesn't turn up at all. So then Father goes to those waiting by our door and tells them — There's no meeting today. On one such occasion, a chap asked, How's that? There has to be a meeting every Saturday. Mean to say, in the next general body meeting, we must table such a proposal. How can the bank manage in this way?

Forget about us if you like. We can even go by the state transport bus.

For one thing the menfolk of our village are an easy going lot. Leave aside women, I don't quite know about them. I can make out from my own Mother that whether rich or poor, all women slave away all the time. Tea to be prepared seventeen times a day. Churn butter in the morning. Do the hair of the daughters, cook well, that means a cartload of bhakris. Cater to each one's likes and dislikes. And always guests and visitors— they are a special group. And still, the women must keep smiling. In the afternoon, they must make a round of the fields. In the evening resume position again before the mud-stove. And late at night with the pots and pans at the washing place. In addition, if there had been a quarrel with Grandma, these chores would get done with more despatch than usual, that's all. When Mother is awake she's constantly nattering — assign chores, keep this here, these bhakris go to the field, that feed to the other field, serve this hand his food, tell that hand to do some other task. A great establishment is our house. Mother says to me, All the same, it's sufficient that your Grandma at least manages the farm hands. Your Father's sold his soul to the business of leadership, being a luminary. And you — what difference does it make whether you are in the house or not? There just has to be yet another woman in the house.

I find it a terrifying idea that one should look for a girl to do the household chores and marry her for that. On this score these people really harassed me.

Indeed, once a girl from Mother's family came to our house to attend a wedding. So my Mother made her stay on, apparently for no particular reason. Seeing this, I began to return home only for my meals. Besides, Mother had told her that no matter what, I was really a good chap. So I started eating and speaking properly. Once, for the first time in the whole week, I spoke in the appropriate manner to her. That happened on an evening when I was sitting on the terrace, right at the top of the house. At that time, because my Mother had asked her to sprinkle water on the terrace, the girl came up somehow all the way up the several flights of stairs with a full bucket of water. Now, since there was no one else up there, I was embarrassed and started staring at the beauty of nature and that outside, hoping that at least Nali or Jai, someone would come along. The clouds were really beautiful.

Then this girl said — Today all of us are going to eat our dinner up here on the roof.

Girls are really bold!

Then I said, Who do you mean by all?

She said, Everyone, of course.

Then skilfully, so as not to let it drip on my feet, she began to flick water everywhere. When I looked at her I saw that she was munching something and smiling to herself. Now, this was the girl they'd brought for me to look over.

So then I enquired after her and all that.

She said, When you came to our village I saw you. My mother thought she would ask you to tea the next day. But when I came to invite you I learned that you'd already left that morning.

I said, I see... I see.

Then I began to look about for a sentence to say that would establish a proper impression of me.

Meantime she herself said, So what did you do after that?

I said, What do you mean?

She said, After you'd been to our village.

I said, Later I went to Poona.

She said, But you did something about a job once, didn't you?

Who told you that?

I know all about you.

Mother must have told her this for sure, I thought.

Again she said, I know all about you. Ask me.

I said, How can you know everything?

She said — Each and every thing.

I said, How so?

She said, Go ahead. Ask.

I said, So then what used I to do in my room?

On this she really laughed, burbling. Then I saw that one of her teeth had a cavity. But that's nothing extraordinary. My own teeth aren't all that good either.

Then with her hand on her hip, she said, What else would one do in one's room? Study. Reading.

I thought, This girl is champion. Besides, she probably reads novels. Moreover, she probably has great taste and all that.

Then, some two or three days after that, this girl spoke to me in front of my Mother about exams. She also said that she had never done anything like that yet.

She said, Why don't you continue your study?

She then said a good deal more — from time to time, in bits and pieces.

Once in the afternoon she was even singing for Mother.

The gist of her message was — Let us get married.

At the same time in my life, some rather odd people visited the well in our field briefly. They were Goddess Ambabai's[20] devotees. Tall caps studded with cowrie shells. And on everyone's back a large, sack-like cloth bag. In these bags, further, many small bundles. Jowar grain in one. Black gram in another. Meal in a third. In one some salt and chilli and such. Because our field happened to be on their way, they were going to have their evening meal there, before going on. There, sitting on the high wooden beam over our well, I was watching their cooking.

There were three of them. One chap, although he was sitting by the three-stone stove, was actually doing nothing. The second one took out of each sack equal amounts of whatever they needed and started cooking. The third one fetched the water and sticks and whatever else was needed. All this was going on so much like a dumb-show that a spectator found it great fun to watch. Two or three curs from the field lolled about, their heads on the ground.

They prepared something that looked like gram meal mess. I said to them, Take some banana leaves. If you need onions, there are some beds over there too.

Then the man who had just sat down went over to fetch some onions. By the time he came back the other two had served themselves and had already started eating. They didn't take the onions this chap brought. However, he served himself and ate his food in silence. No one threw the dogs even a scrap.

When dinner was over they first tidied up everything and, having refilled their sacks, reclined against them. As they smoked their beedies, they raked up some quarrel. All this was going on in the Dangi dialect. Eventually they started snapping at each other angrily.

Cocoon

Then two of them fell upon the third. They knocked him about and hammered and kicked him. And then shouldering their sacks, those two started walking away. The third chap also shouldered his bag and without uttering a word started to follow them.

When he was no longer to be seen, I thought — God, this is really tough. To wander like this, having smeared turmeric powder on their body, and roam from village to village day and night. No land or property. Nothing at all. Dragging their lives along with sacks on their shoulders.

Then I came home and had my dinner.

Some four or five days after this, that girl went away. I said to Mother, This girl won't do in our house. Mother said, Then find some other. But do choose one. I said, But when she went away she must have felt bad. Poor thing. When she went, whatever might she not have felt? Perhaps she had even determined what she would do here, that all things in this house would one day belong to her. She must have thought that she'd change our antique wheatmeal tin. And as she went she might have felt — one wishes to join life-threads... but nay, nothing doing. I pitied her.

So then Mother said, quite happily, So, what shall I convey to her family?

But of course I am not going to do any such thing. Still, her parents would feel — Our girl must have been at fault. That was even worse.

Mother said, You don't feel anything for her, do you? So why are you now bothered about her?

She said, Girls get used to anything.

Girls. Of course all girls are nice.

We are a gang of youngsters who have spent four-five years in the city for one reason or another, and who are just sitting about at home now. I was the last to enlist in this group.

The oldest among us is Lalaji. His real name is Nandlal. But when a chap returns home, his education unfinished, and his behaviour betrays an inner agitation, then the people of our village take great pleasure in attaching some such name to him. When he acquires such a name, he doesn't "agitate" at all. Once you've been named Lalaji, who'd make much fuss about anything? Similarly, the names of the chaps in the gang are — Damu Anna, Sotmya, Dagdu Shet, etc. I haven't yet acquired such an appellation. But once in a way some do call me Pandu Tatya.

The village feels that these are all funny creatures, the sods. But in reality all of us are inordinately disturbed. For one thing, each of us has a conscience that gnaws at him. Mean to say, all our contemporaries have gone ahead, and what is this that has come our way? Anyway, what does "going ahead" mean? Where to? So then, "ahead" means that far away someone is running on all fours, and we are coolly sitting here watching them, that's about it.

But we have realized something. That is, that one should let those who go ahead go ahead. For each one who goes ahead there are naturally several who lag behind, sure there are. Then they should gather together. So it will become clear that even the community of laggards is not negligible.

Now, when I was studying I used not to mix with anyone in our village really. But since my return I've gradually come to understand that forgetting all distinctions among us, we must all gather at Balu's shop. Otherwise, what is there to do except sit at home?

Or, suppose Lalaji starts feeling that only because his father died did he have to leave a really fine job in the Air Force to come back here and vegetate in our village, otherwise he's really top notch, etc. — that would hardly be nice, would it?

When he was in school Damu Anna (real name Dado Muralidhar) used to have fits, so he stayed home. Still, Damu Anna and Lalaji have the same status.

Lakhu Shet (real name Lakshmikant) came here because his work as a lawyer wasn't going well and he was getting bored. And he began to look after his father's shop. And he also gives free legal advice to anyone at all.

But if you leave aside his quirk of lifting his eyebrows, there's very little difference between him and me. So until we have quite conquered the distinction between self and others, it won't do to sit at home alone.

However, if one were to state the one common flaw among us all, it is that at first when we came here we were terribly consumed, sort of pining away. This village of a thousand inhabitants, we felt, was awfully small. And we found the buildings here also too low, sort of squatty.

Nowadays, excepting me, all of these chaps are absorbed in their work. Besides gathering together in the evening before Balu's (real name Baliram) shop, there are hardly any shared occupations for us. Parties, or going to the Ramkunda, the holy tank in the hills, to bathe, to gather at the house of one of us for tea —these things do go on from time to time, of course. But all of us are really bound only by the fact that our time together does not pass too badly. Little else.

Often, as we speak of old matters, do we ask each other — We are not really inferior to others, are we? And within, of course, we always feel that we are stuck, really, but that we must all at this point at least maintain that we are no less, really.

Initially, all of them together took the micky out of me.

A friend of ours from school had become a doctor and was off to England, to "go ahead" further. So he was felicitated on behalf of the village. This doctor was my childhood chum. There was little room in his house so he used to study at my house. Because of this old relationship — why else or what for I didn't understand — in the farewell function these chaps put a chair right next to this friend's and then they bullied me into sitting in it. All of them, however, were prepared to sit on the ground before us, to watch all the fun.

Many people of our village, who were the just-a-few- words-you-know types, gave their speeches and praised the doctor.

I too spoke — In those earlier days, this chap would keep

falling asleep, so then I used to wake him up and force him to study — this reminiscence pleased young and old alike in the meeting.

But what one pensioner said hurt me to the quick.

He said — For higher education one needs not just intelligence but also perseverence. Now look at the doctor's old friend Pandu Tatya himself. There is such a difference between these two. But in this day and age one cannot progress merely because one possesses money, that is all I wish to say.

One chap said, I read the newspaper every day. The gist of all that is that our region is progressing day by day, so much that we are known all over the world.

Another said, In this our village, the number of people who pursue higher education and still prefer to farm is growing. Besides, this year in the matriculation examination a boy from our village came tenth in the Regional Board. This doctor should also in future open a surgery here in our village.

One more said, Only in this way will our country become invincible.

Once there, the doctor married an English woman and even stopped writing letters home.

But thereafter I never again sat in a chair like that.

In our group, everyone had some stories to tell of the past, heroics of their bygone days. But Girdhar had none. He might as well not have been in our village school. After he had worked in Ajmer in Rajsathan for two or three years, he got really fed up with such letters from his father — You seem to forget that you have five other brothers also....

But why he left that job all of a sudden and came home he told no one. He only showed the courage to say that he would do nothing at all, and then sat about at home permanently.

He didn't ask those at home for even a red copper paisa. That's why he didn't spend much time even in our company. Because any of us can manage if we suddenly decide to have tea and such.

Saying, Why should I meddle with you all?

He avoided mixing with too many persons. Of all of them, he behaved pretty well with me.

Girdhar was tremendously mad about puja and worship.

From his family he'd only ask every year for two pairs of pajamas and two shirts, that's all. This too only because one can't very well go about naked — that is, this is what he said when he asked his father for them. Then on Dassera[21] day, like any respectable person, in his new-smelling clothes, Girdhar would go out with us to steal the 'gold' leaves of then Apta[22] tree across the borders of our village, according to our custom, as offering to our elders.

Girdhar's routine was to wake up bright and early in the morning and lie awake in bed. Then he was asked to come to drink his tea and he'd listen to his mother's scolding. Even the younger four or five brothers would say all sorts of nasty things to him. But he would get through all that with ele- phantine calm. Then he would go to just anybody's field and bathe at their water pump. Until the clothes which he'd washed dried, he would pass the time just here and there. With him always was his dog. He would get the dog to climb up a tree along with him, then climb down himself, and then as the dog fell out while chasing squirrels, he would laugh. Frequently he'd touch the clothes to see if they had dried and continue to lark about with his dog. Then later, with his washed clothes as headgear in the hot sun, himself walking ahead and the dog following, he'd return home. While eating his lunch, again, his mother's scolding. Then after lunch he'd lie down wherever there was room and loll about until evening. Come to my house in the evening and if tea was ready, then drink some wordlessly. Then off for a walk. At night again, at dinner, his father's berating. Just like me, he does not like chapati or rice. Then sitting with the usual company until late in the village square. But in our company he'd just sit and listen to us. Never even by accident would he crack a joke or anything.

Once a chap who'd had a drink started to beat Girdhar

without any reason — phut-a-phut. The only excuse seemed to be that Girdhar'd had just said, The fun you get from drinking I myself get without drinking. That chap was really letting him have it — phut-a-phut — and he was just standing there. When the beating ended, Girdhar said — Enough? Any more? Then he took a handful of cowdung and smacked the drunk in the face with it. So then those who had gathered about them drove the drunk crazy by hitting him with dung.

Girdhar would say to me, Of all things, the best is to loll about in the afternoon. And the worst is to go for a walk with you in the evening.

But he liked only me. Because no one else was ready to pay heed to his nonsense. He spoke very little about himself.

Even more funny is Sotmya (real name Sonu). He is a veritable Bheema by build. He is also the least troublesome person in our whole village. He is ready, at any time of day or night, to do any work for anybody. At home, things aren't all that easy for him. But in mixing with us he never feels embarrassed like Girdhar did. But if someone says something wrong to him, he really beats him up.

Earlier, he used to have a habit. While a kirtana performance was on inside the temple, outside in the dark he'd scatter the footwear of the participants here and there and run off. All this he did stealthily. When the kirtana was over everyone would put on shoes other than their own in the dark, and then mutter — This isn't mine, that's not mine, nor this either, that one over there must be mine, etc. And eventually tiring of this, they would say, Let's come back tomorrow morning and then see, and then depart. However, some of them did need their shoes right away. And at least some eight or ten of them, because they were already half-asleep, would put on whatever pairs of footwear they found and go away. So how would the shoes of all the other people match after that?

Once, while he was indulging in this trick, he was caught, that's why everyone gave him the name Sotmya, meaning the boor.

His behaviour continued like this right until just the other day.

Another habit of his was this — people sleep in their yards in the summer, so he would wander down every lane and find out the odd picturesque attitudes in which people slept, and thus entertain himself.

Even as a child this rough fellow had once hit the teacher with his slate and walked away, a permanent truant. Now, others in the school also did indulge in monkey-business. But his parents would say, A poor man's son must learn good behaviour.

He now wished to marry but that couldn't be arranged. For one thing, he wanted a wife who looked like — nothing less than an actress.

Once he was shown a girl who brought him some tea, as is the custom. And suddenly he burst into laughter — khokhokhokho. So loudly that everybody in the girl's house came to see what had happened.

I asked him, I have heard this story — is it true?

So he said, I am sure my father must have told you this. My own people spread all sorts of things about me, sod 'em. But it is true that I guffawed. Hey, how should a sodding wife look? But you really ought to've seen that girl. I am not crazy, am I? This girl was such an amazon, so terrifying to look at, that when I saw her I just couldn't hold back.

And once again he roared with laughter.

His clothes are always clean, ironed. And he never has his hair cut or beard shaved by our village barber. If some car from the bank or a lorry from our village happens to be going somewhere, he goes to some nearby town and returns all shaven and shorn.

Films hold tremendous attraction for him and he has a great love for city life. I haven't, unlike you chaps, lived in cities for years and years. If, by the way, I can go to a city for a day or two, I eat some icecream. Gobble up some fruits. Here, otherwise, there's always the daily chilli and bhakri, sod it. In this way he reveals his contempt for our village.

Some days he comes to Balu's shop and says, I had a hearty meal of khichdi[23] today. Got the chance at last after three or four months.

But whether at home or outside, there's no telling how this brutish chap would behave.

Once he took some acquaintance home for tea. His mother and sister-in-law told him that there was no sugar in the house. Indeed, there was no sugar in the house. Then, having seated the guest he dug up some money from somewhere and bought some jaggery.

The people at home said, You've only brought jaggery for two cups of tea, aren't there ten children in our house, then? Do you expect them to stare at your face as you drink your tea?

Their house is really tiny. So, that meant he wasn't even clever enough to realize that he was being insulted in his guest's hearing.

He shouted at the women — But every now and then you have tea, do you yourselves give me even a saucerful?

Meantime, the guest, of course, left. Then, hugely annoyed, he ate the jaggery he'd bought, and kicked and kicked at the mud-stove until it crumbled to bits.

His father was rather daft, really. He narrated this episode to us, saying, That is our worthless Sotmya, who eats fifty bananas at a time.

Later Sotmya said to us, Why fifty, I can eat sixty. But he says all sorts of things like this about me to outsiders.

He has understood thoroughly that his family reduces his standing in the community. But, that way, no one is at fault really. For one thing, Sotmya is not exactly overburdened with brains. And his great physical strength is also useless, actually. Once a chap from outside our village beat him up thoroughly, thinking that he was a thief.

Of all of us, he's really thick with Lakhu Shet.

So that he should have some strongly built chap with him, Lakhu Shet once took Sotmya along to a merchant who had long been refusing to return some money of Lakhu Shet's. Actually the condition of that merchant was quite bad. Now, Sotmya and Lakhu Shet sat in the merchant's place for quite a while. But the merchant had gone out somewhere, so they had to wait. Finally, the merchant's servant told them that he had just come back. The servant brought them water to drink. And saying that the master would come to them in a moment, he went away. These two sat, sipping water. Just then in the doorway stood the merchant. He had shaved his head smooth. Seeing that, Sotmya's terrifying horse-laugh started. On top of that he was laughing even as he drank. So water started to gush out of his mouth and nose. He was alarmed, suffocating and struggling for breath. Everyone in that house gathered there. They started asking — What happened? What happened?

Then, the reason he himself told us was pretty crazy. He said, After we'd got tired waiting for so long, sod it, suddenly this merchant stood there, with his shining bald nut, like some meek little person. Now how could such a merchant ever produce any money to give to Lakhu Shet?

Lakhu Shet said, From this day, to take this chap along on any important mission would amount to daftness.

When he feels depressed he looks for someone's lorry that is about to leave, and makes a visit to the city. Buys a bottle of attar. Has a hair cut and a shave. He has his shoes polished. Growls in style at the waiter in a restaurant. Buys an expensive ticket and sees a film. And — what is more important — he tells us about all this with a large pinch of salt. What he really wants to tell us is that he too can go about in a city, and is not altogether a bumpkin.

Another thing was that he could not tolerate the scoldings at home, no matter whose. Once in a way he beats his older brother, even his father. Once in a way, when the howling-yowling of women and children is heard from his house, people say — Sotmya must be demanding fifty rupees today!

And when he wants money, he must have it all at once. Then he doesn't have to haggle with them for the next few months. Besides, he heard the same complaint from them whether he asked for one rupee or for fifty rupees any way. So naturally he asks for fifty.

Once his father said. Today, even if you kill me, you won't get fifty rupees.

Then he said, In that case, I shall kill you.

Then his father immediately forked out fifty rupees.

Even his family finds all this entertaining. They already know that they will have to part with the money. Yet they create this avoidable drama.

Once, when he demanded fifty rupees, his brother made himself scarce for the whole day. Even a search of the wholevillage didn't unearth him, because he was actually hiding within the house.

Then this chap collected a few people from the neighbourhood and said, These people find it beyond their power to part with fifty rupees for me even once in six months or so. Right now, before you, I shall break open this trunk and take precisely fifty rupees. I won't take any more. Later, though, they will say he's taken one hundred. And you all are also useless people — you accept whatever they say. That's why I've called you here.

Then he prised open the lid of the trunk from the back and, making quite a show of it, took just fifty rupees from it.

He never really got fed up about the problems and irritations at home, nor did his folks at home get fed up of him. Because during the season, he does the work of ten men all by himself. Thereafter, though, begin these squabbles and scraps.

But once someone said to him, I shall get you the job of a bus conductor in the state transport service. Because that would allow him to live in a big city, he fought with his family, took

Cocoon

two hundred rupees from them, and went to Dhule to attend an interview. When he came back he was very pleased because he was sure of the appointment. But even after two months had passed, he still hadn't got a call, so he sent a letter to his contact there — I gave you a hundred rupees for my job, was that for nothing? So a letter came back from that angry gentleman — You ass, I sent you two letters but received no response from you. Now forget any hope of a job hereafter. So again in his house there was a skirmish.

His brother said, Why should we look after your correspondence?

Sotmya said to us, Sod it, all of them wish me ill. They foil my job opportunities like this. Now, that gentleman in Dhule must have felt so bad!

His father had loaned some money to a chap he knew from another village. But he'd also told him, You may bring the money back whenever you want, only don't give it to Sotmya, that's all.

Sotmya came to know of this.

He said, What am I going to do with *his* money? Yet let me just see how that chap dares to refuse to give me the money. So he went to that chap again and again and demanded the money.

That chap felt, Why did I have to borrow from his father? So he quickly collected the cash together and sent it to his father with this message — I wasn't going to run away with the money, was I?

Sotmya's folk were surprised. Then they came to know the truth from Sotmya himself.

Later when Sotmya'd gone to that man's house, he was told, I've already given the money back at your house. Don't you dare mount the steps of my house again.

Sotmya said, I have come to tell you that you made a mistake. You should have given the money to me, only to me. I merely wanted to prove my integrity to them by taking it home unspent.

Then, feeling terrible, Sotmya narrated the whole thing at home.

His folk said, You are the one who spoils the name of our family.

He said, You don't even have a name, do you? But you have spoilt mine, though.

And he told us, I kept going to that chap again and again! How bad he must have felt! I really am at my wits' end about these people.

Girdharswamy didn't like Sotmya as much as the rest of us do. By way of entertainment, when we are at a loose end, Girdhar said, This man will never achieve anything. Because, after all this he's still attached to his home.

Girdhar's favourite place was the house of Chakradhar, a teacher. None of us likes Chakradhar. If you go to his place and are about to sit down on the bed, he says — You chaps sit just anywhere out there in the village, so don't sit on my bedsheet. Spread that other one and sit on it.

Or if you take one of his tumblers to drink water, he says, Don't touch that one. That's mine. Take another.

Who will visit such a man?

But Girdhar sits there for hours on end. Long ago in the past Chakradhar and his wife had fallen out on this issue of cleanliness. And she'd left him.

Because he's deaf, he doesn't say much to anybody.

Now all three brothers of Chakradhar do sundry jobs in Mumbai. Their father died while young. After the oldest brother had conducted the marriage of their four sisters, he felt his responsibility was over so he went his way to Mumbai, to settle down. Then the remaining three brothers began to curse him.

But his mother loved her oldest boy very much. She'd say, My husband died. But thereafter this one carried out all his father's unfinished duties.

Then these three would say, He didn't finish those marriages for nothing. For that he sold our fields and went off, leaving this worthless house for us to look after.

Cocoon

Then the second brother too went to Mumbai. At first he would send home some five or ten rupees for his brothers' education. Later, as this stopped, the remaining two brothers began to curse him.

Finally, only Chakradhar was left to curse. And just his mother to listen to him.

When he curses his brothers he "invokes" their mother and sisters as well. So, incensed, his mother says, You, harpie — who is their mother to you, then? So he redoubles his curses.

During his life he had been involved in many occupations. He once ran a grocery shop. Learned driving and drove lorries for some time. Then finished two years of training and became a teacher. Now he repairs watches and clocks.

But he says, There's no work as third-class as repairing watches. For one, these are all country bumpkins. They cannot even wind a watch properly. Their watches have to be repaired again and again. Nor do they make timely payments. And if you say even a word about that, they chuck the money before you as before a dog.

But because he is right there in our village, all the watches and clocks of our village come to him. If someone brought him a really ancient watch, he'll deliberately break it and give it back, saying — This one can't be repaired any more.

Once in a way when he begins bickering with his mother, he flings to the floor the watch he may have in his hand and says — Just when I have at last found out what's wrong with this watch, you start your nagging. Why ever did I get into this useless business? I will not survive unless I do some other work.

Girdhar finds it extremely funny when he flings watches down like that and then collapses on the bed and, with his head on a pillow, stares up while continuing to curse the whole world.

His house is really old and almost crumbling. He says, I am just waiting for this house to collapse on top of us. Still, every monsoon he does repair the roof tiles as he mutters curses under his breath.

Cocoon

The mother and Chakradhar go about their house like ghosts. But there really is no limit to the way he makes her life miserable. Did you wash your hands before cooking, did you cover the food, where did you spread my sheet to dry, which chappals did you wear to the bog, why did you clean my plate with mud, wash it again now with ash; you take the mud from the yard, that's where you piss at night, and don't take the cloth from your old sari to strain the drinking water— a thousand grouses. If he sees the least little bit of dirt anywhere he breaks the mud water pot, flings his dinner plate about.

Then as she weeps his mother tidies everything up for him— meanwhile she mutters, He's my arch-enemy. Often people gather to watch all this. Then Chakradhar's mother says to them, Do you think your mothers and sisters are cavorting here? Get lost.

They used to have a cow. When it returned from grazing, it would rarely go to its post with the other cattle. Then the old mother would go all over the neighbourhood and come back with the cow. Then, when she had finished tethering it, Chakradhar would pity his mother. So until the cow nearly bellowed its life out, he would then beat her with a stick — saying the while, *Will* you go off? *Will* you wander off ever again?

Once in a fit of anger he sold the cow to the butcher. At that time, though, his mother raised the roof. Some folk gathered there. And they beat up Chakradhar.

Once this cow was sold, the mother's sole occupation was also gone. At least she'd been able to pass her time in the business of feed and grass, milking and storing cow dung and such. Now all she could do was to Walk about looking for enough dung to plaster her house. In the remaining time she'd sit at her door watching the fun in the street. Then lifting his eyes from the watch in his hand, he says to his mother — Hey, hag, when you sit there like that I feel I must not do anything at all, I feel awful.

Then just for that time the mother would sit inside the house or go to the neighbour yelling things about him. Then he'd shout from within — Go drown yourself, you whore.

312   *Cocoon*

Girdhar says to me, Pandoba, where is your Sotmya compared to this terrific Chakradhar?

Even though I have now myself become a regular village bloke I'm convinced that living in a village is by and large just... living like a beast.

These people really don't care about anything — somehow get through each day that comes saying — Whatever happens happens for the best. If the rich do something, it is said that they have money so naturally they will do these things. If the poor do nothing, these people will say, Poor chaps, what else can they do? These people don't know the meaning of anything beyond the day's needs. A person who owns no clothing might wander about naked, but he needn't feel any shame. The man who squanders his riches is just as shameless.

Such beasts live in cities also. But that's hardly my point.

At least in the city you do find some learned people. Here nothing at all happens that is related to fresh knowledge. There's no conformity here between things that merely help to pass the time and art, etc. Perhaps, in the city, cinema and drama flourish because people actually lack place to sleep. But at any rate that's not a bad way of spending time.

In the past this used to happen even in the villages. Mean to say, during our childhood — thousands of beggars, lutanists, vahi singers, martial powada[24] singers, bhagats who did the spells of Mother Mari[25] — all sorts would come by.

One beggar was just gorgeous.

He would say to us — Ask me my name.

Then we — What is your name?

He — A Bundle of Grass, or Chatrapati Shivaji Brand Beedi.

Then there was another beggar.

He said to us once, Do you know why I didn't come by for the last fifteen days? One day I entered a house quietly. And hid inside a trunk. Every night when I came out of that trunk, I would polish off all the butter and ghee in the house and then — back inside the trunk. But once the woman there noticed this. Then, when I had gone back inside the trunk, she locked me up. I was about to die, having been cooped up in there for two whole days. Then, at last, yesterday from within I started sliding the trunk along the street. The people of village after village were such bastards, no one would unlock the trunk. Then some people from your village finally opened the trunk. There's no place like Sangvi. Now I shall settle down here.

None of that exists now. Now if some bhagat comes by they say — We can't even find enough labourers. Come work on the farm. In those days tamasha shows too would come round frequently.

Now everything revolves round money. That is to say, besides nattering and getting one's children educated, they have no other preoccupation but money.

I do read some things, you know. But these people. How their time goes by in utter contentment, month after month, I am unable to understand. That way, even to cultivate one's farm with some commitment and hard work, that is also a very powerful way to spend time. These people know well how the seed they have sowed — after some rain and sun-shine — slowly grows bigger from the first twin leaf, every day, every fortnight, every year, progressively. If a farmer is seen standing in a crop just about so high, I feel as if I've had a vision. Mean to say, through his fist flowed the jowar seeds and they have become this whole, green, green field. On this crop he spends all his time and leisure. Of all things, weeding is great, freeing each small cornstalk or cottonstem by rooting out weeds with a small sickle — that's really great. To make sure that each bush be distinct and yet all part of a row, all nodding in the breeze. Shift and shuffle, from this bank of the field to the other — grubbing; then turn about and come from that bank to this, just as before, freeing each stalk and stem. And once in a way, glance back at the cleaned rows.

And this goes on until the day is all done.

But I know very little about all this stuff.

I myself have planted just one mango tree and somehow made it grow as tall as myself. I go to the field to see if the hands are doing their work or not — to no purpose really. So why should I make empty boasts about this? After our Grandpa, Father gave up the joy of tilling the land. And I am — a mere observer.

And yet our friends say — Let some more time pass. Everything will become fine once again. Yes, one does get bored, yet why should one allow boredom to occur?

Compared to this, the policy of Gomaji the goldsmith is better — he is a single person. Because he is blind, he stumbles and falls in the street. And on his knees there's always some sore wound or pustule. All day long flies sit on it and make his life hell. Then, sitting on the steps of his house, he has only one occupation — as soon as a bunch of flies settles down on his knee, slowly, cleverly he brings his hands together till the flies are all together caught in his fist. Then, to check whether they have in fact been caught — or just to hear how they sound, perhaps — he puts his fist to his ear and listens to the buzzing of the trapped flies. And then opening his fist he releases the flies, uttering — Huh.

But the method of dumb Onkar Buwa in the temple is even better. Because of great old age his head nods constantly — no no no. And with his mouth he is constantly trying to mutter the name of Ram — Ram Ram Ram. Henceforth, all the time that is left at his disposal will be spent in this way, shaking his head and slowly muttering Ram Ram Ram. No rush.

The ways of spending time that one encounters in our village are astonishing. Tapiram's method was absolutely horrifying. He was a man ruined by leprosy. He lived on until maggots began to fall out of his mouth and nose and only his wrists remained, no hands at all. Until that time, one would see Tapiram sitting on a swing on the way to our field, swinging peacefully. The swing was so low that if his foot even slipped a bit, he'd get bruised. But it was tied low so that he could slide along the ground and climb on to it easily. After great difficulty, when he'd once managed to sit in it, the swing would go from this side to that, from that to this. No matter who was passing by on the road he would raise his stub of a hand and greet them — Ram Ram.

In fact, I was fed up with this Ram Ram. Because, then he would also begin asking, to no purpose really, What's been happening in the village? Is it true that so and so died the other day? A thousand such questions. Until he was done one had to stand on the road and look at this frightening creature. And he himself, swinging — from here to there, there to here. Mean to say, one had to keep moving one's head too all the time just the same way.

Besides, his rotting flesh had made him so unsightly that I used to tremble. When his sons and daughters came to our village they met him only once in a way. And that from a distance.

He had a cousin, his father's brother's son who consumed the produce of this chap's field, and supplied him with curry and rice. Without any hands, this chap ate like an animal. An old woman poured water into his pot, placed his food in his hut and went away.

If one saw him at night swaying on the swing, it was quite terrifying. In his life, nothing at all really happened — absolutely nothing.

But the real limit was that there were people who sat right next to him and chatted with him. I could never manage that. But, slowly I started to say to myself, Why ever not? Once, some day, I *shall* sit close to him and look at his red, pit-like nostrils.

But till the day he committed suicide I hadn't managed to do that. As though to take revenge on people, as he died he fell into the well right beside our village.

No one was prepared to haul him out. Besides, his body had been in the water all night long.

Finally, two or three lepers in our village said — At least for us, our brother isn't a burden.

Even as they tried to get a grip on his corpse, his rotten flesh would slip off his bones — somehow, they gathered his body up and brought it out.

After seeing him, I used to hate myself, recalling that in my

Poona days, I used to occasionally powder my face! The living flesh, with maggots in them — that was a powerful thought.

But once this happened, and even his hut had been torched, we stopped going along that road at night or at spooky times. For one thing, I knew very well just how he used to look. Not that his ghost is likely to do any harm as such. Still, why risk it?

Really, just once I want to hear the speech of ghosts. Girdhar used to say that people like us wouldn't understand that language. What is more, why would someone as worthless as we even get to see such intangible things as ghosts? But I am not prepared to accept that I am unworthy of seeing even ghosts. Now, if I go alone at night to the field, Tapiram's spirit would say to me — So, everything was over while you were still only thinking of coming near me!

Then what would I have left to say? For one thing, a man like Tapiram has lived in the belief that others, healthy people, owe him something. Such people are always angry, raging, always hungry. Why wouldn't they grab me? Besides, I've heard such horrifying tales that even the sight of a ghost would quite stop my heart.

My great grandmother, you see, has built this temple in our field, to Munjoba.[26] If I go by it, I never return without doing namaskar.

A woman of our neighbourhood was possessed by our great grandfather. This my great granny came to know. She then went into the math[27] of the Mahanubhavas to see about the exorcism.

After the usual waving of the aarti[28] lamp and all that was over, my great grandfather's spirit began speaking. Then, in red hot rage, (actually thouing him all the time), great granny said, Thou oldie, thou — as thou lay dying in your son's lap, I gave thee Ganga water to drink for thy salvation, we lit thy pyre after laying thy body on a huge heap of sacred basil sticks, scattered thy bones in seven different holy rivers. Each year on shraddha[29] day thou receivest obsequies and offerings from the holy fire. Now what the devil is it thou lackest here, thou... pest!

Then the possessed woman, humming deeply in her throat, turned venomously upon my great granny and great grandfather's voice roared — Dare you speak to your own husband with such disrespect!

According to great grandfather's demand she took to the river Tapti a procession of warrior devotees. Then, out of the river came hopping into her salver some round black shaligram[30] stones. She had them carried to our field in a procession with song and drums, built this temple over them and planted a peepal tree by the temple.

Such was the lore I'd heard from Grandma.

But my great grandfather was a very religious person. Still, some people do say — once to his house had come two merchants on camels. In collusion with one of them great grandfather had killed the other. And grabbed one half of his riches.

But what have I got to do with that? As long as I am secure, that's fine. Truth to tell, my great grandfather had bartered precious jowar stocks in exchange for each field he acquired, while he himself lived in near starvation during the drought years. But I don't lose anything if I perform a proper namaskar at the temple, placing my forehead on its threshold, do I? Even though the peepal tree creates a barren patch, hampering the growth of our crop under its shade, Father doesn't let the axe touch this tree.

And the other day a Mahar died of snake bite. Now, while dying the spirit that possessed him said — This dying man owed me a life from an earlier birth.

All in all, without God and ritual, man's life isn't secure at all. That's why I did go on the pilgrimage to Changdev, on foot. It was a full moon night and we dunked our bodies thoroughly in the lovely pool of the Tapti there. By and by, I *shall* visit all the religious places in Hindustan.

You and me — our pain is all in the mind. I mean, man has little experience of pure pain.

Someone once abandoned outside our village a moribund cow, left her for dead. She was lame in one leg — it was broken. Besides, she was old. So who was going to bother to keep her? She lasted many many days, hobbling about painfully here and there, looking for some fodder. One saw her all the time, so by and by one didn't even notice her even when one saw her. If, while grazing, she entered some crop in a field, she was sure to be beaten and driven out by someone. That's the sort of time when she *would* be noticed.

But in the summer when there wasn't even a blade of grass left for her, where could she go?

Then for some days she lay all the time under a tree. That was the route Girdhar and I used to take for our daily walk. We'd feel, she must be given a drink of water. If there'd been a well nearby we could have done something. But to fetch a bucket from home, and rope, and then draw water, and make trips to and fro bringing it to her — who was going to bother with all that? That too every day. Besides, it wouldn't have been enough to give her just water, would it?

All the same, once I did approach her. Then I noticed a very big hole on her back. I went closer still. Then, from within the hole rose a buzzing cloud, a whole cloud of flies. Goodness alone knows how many flies had enterd that hole.

She must have been exhausted, flicking her tail over and over at her back. Now not even her tail was moving. That's how close to death she was. Only her eyes and ears would move.

The cow would just look at us. Without even moving her neck. Her vast eyes, boring at us.

Crows must have pecked at her back.

I don't normally feel any particular fear of death. But when one saw that there was such a close kinship between death and suffering, how could one get to sleep? Only chaps like Girdhar. Such are the people who believe that they know what comes after death, the sods. And then — that red gaping hole in the back of the cow.

And, of course, the body and the mind aren't really distinct, are they? That way, of course there's the soul and all that. But all this must originate in the living eyes of the cow and from the flies entering the cow's back. Mean to say, these chaps leave way below them all such things, in the manner of the birds flying over them, and directly enter into matters of the soul and so on. The pain which the body experiences, the mind experiences too. But some, in the grip of attachment, consider that their inner anguish is greater, ignoring the physical pain. Or else, some ignore the physical pain because they take it as a punishment handed down by God.

Tapiram did used to say that he had to pay back some debt from his previous life.

Now, I asked Girdhar — The pain of the soul is real... if that is so then surely the mind must also feel it, mustn't it? For instance — Don't you think that this cow's soul is also experiencing the pain at this very moment?

So then he said, How do we know that? Only the cow knows that.

I go up to Jagan Buwa's farm for a walk, sit for a while with him, and then if he is returning home, do so — he speaking, and me listening to him. He gives me sugar cane and other things to eat. But, then, I do have to listen to a great deal.

This is an old gentleman who lives in our village but it is as if he doesn't, really. He neglects his farm work too. That's why he's a bit of a butt for all the farmers around. But he never misses the winter pilgrimage, in the month of Kartik, to Pandharpur. Go he must. Then let the birds gobble up his jowar crop, or the brinjals all dry up. His sons have all been educated, and they're gone, to work in important positions. He takes it for granted that in the end he will have to sell his land, and so he tills without exerting himself. How can cultivation really succeed with just the labour of hired hands?

320

Besides, nothing he says seems to connect with anything.

The other day he came back from Delhi, where he visited one of his sons. So someone asked him, Well, what's Delhi like? So — what can I say there daughter-in-law and grandchildren all the time in the house speaking Hindi no neighbours ever come or go so all by myself then to Yamuna[31] or Mathura[32] or whatever is nearby otherwise what is there the folk Ganga really there's no place as pleasant as Sangvi....

I've got used to this sort of thing a little, having heard it all the time. Mean to say, one only has to go on chewing the sugar cane. So then, just hearing this stuff I began to feel that this man was not, after all, speaking mere nonsense. If he gets hold of an expansive subject, good. Then he's off —

If you see that way then the self-opening cabinet and then out of it those bangles and this and that being flung out on their own that way some sorcery in all this but these young folk I told that boy that because you do not believe in that but the young ones observe no behaviour but I only just said rather actually I was quite angry really but when those poor fellows present a show then why not just observe but I did say what they were doing now two into two is four this suppose I I mean not really me suppose you or suppose perhaps someone else that way two and two does make four but just suppose someone doesn't perceive that so then what does my third son do in the bank this is just an example you might laugh but the example is really good then....

Then I intervene, But — I say — Jagan Buwa, all this isn't going to last for long, is it? Now the untouchable castes, the traditional balutedars[33] — everything of that sort is gone. Now, does the sanai[34] play in the temple of a morning? Since Bhiku the sanaiwala went, all his sons are after service instead. Later on, the washerman will also vanish. And then the potter too will go. After being educated no one will make the mud-oxen at the Pola[35] festival. Meaning, everything gone. Then, Jagan Buwa — but the point whatever is to happen is to happen to the next generation will happen now you take the new generation but where does the old generation go now right before our eyes our

Kalu Buwa that Chaudhari and Jamna there were seven daughters Rambhi Sumbhi Chembi always quarrelling sitting in front of each other on the steps picking rife lice but what is left a house full of fodder the rats now one of them take Rambhi she could touch her nose with her tongue now we the old folk still look to God so I am happy the halwai's house all during the plague year rich man his son called Huna my own age once he became mad what sitting on the roof of the temple all night long nor father nor mother at home then every day sprinkling water in the yard so much he'd make it muddy but who was to say anything we said it's wasteful drawing so much water every day better sweep the temple each day but no his death was really terrible but the most terrible death was Narayan Pujari's Maruti[36] is not an easy god now even if you make a wish before him that way where there's faith there's God but his only son died still Maruti's eyes to Mother Mari mean to say we got really angry but whatever God does he does besides such a learned pundit tome after tome in Sanskrit besides astrology so accurate if one is so learned what can even reasonable people tell him then night after night after loud shouting in Sanskrit take those rocks off my chest poor fellow yelling vomiting died at the Maruti temple who ever gets such a death the point I mean the older generation has seen so much now my wife if the sparrows come at the door she in a melodious voice come my dear girls may be you are my dead daughters are you not so she flings fistfuls of jowar from the basket profuse to the sparrows I don't object old generation new generation....

Six

Even as I was saying — yes, of course — this year's also gone past. With the exception of the threshing machine it was impossible for anything new to enter the world of our village. Instead, the youth from here go away to the city. And only Gomaji the goldsmith and we are left.

I lived on, month after month, in comfort and luxury.

Meanwhile, there occurred a huge effort to get me married. It is a good thing, of course, that even chaps like me do find wives. If not, who is going to fight duels and such to acquire a beautiful damsel? It's good that custom is now obsolete. Marriage is indeed a good custom. Who invented it? Land and property one receives on account of merit accumulated in one's previous life, that too is a pleasant belief. One doesn't have to struggle to acquire anything. Even then one does find a good wife. That way, once one has found a wife, any wife, she's got to be good, of course. But those who don't marry at all and yet curse the wedded state — they are... bogus. Because they haven't married. Those parents who have got married and have children, they too are bogus. You just have to look at the faces of parents who've had many children. Except those parents who look upon themselves as criminals vis a-vis their children, all others are worthless really.

I said to Mother, You have a son, a jewel. So you are sure to be admitted into heaven. Don't you worry about me.

I told Father, Look for a girl who will not bear children.
Mother got quite scared hearing this.

I don't have any mystical experiences of any sort but I do accept that the soul is immortal. Only Girdhar has slowly started refusing to believe in anything to do with me. He lingered less and less at my place. Still, our walks went on. His main occupation had become God's worship, puja. I only began going into the Mahanubhava math with him before proceeding on our walk. As long as he was doing his puja there, so long would I chat with two or three monks outside the math.

Once into the math came, for a fortnight's stay or so, a new Mahant[1] who spoke to no one. But slowly we managed to get even him to talk. At first, he'd utter only a word or two at a time. What is your name? — Bambas Buwa. From which place? A wave of his hand — From over there. Then until Girdhar arrived I'd keep looking at him and he at me, sliding bead after bead of his rosary through his fingers. He would listen, though, quite happily, to a narration of my life story until then.

Once he said to Girdhar, What you say about Pandurang is not right.

Later, once Girdhar told him — Pandurang's family is well-to-do — I am poor — but both are disturbed. Meaning, there's no real difference between poverty and plenty.

He said, At least Pandurang is interested in something but you seem to be interested in nothing whatever. Otherwise, both of you are disturbed. The distinctions created by birth are hardly real. You can create distinctions on any basis at all. But the thing which you use to make distinctions oughtn't to be trivial like one's birth.

I said, actually I find nothing interesting, Mahant Buwa. You have the wrong idea about me.

Thereafter Bambas Buwa didn't speak.

Next day, Girdhar reopened the same topic — Buwa Maharaj, I find no meaning even in worshipping God. Pandurang doesn't even do puja. There's no difference between him and me.

Bambas Buwa said, You say this after having performed God's puja. He doesn't do puja at all. Your problem is different. You aren't bored with life. He is.

I said, I accept that. I am fed up.

Girdhar said, Which of these states have you yourself been through? At least in the past?

He answered, I too am bored these days. But never before have I felt boredom. This is a recent thing.

Had it ever happened... did you never feel bored before? Only now? — he asked me.

I said, Bored with what?

He was silent.

After some two or three days, Bambas Buwa asked us this question — What in the universe is altogether new?

I gave it some thought. Altogether, meaning absolutely new? What can be altogether new? The Earth of course is old. Vegetation is, of course, the oldest of all living things. That germinates from a seed. Seeds are always old. Then birds-and-beasts, even human beings — even their seed too is of course old. The new-born baby too is already ready-made. So what can be new?

But I said nothing. Because Bambas Buwa paid no heed to me.

Girdhar said, All of whatever the Creator has created is old.

Buwa said, Man himself has been created by God. So all that goes with man, is that also old?

Girdhar said, It is certain that he created man. But now I've found an answer to your question — God is the only ever new thing in the whole universe.

Better think carefully, Buwa said, and come back tomorrow.

Next day Girdhar sat by Buwa even without doing his puja.
Buwa said, First do your puja.

Girdhar said, I did some in the morning. And for quite some time in the afternoon too. Now I don't feel like doing any more.

Buwa said, No, first that.

Then Girdhar went away, performed his puja and returned quickly. He said, God himself is the ever-novel thing.

Buwa said, But he is of course the oldest of all old things.

Girdhar said, Although God has created man, still he does not create ever person himself. The Powers that he has appointed to see to this business do it by means of seed.

Buwa said, He himself created the seed, though. But that God creates man means that he also creates man's soul. You have confused things. The soul doesn't carry on with the help of any other power. God himself brings about whatever happens to the soul. God has created himself, and other gods and goddesses, and devils and other species. If you accept this much, then you may proceed.

Girdhar said, I accept this. But my point is quite different. How will God create the soul of each and every person? Man is of course superior to bugs and ants and birds and beasts in this aspect of creation. But he is also superior to gods, and rakshasas[2] and other kinds of beings. We can say, indeed, that he is superior even to the Creator himself.

Now Buwa really became furious.

Girdhar didn't stop there, though — For one thing, it isn't even certain whether the Creator has created himself or not. Perhaps there is a Super-Creator who created the Creator. But the Creator, when He created man, meaning the seed of man, really bungled. Because any man, if he feels like it, can deny the very existence of the Creator.

Bambas Buwa said, Only an ignoramus would do such a thing.

Girdhar said, Who is, after all, so all-knowing? Knowledge has been created by civilization. But let that be. Whether one has knowledge or not, those who maintain that there's no Creator say so only after having pondered over the existence of the Creator. But at any rate there are plenty of people who live on as though the Creator has no existence — among both savages and ourselves. Besides, the man who commits suicide enslaves the powers appointed by the Creator, such as Death, by destroying their reign over himself. Right at this present moment there are those who actually invite death. The Creator is more powerful than man, that is why he imposes different births on man, and does not let him be. But because he rebels continuously against God, man survives all that. Forget such people, if you like. But man assesses even the power of God only by means of his own imagination. God has no control over the ideas that man creates. Even if different deities are gifted with immortality, in another way even man's being also possesses the essence of immortality Even though man's seed may be destroyed, yet his soul will not be destroyed. He is as immortal as the Creator. He is ready to suffer pain and adversity. Besides, man has such freedom that, in each new epoch, and even during the same life at each fresh moment, he looks at the same Creator differently, with a new vision, in ever new shapes. Actually, man is superior to the Creator because he has not erred by creating someone else.

Bambas Buwa merely smiled. He then said, I haven't obtained the answer to my question from you yet.

Girdhar said, The Creator himself is the new thing.

Thereafter Buwa became silent.

I told Girdhar, Of course, what you maintain is right.

Next day Buwa said, All right. You and I, are both men. That is why when you told us how we think about the Creator you were correct. Now here begins the process of thinking about the Creator himself. But after that beginning we have no ability to go any further. Even Shri Krishna himself was unable to. Still, even such a beginning is not bad really. But later on one begins to feel that even the Creator is an old thing. So now you yourself may begin to see what I mean about the Creator. I shall only tell you what this new thing is. It is Death, yes Death. Which is so fresh and novel that when one experiences it the experiencer himself is annihilated. Perhaps that is why it remains ever new. There are only two things that actually happen in the life of man. Birth and death. Of these two, birth — well, man doesn't experience his own birth. So that leaves only death. That is the only thing therefore that happens to him. When we die we do not die to another, to anybody else. That is the only new thing for *oneself.*

Girdhar was simply, purely petrified.

Thereafter Buwa maintained silence.

Next day I suggested this to Girdhar — But even after dying we continue to undergo experiences. Once one is dead, death no longer remains novel.

Girdhar conveyed this to the Buwa in the evening.

I only listened on —

Bambas Buwa said, The space between death and the life that begins after death — only for that duration may death be stale. Because, once by the fiat of the Creator — or as you put it, by his imposition, whatever that may be — once man is born then his soul itself forgets death, that is how unknowing the soul is. So forget about the next life. Besides, birth is a thing that happens to someone else, as it were. That I have indicated already. Our concern here is only with whether there is any space that would make death itself a thing of the past. The space which we take for granted between dying and being born once again — that space is null. After death all our knowledge about space as such is nullified.

Just at this point I was about to speak. But I didn't.

Girdhar said, That space probably does exist at least long enough to make us feel that death is old hat.

Buwa said, Of course it *exists.* But where do you get this *feel* from? Don't count on matters related to the physical senses. A space in which the soul has no room at all to wriggle, no arms and legs to wiggle, no stomach for hunger, no back even to lie down on — in such space how can knowledge of that very space occur? Even that is not so remarkable. After death even if you kept roaming the space out there for a hundred thousand years, even if you become immortal, still the hundred thousand years there aren't quite as extensive as one single moment. What do you think?

Now it had become dark. That's why he seemed even stranger to me.

Girdhar said, I am not convinced of this. Death after the state of death is like birth. So what seems to you like death now would feel like birth to the soul in that space.

Then turning to me Buwa said — What do you think?

I said, I think you are more right than wrong.

Then Buwa stayed silent.

Next day when I went to the math I learned that Girdhar and Bambas Buwa had already gone out for a walk. I asked myself then — How independent are you in your faculty of understanding? You can at best assent to others' views. That means, Panduranga, things are tough for you. Your knowledge is nothing, nothing. Whatever little you do know has taken you years to acquire. Yours is the way of the ant. Theirs is the way of the winged bird. You climb up, slowly, slowly. Meantime they have flown into another tree. Whatever is to happen to you?

After that Babmas Buwa went away.

Now, day after day, Girdhar hunted out new gurus. If any ascetic came to stay at the Maruti temple, he would catch him before anyone else had a chance.

Once Girdhar met a mendicant gosavi[3] called Jhalnath. He performed some miracles for Girdhar divining whatever came into Giridhar's mind.

Finally Jhalnath said, Son, now what you have in mind is terrible. I shall not take you for a disciple. But, my son, don't you get caught in the maelstrom of being. That whirlpool is terrible. Come out of that. Rely on the rest of the world process. Don't tie yourself to any one thing.

Girdhar said — There was no such thing in my mind.

Next, in a yatra[4] he met a yogi, a bairagi[5] called Thanthanpal. This bairagi, Girdhar told me, was the first Great Man he had met.

Girdhar said to him — ...but Maharaj, why do you go about like this, asking for alms?

He replied, Whatever is in the possession of others is mine too. The supppliant is greater than the donor. I shall demand, by force if necessary. Over and above that the giver may follow his own dharma.

Thantahnpal also said, I have so much power that I can sink this entire crowd into the ground.

But Girdhar didn't ask him to bury the whole yatra.

Girdhar said to me, Sod it, if you sift a thousand, then you might find one who is just about tolerable. Actually, even this proportion isn't really bad.

Then for many days he did nothing.

Then suddenly one day it was all over the village that Girdhar had run away.

Thinking that I might know something about this, his father came to me.

He'd already searched all the wells around. I said, He might do everything else, but he won't commit that act. Don't think that this happened only because of your ill treatment of him. He has become a mahatma[6] in a spiritual order. But you did treat him atrociously. Didn't give him tea when he wanted it. He used to tell me that you believe that a household runs on money. That if a person doesn't deliver something to the household then he should be considered worthless. So it's a good thing really that he's gone.

After Girdhar went there was a big hole in my daily routine. He never used to say much, but once in a way he would say something great — Every person ought to be able to manage within sixty or seventy rupees. Indeed, not a single person in the world ought to receive more than that. And each family ought to have no more than a single room — and so on. With each day that passed, living at home had become tougher for him, but he wouldn't share this with anyone. Right until the end he observed a principle, that he was not going to do anything at all. He'd been terrifically habituated to hearing whatever they said at home.

But what I really felt terrible about was this — that during our last days together, I hadn't behaved particularly well with Girdhar. The reason for that was that his mother and father would keep describing to me the pathetic situation in their home — Tell him to do something, anything, he will only listen to you, they'd say.

I tried my best to tell him — That he must do something. Just lolling about was anyhow pretty bad. At least when one's parents were toiling to death, to loll about shamelessly at home wasn't good.

Once in fact I really lost my temper. I said to him, Karma *is* ordained. Shri Krishna himself has told Arjuna[7] this very thing, etc.

Then Girdhar said, Dear chap, you are not Shri Krishna, nor am I Arjuna. Nor does anyone here wish to go to war. So you'd better shut up.

That wasn't the final conversation between him and me.

After this incident, though, I myself started to avoid Girdhar.

Once in the red-hot afternoon sun I saw him from my window. After him went that dog of his, sniffing along the ground. I saw him walking from this corner of my win dow to that. Then, just like him, his dog too passed by.

He met me once more at a time when I was returning from an evening walk. In the dark he practically collided with me. He said, Turn about. Let's go for a little walk again.

I said, No.

He went alone.

That was the last time.

The next I heard was this news about him.

And I really was scared.

And then I pondered on this.

When — that very last time — he'd said, Come, I ought to have gone with him.

He might have told me something shatteringly great.

Such people pass by one in life, but one doesn't appreciate their worth.

Of course there's a feeling of renunciation, of disgust in one's life too. But that is all barren.

Just as when a lamp is lit in a house we perceive the light from the windows, doors and and even the vents, even so from the behaviour of every great person, must appear some such illumination.

In other words, for others, there's no light within.

Such a man is hollow.

Then I began to say to Mother and Father and to the respectable folk of our village, Whatever you say, I acknowledge as right.

Someone said something. I said, Yes, I accept everything. I will do as you say.

They asked me questions. I answered, Yes, yes.

For instance, no matter what happens, they are sure to bring me to the stake and tether me. It'd be better, then, to arrive there directly and wait in anticipation. Or whatever I do, they are sure to take care of me. It's no use saying "no" and such. That sort of thing, for instance, only Girdhar and people like him can manage. For my sake many terrific things have already taken place in this world. Because of that things become smooth. Precisely. Whoever invented Law and Order? Moreover, for whom? Who is chiefly responsible for the invention of language? At least, for whose sake? Who devised, somehow or other, this thing we call "home"? Everywhere else, too, who set up the custom of marriage? More or less for whom?

I shall do everything. Whatever they say. I did pass all those years, for instance, this way, didn't I? And I do hold my head high that I shall live many more years just this way. I shan't snatch any years away from others. Or waste someone else's father's money. But they say that, for me, the right age has now passed in miscellaneous ways. That's not, for instance, quite correct. There are of course all kinds of years before me, too. Years, of course, are quite neatly disposed — no matter how late one wakes up. Or, relatively, no matter how one behaves. Each one's future years without fail remain before one. These, et cetera, cannot be acquired. So the question of losing them is not, for instance, really valid. Or, to say that years were really wasted, that too is, for instance, wrong. Mean to say, that's right.

One

1. paise : the lowest coin in Indian currency.
2. Krishna's
   Age : in Hindu cosmology the second age in which, people generally follow their duty though they sometimes quarrel and are driven by ulterior motives.
3. anjan trees : tropical trees.
4. bhakri : unleavened hand-flattened sorghum bread
5. Saney
   Guruji : Gandhian freedom fighter, writer of moralistic stories.
6. annas : obsolete Indian currency. Sixteen annas made up a ruppee.
7. Korku : a wandering tribe.
8. halwai : seller of sweets and snacks.
9. bhajis : a savoury, like fritters.
10. Lord
    Ganpati's
    mount : each major Hindu God has a vehicle. Ganapati's is the shrew.

TWO

1. Maushi : mother's sister.
2. Tilak : Bal Gangadhar Tilak (1856–1920), a great patriot from Poona, leader of Indian National Congress, called "the father of Indian unrest," author of *Geetarahasya*, a commentary on the *Geeta*.
3. Bheema : the second of the five Pandava brothers in the Hindu epic *Mahabharatha*. He is the strongman of the story.
4. Arise ...
   reached : Swami Vivekananda's statement. It is a humanistic rewording of the spiritual call from *Kathopanishad*.
5. Tukaram : Tukaram (1608–49) was one of the most revered devotional poets of Maharashtra.
6. Peshwa style : floor-seats in the style of seventeenth-century Brahmin prime ministers who were the virtual rulers of Maharashtra.
7. tabla : drums used as an accompaniment to Hindustani music.
8. neera : fresh palm sap before fermentation sets in.

Cocoon

9. shardoolavi-
   kridita : a kind of metre, for a lofty, long verse line with
             nineteen letters.
10. *Geetarahasya*: Tilak's philosophical treatise on the *Geeta* written in
             the Mandalay prison.
11. *Vikaravilasita*: the title of Agarkar's adaptation of *Hamlet*.
12. Naushad ...
   Kumar : actors, actresses and lyricists.
13. Aurangzeb : the fifth Mughal emperor (17th century).
14. Shivaji : legendary warrior chief of Maharashtra who
             challenged Aurangzeb's rule.
15. Dr. Ambed-
   kar : 20th century social reformer.
16. *Sakuntala* : one of the greatest literary masterpieces of
             India by Kalidasa (350–470 A.D.) The full title of the
             play is *Abhijnanasakuntala*.
17. Bhup raga : set compositions in Indian classical music.
18. pice : smallest unit of predecimal Indian currency —3 pice
             to a paisa, 4 paise to an anna, 16 annas to a ruppee.
19. shloka : a stanza of generally religious verse in Sanskrit, in the
             anushtubh metre.
20. exams
   externally : a system of adult education in which one can take
             certain degrees without actually attending classes.
21. Upanishads : the final chapters of the Vedas known as Vedanta (the
             end of knowledge). Literal meaning upa = near;
             ni = below; shad = sit. Meaning the position of the
             student vis-a-vis his guru.
22. Sarvetra
   sukhinah
   santu : Sanskrit for "Peace and happiness to all beings."
             (Rig Veda).
23. namaskars : conventional greetings, palms pressed together.
24. malik : employer.
25. chapatis : grilled, unleavened bread made of wheat flour.
26. amti : fried dal in a thin tamarind gravy.
27. shrikhand : dessert made from partially dehydrated yogurt.
28. pat : a low wooden seat, a couple of inches high.
29. bhayya : a term of affection, used by North Indians, meaning
             brother.
30. saheb : a superior.
31. Charminars : a well-known brand of inexpensive cigarettes.

THREE

1. Kolhapuri : Kolhapur is famous for its distinctive style of footwear called Kolhapuris. Patil used the least expensive chappals.
2. Collectors : important civil servant.
3. Dr. Radha-krishnan : India's philosopher-statesman and one-time President, author of several books on Indian philosophy.
4. *Shyamchi Ali*: Marathi classic novel by Saney Guruji.
5. Aurobindo Ghosh : Indo-Anglian mystic writer, a yogi and founder of the Ashram at Pondicherry.
6. Konkani : the language of the region lying on the west coast of India, south of Mumbai and adjacent to Kerala.
7. convert : a convert to Christianity, possibly from a lower caste than the others, therefore held in some contempt.
8. seer : a pre-metric measure of about one litre.
9. Asoka : Asoka (270–32B.C.) Emperor of India and of the Mauryan dynasty.
10. *Dnyanesh-wari* : commentary on the *Bhagawad Gita* in Marathi, by Dnyaneshwari, 13th century poet-saint of Maharashtra.
11. Keshavsut Phadke : the first two were makers of modern Marathi poetry; the third, a romantic novelist, all considered at that time rather "risky."
12. Mahamaho-padhyaya : literally, master teacher.
13. shira : a semolina dessert.
14. Vetal Hill : a hill with a temple of Vetal on its top. Vetal is a king of the demons, wildly mischievous, malevolent. He is often found in folklore as a hero of superhuman strength (see *Vetal Panchavirhshati*).
15. bhel : a dish of rice flakes mixed with onion, dal and various savoury sauces, a much-relished snack.
16. Raksha-bandhan : literally, a seal or bond signifying brotherly protection. It is a ritual practised in many parts of India.
17. gulmohar tree : a tree with reddish gold blooms. The name means "gold coin."

Cocoon

18. Sinhagad : one of the most famous Maratha mountain forts.
19. batatawada : savoury potato fritter.
20. basundi : milk dessert made of sweetened, thickened milk
21. laddu : a sweet made of sugar syrup and fried gram flour etc. packed into round balls.
22. shev-chivda : a savoury of mixed, crushed nuts, and fried.
23. lungi : a sarong-like, ankle-length cloth worn by men.
24. paan lime : fine, creamy, soft slaked lime chewed with betel-leaf.
25. Aaee : mother.
26. ija, bija, tija : one, two, three.
27. Kartik : eighth month of the Indian calendar, usually October.
28. Devi : pre-Vedic belief that chickenpox and smallpoxare the visitations of the Mother Goddess to test a family's devotion.
29. viharas : Buddhist caves/halls for meditation.
30. Maha-
nirvana : the Great Emancipation used figuratively for Lord Buddha's death.
31. ahimsa : non-violence in speech, thought and action.
32. Yashodhara : Prince Gautama's wife.
33. Gautama : Lord Buddha's name before he renounced his kingdom to practice a new way, i.e., Buddhism.
34. bhikku : Buddhist monk.
35. Rahul : Prince Gautama's son.
36. dharma : the complex code of Hindu ethics underlining the importance of duty and right conduct.
37. karma : variously interpreted as destiny, work (actions) or the sum of a person's actions that determine his future births.
38. rangoli : decorative patterns drawn on the ground with rice flour or similar coloured powders.
39. Samadhi : place of burial which attains the status of a shrine.
40. gunja
creepers : the creeper *Abrus precatorius.*
41. chowky : police station.
42. gulal : vermillion powder used in rituals, celebrations and magic rites.
43. kumkum : vermillion powder made sticky with oil and used to place a decorative dot on the forehead.
44. sabhash : "well done" or "good for you."

45. Lakshmibai : Reverend Tilak's wife. Writer of the first, powerful autobiography in Marathi.
46. champak : temple flower.
47. tamasha : folk theatre peculiar to rural Maharashtra, with dance and music.
48. Gandharva : mythical beings, sons of demigods.
49. Kinnara : celestial musicians and singers.
50. Yuck : the left is used for washing after defecation.
51. mantriks : those who through penance and special austerities harness certain supernatural powers.
52. *Rukmini-swayamvara* : that portion of the great poem *Bhagavatam* that describes the wedding of Lord Krishna and Rukmani.
53. tail : actually, Hamuman is a character in the *Ramayana*. Khanolkar is so ill-informed he gets even Indian religious literature and popular stories mixed up.
54. dev cowrie : in a set of cowrie shells, one is designated as a special piece and, like many other special things, named for the divine, "dev."

Four

1. *A:doramata-povanadiga-manam* : quotation from the Sanskrit summary of the epic *Ramayana*.
2. *Shateshu jayate shurah Ramayana.* : quotation from the Sanskrit summary of the epic
3. Swaytrees : pole to carry shoulder loads of water, etc.
4. Chakradhar : 13th century founder of the Mahanubhav cult (anti-vedic and anti-Brahminical).
5. *Leela-charitra* : a biography of Shri Chakradhar, an account of his actions.
6. Sangam : confluence of Mula and Mutha rivers in Poona.
7. Bhandardare : Bhandardare his old classmate referred to earlier as one of the many expert parodyists in the class.
8. sati : a widow who immolates herself on her husband's funeral pyre.
9. Krishna-murti : great theosophist and philosopher.
10. Shaitan : Satan

FIVE

1. Dada : elder brother.
2. tiffin carrier : a food carrier of stacked containers.
3. varkaris : a dominant religious sect in Maharashtra for whom liquor and meat are taboo and which worships Lord Vitthal of Pandharpur; antivedic, it has produced saints like Namdev, Dnyaneshwar, Tukaram.
4. kirtanas : musical performances that retell stories of religious epics.
5. Mahajan : meaning "honoured Sir."
6. Marwadi : trading community from Marwar.
7. bajri : yellow millet.
8. baiji : respectful way of addressing a Marathi woman.
9. bhai : brother
10. Nath : an anti-vedic sect that professed equality among castes and worshipped Shiva. Known for their supernatural yogic feats.
11. tulasi : sacred basil.
12. bhagat : a worshipper of a primitive deity, one who exorcises spirits.
13. vahi : folksongs recorded on paper.
14. Maharwada : a separate area on one side of the village for the untouchable Mahar caste.
15. Meru : in Hindu cosmology, the centre of the world and Brahma's heaven.
16. Vanji : a goddess who requires human sacrifice.
17. Satpura : one of the mountain ranges that lies across the middle of the Indian subcontinent.
18. taluka : an (administrative) division of about a hundred villages. States are divided into districts and districts into talukas.
19. Kaikadi : a wandering tribe.
20. Ambabai : one of the three main forms of the Mother Goddess.
21. Dassera : one of the most important festivals, the tenth day of the ten-day festival meant to commemorate episodes from Hindu religious lore.
22. apta : a tree; the leaves are offered as 'gold' to teachers and elders on Dassera day.
23. khichdi : rice and pulses cooked together, mashed and seasoned.
24. powada : a ballad, a kind of alliterative poetry, recounting the achievements of a warrior, a narrative of a battle usually about a hero sacrificing his life.

25. Mari : a primitive, pre-Aryan Mother Goddess capable of inflicting deadly punishments, epidemics, etc.

26. munjoba : fiendish spirit, young uninitiated (unmarried) person turned spirit.

27. math : a centre of learning and a seat of a religious leader.

28. aarti : ceremony of waving a wick-flame before a deity or an honoured person.

29. shraddha : anniversary of a person's death.

30. shaligram : ammonite fossils found in river beds, considered sacred and worshipped by Hindus.

31. Yamuna : one of the holy rivers of India, associated with Lord Krishna.

32. Mathura : a holy place also deeply associated with Lord Krishna.

33. balutedars : baluta = share in the produce; dar = holder. Traditional public servants, twelve in number, such as the carpenter, ironsmith, potter, cobbler, etc., each of them is entitled to a fixed allowance of corn annually in return for their services to the village community in Maharashtra.

34. sanai : a wind instrument like a clarinet.

35. Pola : bull festival. The new moon day of Shravana (August) when bullocks are exempted from labour, beautifully daubed and decorated and paraded about in worship.

36. Maruti : another name for Hanuman, the monkey-god, Lord Rama's greatest devotee in the *Ramayana*.

SIX

1. mahant : an accomplished, acknowledged religious man.
2. rakshasas : an order of beings, demons, in Hindu mythology.
3. gosavi : a Shudra mendicant who wears ochre robes and has renounced the world.
4. yatra : a religious fair.
5. bairagi : a Vaishnavaite mendicant who practises austerities.
6. mahatma : great soul, a great being.
7. Arjuna : the third Pandava, one of the heroes of the *Mahabharatha*, Lord Krishna's friend to whom the outpouring of wisdom in the *Bhagawad Geeta* is addressed.